THE DEVIL'S A LEARNING

Book four

P and K Stoker

Amazon

To our beautiful Charlie Bear xxx

CONTENTS

THE DEVIL'S A LEARNING

CHAPTER ONE

Nora, despite her flat feet and ever-present cosy grey duffle coat, was having a good old go at energetically skipping as she joyously entered a charity shop in the centre of Falkirk, Scotland…

"Hiya, my Outstandingly Oxen-type, devilishly handsome husband. How are you doing? Oh, you've got something on your face." Nora said in greeting and did another couple of lopsided leaps over to the dusty and murky glass counter, that was haphazardly lurking in the centre of the cluttered room. That counter contained the more expensive charity items, for the more discerning customer, that were marked £2.50 each or three for a tenner. It was a great honour to be in charge of the treasures hidden within, rather than being relegated to the back of the shop where the mysterious, and sometimes smelly, sorting of items occurred.

"What? What? Get it off me," and Devil Keith, the Devil, started frantically dancing around, slapping at his face and blinking rapidly. He wasn't entirely sure what the blinking would accomplish but he was giving it a good old go. So he was.

"Stop with all the leaping about and skelping at yourself. It's my lips, you Silly Buffalo." Nora did another of her strange, unbalanced jumps up: at a startled Devil. She then slapped her hands on both of his cheeks and leaned in for a hot, passionate kiss. He yanked her over the counter and grabbed her cheeks too. Her more southern cheeks. Meow!

"Ohh, you know how to make a girly feel truly welcome." She gasped then giggled whilst wrinkling up her little nose. She

was quite enjoying this old marriage lark.

"So how did it go, my Sturdy Strumpet? My Christmas Pudding, Silhouetted Stunner? Did you get them? Are they scoffing down some disgusting, salt encrusted porridge as we speak? Are they discovering that orange ***really*** *is the new black? Eh, my beautiful, clever Crime-busting Caterpillar?"* Devil Keith, the Devil, excitedly enquired whilst furtively going back to his current task. Namely plucking his shapely, pale pink eyebrows into a seductive arch. A job he chose to do that morning, in order to help keep himself busy so he wouldn't worry too much about his Nora and her recent adventures. A choice he now regretted as he may have, in his extreme anxiety, overplucked his eyebrows and went onto remove his splendid goatee, delicate toe hair and a fair bit of his nose hair. Oh, nippy!

As an aside. Devil Keith didn't suffer any qualms about using or abusing pet names. Unlike his twin brother, Bub, who was still lovingly and laughingly known as Groomy-woomy or Groomy-wormy or just Wormy. But only by those individuals whom loved him dearly: his wife, Harry, sat firmly in that camp. Or by cowardly enemies, who were too far away to be thrown into a moat containing some mighty fine but awfully savage, Hell number three, crocodiles. Devil Keith and the crocodiles were best mates now as Devil Keith had started, with the help of Stan, a dating website called *"Chompster".* You didn't have to swipe left or right to demonstrate your dating preference rather, due to facial recognition technology, you just had to show them your teeth: if you were interested in hooking up. Or sensually chomping it up, as the adverts flagrantly boasted.

"It all went surprisingly well. We did good, we did. They're both 'banged to rights'... as they say in the old Ealing crime caper movies. Those conniving Grannies have knitted their last jumper, stitched their last sweater and crocheted their last cable-knit cardigan. For a while anyway. Unless they take up the unhealthy

habit again in prison. Devil Keith, my Cock-eyed Canoodler, is that even possible?" Nora, like her sister-in-law Harry, was a complete novice at the old pet names business but Devil Keith thought her naivety was rather endearing.

In fact, he thought everything his Nora did was unbelievably cute and adorable and wonderful and mesmerising. He told her that irrefutable truth seven to ten times every hour. He even set his alarm clock so that he could also remind her of this indisputable fact during the night. Nora gently suggested that instead of the one, two, three, four and five am *"cuteness and adorability reassurances,"* Devil Keith could tell her ten times when they both woke up. Naturally waking up, in the morning, when most civilised people awoke, she then stressed.

Devil Keith wasn't entirely convinced that this was adequate for his husbandly needs so he was still secretly setting his alarm, on vibrate, so he could watch his Nora sleep. Then quietly whispering to her how much he loved her. However, there still was the occasional, nocturnal shouting at her of... *"you're the very best thing to ever happen to me so stop with all that aging malarkey, and all the slowly sliding towards death habit. I'm not a fan. So just stop it this minute, lady."* The startled Nora was less appreciative of the *"louder whispers"* than Devil Keith expected but he read an article that said if something happens for fifty-nine to seventy consecutive days then it becomes a habit. Only fifteen days to go before his Nora craved this essential feedback. Wish him luck.

Plus, due to his Nora's gorgeous Scottish accent, he couldn't actually understand precisely 37% of what she said. In Devil Keith's head, the pet names frequently sounded like odd but adorable grunts, squeals and random oos. So he just smiled and distracted her by breaking off her split-ends and keeping the broken ends to sprinkle on his scrumptious, homemade plum and sherry trifle. Devil Keith had been saving the pieces of her hair as love tokens, but his Nora correctly assessed the situation and declared that they did not have enough space for another one of his bodily fluid or bodily waste collections. Devil Keith's large mason jars full of Nora's bitten toe nails, her ear wax and used dental floss were already overwhelming the bathroom shelves and overflowing into their second spare bedroom.

Oh yes, back to the *"banged to rights"* conversation...

"I know the singularly brilliant Stan can whip up a pretty impressive, knitted suspension bridge but that's purely his skill? Right? Devil Keith, please don't get jealous. I think you're totally brilliant too. And gorgeous and the centre of my world. Is that better? So, can I ask a question about the dull and extremely ugly Stan? Right?

The extraordinary knitting, it is just **his** *skill? No one else's? The conning Grannies won't be able to knit a set of ladders to scale a high prison wall or embroider a fully functioning helicopter to fly away, or maliciously darn together a really big spoon for tunnelling out of the prison block to freedom?"* Nora was mildly concerned that she might be *"taken out"* by a particularly sharp crocheted shiv due to her recent role as an *"ultra-super-grass"*.

Devil Keith, due to his relentless scouring of relationship advice websites and completion of their scientifically backed questionnaires, instantly recognised her need for reassurance and gave her a big, squishy cuddle. He then, ever so gently, kissed the rumpled hair piled on top of her head. He loved being her cuddle monster. Correction, her **manly** cuddle monster. Correction again... her **glamorous, manly, delightful** cuddle monster who is miles more handsome than that grotesque Stan. Yet another Devil Keith, the Devil, hostile laptop takeover is occurring at Maison Stoker.

So, why was Nora an ultra-super-grass and why were the Grannies *"banged to rights"*? And, why were they no longer wielding their naughty knitting needles and criminally-insane crochet hooks around Falkirk district?

◆ ◆ ◆

CHAPTER TWO

Cue backstory...

Following their purely accidental discovery of America, Nora and Devil Keith had briefly returned to Hell number one in order to give their family and friends the good news regarding their, ever so, recent nuptials. And, if Nora and Devil Keith were being totally honest; to ever so slightly, hide from the custodians of Stonehenge. Devil Keith is a big, big, big fan of the words *"ever so,"* so expect to see that phrase a lot in this book. He's holding the authors' corkscrew ransom, and you don't want to know what he's done to their innocent fish-slice. So, ever so, is going to appear ever so often.

Back to the Stonehenge wedding...

Those pencil-pushing, jumped up janitors (Devil Keith's at the laptop again and there's been a bit of a scuffle) were mighty upset at Nora and Devil Keith's wedding arrangements. Well, they were really Devil Keith's arrangements as Nora would have just nipped down to the local registry office and be done with it. Nonetheless, she was touched by Devil Keith's thoughtfulness and romantic gestures. And, as she began to know him better, she also appreciated his truly unique and talented design skills. So long as the designs weren't entirely focused on her, she'd quietly whisper to the nearest mannequin. Devil Keith very nearly understood Nora's reticence and attributed it to her very attractive shyness, so he left her to choose her own simple lace wedding gown.

n their wedding day, Devil Keith proudly donned a brand new neon yellow mankini, as a reference to the rising sun and the symbolism of a new phase in his life. This was complemented by a pair of khaki green fisherman waders: a hideous necessity due to the need to navigate through the mounds of sheep poo. The dashing outfit was finished with a simple circlet of lavender flowers for his flowing locks. He liked the smell of lavender. Traditionally he would have gotten married in the scud, as the ancient officiants were right sticklers for making sure the bride and groom were unequivocally male and female. No same sex unions allowed. No siree. But interestingly enough, those exact same bureaucrats weren't too fussed when the Greek God, Zeus, turned into a swan. The sleazy God did this for his frequent episodes of the old, and frankly deeply disturbing, hanky-panky with a fair maiden or two.

Anyway, back to the wedding day: it was just too bloody cold for nudity that early in the morning so Devil Keith also added a warm sky-blue woolly jumper to his ensemble. Just loosely tied around the waist, he wasn't some kind of heathen. Sheesh. He wanted the dazzling mankini to be the star of the show. All of that was perfectly reasonable and could be a part of anyone's wedding getup if they had the style, the vision, the athletic build and an adequate waxing regime, he assured his stunned Nora.

Back to the "*ever so*" controversial part of the wedding arrangements: namely the truly gigantic scarlet balloon arches, forklift buckets crammed with biodegradable mauve confetti, and the miles of gaudy, acid-green bunting encircling the UNESCO world heritage site. This caused some raised eyebrows and a little bit of regurgitated sick to appear in the unfortunate spectator's mouth. However, it was the humungous wedding cake that really stole the show. It was an eighteen-foot monolith of dried-fruit and icing, that unfortunately topped over and took out the outer ring of the prehistoric, vertical Sarsen Standing Stones. Devil Keith blamed the wedding photographer as he believed the camera flash had startled the innocent cake into a dead faint.

The catering mishap, and Devil Keith making their wedding rings from trinkets he *"found"*, tightly clutched in the hands of the skeletons buried under the ancient stones, didn't help matters much either. Devil Keith later swore that he knew the skeletons very well; when they were actual functioning people, and not quite so fashionably skinny dead folks. He also insisted that Timothy and Prudence, when alive, were a couple of real hip characters. Always up for a good old night out at an up-beat comedy cave. They enjoyed some high jinks with the inventors of the wheel, and they were utter connoisseurs of a gory blood sacrifice or three. They would have loved the *"in yer face,"* wedding decorations and ceremony. And Devil Keith knew they would have totally approved of the re-cycling of their jewellery and re-touching of their crumbling metacarpals. Devil Keith was emphatic about that as he wasn't a big fan of museums, galleries and the likes. He knew they were just fancy buildings jampacked with his old junk, generally unwanted castoffs and pounds of exfoliated dead skin cells. They are yucky places, and so unbelievably unhygienic: you just have to look at how often the experts have to use white gloves to protect their hands from the dirt, he frequently argued.

However, Devil Keith believed that people with more sophisticated palates would want to explore his 1930's glass fronted, wooden China cabinets. That's if you really wanted to experience some truly awesome and unbiased history, he'd boast. The dusty, cramped cupboards were jampacked full of stimulating and gruesome items that would guarantee that you would never again enjoy a full night's sleep. But you'd be ever so popular on camping trips. After reading the item's description label and digesting their history, the torch lit stories you could tell would be, in equal measures, both ary and petrifying. Just ask the overly tall people who w… native to Easter Island. Oh, you can't as they were all frozen in fear, then calcified and buried up to their necks, following a singularly horrifying rendition of *"Ging, Gang, Gooley, Gooley, Gooley, Gooley what's it?"* The *"what's it"* part of the song was one of Devil Keith's more inspiring and ghoulish items from his cupboard. Therefore, just proving Devil Keith's irrefutable point regarding the veracity and impact of his amazing treasures.

Back to Stonehenge and the wedding to end all weddings...

The loved-up, energetic elopers would have used the Time Scavenger to rectify their mistakes. Devil Keith has hissed in one of the author's ear that there were no mistakes... just misunderstood and bodacious style choices that small minded folks would never, ever appreciate. Back to the story, and away from all the devilish Devil Keith huffing. However, the magical tool had gone a missing. Only to reappear in the grubby, but surprisingly strong hands of Fachance, the Horsewoman of Famine and Angel Gab, who just as the name suggests is an Angel. Hands that were currently encouraging the citizens of Florence, during the Renaissance period, to embrace the art of karaoke whilst supping on a pint of warm lager and nibbling on mounds of pesto filled, crispy filo pastry bar snacks.

CHAPTER THREE

Still on the longest backstory, ever...

So, as they were technically on the lam from "*Visit England*", and wanted a break from Hell number one, Nora and Devil Keith had decided to hang around Nora's place in Falkirk. Devil Keith was still mightily taken with Nora's plastic gorilla garden ornaments, so he was quite content to honeymoon by the meandering canals, chat with the surprisingly chipper Kelpies, and gobble up deep-fried Mars bars dipped in HP brown sauce. HP sauce watered down with just the right amount of malt vinegar. It's a secret Scottish culinary art, you know.

Whilst blissfully honeymooning in sunny Falkirk, Nora had decided that she'd try to capitalise on her recent weight loss. Weight loss courtesy of a bout of debilitating scurvy, and the dysentery induced dietary programme that had been forced upon her during her historic *"discovery"* of the Americas. Before that particular sea journey Devil Keith had been an avid pen-pal with three native American Indians and one very chatty Viking called Cecil the Paddler, so he knew this journey was less of a "*discovery*" and more of a *"happened to come across a great big bloody continent, again"* scenario.

Anyway, back to the reason for Nora's significant weight loss and need for new clothing. The La Santa Maria, old Chris Columbus' fifteenth century tall ship was less than hygienic, and the all-inclusive meals weren't as all-inclusive as the body ideally required. Hence the terrible scurvy. Even with all the rition, the hiding from randy old sea-dogs and the rope Nora looked on that journey very fondly. Very fondly indeed. It was on that raw sewage, smelling deck that Nora had gazed over at Devil Keith and realised that the sight of him no longer made her want to gag. He was also so sweet when she held back his hair, so he could barf over the side of the ship again, that she lost her heart to the big lummox.

Back in Falkirk with the besotted wee honeymooners...

So off the, nearly, slender Nora went one sunny Tuesday morning, with a song in her heart and a tenner in her back pocket. She tried to squeeze herself into Falkirk, Matalan's finest size 14 skinny jeans.

Whilst pulling the denim torture garments up her, still, podgy thighs Nora heard the women in the next changing room laughing uproariously about *"a poor sucker taking the fall".* The noisy women then began bickering about a high-risk heist they had engineered. The argument centred around a crucial wardrobe malfunction. It turned out that one of the ladies had discovered that all of her black ninja, criminal, work-gear was still in the wash. She had cleverly improvised and turned up at their latest break-in wearing a giant, black cat Halloween outfit. It was the only black outfit that had passed the laundry *"sniff test"*, she hotly argued. To make matters worse the lady in question, who went by the name Granny Kitty, had been wearing the outfit back to front and unfortunately tripped the alarm with the rapidly swinging and rather naughty tail. Unfortunately, Granny Kitty had also taken quite a shine to helicoptering her stiff tail and began blithely shouting *"get a load of the blade on me"*. So, the ladies had just made it out of the jewellery store before the *"fuzz"* had arrived.

The ladies had also mentioned the bleep, bleep, bleep *"filth and pigs,"* so Nora thought the ladies, although criminal masterminds and highly creative swearers, were very particular about their cleanliness and obviously hated dirt an_ grime of any sort. They also appeared to be concerned about the welfare of farmyard animals and didn't appear to want them crammed inside a police van. That was two large ticks in the positive list Nora was mentally writing but the negative list was pretty much overwhelming. She wondered,...how did the Groovy Grannies manage to cartwheel and limbo-dance through the laser beams and avoid the security cameras? There must be a story, and several pints of cod liver oil, behind that particular skill set.

Nora then pressed her right ear against the wall of the changing room and was utterly gobsmacked by the audacity of their next brilliant scheme. So when she heard them leave, she quickly chased after them. Well, less chased and more stumbled with her new jeans at midthigh and her second-best pair of black flowery knickers covering her quivering, cellulite loaded bum cheeks.

Meanwhile, Devil Keith was innocently loitering outside the changing rooms trying to come up with another two-hundred reasons why Nora shouldn't wear jeans. He knew Nora looked absolutely great in everything she wore but he just couldn't stomach...gulp...denim. Nor could he understand people's fascination with the odd fabric. It was stretchy but stiff, and soft but hardwearing. It was, in fact, an unpleasant conundrum. A riddle wrapped in a mystery inside an enigma.

Still in Matalan, Falkirk...

The semi-clad Nora, from under a couple of robust security guards, stage whispered, *"Devil Keith, follow those heisting harridans"*. Devil Keith initially followed the panting security guards, then he realised that the security guards in question weren't going anywhere other than to sit on his squidgy but adorable Nora. Devil Keith then decided that the offending security guards needed a good old tearing limb from limb, but then he remembered that Nora had vetoed that ıusbandly duty. She had stated that she could look elf and Devil Keith didn't need to go after everyone wno ... ed at her a bit funny. This was especially true of the local lollipop man, and Devil Keith's belief that he was a top-notch spy sent to keep tabs on the newlyweds. The elderly lollipop man had some serious core strength in order to deftly wield his big lolly as well as the wrinkly wisdom to do some serious intellectual damage to some unsuspecting folks, according to Devil Keith.

Just in case you haven't noticed: Devil Keith has some wild and unusual theories. He holds the firm belief that as the human brain has wrinkles and cracks and crevices, everyone who has wrinkles on their face are just sweating out bits of their brain because their brain was getting too big for their skull to contain. So furrows, crow's feet and skin folds equate to a higher IQ. He also believes that as Botox and Fillers reduces wrinkles then everyone who uses it is reducing their intelligence. His theory was a work in progress and was awaiting ethics approval before being considered for some top-notch medical research. No, no.... the whole research lab thingy was a dream Devil Keith had last Thursday after he ate too much chicken korma that he found under the sofa. Not real at all. Phew.

Oh no, still trapped in Matalan...

Devil Keith, very nearly, quickly realised his mistake regarding the whole following of the security guards and, instead, discreetly followed the two gossiping ladies to a local charity shop. By discreetly the authors mean that Devil Keith stopped shouting *"cooeey, wait for me, oh wonderous thieves,"* after the fourth heavily tutted, granny rebuff and after receiving a particularly spicy, dirty look. Turmeric was the spice in question.

Outside the Falkirk charity shop...

Cheese and onion crisps in hand, Devil Keith watched the charity shop door in case the vixens decided to escape from the rather charming prison of second-hand goods. On reflection, Devil Keith thought that he really should have brought his Nora with him as his twenty-eight-hour stakeout was really rather boring. He spent the first three hours playing eye-spy but realised that the *"something beginning with the letter C,"* was nearly always a car, and he got fed up of constantly losing to himself. It was so embarrassing when a stray pigeon won a game, although Devil Keith thought that round was fixed. Plus, he really shouldn't have nipped off for that seven-course taster-menu meal in the middle of said stakeout as the ladies might just have made a dastardly dash home during the delicious pudding course. He did so enjoy a pudding. Mmmm pudding.

Meanwhile, in Matalan...

After pulling up her black flowery drawers and promising to buy the nearly stolen jeans, Nora went home to wait on her jacket wearing crusader. She had, with the unsolicited assistance of Harry, previously burnt all of Devil Keith's crushed velvet, hero capes. Even the eight, identical purple stripped ones: trimmed with fake fur weren't safe from the white hot embers of the back garden barbeque. The vindictive capes kept getting caught in train station doors and viciously yanking her poor Devil Keith backwards, to the side and occasionally upside down. Nora had rapidly intervened on thirty-four occasions to ensure that her Devil Keith wasn't permanently decapitated. She really liked his lovely head attached to all his other equally lovely bits and pieces, so she decided enough was enough. As she couldn't commit arson against all train doors (Devil Keith's nearly helpful, and frequent suggestion) she decided a wee bonfire of the offending capes was in order. Nora had also kindly requested that, in future, he wear his under pants under his pantyhose not on top, as was his want. It continued to be a ogress but Nora felt that the nagging was justified eith's fainting, due to excessive layering, was getting dangerously out of hand. Plus, Nora couldn't source enough burgundy coloured brocade chaise longs for Devil Keith to artful drape himself across. The polar bears in Hell number three had cornered the chaise long market and they weren't for sharing. No, not at all.

No longer in Matalan...

A few days later, and still unable to squash herself into her new jeans, Nora had used the excuse of donating some of Devil Keith's more unsavoury items: in order to visit the charity shop. Whilst wresting a particularly stubborn flaming orange feather boa (it had also been caught in a train door and nearly guillotined her darling Devil Keith) and a flamboyant diamante peacock brooch (it gave Devil Keith, the Wee Sweetie, terrible flashbacks of the Peacocks of Hell) out of a Tesco's Bag for Life, she politely enquired if the charity shop needed any volunteers. They did, and Nora started her dangerous undercover work. Work that she hoped would catch the baddies and save the *"poor sucker"* who was so wrongly accused of theft.

◆ ◆ ◆

CHAPTER FOUR

The crime caper discovered...

Nora quickly discovered that Granny Kitty and Granny Fifi were the two ladies she had overheard outrageously crowing then viciously arguing in the Matalan changing rooms. As it turned out, that pair of scheming hoodlums had quite the racket going on. Quite the racket indeed.

The racket...

In preparation for their light-fingered re-distribution of wealth, the Grannies would sort out jars of woodlice: using dexterity training chopsticks to pick up the fidgety creatures and organise the clicking insects according to their overall attractiveness. The homely woodlice were savagely chucked into the garden waste bin. However, the comelier woodlice were lightly pampered with baby oil and talcum powder, then funnelled into brightly coloured maracas for the Grannies other business: exotic baby rattles.

The Grannies used their heavily leashed and saliva frothing, cannibalistic chickens Doris, and Henrietta to aid in their audacious thefts. The crafty Grannies would cobble together, what looked like a makeshift chicken obstacle course in their overgrown back gardens. Their excuse being that the Grannies were entering their hens in H-rufts: the avian version of the famous dog show, Crufts. The crumbling wooden wine boxes, collapsing garden shed, old coal bunkers, log piles, broken lawnmowers, rusty swings, groaning slides and old

.ne ropes were an ideal way of hiding the floorplan of ıded victim.

Grannies, high on cod liver oil supplements, then negotiated the fake floorplan. They limbered up, readjusted their respective bosoms then flamboyantly cartwheeled, summersaulted, tiptoed, crawled, limbo-danced and generally chased the nimble fowl in, over, around and under the wonky obstacles. Craftily honing their geriatric gymnastic skills whilst carefully timing their nefarious caper and ensuring that the Grannies could successfully avoid the sensitive laser beams, loaded dart guns, tanks of voracious piranhas and thermal imaging contraptions. This preparation also helped to make sure that their panty-girdles didn't ride-up and cause a nasty wee yeast infection. The Grannies' panty-girdles not the chickens, just to be clear. The chickens preferred a thong style of underwear, when they reluctantly agreed to don **any** underwear, as the totty pink thongs didn't get in the way of their lucrative egg releasing mechanism.

The Grannies also brought their ferocious chickens on their jewel heists as the Grannies had quickly discovered that the cannibalistic hens were addicted to sandwiches filled with diced chicken, shredded rocket salad and tinned tuna... always mixed with light mayonnaise. The chicken thongs weren't very forgiving. The Grannies would catapult the small, crustless, triangular sandwiches onto the top of the security cameras and the chickens would be unable to resist roosting on the cameras and enjoying a rather pleasant, if very basic, picnic. The chicken feathers, rumpled wings and breadcrumbs completely obscuring the antics of the limber thieves. And causing the local police to shake their heads in total disbelief and ask who was committing these audacious crimes and where was the loot?

The real reason the Grannies worked in the charity shop...

Following their very successful thefts, Granny Kitty and

Granny Fifi used the charity shop as the centre of their fencı operation. They would choose truly ugly cardigans, sweaters and jumpers then ever so craftily and charmingly sell them to unsuspecting, fellow grandparents. The thieving Grannies would then offer to gift wrap the hideous woollen articles and send them on to the naive grandparent's grandchild. But in order to do that, the unsuspecting grandparent was told that they must return to the charity shop the following day so that the doting grandparent could add a note to the parcel. Afterall, the grateful grandchild would want to know who had been so thoughtful and kind as to send them such a considerate gift. During the night the felonious Grannies would quickly unravel part of the hideous knitwear and stitch their ill-gotten, stolen diamonds and other jewels into the gruesome garments.

The following day the innocent grandparent would return to the shop and attach their loving note to the exterior of the wrapped item. A note that was usually full of complaints about the ever-decreasing size of a Mars bar and the scandalous price of postage stamps. And how young people needed to pull up their jeans as too much air on their exposed bottoms turned them all into gun totting criminals, and how the price of pegs was going through the roof so they had to resort to pegging their washcloths together on their sagging washing lines. And lastly, how their chronic indigestion and debilitating back ache was all caused by that global warming malarkey. There appeared to be a tick list of complaints that all the grandparents used in their long and meandering letters to their grandchildren. A tick list that was, in all probability, attached to the grandparents first pension payment.

The menacingly mature, criminal masterminds would then post off the sparkle filled parcel, with the ever so useful (?) note. The unsuspecting grandchild would receive the well-meant gift, and unless burdened with truly poor taste, the grandchild would quickly take the offending article to their nearest charity shop. In the meantime, Granny Fifi and Granny Kitty would have already pre-warned their colleagues, in that shop, so when the offending item was donated idden away until it could be unpicked later that sing the jewels from their knitted prison. Ready for the loc licit gem market. What rotters!

The villainous Grans had pulled this stunt off four hundred and ninety-six times. Effectively fencing their hot gems in eighteen different countries. Crossing international borders with impunity and downright cheek. On the three occasions that the grandchild had kept the grotesque jumper, Granny Kitty and Granny Fifi had employed particularly forthright pensioners to make derogatory remarks and tuts, until two of the grandchildren had given in and handed the offending jumpers into the local charity shop. One grandchild had the audacity to re-gift their ugly jumper to a friend. Well, hardly a friend as the jumper was vomit inducing and destined for the very back of a wardrobe. However, an anonymous call to the local copshop had seen him perp-marched all the way to the local jail. Hence the *"poor sucker"* comment, and the grannies cruel laughter, in the Matalan changing room.

CHAPTER FIVE

Back to the present day, in the charity shop, and the reason for Nora's delighted skipping...

Nora had just handed over the overwhelming evidence, that proved the Grannies guilt, to the previously puzzled local constabulary. The Grannies were very fortunate that they were handed over to the police at all. The Brownies, from Hell number two, had used their Interdimensional Badge to visit Falkirk the week before: in order to achieve their Orientation in the Wilds badge. The Brownies were also curious as to what the honeymooners were up to, so popped into see Nora and Devil Keith for a blether...and to steal some of their delicious Tunnock's tea cakes. The Brownies laughed so hard, and slapped their chubby dimpled knees when they heard about the Stonehenge wedding debacle and were positively delighted when they found out about Nora's criminal investigation. Brownie Mary Jo was shocked that the poor birdies were being treated in such a haphazard and unkind way: cannibalism is taught not inherited, so the Grannies were out and out baddies, she firmly stated. The other Brownies were equally incensed and had joyously cackled as they offered to bring forward their Rotisserie badges and put the Grannies on a hot, roasting spit. That would make them Grannies talk...and possibly crisp-up and char and mostly be no more. The Brownies hooted with glee.

Nora and Devil Keith had appreciated the Brownies bloodthirsty proposal but felt that the Grannies needed to stand trial and be locked away for their crimes. Well Nora believed that, and Devil Keith agreed as he didn't like the way the Brownies were eyeing up his comfy recliner chair and discussing how hot it would burn. The deeply disappointed Brownies put down their bundles of kindling, tidied away their sharpened sticks, unscrewed their balls of newspaper and re-boxed their firelighters. They then reluctantly dragged their little feet away from the flammable furniture. They were generally pretty morose and doing a fair bit of sighing. However, after pocketing the last packet of coconut snowballs they happily left their calling card and told the honeymooners to holler if they changed their minds.

Nora and Devil Keith had reviewed their mound of condemning evidence. Evidence gathered during hours of painstaking surveillance of the chicken obstacle races, where Devil Keith honed his eye-spying talents to new heights of skills and untold mastery. The letter C now stood for more than just cars as there were chickens and a coup to consider too.

Devil Keith and Nora had went onto accumulate other damning testimony: that included seven different types of wool, an array of blunted knitting pins and four well-used darning needles. Plus, there was the run of the mill evidence consisting of videos of gloating confessions: made by the horrendous hens. The offer of several packets of the white-suited Colonel's eleven secret herbs and spices proving to be too tempting for the gluttonous poultry and their loose beaky, beaks.

The Grannies' many receipts for large purchases of family-sized bottles of Chanel Number 5 perfume and colossal bars of Cadbury's Dairy Milk chocolate had also been a blatant clue. The Grannies had bought enough of the expensive perfume to bathe a camel, according to Devil Keith. And Devil Keith would definitely know that strangely useful fact. Afterall, he was a zoo visiting aficionado: just ask the ever so grateful and terribly frisky pandas at Edinburgh zoo.

Back to the present day in the charity shop and all that skipping, again...

Nora had proudly handed over their investigation file earlier that very day, but not before being cruelly attacked by Granny Fifi who had been brandishing exhibit A. The diamond tipped, size 12 knitting needles that were so coveted by the Grannies. The mobster Grannies were put in a nippy sore head lock and perp-walked into Falkirk Police Station. The delighted and relieved poor sucker was due to be released any moment now.

Nora fantasized that she and Devil Keith would get a crime buster's medal, although she wasn't sure they were worthy of a ticker-tape parade but you never can tell. She'd book a hairdresser appointment and get her corns sorted, just in case. Devil Keith excitedly grabbed an empty mason jar.

CHAPTER SIX

Still in the present day, in the charity shop, and Nora's recent delighted skipping...

"I feel sorry for wee baby Charlie," whispered Devil Keith. He was really quite fond of the curly haired, chirpy, totty wee boy. Devil Keith was seriously considering having a little ankle-biter himself but he wasn't sure where he could order one. He decided to ask the illustrious Mr Hamhands. He was such a sound chappy and was sure to understand the mechanics of it all. Dr Riel had made it sound all yucky and bloody and moist and generally quite damp. Devil Keith didn't think Nora would like all the indigestion and stretch marks he was sure to get. And he was adamant that his Nora wasn't going through all that nonsense either.

"I feel really bad too, but they were going to convict an innocent man of grand theft and leave him to rot in jail. The poor guy was clearly terrified and no one else seemed to want to help him. His friend was no use. We had to do something to get him out of prison. He didn't suit orange. Not at all. Not with his putty-ish colouring and bright red hair.

Plus, they really should have thought about their grandson before feathering their nests. Get it? That's a good one. Ok, don't laugh. I'll explain it later.

Why exactly am I having to shout this back story?" Nora loudly yelled whilst cradling her heavily bandaged hand. A hand that Devil Keith had tried to kiss all better, but he had only made the bandage soggy wet and a bit smelly.

"Ah, well about that..." Devil Keith blushed and rubbed

the back of his neck. Yes, he actually blushed a delightful shade of sunset orange. *"We were invaded by the delightful Queen Lucy, and she brought her gaggle of heartless henchwomen with her. I was overwhelmed before I even realised who it was. They're very sneaky, I'll have you know. Those brutish, frightening Faeries."* Nora realised that Devil Keith wasn't actually blushing. He had been experimenting with pots of rouge and Marie Antoinette's beauty spots, yet again. When will he realise that *"Profound Adolescent Embarrassment"* was the only shade for him? Also, when will he learn that beauty spots look like big blackheads? Yuck.

"When you knew who it was, why didn't you stop her?" Nora puzzled and picked at the edges of her blood-soaked bandage. Why do people pick at things when they know it will hurt? It's a mystery, that if solved, would be awfully useful to know, Nora decided. It might win a prize. A big prize.

"My Melodious Melon Mouther, she was in disguise. I was prepared for her candy floss pink hair so didn't recognise her with her pretty aqua green tresses. I thought she was just a normal customer. 'A wee Falkirk Bairn out for a daunder', as you'd say." Devil Keith studiously nodded and pulled an orange boa from the *"ten pence only"* bin. That little gem was going home with him tonight as he just knew that his Nora would absolutely adore it. He added that to a beautiful peacock brooch he had unearthed and secreted in his cavernous, patch pocket. He was always amazed at the treasures people would throw away. Amazed and delighted. So amazed and delighted that he decided to start his quest for purple satin-lined capes a day earlier than originally planned.

"Erm, Queen Lucy is, at most, 8 inches tall with fluttering wings and a skirt made entirely out of delicate pink peony petals. She's uncommonly beautiful with all that slender, ethereal look going on. She's also constantly surrounded by honey bees. Bees that sing 'Kiss me Honey, Honey kiss me', by Shirley Bassey. Devil Keith, sweetie, wasn't that a blatant clue?" Nora questioned whilst gently tugging an orange feather boa from Devil Keith's

cavernous pocket. They were taking the train to Stirling later, to tour Stirling Castle, with her friend Andrew, and she didn't want to disrupt the service yet again.

"No, my Lardy Lady, the bees weren't a clue at all. The harmonious bees were singing, 'Come fly with me' by Frank Sinatra. I thought they were just Falkirk locals. A new crew with nothing in common with the luscious Queen Lucy." Devil Keith re-adjusted his twenty-one beauty spots then sighed when he realised that they resembled the *"Great Bear"* constellation. Astronomy. One of the coveted Brownie badges. He so missed Brownie Rachel, and the other little Brownies so he popped a packet of brightly coloured hairclips in his pocket and decided he and his Nora really should think about heading home to Hell. Their mission had kept them away for quite some time and he was becoming terribly homesick. He could nearly smell the whale blubber coffee calling his name. He pondered this for a long time then agreed with himself that the coffee was, indeed, able to call his name. And whistle. He was the dashing Devil afterall.

The bees in question, yes, we're back to the bees. They were part of Queen Lucy's permanent entourage. They had recently been taken over during a particularly rough, and honey squandering coup, by a distinctly rougher element. Bullies who insisted on mixing up their established bee choir and demanding a wider repertoire of songs. The new choir master felt that the bee's constant bass and baritone numbers were putting off their audience, so he had agreed to add a squad of pushy wasps to their number. Wasps who could sing distinctly higher tones and notes. There was also an unsubstantiated rumour that one of the wasps was able to sing falsetto and could do a remarkable Freddie Mercury impersonation of, *"I want to break free."* Although he had substituted the lyrics with the clever and original *"I want to break bees; I want to break bees"*. This all just added to Devil Keith's Faery confusion and his complete lack of recognition of the babelicious Queen Lucy.

Back to the charity shop and the reckless Faeries...

"Ok, I can nearly understand your logic, my Kiss Kidnapper. But again, why am I having to do all this shouting?" Nora tried to prise a turquoise, sequined polo neck jumper from Devil Keith's clenched fist. Nora had put that aside for his upcoming birthday. He was quite difficult to buy for as he was forever unearthing stylish treasures. That very morning, he had combined a rather skimpy mauve bikini top with a red Stewart's tartan kilt, and an emerald green bowler hat. A hat that had the crown removed in order to fit multi-coloured, flashing Christmas Faery lights in the space created. The combination was startling, yet totally worked as it was all pulled together with green and white wedge-heeled trainers.

"Oh, the noise. That's nothing to worry about. That's all down to Faery Layla and her wild ways." Devil Keith added a pre-owned flea collar to his treasure trove. Devil Keith thought that his wee Brownie Nelli was just the gal to wrestle that onto bug infested, old Periwinkle. Devil Keith then realised that he was bringing back gifts from his holidays. He was quite charmed by his own thoughtfulness so added a pre-used blackhead remover, for Harry, to his bulging sporran. A blackhead remover that could double as a robust BBQ scraper. He decided that he was an absolute gem of a friend, to that ginger messy gal.

"Damn and blast it. Not Faery Layla again." Nora tentatively looked around for the frightening Faery. Faery Layla had big brown eyes rimmed with long, long eyelashes. Eyelashes that were tipped with micro-hypodermic needles. Needles that were pre-filed with Botox, by her cousin Faery Natasha. This was so the feisty Faery Layla could rapidly fire off the needles and literally freeze you with a certain look. The dreaded Faery Layla also struck fear into the very soul of all customer service representatives when she requested to speak

to the manager. She was widely known to be very opinionated and unwilling to take any nonsense. She had also recently decided on a change in career and was currently indulging in a whole lot of Life Coaching. Whether the person wanted coached, or indeed wanted a life.

"So, the noise? Is that all her doing? I hope not. I think my ears are bleeding." Nora grimaced and sort of whispered above the din. A challenging skill that she now used more frequently than she ever thought possible.

"Yes, that's all her doing. She brought the whole bric-a-brac shelf to life and is currently encouraging them to express their feelings and innermost thoughts. It's pretty funny when you give it a listen." Devil Keith added a nit comb to his holiday gifts. Another Harry gift? Probably.

CHAPTER SEVEN

Nora cocked an ear and gave it a listen...

"Only the truly rich and incredibly privileged understand me. Me, me me.... the regularly polished and rarely used true King of the cutlery drawer. The special occasion accoutrement, as I'm known in the trade. The dining table bling, extraordinaire." An obviously narcissistic fish-knife drawled as he boasted to his four fish-knife brothers. Brothers who were enthusiastically nodding and were delighted that he was presently their credentials with such unequivocal style, pose, shininess and je ne sais quoi.

"You're a bit full of yourself, aren't you? You can't be that good. There are full boxes of fish-knives under the counter and I saw at least eight of you in the '10 pence only bin'. You lot need to get a life and be more versatile, or you're never gonna get outta here. Tinned tuna, in fresh spring water, and sushi bars are the future of fish cuisine. Keep this up and you're so gonna get melted in a vat of mixed metals then turned into over-priced camping mugs. That's your fate if you're not careful and do exactly what I tell you.

You need to get out there and diversify. Have you thought about trying your blade at being a screwdriver? Everyone needs a screwdriver tucked away in their toolkit." Faery Layla pointedly suggested. The fish-knives threw her a dirty look then formed a small cluster to discuss their options. They thought screwdrivers were uncommonly...well common. However, hanging out at sushi bars sounded suitably exotic so they did a bit of rapid rebranding and scratched *"Sensational Sushi*

Accoutrements" into the lid of their dented box.

"Are you happy now?" the newly adapted sushi knife asked with attitude, and a side order of huffiness.

"Yep, you'll do for now. So just get on with the rest of your Life Change, and don't bother me again. You're as sorted as you'll ever be." And with that tricky problem dealt with, Faery Layla rubbed her well-moisturised little hands together and thought about buying a campanula, flower handbag with all her lovely Life Coaching earnings.

"Faery Layla, excuse me. Can we talk about the quality of the coaching you're offering? Faery Layla...." Nora tentatively, and bravely enquired whilst wondering what role the obviously fish-knives would have in a sushi bar.

Faery Layla rolled her eyes then ignored Nora's polite request.

"Me, me. Do me next. Please. Please, Miss Faery Layla. Me next." Screamed a chipped, and ever so polite champagne flute as it ran to the edge of the shelf and precariously wobbled. *"I'm truly wonderful and already sooooo versatile. I hold champagne and prosecco and Babysham and, oh my, did I say champagne? Oh, dearie me, I think I may have. Shall I continue to wow you with my skills? I also cradle raspberries on my rim, and I hold freshly squeezed orange juice in my slender sides. I'm on everyone's picnic list and I'm really good during special occasions. I'm so, so wanted. Really wanted. I'm never stuck in a cupboard for long. I get to travel in wicker basket style or placed on a silver tray with crisp linen. And everyone, but everyone, just knows that I'm awfully special.*

Ohhhh, woe is me. Why am I even here? This is all a mistake. A miscarriage of justice." The flute was manically laughing and crying.. all at the same time. The glass began rhythmically rocking and knocking off the edge of a matronly casserole dish.

"You're here because you're obviously cracked. Next client. Come on, I don't have all day." Faery Layla rolled her sparkling

eyes and went back to painting her nails a lovely metallic shade.

"Faery Layla, excuse me. Can we talk about the coaching you're offering? Faery Layla...." Nora more assertively enquired, and nearly tapped Faery Layla on her arm.

Faery Layla rolled her eyes, again, then ignored Nora's polite but pointed request. The Botox was surely coming out today...both Nora and Faery Layla thought.

"I'm next, but I can wait. There's no one wanting to take me home. I have all the time in the world. I remember when I was in every China cabinet, on every mantle-piece and on every bar in the country. Precisely lined up on every dusty, old oak beam and looking out at the customers as they had a after work catch up. Those were the days. I was useful. I would hold pins and scissors, or hopefully carry a full pint of frothing ale in my pottery belly. Now I'm old and obsolete. No one wants to dust me, and everyone drinks out of bottles or cans or glasses. Even goblets and stainless steel tankards are more popular than me. I never thought I'd see that day coming. No siree.

No one needs me to hold pins, or mini tape measures from Christmas crackers, or thimbles anymore. No one bothers to take up a hem anymore, or sew on a missing button anymore. People just throw things away. Things like me. I'm just a used up old nick-nack." The robust Toby jug was perpetually smiling despite his deeply depressed tone and woeful tale. Which was ironic, and ever so slightly disturbing.

"You need to buck up your ideas and get back out there. Have you thought about the great outdoors? You'd make a great bird feeder. That would solve all your problems." Faery Layla had moved onto applying nail polish to her other hand. She was exceedingly confident that her advice was truly excellent and, to celebrate, she decided to treat herself to an extra spicy kebab for her tea.

"I hate wildlife. And feathers make me sneeze. Ask any feather duster, they'll tell you. I give them such a fright. I'm just

sooooo useless but I'm too heavy to throw myself off the shelf." The old jug sniffed and looked longingly at the edge of the shelf. Well with all the smiling it was difficult to say how longingly the jug looked at the potential means of his splattered destruction, but it was all very likely.

"Right, I'll come back to you but stay away from the edge. You're full of purpose and potential so pull yourself together and give me some time to think. Sheesh. Now you, lurking at the back. Yes, you. Come on out and stop with all that whispering and cackling." Faery Layla said whilst blowing on her nails.

"Faery Layla, excuse me. Can we talk about the coaching you're offering? Faery Layla.... now." Nora stepped towards Faery Layla and indicated the pint-sized termagant should follow Nora to the corner of the shop.

Faery Layla did her usual answer of an eye roll then ignored Nora's trembling pointed finger.

A stainless steel can opener confidently sauntered up to the front of the shelf then wildly screamed, *"I'll cut you. I'll cut you. I'll open you up like the last tin of Spam. Ever seen your own beating heart? Well, you will. You will."* And with that the can opener launched itself off the shelf and at the opinionated Faery.

"Get back you fudging lunatic and behave yourself, sheesh." And with **that** Faery Layla flicked the metal psychopath into the closest umbrella stand. *"And you made me chip my nail, you manic. You're getting melted first. Fish-knives, and the newly branded sushi knives you're safe for another day. Bloody lunatic has tetanus or something."*

Nora carefully removed the furious can opener from the stand and openly glared at Faery Layla. Nora then sat with the tin opener in order to help him to de-escalate his anger and discuss possible outlets for his quick temper.

"It's us next. We know it. Everyone knows it." squeaked a delicate cup and saucer duo. *"We want to be heard. We're the last*

of our kind. We are unique. They're all out to get us because we are individuals. There's no one else quite like us. We've been singled out for months and months. There were thirty of us to begin with, but we're being singled out, I tell you. Purchased one item at a time. We're next I tell you. They're coming for us. Breaking our spirit. They want to fill us with scented wax and set us ablaze. Burn like the fires of Hell." At that the terrified best, bone China crockery squealed then ducked behind the rotund casserole dish.

"Everyone but everyone uses dishwashers these days. No one wants to handwash China dishes. You need to get with the times and stop being so bloody delicate all the time. So, what if you're filled with candle wax. At least you're useful. Unlike fat Toby there. No offence Toby." Faery Layla was busy buffing out her chipped nail and shooting daggers at the can opener. Faery Layla decided that she preferred the thought of shooting actual daggers, so she was going to swap out the Botox vials for some seriously sharp steel swords. She just needed to pop into see her "*Blade man*" before she picked up her dinner.

"None taken, Faery Layla. I'm just glad you remembered me at all. I'm usually forgotten and relegated to the monthly swipe of a damp yellow duster. That's the highlight of my life." The magenta waistcoated Toby jug softly murmured, and thought longing of the caress of a lemon scented cloth.

"Yeah, well I'll get back to you. You're a bit of a difficulty one, ya grinning weirdo." Faery Layla screwed up her button nose and contemplated the Toby jug's fate. She wasn't hopefully. Maybe the ledge was the best idea afterall.

"Hic, hic. Me next if you please." Slurred the polite but ever so drunk corkscrew.

"Why are you here? I thought a corkscrew would break before it was handed into a charity shop. Now the bottle stopper beside you is still in its original wrapper because no fudger from Falkirk would ever need one. There's never any wine left to save and stopper here. Erm, but you. What's your game?" puzzled the impatient Faery Layla. She was going to have to take off all the

nail polish and start again. That temperamental opener!

"Well, my flighty lady, hic. I was part of the temperance movement and would back away from opening the evil: that is a bottle of wine. The lady of the house became increasingly impatient with my stubbornness, and instead of trying to see my point of view she handed me into this prison for the unloved, hic.

I needn't have been so highly principled as I have since found out that I am allergic to cork, so I have no purpose. None what so ever, hic. I was unable to even open the fancy bottles of spice infused oils that are so popular nowadays. Being handed back in here for a second time... well that broke me. My resilient spirit was no more, hic.

There was a lovely, young ceramic haggis sitting beside me on the shelf. He was minding his own business, but he made the mistake of still being half-full of whisky, so in my time of need, I drained him dry. He gurgled and cried out as I drained his last drop of nectar. In the sma' hours I can still hear his watery cries, hic. I'm so ashamed.

Since then, I've been raking the shelves for the remnants of alcohol, and licking the sides of the hand-disinfectant dispensers. I've completely given up on my temperance principles and I'm a mess, hic." Sobbed the screw. He felt that he could no longer claim the title of a *"Corkscrew"*. The shame of it all.

"So, let me get this right. You wouldn't do the one thing you're meant to. So, you were sent here, where you now do the one thing that you're meant to? Am I correct?" Faery Layla stared at the baffling screw then did a really slow blink. The Faery began shaking her head and rubbing her left eye. She was beginning to think that Life Coaching wasn't all it was cracked up to be. She should have stuck with something easy, like the marine corps.

"Well, when you put it like that.... yes." Whispered the embarrassed screw. His gaze shifting to a packet of, out of date, brandy butter. He coiled, ready to pounce.

"Next!" shouted, the impatient Faery Layla.

A gaily painted bonbon dish pushed its way to the front of the distressed items, and gave a decidedly gallic shrug. *"Bonjour, I also am in need of a little, itty bit of, what you call, assistance. I was tragically ripped from a sunshine drenched windowsill in my French Chateau and bundled off to this forsaken place. I use to hold the most delicious sweets, chewy bonbons and petite fors, but here I was so misused. I had to hold... nicky nacks. These heathens do not understand how to present food. Food should feed the eyes, then tempt the tongue then nourish the body. Here they just open a packet of bargain biscuits and scoff them all. It is tres unpleasant."* The bonbon dish lifted her delicate, lacy rim and sighed.

Faery Layla thought she might, just might, have felt a little bit of sympathy for the bonbon dish if it weren't for all the lying and heavy sighing.

"Who are you trying to kid? My head doesn't button up the back. I bet you're not even from France. You have an English accent. It's familiar. Where have I heard it before? Oh, I've got it. You sound just like the singer, Adele. I bet if I turned you over, you'd have a sticker saying 'made in China' or 'made in Tottenham' on your deceitful bum. You, young dish, need to be true to your roots and hold those Knick-knacks with pride. And you so know that Knick-knacks start with a K. Stop being such a spoiled madam and embrace the common people. Biscuits are biscuits. They taste good and are terrible for the waist line. Next." Faery Layla had regained her coaching confidence. This was a piece of cake or a bite of biscuit.

Nora was still working with the tin opener, but felt she really needed to have a serious chat with the terrifyingly blunt Faery Layla. Nora was positive that Faery Layla wasn't fully qualified to offer this type of advice.

"Right, I have a couple of minutes left to sort you lot out, so I'll cure the fake fruit next. Out with it. Your time starts now." Faery Layla set an alarm on her smart watch. She still had

nearly all of her 10,000 wing beats to fit in that day.

The highly polished, plastic banana rose from the fruit bowl. *"As salesperson of the year I feel that we probably don't need any help. But for a small commission, Apple here, could do your taxes and Bunch of Grapes, over there, could be your own very personal shopper.*

I am a well-known and much-loved telephone, but I also do a bit of stunt work on the side. My slide on a banana skin is legendary. It's all due to the secret flick: my own invention, with patent pending.

Ahh, yes. We do not need your help but you definitely need Orange's help. He's a world famous psychic and dabbles in a bit of bison breeding, but only every second Monday." The banana finished with a strangely, skewed bow. He forcefully offered an autographed photo to Faery Layla, for the princely sum of £1.73. Per letter. He obviously could not read the room and Orange's psychic abilities weren't helping. Not one little bit.

"Well, that got strange very quickly. I'm not in the market to deal with fake fruit, who are all compulsive liars. Yes, you lot. You fibbers. Oy, Toby, you should take a leaf outta their book and tell folks that you're a TV remote control holder. You're so plump that no one could lose you down the side of the sofa. No way, Mr Chubster. Problem sorted, so keep away from the edge until I get my money.

No, I don't want the autograph, you lying banana and I don't believe you were ever a phone. Where would I plug you in? Stop, please don't show me...it'll put me off ma dinner.

Now, your bills for my services." Faery Layla rubbed her hands together again, smiled gleefully then got out her calculator and her big change purse.

"Ahem, before you do that, we ***need*** *to have a chat and I'd like to look at your credentials. I'm not sure you're really a Life Coach but I'm really sure that you shouldn't tell your clients to 'pull themselves together'. Advising clients to lie and referring to Toby as 'Fat Toby' or 'Mr Chubster' isn't acceptable either. So, we*

need to talk." And with that Nora strongly indicated Faery Layla should come with her. When that didn't work Nora gently-ish grabbed Faery Layla by her long stream of flower entwinned, dark brown hair and hurried her to the corner. Keeping Faery Layla's eyes pointed away from her face. Nora didn't fancy having a permanent Botox frown as she and Devil Keith, aka the Thief Taker Downers, were being interviewed by the Falkirk Herald later that day. Nora really hoped the Herald had decided on a better nickname for them by then. Something sexy like, *"the Granny Grabbers,"* or *"Pensioner Pullers"*. On second thoughts, Nora decided she'd stick with the original name as it was a lot less pervy. Nora just hoped that Devil Keith could cancel the run of forty-seven personalised tee-shirts they had ordered.

The conflicted sporks felt that their identity issues could wait until the Nora and Faery Layla discussion was finished. Then the sporks disagreed and asked to join the plastic fruit, then they asked to live in Toby's tummy, then they wondered if they could serve sushi and finally, they tried speaking with a London accent. Nora was a strong believer that the sporks needed to recognise their worth, but she also realised that they had a long journey ahead of them. A journey of discovery, support and potential change. If they wished.

CHAPTER EIGHT

Still in the charity shop and not nearly as cheery...

"Devil Keith, whilst your lovely, lovely Nora is chatting with my gloriously clever Faery Layla, I think we have a few things we need to discuss. Eh? For sure." The stunning Faery Queen Lucy purred and fluttered her very long eyelashes. She puffed up her delicate flowery skirt and primly perched on a *"Visit Falkirk,"* ceramic thimble.

"Ah, well. It's stocktaking season at the moment, so maybe... sometime in the next decade? I could certainly fit you in then. I'll get my appointment book, shall I?" Smiled a very nervous Devil Keith as he furtively taped down some frustrating board games and munched on a couple of die. He choked, a little, but just kept on chewing.

"Faery Ritamay, Faery Jax, can you persuade Devil Keith to take a break from pricing up the jigsaws with the missing pieces? We have some business to discuss, for sure." Nodded Queen Lucy, as she rested her red suede platform boots on a dullish silver button.

Faery Ritamay, the harridan, feverishly grinned then pursed her glossy vermillion coated lips and harshly licked the excess lipstick from her front teeth. She straightened her tight black leather corset then tipped some lilac scented talcum powder down her cleavage to reduce the horrendous chaffing. She patted down her jiggling bosom then re-lifted her breasts and gave them a bit of a shoogle. *"Ah, just right,"* she sighed. She then tightly tied her no-nonsense rubber soled nurse's shoes, removed her black-rimmed spectacles and fluffed her humongous moth wing hat before striding over to the frightened Devil Keith. Ritamay was an excellent flying Faery but the strutting was just so much more… eviller.

Faery Ritamay slowly unholstered her small but mighty puff gun, she admired the gleaming shell handles and tested the grip. Her adapted gun fired gas pelts containing deadly mushroom spores. The fungi, most foul, were a closely guarded secret. Her own homemade and highly illegal concoction of Funeral Bell and Panther Cap mushrooms. A small whiff of the gas incapacitated its victim by inducing projectile vomiting, inflicting liver damage, producing vivid hallucinations, created feelings of confusion, then there were the delusions of greater strength and finally, the fatal convulsions. On reflection: not the most pleasant way to spend a Tuesday afternoon in rainy Falkirk. As an aside: the weather changed as often as Devil Keith changed his pantaloons, so that was often.

"Devil Keith. I don't really want to use this gun, but I will. Because contrary to your misguided beliefs and your feelings of entitlement… I don't love you to the moon and back. In fact, I'm not keen on you at all just now. Not at all. You big, fat cheater." Sneered Faery Ritamay and with that pronouncement she bopped Devil Keith on the nose. She packed quite a punch for a little one. She then followed it up with a swift pull of Devil Keith's few remaining nasal hairs. Ohhh, eye watering stuff.

"She's telling the truth, for sure. Well, apart from saying she didn't want to use the gun. She does want to use it, for sure. She's been giddy all day with the thought of it." Clarified the very helpful and glamorous Queen Lucy. She nonchalantly wiped a spot of dust from her normally pristine shoes. The shop could really benefit from a spot of dusting and a lick of polish.

"Oh, she is telling the truth, my flower. Now we usually wing it, but I think Faery Ritamay may already have a devilishly good plan hidden under the plume of her unusual hat." Faery Jax demurely whispered and sighed. She warmly thought about all of the odd conversations, lively debates and dastardly plans

the Faeries had indulged in over her many henchwoman years. The dandelion clocks that had been repurposed to produce a fatal cases of the giggles when blown upon, and the rigid frozen worms that could dislodge a stubborn fingernail from its nail bed. Then, after that wee touch of silent reminiscing and a great deal of grinning, she purposefully adjusted her own hat. An attractive thistle flower was prettily perched on her head and tied beneath her chin with an orange and yellow striped bow. She then followed closely behind her scheming compadre. Faery Jax tapped her pretty Faery foot, looked up through her lashes and waited for all the gooey action to begin.

The Queen's Faery body guards worked as a tag team. Faery Ritamay would rough folks up, whilst Faery Jax would use her Bodyshop compact, full of coconut butter and other soothing balms, to smooth out the injuries. Well, some of the injuries, so long as body parts weren't completely severed then maliciously hidden. Faery Jax was blissfully unaware that the fragrant pots of moisture didn't exactly cure Faery Ritamay's poisons. Although she would have been absolutely delighted to know that coroners and morticians have been known to note how soft the cadaver's skin is. In the serial killer world Faery Ritamay is known as the '*Hawaiian Sunset Sender-offer*'. If Faery Jax had been party to this information, she would seriously have to re-think her career. Afterall, she was a peace-loving, peach and cream skinned story teller. Well apart from all crushed beetle exfoliants hidden in the bottom of her handbag. They're all crunchy and ever so good for sloughing off dry skin. At a push, they also double as a lovely pizza topping.

A wee aside...

The Tooth Faery aka TF use to be Faery Ritamay's most ruthless and trusted sidekick. TF's roll was to locate fresh teeth so that they could be ground into healing calcium poultices to aid the re-growth of torture related crushed and broken bones.

Unfortunately, the Tooth Faery began experimenting with the ground up teeth and now has a significant substance misuse problem. You do not want to know what TF does to earn the under-pillow money that she leaves for the recently toothless. Oh, dear me. For sure, you do not.

"Before I let Faery Ritamay and Faery Jax do their beautifully scented thing. I think we should have a little discussion regarding how you're going to grovel, then pay me back my winnings. Oh yes, and cut me in on all the lovely action. For sure.

Oh, and before you start spinning a yarn. I've already called on Mr Havel, the crafty bookmaker. After a bit of gentle-ish persuasion he talked. In truth: he's a good guy to have on your payroll. Very brave and extremely loyal. Nearly as loyal as my Faery Ritamay, Faery Layla and Faery Jax. He withstood hours of intensive interrogation, multiple imaginative threats to his person, nap deprivation torture, hundreds of disappointed sighs and the odd re-run of badly dubbed Dr Who. I thought he was never gonna break, for sure. Even when my awesome ogre slammed the rusty hacksaw, brutal hammer, the trusty tile-cutter and a pre-owned tyre-pump on the scarred table, Mr Havel was stoic. Stared straight ahead without as much as a blink. We were so impressed and were about to stop the process... to let him go home for a portion of cottage pie and a pint of frothy ale.

But Faery Layla made a truly inspired suggestion. She rummaged about in her peach lacy bra and slowly smiled. You know the smile I mean, for sure. A small, cream, plastic tube was placed in the centre of the table, and it was Mr Havel's undoing. Faery Layla so enjoyed slowly unscrewing the lid to expose the razor-sharp tip of the sewing box staple. The Quick Un-pick lay there in all its glory. A surprisingly underused torture tool that is delighted to mercilessly slit an innocent stitch from its thready moorings.

It only took the vicious removal of one of Mr Havel's much-loved patch pockets, from his beige shorts for him to crack. By the time Faery Layla had loosened one tiny stitch on the second pocket he was undone, for sure. He spilled all the betting slips and the beans. For sure he did. So, your story better match up. For sure." Beamed Queen Lucy. Her customary *"for sures"* were popping up all over the conversation so it was clear that she was confident that she had won this round with the rapidly wilting Devil. She patted then stroked the shop counter, and heavily hinted that Devil Keith should pop up beside her. Within striking distance, for sure.

"They're not beige shorts. They're ***khaki*** *shorts. Manly khaki shorts."* Devil Keith was trying to put on a brave face, but he couldn't stop a stray gulp from escaping. Then he gulped some more. The unsanctioned removal of a piece cloth from a fully functioning item of clothing, for the purpose of torture was low, so low. Even for the ferocious Faeries.

CHAPTER NINE

So, what did Devil Keith do with the bookmaker that upset the Faeries?

A few months ago, Devil Keith had gone out for a walk one day to break in his new lilac, ballet flats. He needed them for a special date later that week, and Bub had refused to do it for him. Bub, was being totally unreasonable and it turned out that he was under some spell or something. Yawn... who wants to know about all that? If you do you'll find all the wonderfully entertaining details at *"The Devil's a courting,"* by P and K Stoker.

During Devil Keith's daunder and by pure luck, he spotted some huge hairy mammoth tracks. He hadn't seen a mammoth for quite some time so he initially thought they were just ordinary elephants wearing ill-fitted Ugg boots. He then decided that wasn't the case as it was too hot for Uggs. And anyway, elephants absolutely preferred wearing vertically stripped flipflops. They're so slimming. Everyone knows that.

However, he was intrigued by his rediscovery of the mighty beasts, and he thought there might just be a bit of money to be made. Afterall, King Kong was rolling in dosh following the launch of his very successful bug spray. A bug spray that could vanquish mosquitoes the size of single engine airplanes.

So, whilst Devil Keith was hotly debating and deliberating on how he could possibly bundle a non-consenting mammoth into the back of his Ford Corsa, he had come across a couple of robust guys hanging out in a cavernous cave in the Bashelaksky Range of the Altai mountains, in coldest Siberia.

Devil Keith really did walk a lot when he was pondering and solving Tetris like problems with his car's boot capacity. And he could complete full Marathons when he was breaking in particularly tight shoes. He really should consider buying a half size bigger but his vanity wouldn't allow him that comfort, and he didn't want to have bigger feet than Bub. For some reason he thought he'd never live that down. Didn't he realise that men with big feet just needed bigger socks?

The encounter with the robust guys...

After a bit of sketching in the snow: please note that none of them would have won any prizes at Pictionary. Then there was some general grunting, a bit of vague pointing around, a minute of hiccups and a few seconds of high impact Zumba. Well, it turned out the guys were a missing tribe of Neanderthals. Then, with the help of Google translate their full story emerged.

So, there was the getting cut off from the rest of the mountain range due to an unforeseen avalanche. The avalanche should have been expected as the guys had just finished their annual chilli eating contest and, as a result, the air was unseasonably warm. Then there was the constant bickering over when winter was officially over, so they could wear their spring collection of furs. Plus, the unrelenting boredom of always wearing the same style of high-leg loincloth. If it's not broke why fix it? Was the overwhelming ethos that was heartily disliked by the vocal, and fashion conscious minority. And the now dwindling hunting grounds that had drastically reduced their Neanderthal numbers, and were making them consider commuting to work. A typical lost tribe story, blah, blah, blah. Devil Keith has ambushed the laptop again, in a bid to avoid facing retribution from Queen Lucy. For sure.

The shy, isolated Neanderthals had no idea that they were now in the minority, and those pesky humans had over run the wilderness. Well, the Neanderthal world was really just a bloody great big cave with hot and cold running stalactites; with a couple of feet of softish snow beyond said cave. So, after quite a bit of discussion, a hoola dancing competition and some counselling to explore their abandonment issues, the Neanderthals all agreed that they didn't want to join the human race. They had never been fans of the smooth fore-headed, patchy hair brigade: as the humans were so loving referred to. The Neanderthals were a surprisingly conservative bunch and heartily disapproved of the humans and their relatively hairless ways. Who goes out showing that much bare skin on their back? A self-centred male hussy, that's who, was the Neanderthals unanimous response. Devil Keith thought that the notion of waxing might cause the Neanderthals to spontaneously burst, so he decided to hide his legs, back and other bits.

However, the Neanderthals did quite fancy the idea of being able to microwave their hairy mammoth steaks. They were fed up with arguing over whose turn it was to rake out the ashes and set the following morning's kindling. It was such a tedious, repetitive job and it was difficult to keep a modesty-covering loincloth in place whilst scrambling around the smoky campfire.

Devil Keith explained that in order to revamp their kitchenette cave to accommodate a double Belfast sink, a coffee machine and an air-fryer they would need some money. And some viable skills to get that money. In response the Neanderthals offered him some old bone needles, and some chipped out cave paintings. Devil Keith felt that due to the Neanderthal's shoddy workmanship, and lack of depth perception, a bunch of five-year olds had more artistic talent and probably had the cave painting market all sewn up. He politely declined.

After some elegant debating, and some excellently

brewed, frothy mammoth milk ale Devil Keith had a eureka moment. He had discovered, in his extremely inebriated state and hanging upside down from the cave ceiling, a gap in the sports market. Namely Neanderthal racing. The Neanderthals were initially sceptical, but Devil Keith then showed them some temptingly bespoke, kitchen floor tiles that he carried about on his person. Devil Keith had used the emergency tiles on a large number of occasions, and was always pleasantly reassured to find that a lot of other people carried their own set of glazed terracotta's. The Neanderthals were convinced. They thought it was a grand idea, so long as they got to design their own sports strips and could vet the sponsorship deals. They were surprisingly business savvy considering they normally traded in misshapen rocks that resembled Channing Tatum, and swapped hardened mammoth poop.

Let the money roll in.

CHAPTER TEN

Somewhere warmer than Siberia...

Devil Keith put out some feelers and was confident the Neanderthals would draw a crowd of the very bestest, betting enthusiasts. With the help of Mr Havel, the illustrious bookmaker, Devil Keith set up his moneymaking scheme.

Mr Havel would don his multi-pocketed khaki shorts and enticingly call out the racing odds. The fluttering Faeries were entranced by Mr Havel's booming laughter and his nifty knee support. The Faeries believed that Mr Havel kept his very best Faery Dust in the elastic bandage so they would flock to place their bets and ping the compression stocking for luck. Little did they know that Mr Havel had no such Faery Dust, but he did use his bandage to store his delicious beef jerky. Jerky that Mrs Havel lovingly pre-chewed for her husband and tucked into the support bandage each morning.

Now this is where it all got a little bit tricky because there weren't enough Neanderthals to create enough viable racing teams. Devil Keith, was initially perplexed then he had another mammoth's milk ale eureka moment. And in his drunken wisdom decided to *"flavour and enhance"* the racing teams with fit, human males dressed as Neanderthals. He had a surprising number of aspiring youngish soap actors, who had been inexplicably bumped-off in their TV world, to choose from. So, with some emergency method acting lessons, that mainly comprised of mammoth wrangling and twerking. And with the addition of toupees and tufts of dander, Devil Keith thought all his problems were solved. Unfortunately, the Real Neanderthals reacted badly to the starting pistols and all ran off to check there were no further avalanches. They did not want to be locked in with the highly critical Devil Keith. No siree.

When the Real Neanderthals calmed down and started racing, they were unbeatable. Winning every race and developing quite a fan girl following. Not as much of a fan girl as Brownie Mary Jo's crush on Luke Bryan, the country singer, but close enough. This predicable winning seriously disrupted Devil Keith's ability to rake in the cash as the odds were mercilessly slashed and the pay-outs were crippling. No one, but no one would bet on anyone but the favourite Neanderthal racer.

Devil Keith, in his desperation, tried branching out in order to re-coup his losses. He bought a job lot of Ugg boots as the hairy-footed mammoths looked so good in fur, and they had their very own robust fan club. Unfortunately the sales were dismal as no one wanted Ugg boots during the hot summer months. He had sunk quite a sum of his own money into the sweat inducing boots, and was facing immediate liquidation of all his assets. This included his corsets and prized China cabinets. Devil Keith was so out of his depth, but was pretending everything was hunkidory and spending like a man with six arms and no sense. So no one suspected a thing.

However, this all came to a head when an unsuspecting Mr Havel took a considerable bet on contestant number two. The firm favourite and guaranteed winner, for sure. The bankrupting bet was placed by none other than Queen Lucy. Devil Keith was worried. In fact, he was very worried. He had two days to the cover the astronomical bet, and he was quickly escalating into full-blown panic mode.

Whilst sweating and generally becoming very unwell; he was nearly convinced that he had sweated a good half lobe of his liver out through his skin, such was his fear. Devil

Keith began his usual routine of nightly haircuts and trims to fill his dander quota. This was normally limited to donations from his unsuspecting, and slumbering brother. Ah...so that's where all of Bub's hair was going? Cuts and snips to provide the follicles for the actors. Glad that question was finally answered. Harry will be relieved and a little disappointed as she had her fingers crossed for Devil Keith to have a wee touch of male pattern balding. She was convinced that he would be needing the random clumps of hair for his own head. She'd also seen a couple of toupees in one of Devil Keith's China cabinets.

After sheering Bub, Devil Keith discovered that Stan was also available for a bit of scissor action that night. Devil Keith was unaware of Stan's unusual lineage and he pinched some locks from the lucky Irishman. These were sewn into a new toupee for contestant number three and, Holi moly, that non-Neanderthal racer won. He should never, ever have beaten the Real Neanderthals as he was a rank outsider. Devil Keith had finally made some money. In fact, he made a lot of money that night and a shocked Queen Lucy did not. Devil Keith made so much money that he began fixing all of the races. He didn't make the mistake of using Stan's hair in a full toupee again as racer number three had won by a suspiciously, ridiculous margin. There was smoke trailing behind the racer's...well, behind.

Rather, Devil Keith glued tiny tufts of hair on the actors pretending to be Neanderthals so that he could predict exactly who would win and who would place in each race. The results were phenomenal and highly illegal. Devil Keith also, totally by accident (he says), then deliberately used the tiniest slivers of Stan's hair to increase his generally luck so things were going very well.

When Devil Keith married his Nora, he tried to share his successful sporting venture with her but Nora was no freeloader (her words) and insisted on buying shares in his business. He was delighted to share the positive aspects of the business, but not the race fixing, with his lovely Nora. He correctly predicted that she would have worried for his safety and might not have approved of his methods. Nora was less impressed with the gambling, winning, infamy and being a WAG, but she was delighted with the constant cash flow. Money she could and did share anonymously with a number of local charities and good causes. She even refused the offer of a brand-new duffle coat, stating that her current jacket was only four years old and still had another couple of good years of wear left in it.

The stunningly striking Queen Lucy is no putz. She began intently studying the racing and watching how Devil Keith was interacting with his eager squads. She noticed that most of the Neanderthals were investigating lucrative modelling careers whilst swaggering around and boasting at the after-race parties. Whilst a smaller group of Neanderthals appeared quite shy and timid... positively coy. They were spending a great deal of their time with their trusty measuring tapes then intently critiquing kitchen appliances. They also spent their Sunday's off browsing homeware stores, and they appeared to be glued to night-time shopping channels. The smaller group of Neanderthals were also engaged in a surprising number of highly vocal arguments over the shopping channels' puzzling postage tariffs. A watch and golf clubs incur the same postage? Absolutely preposterous!

The Faery Queen also noticed that most of the Neanderthals were very conscious of their complicated grooming regimes and wheeled full length mirrors around the sports stadium so they could check on their eye-liner. Whilst the smaller group of Neanderthals were utterly intrigued by the concept of conditioners for colour damaged hair. So intrigued that they not only used it on their hair but they had also published a highly successful book titled, *"Conditioning in Cocktails"*. The book made it to the top of the New York Times best seller list for eighteen consecutive weeks until someone used too much conditioner in their strawberry daquiri and found their tongue to be too bouncy and full of body to fit back in their mouth. Queen Lucy noted that there was also a random splinter group who were utterly intrigued by the structural integrity of loofas. This group comprised equally of the boastfully vain Neanderthals and the timid Neanderthals, so she wasn't sure what was going on there.

All, in all, the Queen realised that for all the stories of the Neanderthal's enforced isolation they didn't appear to be one truly cohesive tribe. There wasn't nearly enough hairpulling, early morning underwear stealing and arguments over the TV remote control, for her peace of mind.

Queen Lucy reasoned that people would think that Nora was probably the weak link regarding solving the racing mystery, as young Nora was new to the supernatural world. However, the Queen recognised Devil Keith's utter devotion to his Nora, and how protective Nora was of her Devil Keith. Nora would never betray Devil Keith. Plus, no way was the Queen getting in the middle of the hot and handsy honeymooners. She acknowledged and respected true love and true lust, when she saw it. And she was seeing it big time and often and graphically, for sure, when she was with Nora and Devil Keith.

Queen Lucy had her very own prince charming at home: vacuuming their shared mushroom palace, dusting their collection of Cliff Richards memorial dinner plates and bringing her a cup of morning dew every morning in bed. Just to be clear. Not **The** Prince Charming of the Fairytale fame. Oh no, not that weirdo. **The** Prince Charming had a thing for shoes, and he was currently banned from the shoe aisles in Shuh, Gucci and Sports Direct, following his highly publicised shoes caressing debacle.

So, the Queen of the Faeries had decided that Mr Havel, the booming bookmaker and his intriguing shorts were going to provide the answers to all of her questions. And she had many questions.... like where was all her money, are people really putting hair conditioner in their *"Sexiness on the Beach"* cocktail, and lastly was the exorbitantly priced spying lollipop man a tax-deductible business expense?

CHAPTER ELEVEN

Present day and back in the charity shop, still with those Faeries...

It took some doing but Nora convinced Faery Layla that she had taken on quite a lot of work, with no guarantee of payment from the unemployed and abandoned items. So, the huffy Faery reluctantly allowed the charity items to go back to their silent, non-sentient selves. That is until a monthly direct debit could be set up to stream some much-needed dosh from the *"moaning minnies,"* into the Faery's bank account. Faery Layla was scheming again and using some, justifiably, frowned upon descriptors for the charity items.

In reality, the wait for the direct debit would give Nora some leeway to access some proper, licensed and evidence-based therapy for the distressed and deserted items. A way to put them on the road to support, rehabilitation and recovery. And Nora was hopeful that Faery Layla would lose interest in the items by then. Nora was also going to look into Botox poisoning, and how to recover your facial expressions, as she thought that she probably hadn't seen the last of the gobby Faery.

Devil Keith was hunkered down and backed into a corner of the shop. Faery Ritamay had the puff gun back out and pointed directly at his face. He had agreed to sign over the controlling interest in the Neanderthal racing to Queen Lucy, but he feared that might not be enough to keep his Nora's pockets completely intact. He needed lots of money and he needed it fast.

Nora was also trapped in a corner with the still scowling Faery Layla. Things were exceedingly tense in the shop. Nora looked around and realised that she had been tricked into physically separating from her Devil Keith. The Faeries must have known that she'd want to protect the distressed bric-a-brac items and used this information to isolate Devil Keith from her support. Those sly flighty ones had been playing her from the start.

One wrong move and Faery Jax would whip out her compact of coconut balm and start a rubbing. There was no escape for either of the lovers when a white tube whooshed across the shop floor. Devil Keith dived over the menacing Faeries and on to the rolling tube. He quickly, and gratefully unrolled the scroll.

To the voices of a Welsh male choir: singing to the tune of Twinkle, Twinkle Little Star.

"Congratulations, you have gained
a second horn to put on your shelf.
Come home, come home and celebrate
your wonderous achievement. You are great
You are a person without equal.
Well not quite as good the other Hells
They already have at least two horns.
But off you pop and collect your prize.
Congratulations, you have gained
a second horn to put on your shelf."

"Good old Karen and Dr Riel! And what a great tune and lyrics," and with that Devil Keith grabbed his Nora and gave her a lusty cuddle. They happily jumped onto the cockroach moving pavement and hotfooted it back to Hell number one.

CHAPTER TWELVE

On a hidden balcony...

"Oh, I think I might have a tan. Bub, have I got any white bits? Can you have a wee look for me?" Harry whispered naughtily and winked at her man. Bub gladly, and painstakingly, searched for Harry's non-existent white bits. The joys of a belated honeymoon in the sunshine and a luxury hotel suite with a secluded balcony. Bub and Harry enjoyed the utter contentment of not having to explain every single thing to a loveable idiot. Then explain again, to a now less lovable idiot. The joy of not having to guard your dinner from roaming, greedy hands. Of not having to use specially sharpened fork tines to impale those intrusive hands. The utter delight of finding your items of clothing still hanging in the wardrobe, and not smouldering on a blistering BBQ grill. The surprise of still having hair on your head instead of crumbs of blackened, gingerish follicles floating in the bathtub. In fact, the out and out shock of actually having any hair at all was idyllically intoxicating.

The loved-up Harry and Bub had decided to tour Italy for a few weeks. This was because they were intrigued by the culture and history, and by now, everyone who knew of Harry's slight (cough) misdemeanours were dead. Positively and unequivocally dead. Bub and Harry, clipboard in hand, had toured the mausoleums to make sure of that. Ticking off the names of the deceased with obvious relish. Bub has now learned never to underestimate his Harry's, let's call it impact, on people, places, and things.

They roared through the Italian countryside, in their bright yellow Lamborghini, with their roof down: admiring the lush vineyards, rolling hills, tall cypress trees and crumbling but noble villas. They gaped at the intricately carved stonework that was gracing castles, clock towers and piazzas. They marvelled at the ruins of the roman empire and were inspired by the medieval architect of *"modern"* Italy. They visited tiny bustling fishing harbours, feeding the squawking gulls and paddling in the warm, clear seas. Splashing like tots, then exploring the rock pools for hidden treasure, sparkling shells and crabbit crabs. The infatuated honeymooners had completely forgiven the big boy crabs for stubbing out their cigars in their lovely wedding cake.

Hand in hand the golden couple, well reddish and sort of golden-ish to be fair, slowly strolled through the scent-soaked majestic gardens and uttered gasps of wonder at the glorious Italian churches. They toured the eternal city of Rome and frolicked in the cool fountains. Well, less frolicked as that was frowned upon, and more enjoyed the glistening water as it touched their upturned faces. Harry also sneakily pointed out where Nero had set his fires and Bub added his architectural know how by pointing out why, the places Nero had chosen for his blazes, were totally inadequate for the job.

Bub and Harry ate tiny, but expensive portions of mozzarella pizza, plump pink prawns and creamy pastas in noisy, crowded pavement cafes. Gasping at the rich, aromatic coffees, sharing plates full of steaming hot garlic bread and fighting over the last delicate, cream pastry. Bub always let Harry win, then ate half the scandalously good pudding anyway. Then, whilst delving into the history of the soaring cathedrals and intriguing palaces, the lovers decided to settle for a few days in the awe-inspiring Venice. A city like no other. A city of endless canals and deep blue scenic lagoons. Lagoons dotted with tiny charming islands. A city positively bulging with history, music, culture, class, the occasional decrepit crypt and beautiful, arching bridges. A city, full to the brim with romance, where they could gaze into each other's eyes, to their hearts' content. And they could help each other pick out basil that was obstinately caught between their back teeth.

They accessed the islands of Torcello, Murano and Burano by motorboat, (Bub said it made him feel like James Bond, unfortunately there was a little less Glock action than he had hoped for) so they could admire the fragile, but bloody stiflingly hot, glassblowing and *"oo"* at the exquisite handmade lace. Expressing wonder at the traditional craftmanship and the cleverly preserved artistry.

They whispered reverently whilst touring Doge's palace, the Basilica San Marco and St Mark's Basilica. Expressing wonder at the exquisite mosaic floors, finely carved statues, effigies and the bedazzled Byzantine treasures. Gazing at the panoramic views over the gloriously unique city. A city of warm honey stones, sun dappled terracotta tiles and captivating hidden gems. Well, hidden apart from the myriad of tourists that flocked to the city every day and created looooong queues. Really looooong queues.

They giggled as they navigated the maze of narrow-cobbled streets and cramped brightly coloured townhouses. They traversed town squares to learn the history and walked along the ancient Ponte di Rialto and Ponte degli Scalzi bridges. They sauntered across the tiny, enclosed Bridge of Sighs and viewed Casanova's poky prison cell. He wouldn't have done much seducing there, they concluded, then snogged against the cell wall until they were told to leave. They toured an old gondola factory in Squero dei Muti and admired the old but very effective tools.

They spent their glorious sunny days gliding along the Grand canal in a brightly painted gondola whilst indulging in sinfully delicious, tart, strawberry gelato. Sipping perfectly chilled crisp white wines, chewing fresh artisan breads and gobbling up podgy, glossy, black olives whilst chatting long into the night. Harry donning her wispy cotton, summer dresses and high-heeled strappy sandals: despite the uneven cobbled streets and mounds of abandoned bicycles. Listening to the raucous street vendors and being tempted by traditional masks, on sale at the ancient gaily decorated, market stalls.

CHAPTER THIRTEEN

End of week two…

"I absolutely love history and I'm so sorry to say this, but I'm bored. So, so bored. I can't look at anymore pert, marble bums or admire yet another artfully placed fig leaf. I've totally ran out of adjectives...and I don't care if that makes me an ungrateful, uneducated pleb." And Bub slumped forward onto the 5000 thread, white cotton Egyptian sheets. It really was a luxurious hotel complete with excellent room service, fabulous food, 24-hour cat-calls and salacious winks. The last two items were all courtesy of the besotted and buxom Harry.

Bub was also looking forward to swapping his rumpled, cream linen chinos and loose white shirt for his signature three piece suit. He so liked a single breasted jacket, a brightly lined waistcoat, a subdued tie with platinum tie clip and a shirt that could accommodate his wide array of tasteful cufflinks. And don't get him started on the need to wear loafers, without socks, whilst holidaying. Give him a sturdy pair of ox-blood red coloured leather shoes with woollen Argyle socks any day of the week. The holiday loafers caused some awful chaffing and truly terrible foot odour.

"Oh, thank goodness. My feet are gowping in these silly cookie bun sandals. I really, really need my old Dr Martens back. And no matter what I do I just can't keep these stupid white dresses clean. The cobbled stones make the cafe tables and chairs so wobbly. I drop things on myself all the time then I keep having to suck all the stains out of the gauzy fabric, before someone notices. When they do notice they look at me all funny. Like I'm some kind

of sugar saturated, wonky toddler.

Oh, and if I have to smack my lips and extol the merits of sipping another glass of crisp white wine I will explode and take out a whole vineyard with my handy blowtorch. I need a Falkirk Sewer.

And, don't get me started on those twitting, slippery olives. I'm forever chasing them under tables and onto the busy roads. I nearly kissed the wheel of a moped yesterday and to make matters worse, everyone was checking the olive for injuries. I had a really sore skinned knee and not one person noticed it. Well not until the blood and gore stained my dress then they were all... 'use white wine to get the blood out'. When I used the wine, I was told off for using vintage wine. Seemingly, my horrendously injured knee wasn't worthy of a forty-year-old chardonnay. I just couldn't win." And with that, Harry also slumped onto the bed in a bored, exhausted and sore, heap of messy ginger curls. She failed to add that after soaking a hankie, a couple of times, in the glass of expensive wine she had gulped down the remaining blood infused booze. She drank down that double dipped wine with obvious relish, a few loud burps and stuck her finger in the glass to make sure she caught every last drop of the expensive liquor. That's what **really** upset the flustered locals.

Bub was truly amazed that Harry had lasted as long as she had on this culture loaded holiday. He was the history buff and she was...not. Apart from a bit of light-hearted bickering, threats of division of property, visiting divorce lawyers and them storming off for a few days, to get a much needed break from one another, they had spent a tranquil and educational time together. However, Bub knew when his honey-bunny had reached the end of the line with the old being civilised affair, and she needed to do a bit of the old carnage affair instead.

"Well, my beautiful bride, how about we play some hooky on this whole arts and culture business? We could get us some tequila and a visit to a shady side street to pick up some... playing cards or a couple of board games. Strip poker for two? Can I interest you in a Curlywurly and some cashew nuts? A Twinkie or ten? Some Reece's

Pieces for my wee, injured Lambikins?" Bub wiggled his perfectly arched eyebrows suggestively and rolled off the bed, and onto the floor. He noted that the hotel was so nice that there wasn't even a speck of dust under the bed, but there also wasn't the utter necessity that was barbed wire either. No hotel was truly five stars without the useful wire.

And that is how the completely naked, and buffed up, Bub and Harry were caught blind drunk, raucously singing and generally, well, brutally carousing in the breath-taking city. Not too bad you say, especially when you consider what Harry and Devil Keith previously did to the Colosseum in Rome, the city of Pompei and the statue of Zeus: no civilisation was truly safe from the mental menaces. Oh yes, and the Leaning Tower of Pisa. That is until you realise that Harry and Bub had just finished wildly, and savagely, space hoppering (is that even a word?) across the medieval city of Venice at 3 am in the morning.

They had bought the orange, smiley faced space hoppers at a flea market and decided to liven them up... just a wee bitty. The old Cessna engines were just, ever so, lying around and begging to be re-cycled. So, Bub and his recently acquired engineering skills got a working. Smeared with engine grease (and not much else) and smiling manically, the pair of hoyden honeymooners were off! That is also why parts of Venice are now slightly more underwater than they were prior to the honeymooners' reckless shenanigans and ferocious bouncing.

Oh yes, and that is why certain members of the mafia hot footed it from Rome and are about to readjust Bub's hair parting with a bloody great big axe.

Corralled into a dusty, airless crypt by the suave suited, gun-toting hoodlums: Harry and Bub, wearing hastily donned shower curtain togas, thought the game was well and truly up. They had hoppered their last hop and totalled their last Venetian palace floor. There was no escape in sight, when a white tube whooshed across the floor. A nearly naked Bub dived over the startled Dons, onto the tube and gratefully unrolled the scroll. People would pay good money for that view of perfect maleness!

To the voices of a Welsh male choir: singing to the tune of Twinkle, Twinkle Little Star.

"Congratulations, you have gained
a second horn to put on your shelf.
Come home, come home and celebrate
your wonderous achievement. You are great
You are a person without equal.
Well not quite as good the other Hells
They already have at least two horns.
But off you pop and collect your prize.
Congratulations, you have gained
a second horn to put on your shelf."

"Good old Karen and Dr Riel!" and with that Bub grabbed Harry and gave her a cuddle. They tumbled onto the cockroach moving pavement and escaped back to Hell number one.

CHAPTER FOURTEEN

In a clinic, with just enough outside space to stable a larger than average sized horse. Well, it's really just an awfully big bike shed but when you have a forty-two-hands high horse and require a cherry-picker to reach the saddle on said horse, you're pretty gratefully for anywhere you can safely park it...

"So, have you got everything you need? Everything you need? We got here at 9.30. I said we'd get here for 9.30. Just in time for the appointment. I say, just in time for the appointment." Checked the nervously, expectant father as he tightly tucked the prickly horse blanket around his rotund wifey. He was more anxious than usual as he was still, slightly, in the dog house after accidentally being caught calling his wife *"obscenely massive"*. In his defence she was a tad bigger than the pregnancy books suggested: hence the need for this urgent clinic appointment.

"Yes, now stop fussing and yes, I have forgiven you for your slight faux pas. I agree: I am a little bit bigger than I expected to be at twenty-two weeks pregnant. I thought, at this stage, I'd still be able to tie my own shoe laces, make my oatmeal face packs without eating them all and continue my research into the cure for the common cold. And reach that awkward breakfast bar to put a dab of steaming hot road tar on my slightly burnt toast. Oh, it's so delicious: I can't believe you won't try it." Stan quickly shook his head and mutinously compressed his lips together. He'd tried the Woodland Scents talcum powder liberally sprinkled on prawn cocktail crisps, so he wasn't falling for any more of Dippit's pregnancy craving snack suggestions. No siree. They

were hoaching!

And there was absolutely no way that Stan was trying Dippit's incinerated toast. Stan had a habit of adding songs or phrases to kitchen items in order to enhance the whole cooking, drinking and dining experience. His kidnap-proof, screaming bar glasses were going down a storm in Falkirk's pubs, so Stan had expanded his repertoire to include ovens, kettles and toasters. When perfectly cooked, Stan's toasters burst into a song based on the tune *"I'm so pretty,"* from West Side Story. They would merrily belt out: *"I'm so ready, I'm so ready, I'm so ready and crispy for you. I'm so brown, oh so brown."* Unfortunately, when the singing toaster made Dippit's breakfast treat it now sang a melodious version of *"Ring of Fire,"* by the fantastic Johnny Cash.

Admittedly a great, great song but the toaster wouldn't stop crooning until the fire brigade gave it the all clear. In writing. In triplicate. Dippit made toast several times a day, so poor Stan was up in front of the court on a weekly basis, for wasting fire officer's time and Grievous Bodily Harm. All the twitting writing was giving the fire officers repetitive strain injuries hence the harm offences. Stan predicted an orange boiler suit in his near future as he couldn't possibly disappoint his Dippit and her insatiable need for seared toast.

"Now, where was I? Damn this pregnancy brain and its sieve like qualities." Dippit crunched through a wooden school ruler smothered in peanut butter and lashings of Brasso.

"Moaning?" Stan very, very quietly whispered. Dippit was usually such as easy going person and very, very laidback. Always smiling and ready to help others, but that had all changed a few months ago: once junior boarded the Dippit womb transportation system. Since then Dippit had been a tad testy and, ever so, mildly argumentative. If you call throwing a 72 inch TV clean through the living-room window because she didn't like the end of Star Trek III, mildly argumentative. However, she was still adorable and Stan's cute little wombat.

"Ah, yes. Moaning. Was I moaning? I don't remember.

Moaning? Me? Are you sure? But, most of all, I'd hoped to still be taking my belly dancing lessons. Those tricky omnis won't do themselves, you know. But it wasn't to be, and I'm just a little bitty touchy about that. Maybe it was me moaning? Where was I? Oh, yes. Moaning. I miss my dance sisters and their wiggly ways. That's why I chose Karolyn to do the sonograph. She's a great dancer and ever so patient. It's such a pity that she can't remember me, but when CC turns back time the whole dance session is forgotten, not just my Incredible Hulk impressions. Stan, do you think you could help CC refine his time reversal skills? I'd like Karolyn to recognise me after the class." Dippit fluttered her long, curly eyelashes and chewed on a family-sized packet of crispy cocktail sticks. This was her third pack today and it definitely wouldn't be her last.

"Erm, no. I say no. I've offered but he says that he can't bend the rules, or he'd risk erasing all of history. All of history, I say." Stan had spent a great night with CC. Drinking room temperature real ale, eating many bags of delicious Quavers and scribbling on a very convenient blackboard, that the local dart's team quibbled was theirs. With the help of the intrigued, and slightly squiffy dart's team, they'd nearly located Bigfoot's lair: it's either behind a chemist in Camelon, Falkirk or somewhere else entirely. They'd also worked out how to successfully divert the path of lava flows and potential save many islander's lives. However, they were still no closer to understanding why Stan couldn't stop referring to his wife as massively obscene. The dart's team were flummoxed and feared for Stan's ongoing safety.

"I'm also really hot. Are you hot? I'm so hot in here and think my horsy really needs this blanket more than I do. I feel awful leaving him outside, all alone, especially when I'm a little bit concerned that he might be jealous of the baby and all the attention the babe will get. He's still so, so little himself." Dippit was trying hard not to cry: damn these pregnancy hormones. She was smelling the horse blanket and fondly remembering when she'd given the cute, twenty-hands high, newborn foal

his first ever blankie.

"I'm sure our wee Ducky is just fine. And he can take care of himself. He's over twice the height of a normal horse and he has all those ten-inch spikes instead of a mane. Spikes instead of a mane, I say. But if it'll make you feel better, we can make sure that every time we buy junior a gift, we'll make sure our darling Ducky gets a little something too. I say, a little something too.

But we need to concentrate on today and not borrow trouble. No trouble, I say. How are you? I say. How are you?" Stan was subtly leaning to the right so he could sneakily look out the window in order to check on their wee Ducky. Stan really regretted not bringing another horse blanket with him. And not carrying a hessian sack of peeled carrot sticks for Ducky to munch. And not packing a box of eighteen firelighters for Ducky to munch. And not lugging a crate of pre-cored Granny Smith apples for Ducky to munch. And you guessed it…not bringing some cans of WD 40 for Ducky's cute wee spikes. And to munch: well the empty cans would just go into landfill without little Ducky's convenient and ecofriendly re-cycling mastication. That colossal horse was such a wee doll.

"Now, you stop fretting about me. I'm positively glowing with health. I've just had six pints of creamy Guiness for my breakfast, so I'll be fine for the next hour or so. So don't worry, and go eat your bag of tulip bulbs. I know they calm you." Said a surprisingly upright and non-green Dippit. Stan kept a Dulux paint colour chart with him at all times so he could monitor Dippit's various shades of green. It was one of the easiest ways of knowing when the herb infused Guiness was wearing off, and Dippit needed an emergency top up. She was currently edging into *"Crafty Cabbage Green,"* so everything was, indeed, alright. Although Stan wasn't completely convinced that the colour chart depicted actual Dulux paint shades. The Dulux range of Kitchen's and Bathroom's eggshell paint in the, *"Kuddly Komodo Dragon Green,"* colour was truly ghastly. Dippit occasionally sported that shade just before a fainting spell.

"Hi, I'm Karolyn, your stenographer. Lovely to meet you at last. Excuse me, but did I just hear you say six pints of Guiness for breakfast? Six whole pints? That's a lot, even for non-pregnant women to drink.

I know I sent you a leaflet explaining what would happen today, and my role in your pregnancy, but I think I'll just go over it again. Shall I?" Smiled Karolyn, whilst tucking her bobbed blonde hair behind her tiny ears. An indication that she did, indeed, mean business. These expectant parents had missed a few appointments and that was quite a worry.

"My principal role today is to conduct a sonograph so that I can examine your baby's development, but I would be remiss in my clinical duties if I didn't offer some lifestyle choices during this joyous time. Erm, alcohol during pregnancy is very much frowned upon due to its negative impact on both the mother and the baby. I can signpost you to some excellent resources that can help you during this stressful time. That may assist you reduce your alcohol consumption and help you make healthier choices." Karolyn used her keen wit and naughty sense of humour to put anxious mothers at easy but even with all her experience she hadn't heard anyone talk about their excessive alcohol intake with such reckless abandonment.

"Sorry, I'm not quite sure how to explain all this. Can I think about it while you do the scan? I'll get back to you." Dippit whispered with every intention of getting CC to do his whirly thingy so that the efficient Karolyn wouldn't remember this appointment.

Gel on stomach as Dippit laid back on the reinforced bed: Karolyn had quietly requested the more robust bed when she spotted Dippit's, let's call it, *"unusual shape"*. Dippit made herself comfortable and cheerfully waited on seeing their little baby for the very first time. Stan put down his yellow net bag full of bulbs, swallowed a mouthful of the delicious Dutch treats and held Dippit's clammy hand. They had missed all the previous scans due to Dippit's horizontal antics and the need to find Roger, the cheating, horrible pig. Calls himself a father? He, him, he needs a good thump. Oh, Harry has now grabbed the author's laptop and is typing away furiously.

CHAPTER FIFTEEN

So, this was it!

Karolyn's face drained of all colour. *"Erm, this isn't quite what I expected to see today."* Karolyn, in her defence, expected to see distinguishable features such as hands and toes and the shape of the baby's face on her black and white screen. And if they were lucky, and the baby was lying in the correct position: possibly the sex of the foetus.

However, Karolyn did not expect to see a miniature West End theatre stage: with crushed red velvet curtains tied back with plaited golden tassels, several highly intrusive spotlights and a fully functioning orchestra pit. But no musicians, or come to think of it, backing dancers, were currently in view. Oh, thank goodness, or Dippit would have needed a tractor and trailer attached to her burgeoning tummy for that entourage.

And Karolyn certainly never, ever, ever expected to see a small baby riotously dancing across the brass-inlaid stage.

Stan and Dippit's baby was giving it laldy as it leapt, spun, shimmied and jigged around the stage. It was gleefully carefree and so thrilled as it violently bounced off the bobbing pink uterine walls. Pirouetting and prancing, then doing a cheeky cha-cha-cha number. And flinging its wee pudgy legs (with elegantly pointed toe) out to the audience. The audience being the bewildered, but proud parents, and a mildly panicking sonographer. Before this appointment Karolyn had often wondered how the babies spent their time, when not being paparazzied by her. So much sleeping, eating, gently rolling over, kicking and growing sounded kinda...boring. She was now quite happy with the concept of boring as the alternative was alarming. Alarming, and very cute, but overall alarming.

"Don't panic. I think I know this one. I say, I think I know this one. It was playing on the radio the other day. I say, the other day." A now unflappable Stan said, as he cocked his ear to an imagery tune. Stan fumbled with his phone until he found the song in question. Michael Flatley's Riverdance. He played the song at full volume and the baby became even more animated: flamboyantly conducting an imagery orchestra, blowing huge double-handed kisses and finally doing a wiggly fingers wave, then bowing as it picked up bouquets of long stemmed, pink roses.

The large bouquets of flowers were slightly more difficult to explain until Dippit remembered that she had recently added eating wicker baskets, full of fragrant potpourri, to her pregnancy cravings. Her other pregnancy cravings of triple A batteries, several small flashlights, a tin of Brasso, a pack of school rulers and many packets of cocktail sticks, also made more sense now. Her expectant body was building a rather splendid Broadway type stage. However, she couldn't recall eating any red velvet curtains, although they did look awfully familiar. Dippit thought for a few seconds...ahhh, the multiple holes in Stan's boxer shorts now made sense. And, to think, she had blamed some innocent moths for chewing through the garments during the night.

There was utter silence in the room as the teeny, totty baby lay down on its side. It curled up and drifted off into an exhausted sleep. Smiling and cuddling the celebratory roses to its wee, chubby cheeks. Probably dreaming of curtain calls, wardrobe fittings, artistic rivalries and baby fan clubs. Fan clubs where autographs were scrawled using multi-coloured finger paints. The baby couldn't write yet. It wasn't some kinda of genius, afterall.

Karolyn, a dedicated professional, managed to quickly

scan the babe and determine its size before the sumptuous curtains swished closed on a truly unique opening night.

"Well, that was certainly different. Did everyone else see that? It wasn't just me that witnessed that stellar performance?" The dazed Karolyn whispered in wonder. She rubbed her awestruck eyes and looked around the room for hidden cameras. Those physiotherapists could be right little minxes when the occasion arose.

"Yes, we saw it all. Awesome. So, that's my boy? Or my girl? Did you happen to notice?" Enquired, an unfazed Dippit. She stopped rubbing the sticky gel from her rounded belly, and looked at Karolyn for confirmation. Karolyn shrugged and slowly shook her head, as checking the sex of the baby had been way down on her list of priorities. Surprisingly, Karolyn's priorities now included wondering how the baby got its legs up so high. Those kicks were truly phenomenal.

Dippit was just so proud of her talented wee sprog and very relieved about the whole stage thing, as it now explained her, "*obscenely massive*" tummy. She had remained a little bit miffed about that much repeated comment. Stan knew it!

"I'm sorry that I didn't notice the sex of your baby, but I did manage to grab a quick measurement at the end of the performance. When you made the appointment you said the babe would be 22 weeks along, but according to my scan your baby is coming in at 30 weeks. Did you happen to get your dates wrong? I don't appear to have a lot of notes here for you." Karolyn started writing up her forms in order to capture the information and, more importantly, to give the parents time to absorb that update.

"Erm, no. We're pretty sure our wee cub is 22 weeks. I say, 22 weeks. But if he or she is 30 weeks then that would explain Dippit's humungous stomach. I'm glad I locked myself away in the nursery for a couple of days and finished all the painting. Finished the painting, I say. So, what's next? I say what's next?" Stan queried as he nonchalantly went back to eating his tulip bulbs whilst rubbing Dippit's distended belly with beeswax furniture

polish. He was totally unaware that he'd just added yet another hurtful description about his wife to his repertoire, but he'd learn. Oh, how he'd learn! The dart's team are about to fear for his life.

The ever-professional Karolyn suggested adding additional calories to Dippit's diet as the darling babe was obviously using a great deal of energy in its pursuit of dancing perfection. She also heartily recommended a repeat appointment as she needed some time in order to check her medical text books and see if this had ever been previously documented. She also, maybe, wanted to get herself a brain scan or two and more sleep. Definitely more sleep.

A small white tube whooshed across the polished linoleum floor and Stan quickly picked it up. Well, the rotund Dippit certainly couldn't manage that act of death-defying gymnastics. Stan wisely decided not to mention that.

To the voices of a Welsh male choir: singing to the tune of Twinkle, Twinkle Little Star.

"Congratulations, you have gained
a second horn to put on your shelf.
Come home, come home and celebrate
your wonderous achievement. You are great
You are a person without equal.
Well not quite as good the other Hells
They already have at least two horns.
But off you pop and collect your prize.
Congratulations, you have gained
a second horn to put on your shelf."

"Good old Karen and Dr Riel! They must have finished up sooner than they planned. I say, sooner than they planned.

I think I might have to have a look at the talking scrolls again. The talking scrolls, I say. The tune and lyrics aren't very good. They're nearly as bad as all the poems in these P and K Stoker books. These books, I say. The singing is top-notch though.

I say top-notch. You can always rely on the Welsh for a good old time." And with that sage pronouncement, Stan and Dippit did not waddle onto the cockroach moving pavement, and they did not go back to Hell number one. The cockroaches were quite relieved as they had clocked Dippit's burgeoning bump and they hadn't packed their JCB that morning. The expectant parents went pram shopping then dropped into see the Falkirk Honeymooners. They also planned on looking into finding a talent agent for their clever baby girl or baby boy. But not before CC. did his thing. The wonderful CC., and his equally wonderful wife, were so getting an invite to the baby naming ceremony.

Karolyn couldn't believe that her last patients had cancelled on her, yet again. She stopped and thought she could detect the faint smell of... sweaty horse? She surreptitiously added a little dab of Vicks under nose as it was not good practice to vomit on the patients.

CHAPTER SIXTEEN

A warm and dreamy beach...

Karen was the most beautiful shade of warm, trickling honey mixed with thick double cream. Her long hair was streaked with blonde highlights. It was tied back with a navy blue ribbon and pulled into a high pony tail. Whilst the intoxicatingly gorgeous Dr Riel's skin gleamed with health, relaxation and a glistening deep blue/black tan. His twinkling amethyst eyes were shaded with blue rimmed designer sunglasses and a battered straw, Panama hat. The hat was trimmed with a pineapple and orange themed bandana. He was feeling rather rebellious with his wardrobe choices.

This holiday was one of the best ideas Karen had ever had. It was the perfect opportunity to decompress and chill after their recent Hell number three wild adventures. A few weeks of soaking up some hot rays after the scrumptious Dr Riel had won the much-coveted, and very much contested, Monarch of Corfu wet tee-shirt tournament. He'd posed, pirouetted and pouted, in order to beat all of the silicon enhanced beach bunnies. He'd solemnly vowed to rule the prestigious Greek island's sandy beaches with care and consideration for the next fortnight. The paltry twenty-euro winnings, the polyester-mix crimson sash and the cheap bottle of retsina wine were the icing on the cake, as Karen had made all the real money on a bit of savvy side betting. She knew Dr Riel's magnificent tush was a surefire winner so it wasn't even really gambling. The chumps!

Day eight in paradise...

Karen and Dr Riel had slurped their delicious, icy cold cocktails and were taking yet another well-deserved nap on their pale pink, striped beach towels. Pert-ish bum stuck in the air: Karen felt a sharp knock across her lower back. Startled awake, she quickly pushed herself upright into a seated position. She squinted up and then up some more. She quickly realised that one of the beach volleyball players had over-reached, in order to slap back the slippery ball. In the process he had tripped over Karen's prone body and face planted into the soft, warm sand. The guy was unhurt but deeply embarrassed by his misjudged gymnastics. Whilst apologising profusely for his clumsiness, checking on the condition of Karen's back, doing a one-handed push-up off the ground and brushing off the intrusive sand he stopped, dead.

"Sorry for the ogling but have you seen this?" the bleached, blonde Adonis enquired whilst excitedly pointing at Karen's legs. Karen didn't respond as she was momentarily blinded by the sheer number of muscles this guy carried about his person. Flexing pectorals, hugging external obliques, the tight serratus anteriors and a twelve pack of truly superb abdominals were just lying there minding their own business. Abdominals that were so well cut they would show through at least four layers of thick thermal vests. Karen would lay good money on that. And she would know. Well, when you're mis-filed and locked in a battered cabinet by Eva Braun for over ten years you're inclined to read pretty much anything you can get your greedy little hands on. Karen had got her hands on Harry's, much thumbed and heavily underlined, old medical text books. Karen had turned the gruesome anatomy diagrams into her very own boy-band of much loved friends. Karen sometimes missed them and their imaginative soft tissue gossip. Although, Mr Adolpho Abdominal was always very bitchy towards the others, and he would sometimes reduce the

sensitive Mr Enrique External Obliques to tears. The totally gorgeous cad!

"Oops, sorry again. Forgive my terribly bad manners. I'm John Owen, although I prefer John O. And you, my lovely, have the most amazing calves." John O flicked out his smooth, shining hair and held out his gorgeously tanned hand. The trio completed their introductions then furtively wiped off the transferred baby oil. It's acceptable to have your body drenched in your own baby oil but hell mend you if you feel so much as drop of a stranger's warmed oil on your skin. Yuck! Just yuck!

"I do? Really? Honestly? Really? I always thought they were a bit chunky. And really veiny." Karen popped her tee-shirt on over her red bikini top, and wished she had a pair of sturdy woollen, heather-knit tights handy in order to cover the offending limbs. She really didn't like her legs and their Grand Canyon type vista of dips, peaks and troughs. Dr Riel thought it was a crime to cover up all that luscious skin but he wasn't all that keen on John O looking at his woman. And calling her lovely... the bare-faced cheek of the man: that was Dr Riel's job.

"You most certainly do have the most amazing legs I've ever had the pleasure of looking at, my lovely. I know this sounds decidedly shifty, but would you mind if I grab my phone and take a photo of your calf? With your permission, I'd like to have a closer look at it." John O asked, with a stunning white tooth smile gracing his awfully lovely face.

Dr Riel did mind. He minded an awful lot, but Karen was so charmed by the, ever so, polite request that they happily (ish) agreed. But only on the proviso that Dr Riel was given **all** the negatives. Negatives? Do they still exist? Can you even get negatives on a mobile phone? The authors are sometimes amazed at the innocence of the Hell characters, and their technical ineptitude. They also wonder how the Devils and their associates manage a Hell...at all.

John O quickly nipped off and grabbed his mobile phone. He took a photograph of Karen's craggy calf, and asked to sit beside the happy couple. Dr Riel grumbled but agreed.

John O zoomed in on the photograph. *"This purple vein, here, looks like the coast line of Corfu. Don't you think? Plus, this other pulsating vein looks just like the rugged Albanian coastline."* John O said all this, in a rush, without taking a full breath.

Dr Riel and Karen didn't have a clue: who would know those strangely, unique facts? So, after consulting a map, on their phone, they all agreed that the engorged, knobbly varicose veins did look very much like Corfu and the distinctively craggy coastline of Albanian. Bizarre but true.

"See here. There's also a suspicious looking freckle at the side of this extra thick vein. I think there's something caught just under the skin. It's pale orangish, and it's slightly raised.

This is odd, don't you think? This is crazy, but is that a tiny piece of brown amber embedded in the freckle, my lovely?" John was positively bouncing with excitement as he tried not to grab and rub Karen's calf to test his strange theory. Dr Riel would only tolerate so much, and poor John O wasn't keen on all the low growling and small yelps emitting from the handsome doctor.

It was a tiny fragment of amber, and Karen confirmed that it had always been in her leg. She had tried to remove it by plucking it out but it was stubbornly stuck. And it was forever catching on her pink lady razors, when she deemed to shave her stubbly legs, that is. Dr Riel and Karen were excited by the discovery but they were trying to play it cool. They had heard, via Devil Bub and his Deadly Sin of Lust stupor, that Karen's varicose veins were a treasure map that would lead them to the Lost City of Atlantis. Bub had discovered this secret whilst licking and sucking on Karen's bulging blue veins: that is another story. (The Devil's a courting, by P and K Stoker, just in case you need any ideas for a truly brilliant birthday gift for your very discerning friend or relative). Karen and Dr Riel had dismissed Bub's, frankly cuckoo, claims as hokum but maybe, just maybe the drug addled Devil was correct.

Karen and Dr Riel could be sitting or, to be more accurate, walking on a veritable gold mine.

CHAPTER SEVENTEEN

Still on the warm sandy beach with Karen's calf the most exciting thing ever...seemingly...

"This is phenomenal. Truly phenomenal. Now, I know this sounds completely mental but give me a minute and suspend all previous concepts of reality... I think you may have a treasure map on your leg. A real-life, honest to goodness, treasure map. I know, cool, eh?" John O held his breath, again. He really should try breathing regularly: all this hypoxia is awfully bad for the old brainbox. He waited on them calling him an idiot and walking away but when they didn't, he added. *"You're also not gonna believe this, but I'm here with a group of my new mates. Those guys over there: making a complete tit of themselves trying to impress the local hotties. We're on our holibobs, but in our day jobs we're a small team of marine salvagers. We're just starting out really, but we're good. Professional, like.*

I've heard of old maps and stories being inscribed onto leathered animal skins, but as far as I'm aware they don't lead to treasure or anything of real value. I've also heard of obviously made-up treasure maps, with directions to the person's private body parts, being tattooed onto human skin. That's normally done as a bit of a joke. Or as a result of too much of the old falling down juice on a lads holiday.

This, my lovely, is mind blowing: totally unconventional. I've never heard of anything remotely like it, so would you like to investigate this further? I mean investigate it with me. Us? It won't cost you anything but your time. We sailed over here so we have all the necessary equipment with us. Ready to go as it were.

I know, I know, this all sounds like a suspicious coincidence but sometimes things just come together. It's like...fate. You believe in fate? Don't you? Eh?

Just think. At the very least you'd have a weird story to tell to your friends and family. Your grandkids. But you might also have the most amazing adventure, and hefty bragging rights to boot. It could be awesome. Life changing even, my lovely." John O looked so hopeful that it was extremely hard, but not impossible to say no.

Despite Karen and Dr Riel finding it a very suspicious twist of fate that they had met the knowledgeable and enthusiastic John O, they both agreed to join his exciting search. Afterall, with all their skin sizzling, copious basting and generally smelling like overcooked burgers currently going on, they thought that they'd probably tanned enough. Well, for the moment.

Plus, a free mini holibob adventure, how bad can it get?

CHAPTER EIGHTEEN

It got very bad...

Karen was trapped on the sandy sea bed with her oxygen gage gradually edging into the red quadrant. She tried to calm her racing heart and breath slowly but she was panicking. Where was Dr Riel?

A few days before the unfortunate trapping incident...

Karen and Dr Riel had decided to continue to keep the whole, "*Lost City of Atlantis,*" to themselves. They thought that the calf map was peculiar, but adding the whole legend of Atlantis would have taken it to a whole other realm of odd. Plus it gave them some leverage. John O was so busy trying to convince them of the veracity of his hairbrained scheme, and their need to work with him, that he didn't stop to ask himself why they were so willing to cooperate. Why they didn't question the unbelievable pile of coincidences.

Karen, Dr Riel and John O had spent a few days poring over maritime maps, old tomes and searching the internet and local libraries. Looking for any clues related to lost treasure, myths, local legends and folklore related to the Greek Islands. There was a great deal of information out there, but nothing linked to living skin maps and absolutely nothing definitive with regards to a hidden treasure marked with amber. Come on guys...If it had been definitive, the treasure would have been found already and wouldn't be lost anymore. Duh!

After a frustrating couple of days of debating, theorising, making lists and then crossing items off the lists, they decided to just go for it. Dr Riel, Karen, John O and the guys chartered a second smaller boat and began their sea search. The strait between the island of Corfu and the Albania coast was only three kilometres wide so Karen was confident that they would be home in plenty of time for some yummy baked fish and horiatiki salad and wine and cocktails and wine and brandy and liqueurs and more wine: all surrounded by piles of lovely loot. Dr Riel didn't want to burst her happy bubble so refrained from telling her how difficult a three-kilometre square grid search was. Even with two boats at their disposal, GPS, magnetic lures and some very high-tech sonar on the case they would struggle to determine the location of the treasure. Possibly, and hopefully, with some much needed luck they would chance upon it.

After a couple of very frustrating days of searching the seas they were now confident that they had pin-pointed the area where the *"Freckle Treasure"*, that's what they were all currently calling it, should be.

Dive day…

As Karen stepped onto the rusty, but well-equipped boat, she felt a searing sting in her left calf. Although in tremendous pain she thought this was a clear indication that they were on the right track. The sea recognised her amber freckle and was warning them off. Dr Riel removed the offending crab's pincers from Karen's calf and assured her that the delicious crab was going to be their dinner that night and was not in fact a portent of doom, or otherwise.

Karen and Dr Riel had completed a diving crash course so they all drenched themselves in Lily of the Valley talcum powder then suited up. Due to Karen and Dr Riel's limited diving experience, mainly occurring in the local swimming pool and just off an old rickety jetty, they were each paired with a more proficient deep-sea diver. Prior to diving Karen and Dr Riel were both given clear and detailed safety instructions.

Karen was not to lose sight of John O, her diving partner and her life line. She and Dr Riel repeated this until John O was satisfied that they would follow their respective partners and not do anything risky.

In they all plunged...

They excitedly dropped into the clear Ionian Sea. Surrounded by the warm waters Karen was immediately entranced by the shifting colours of the sea, the myriad of flashing fish that zipped away from her searching fingers and the gently undulating, floating pieces of seaweed that licked her outstretched hands. She tickled a curious little fish that had decided to hover in front of her face. When the fish refused to swim away she decided to followed the brave little fish on its watery adventure. The fish stared into Karen's eyes and then darted down into the darker depths. He stopped and appeared to wait on Karen catching up with him. John O noticed the strange interaction and tried to stop Karen from swimming away without him, but he was too late. She was gone.

The smarting John O tried to catch up with Karen but he got caught up in a large piece of discarded fishing net. Anxiously he began roughly cutting himself out of the intrusive old net but by then Karen was nowhere in sight. She was long gone by then. John O was worried about Karen, and angry at her poor judgement. She was in for a tongue lashing from the furious Adonis, yes she surely was.

Karen kept following the charming fish until her vision was obscured by the lack of sunlight filtering down through the sea. She had gone further than she was meant to, but she knew John O had her back. Both figuratively and literally.

Karen turned to check in with John O and found, to her dismay, that he was nowhere to be found. Slightly alarmed, she turned and began swimming up to the surface but there was still no sign of John O. In her panic she swam down again to find the fish guide. She misjudged the speed of her descent and slammed into a mound of rocks. The rocks, that were pilled higgledy-piggledy, slid to the right and into a small skewwhiff pillar. That too lost its structural integrity and wobbled. The top boulder of the pillar fell, then a second crashed and by time the third rock was dislodged, Karen was securely pinned to the ocean floor. Stunned: covered by a mist of sandy water and in a great deal of danger.

Her oxygen rapidly depleting, Karen stretched out her arm and scrambled around to find a makeshift lever so she could prise the oblong rock from her painfully, crushed thigh. Minutes away from slow suffocation, a gasping Karen saw the most amazing and welcome sight. The wonderful, fantastic and overall very handsome John O was shining a large underwater torch in her face and miming for her to breath slowly. He swam around in order to assess the situation and to check the level of her tank. He signed "*Ok*", and began slowly and steadily pulling at the confining rock. He was gently holding Karen in place with his other hand as he didn't want any more debris falling on the anxious, inexperienced diver.

After a few frantic seconds John O dislodged the offending rock and helped a shaken Karen to the surface. John O had placed the imprisoning large brick in a mesh diving bag so it too, was taken to the surface so it could be investigated further.

A terrified Dr Riel grabbed Karen and checked her for injuries. Scolding, hugging, patting and poking her thigh, all at the same time. Dr Riel was a loved-up mess. He was pushed aside so one of the guys could coolly take charge and administer first aid in his place. All the while, John O was pacing the deck and doing a fair bit of yelling at the shaken diver. Karen thought that she probably deserved a bigger row and was surprised by John O's ability to control most of his temper.

Karen was very grateful for the team's speedy interventions and lashings of hot, sweet cocoa. However, Dr Riel probably received and required more care than she did.

The poor wee scone was distraught. Her thigh was badly bruised but there were no signs of a fracture so she would make a full recovery, but her diving was currently curtailed. Rather than being frightened by her experience she was intrigued by the trapping rock and the cute beckoning fish.

CHAPTER NINETEEN

On a salvage boat in the Ionian sea...

"Have you ever seen a piece of rock this shape before?" John O was holding the rock up to the light so he could, more clearly, see the cutting profile on the brick. His eye squinting and frown lines were very, very cute: in case you wanted to know. The additional sunlight only confirmed what his trusty magnifying glass had found.

"See here, this part of the rock has been carefully shaped but rather than rough chisel marks there appears to been clean, precise cuts. Razor sharp edges. It looks like it was recently machine engineered, but on this side of the rock the natural wear and tear of the sea tides contradicts that theory. It's probably thousands of years old. This makes no sense. How can it be that old, but still have that type of precision cutting? Any ideas? Karen, you've had this map on your body for a while: have you ever looked into it? Have you any notion of what this could mean?" John O was rhythmically stroking the smooth surface of the rock. There were no blemishes on the even, glass like surface. He was baffled but he wasn't going to let this puzzling discovery defeat him.

Dr Riel and Karen couldn't answer how it was made, but they could hazard an educated guess as to whom had made it. They decided to continue to keep their secret for the moment and see how John O was going to proceed.

John O decided he was going to proceed by taking a plethora of underwater photographs, completing as many dives as was possible each day, mapping out his finds and scouring the sea bed for more pieces of the rock. He was completing a complex *"Sea Jenga,"* as he laughingly called it. After many more dives the boat decks were covered in pieces of complicated shaped rocks. John O had hired in an extra barge, as the underwater find was proving to be colossal and unwieldy.

As the days rolled into one another Dr Riel, John O and his mates were becoming increasingly exhausted. The physical labour of dragging themselves into wetsuits, diving, fingertip searching and then dragging up every rock was relentless. They were also fed up with the scant supplies in the mess hall. Fresh fish and copious rations of rum had lost their appeal after consuming them for every single meal. They really wanted a bowl of Caesar salad, a light souffle and some raspberry jelly, washed down with several glasses of freshly squeezed orange juice.

They voted, then took a short break to laze in the morning sun. Afterwards they briefly surveyed their staggeringly high piles of boulders and sighed. They sighed a lot. They then made the decision to stop diving for a few days and concentrate on trying to make sense of their collections of "*debris*". The constantly upbeat John O wasn't keen on the term debris but he was out voted by the subdued and disheartened team. The team painstakingly divided the rocks by size and shape but that didn't help them *"see"* an ancient structure. They just couldn't fathom what they were looking at, or looking for. Karen suggested to the beleaguered team that they should give it one more go. Complete one more dive then head for shore so they could get help from more knowledgeable divers, and access a few geologists. The salvage team were understandably disappointed, but agreed with the revised plan. That raspberry jelly sure was alluring.

CHAPTER TWENTY

The last dive…

John O told them that one last dive probably wasn't going to make any significant difference to their haul. However, he thought that as Dr Riel and Karen had been such good sports, about the whole treasure hunting business, then he would oblige her unrealistic whim. He also agreed that her leg was sufficiently mended so she could join them, but she had to promise to stick close to Dr Riel and himself.

"I know I worried and disappointed you during my last dive. And I'm so, so sorry for doing that to you all, but can we do something different today? Mix things up?

I know this sounds dangerous and unscientific, but rather than follow our seabed set grid pattern to find clues how about you just let me swim wherever the notion takes me? It worked before, when I was on my own and became trapped. That turned out to be our first solid clue. Is it worth trying that again?" Karen crossed her fingers and gave her most winning smile. Dr Riel baulked at Karen's idea but he knew that she wanted to see this hunt to its natural conclusion. Come what may. He also wasn't completely convinced that Karen could identify a specific fish. He thought that they all looked basically the same when wrapped in hot crispy batter and accompanied by a slice of fresh lemon.

Dr Riel and John O were escorting Karen, as the remaining sailors said they had last minute tasks to complete on the boats. A tingling Karen entered the warm water, stopped and closed her eyes. She floated until she felt a small, inquisitive fish brush against her fingertips. She opened her eyes, grinned and recognised her little fish. Dr Riel was charmed, delighted and gobsmacked, in equal measure, when the fish gave his Karen a saucy wink. The sauce in question was hollandaise.

Karen made an ok sign at her fellow divers and they followed the ever so friendly fish. The fish travelled down to the sea floor but at the last moment it turned away from their previous search area. The fish kept swimming then stopped, looked back at Karen and wiggled his cute little fin. The obliging fish was gobbled up by a bigger fish. He really should have spent less time flirting and more time minding his own business. Oh, and keeping an eye open for predators.

A startled Karen, Dr Riel and John O stopped too. The little fish deserved a moment of remembrance and... before them, on the sea floor, lay the remains of a huge, sunken, oval amphitheatre. Karen concluded that the previous rock finds were probably no more than damaged wandering paths leading to this stately structure. Ah, that would make it ancient crazy paving: well that makes a lot more sense. No wonder John O couldn't make head nor tail of the pattern of rocks on the boats. It was never meant to be a sensible structure as the piles of debris weren't a temple or a palace or a banqueting hall. Not at all. Now John O, with a clear conscious, could call it mere debris.

A great deal of the bricks were missing from the ancient amphitheatre but enough remained to indicate a maze of luxurious rooms that surrounded the central theatre and the tiered seating galleries. Rooms that appeared to be opulent dressing rooms and sumptuously decorated bathing rooms. Bathing rooms that came complete with deep sunken baths, pre-fitted gleaming crystal bath plugs, gold taps topped with multifaceted glistening rubies, long elegant seating areas and marble reclining benches. The benches had built in shelving units; big enough to hold a goblet of wine, or a tray of cubed cheese and pickled onions skewered on cocktail sticks. Plus there were some mighty plush toilets with, what appeared to be controls, for heating the seats and rinsing bottoms. The loo brushes and bidets were all decorated with sapphires, emeralds and seed pearls that completed the glamorous look. On the bathroom walls were hieroglyphics that indicated the person should wash their hands after use, and warnings that the theatre patrons were not to steal the two-ply toilet roll.

There were also kitchens with adjourning dining halls filled with opaque glass thrones, marble topped tables and finely carved tall shelving units. These dining rooms followed the points of the compass to ensure that a theatre goer could easily find sumptuous repast between the acts of the play. The dining rooms had their own instructural hieroglyphics on the walls. They appeared to inform the diners of the "*specials of the day*," and contained warnings that the diners shouldn't sneak their own alcohol into the venue as there were random toga searches taking place.

The curious trio swam closer and noted the multicoloured, complex mosaics covering the floors and approximately a two-thirds of the way up the dilapidated walls. Mosaics depicting beautiful frolicking mermaids using sea urchins as balls, whilst playing catch with sleek, diving seals. Pictures of laughing people excitingly waving their arms in the air whilst riding on the back of a grinning sperm whale. Surely not the equivalent of an early banana boat ride across the waves? There were scenes of happy couples holding hands and walking six foot tall penguins, on plated leashes, in children's playparks. One corridor contained evenly spaced mosaics of hearts with portraits of attractive and dramatically posed people within each heart. Every heart was topped by a golden star constellation. Early theatre posters? The trio could barely believe their unique and very bizarre find.

They excitingly motioned for John O to take some photographs but the explorer, in his rush to dive, had forgotten to pick it up. And just in case you don't know: diving suits don't have many pockets, as pockets look fattening and ruin the sleek lines of the mighty tight suits.

The trio left the theatre and continued their exploration. Karen pointed to a minute, intact, structure nestled to the left of the distinguished theatre. They indicated that they would investigate her new find and swam over. It was a smallish, perfectly round temple complete with interlaced rows of flawlessly straight columns: creating the impenetrable exterior walls. The columns had been covered in intricate carvings but these were nearly completely obscured, with pits and craters dotted all over the marble surface. This damage was not consistent with natural aging and washing sea tides. It looked as if someone had taken a pickaxe or a hammer or a heavy mallet to the delicate carvings. A deliberate act of vandalism to hide the symbols from view.

It was extremely difficult to discern what had originally been etched onto the columns but Karen pointed to an area, near the bottom of one of the uprights. They squinted, through their masks, at the desecrated column. It may have been carvings of vine leaves cradling bunches of ripe grapes but there was extensive damage, so it wasn't all that clear. Dr Riel scanned the sea floor and rubbed away some lose sand, then he picked up a small piece of debris. It was relatively unscathed. It had the top of a pineapple, a segment of an orange and what appeared to be a small group of ripe cherries stamped on it. John O had also been searching and found a fragment of rock covered in tiny, bobbing circles. The trio concluded that the spheres may have been floating bubbles. John O carefully bagged the two pieces of delicate rock. They would exam them more closely when they returned to the boat.

They swam around the temple searching for an entrance to the intriguing structure. To the left of the building they found a doorway. The entrance was guarded by an imposing statue of the Greek God Poseidon, astride a humongous, snarling horse. He was raising his stone trident menacingly in the air. The other side of the entrance was guarded by the

Roman God Neptune and he was riding a sweetly, smiling dolphin. To negate the impact of the cheeky grin, on the dolphin's face, the Roman God was waving an even bigger trident. Even more menacingly, if that were possible. The trio knew the names of the Gods as each statue came with a handy plaque attached to the base. A plaque written in English and in comic sans font. Quirky.

A Greek and a Roman God together, was highly unusual but what was really confusing was the certainty that these God's weren't original to the temple. They looked to have been added on many centuries later and attached using a terrific amount of Blu-tac. The God's pairs of Nike Air trainers were also a blatant clue. Karen looked closely at the faces of the angry God's. They looked somewhat familiar. With their large noses, protruding eyeballs and exaggerated eyebrows they sort of looked like caricatures of people she nearly knew.

The puzzled trio entered the petite building in, single file, and traversed through a stark, modest anti-chamber. From this narrow hallway they could see into another, larger, room. A room with a dazzling podium set in a raised central stage. They entered the decorative room and suddenly dropped onto the highly embellished mosaic floor. The room had no door separating it from the watery hallway but this room was absolutely dry. It appeared to have been untouched by the sea, time and the elements surrounding it.

A mesmerised John O took out his mouth piece and slowly looked around the room. *"How is this even possible? This room should be flooded with water but there's some kind of barrier keeping all the water out."* The wall of sea water shimmered and stopped abruptly at the entrance to the chamber. Held back with an unknown force or forces

The trio looked about in complete and utter awe. Speechless and happily stunned. They looked up and excitedly pointed. The ceiling was composed of a single, large, stained glass dome depicting ferocious hunting scenes. Dinosaur hunting to be exact. A smug clan of tyrannosaurus rex were clearly winning the hunts and devouring the barbeque sauce coated, screaming villagers with obvious relish. There was a greedy dinosaur in the bottom corner of the tableau and he was thumping the bottom of the sauce bottle to make sure he retrieved every last tasty drop.

The walls were equally dramatically illustrated. They were covered in glowing panels of beaten gold, glittering silver, opulent platinum and warm bronze. Each panel contained detailed drawing of slushy machines, traffic cones, hot air balloons, bunk beds, clock springs, bi-planes, Viking long ships and busted car radiators. There was a set of ornate ladders propped up against one of the lavish walls. John O climbed up to find yet more sketches on the majestic walls. There were poodles wearing bowties, stiletto heeled shoes, manhole covers, crock pots and several Rubik's cubes. To name but a few of the bizarre items on display. How had an ancient culture seen these modern inventions? How had they managed to capture these unrelated images in such detail?

Dr Riel and Karen agreed to investigate the bedazzled podium whilst John O took to the ladder. They tentatively walked across the floor, avoiding any boobytraps and trip-wires, in order to see the carvings on the edifice. In preparation for the treasure hunt they had all watched the Indiana Jones movies, so they were worried that any second now a big old boulder was going to come hurtling towards them and pancake the lot of them. Hence the tentative walking, and the frantic pre-dive Last Will and Testament writing. Harry was NOT getting Dr Riel's medical journals as she worried about her health far too much as it was.

The podium was covered in fist-sized, sparkling jewels depicting the earth, the moon and the sun. These heavenly bodies were surrounded by tiny, spinning hourglasses and clock springs. There was a flat, smooth rock perched upon the podium and in the middle of the rock was a marble box depicting shifting tides and decorated with glistening shells. The scenes were so realistic that they could, initially, have been mistaken for a series of photographs. The highly decorated box was, unfortunately, empty and the lid appeared to have been ripped off it. What had been in the box? Who would take the item in the box but leave all this wealth behind?

They were blisteringly excited with their discoveries and would have spent hours exploring and documenting the fantastic temple. But they decided that as they didn't have the camera with them, and they had limited oxygen supplies with them they needed to keep going. Well John O had limited oxygen supplies, but Karen and Dr Riel could hardly admit that they could have stayed underwater indefinitely. Karen had previously panicked when she was trapped under the boulder as she didn't want to spend eternity imprisoned on the relatively boring seabed. Plus, she was worried that John O would discover her and Dr Riel's immortality secret identity if she was found alive with a depleted oxygen tank. So they concluded that they would continue exploring the other buildings then do a second, third, fourth and fifth dive to gather photographic proof. No one would believe them otherwise.

The trio reluctantly left the stunning temple and moved on to a large building, to the right of the amphitheatre. This huge building had two towering pillars on either side of its entrance but again, they had been attacked and left with significant damage. The arch above the entrance way was entirely obliterated and a large section of stone facia appeared to be completely missing. The trio raked around the sea floor but there was no useable debris remaining on that site. It was evident that this building had been viciously attacked then tidied up, in order to hide its purpose or possibly suppress a damning secret.

The trio tentatively swam into the vestibule, as they weren't sure what horrors they would face this time around. Instead of the anticipated boobytraps and sharp swinging axes, the only article in the hallway was a large piece of broken pottery. Sharp edges that would have caused a really nasty cut, but thankfully there wasn't a small dart wielding pygmy in sight. Oh, goody. They stopped to investigate the crockery. The sliver of pottery was beautifully decorated with the letters L, A, N. They scoured around the tiled floor but the rest of the glazed clay was smashed beyond repair and of no use in their pursuit of the elusive, ancient word. They bagged the pottery clue for further investigation.

There was door at the far end of the long hallway and to the left of the doorway was a simple clock face and a series of small hidey-holes. Some of the dookets had small, square buttons propped in their centre. Karen was initially puzzled, then following a more thorough search, she thought that it may have been an ancient timeclock with button time cards. Why was that required? A factory? Surely not she decided, but she added that preposterous idea to her ever expanding mental list titled... "*What is going on here?*"

The trio continued through the hallway and into the main reception area of the large building. They braced themselves as they were expecting to plummet to the floor, but this room continued to be flooded with sea water. The reason: the back wall of the room was completely missing and open to the tides. It was ripped out, with clear evidence that someone had used heavy chains and winches to drag the wall from its secure mooring. Multiple holes had been gouged out of the walls in order to attach the destructive chains and the sea bed was pitted with deep craters. This act of annihilation and destruction appeared to be the main target of the marauders.

In the very centre of the damaged room was a series of long marble tables surrounded by high, uncomfortable looking stools. There were pestle and mortar, measuring cups, juicers, knives and chopping boards scattered across the scarred table tops. The remaining two walls contained large sinks and were lined with row upon row of ceiling high marble shelving. The role of the shelves was to hold large clay pots topped with wax sealed stoppers, but all of the ancient pots had been smashed into tiny pieces. Their purpose, and contents, obliterated with absolutely no chance of repairing this act of wanton destruction.

Behind the central table was an elegantly crafted but relatively simple, unadorned podium. Karen picked up a large piece of pottery that was lying at the base of the podium. Under the pottery shard was a broken piece of glass with the letters RR clearly etched into the curved surface. She bagged the fragment of glass as she thought that it may have been part of an old bottle. On the top of the plain column was a flat rock covered in writing. They beckoned John O over and the eager trio went to investigate.

Instead of the expected ancient hieroglyphics, that would undoubtably issue a dire warning, the carving revealed the words... *"Ha, ha, ha. Jock Mackay was here, 1900. Better meddle with the de'il than the b"*. The last sentence appeared to have been cut short due to lack of space on the tablet. However, it was accompanied by a rough estimation of a thistle, roughly hewn beneath the bewildering words.

Who was Jock Mackay? What happened in Scotland in 1900? Why was Jock laughing? What had the de'il to do with it?

CHAPTER TWENTY-ONE

John O's boat...

"I can't believe the guys left with the other boat, ***and*** *they took all the jet skis with them. I just checked the mess and there's more bad news. They took the last poke of cheese balls; the open packet of stale hobnobs and the full barrel of rum. I was so looking forward to celebrating tonight."* Karen huffed and planned on skelping their thieving legs. She so wanted a wee rum and diet coke to toast their enigmatic find.

"Even taking into account the tragic loss of the savoury balls that's still so much better than our first thought. A deserted ship and a Marie Celeste type mystery, on top of what we just found, might have just tipped us all over the edge. Plus, you have to admit that it's a bit of bonus that we now have time to figure all this out in peace. I couldn't have concentrated on playing another game of Exploding Kittens tonight, my lovely." John O was surprisingly upbeat considering they had no photographic proof of their archaeological find and they didn't actually know what their find was. And they had no cheesy balls.

Just in case you're worrying that things have taken a dark turn and there's been some kinda sailor cannibalism or hostile mermaid take over or such. The missing sailors had left a note, signed with thirty kisses. They were off to get a pint and pull some lovely ladies. They **were** on their holibobs afterall.

In the back room of a Greek taverna...

The bamboozled trio laid out their mysterious clues on the wobbly wooden table. There was no way that they had finished their incredibly curious hunt, and they weren't handing over their treasures to anyone else until they had more information. On the table sat a piece of broken pottery, a glass shard with the letters RR, the damaged pieces of the temple's column and the crudely carved tablet. John O had made several rough sketches of the structures so they could add notes to the margins. They had also carefully marked the mariner's map with detailed coordinates so that they could revisit the site at a later date and take some much needed photographs. However, they had all agreed that solving these mysteries would be their first priority.

"After spending a few hours combing through our copious notes I can't find anything that even remotely explains the writing on the tablet. It might just be a practical joke. Something left by a previous diver who had a bit of a strange sense of humour. And to be honest the pottery and glass could be anything. Archaeologists are forever digging up old, discarded bits of marmalade jars. It may not even be that important." Dr Riel solemnly stated and sat back in his rickety, wooden chair. He quite fancied going home and drinking some pee infused tea, then chatting with the Hounds of Hell. He missed his gossipy wee guys and their happy, chompy ways. Plus, he was bone tired and fed up with mysteries. Dr Riel found that they never ended well. Someone was always left unhappy, or in jail, or illegitimate, or down a well, or in love with a rabid racoon. The authors are now concerned about Dr Riel's bizarre reading habits.

So to brighten himself up, and collect some much needed clean underwear, he'd nipped off to Hell a few days before. He was tempted to stay away longer as the word treasure now brought him out in hives and he'd completely run out of his antihistamines. It was only the thought that John O would be alone with his woman that had cut his Hell visit short.

As an aside... John O wasn't completely immune to the

tension in the air so he also popped off to re-stock their stationery cupboard and give the couple some, much needed, alone time.

"Ahem, what about the amphitheatre? Are we leaving that out? I really, really think we need to include that in our questions. In fact I insist. Who went there? Where are all the buildings that should surround it? There are a lot of paths but no entranceways to buildings. You can't have a theatre as big as that without an audience. It would have had to have some means of earning a crust. What about the actors and musicians? Where were they housed? Who needed all those baths? Why were the path plugs in the plug holes rather than hanging over the taps?

Where has the city gone? Has it been moved? Stolen? That sounds stupid now that I've said that out loud.

And why are there Greek and Roman statues at the entrance to the temple? Why were they added later? Who decorated the temple and what was in that expensive box?

Was that other building a factory, and who would have stolen that wall? Why steal the wall and leave all that gold, silver and jewels behind in the temple? What was in those pots?" John O was stressed and might just need a wee cuddle. He also desperately needed some answers, but Karen and Dr Riel were still keeping the whole Lost City of Atlantis to their respective chests. However, John O did raise some mighty good points. If this was the Lost City of Atlantis and it's now been found. Where is the rest of it?

CHAPTER TWENTY-TWO

Still in the back room of a Greek taverna...

After yet more head scratching Karen made a bold decision. *"Ok, we'll include the mystery of the 'missing' city but I'm not convinced that it's relevant at this time. Someone might have taken the stones to build something else. That happens all the time. The Great Wall of China has a lot of patch jobs, and the locals have some mighty fancy brickwork surrounding their raised garden beds.*

However it would have been useful to have some photographs to add to our file, just in case we come across similar brick work or structures. That would probably make you feel better, John O. Although your sketches are excellent.

Anyway, this isn't getting us anywhere. I know we agreed not to disturb the expectant parents but it's time. I'm phoning Stan and Dippit. He might just have a small suggestion as to where we should start. Or failing that, he might be able to get his brothers, Liam and Patrick, to make us some type of device to point us in the right direction." Karen nipped off to phone the studly Stan and Dippit.

Thank goodness she had free European roaming on her mobile phone plan as the call went on for a long, long time. Stan and his anxiety ridden repetition was getting worse. Karen quickly ordered him a huge pack of tulip bulbs, that was large enough to cover the entire garden of a National Trust

Stately Home, as a thank you for his unconventional advice.

"Stan suggested, and Dippit piped in from the background, that we should stop diving until we have more information about the city, as it could be dangerous down there. But Stan was relieved that, so far, there were no poisoned darts or pygmy assassins on the loose. He's been watching the Indiana Jones movies in preparation for the arrival of his baby. That weird pregnancy development needed more questions and answers than I currently have time for, so I happily left it well alone." Karen then broke into a massive grin and she was positively vibrating with excitement. *"Hold onto your hats, guys. This is the absolute best part of the conversation with Stan and Dippit. The saying 'Better meddle with the de'il than the b.' They think the full saying is… 'Better meddle with the de'il than the bairns of Falkirk'. Stan was confident that was the secret to unlocking this mystery.*

Taking that into account, he also recommended that we leave the 'stodgy intellectual research' behind and search through the newspapers of the time for any likely stories. 'Some oddities like space invaders planted carrots in my back garden and now I lick greengrocer windows' or 'I love sushi cos I'm the long-lost lovechild of a misunderstood Krachan'. That type of news story, were his much repeated words. I think. He said an awful lot. Most of it unrepeatable, as he wasn't all that keen on being disturbed whilst he and Dippit were feathering their expectant nest." Karen shook her head and sighed. She wasn't sure she had ever read stories remotely like that.

Then she remembered the newspaper articles about the village of Bonnybridge, their multiple flying saucer sightings and their ill-fated bid for a Scottish Space Themed amusement park. Stories like that…that's the very ticket.

"Karen, my love, that could take us forever. There are some mighty strange folks out there and some really fanciful tales make it into print. And we've already blasted through all my wet tee-shirt winnings. Don't you want to go home for a while, then re-visit this all later?" Dr Riel really, really wanted to go home and not because he was, at all, intimated by John O and his polka dot

Speedos. Oh, no. And John O's unnatural fixation on his Karen. Oh, no to that either. Bet John O, the pompous jerk, couldn't get their adult swing to work.

"Please, can we stay just a little longer? Stan suggested that we start with a couple of the local newspapers that were around at that time. He also suggested including the year after the date on the tablet, just in case the carving happened at the end of 1900 and was delayed in making the news. So 1900 and 1901 are our smallish search window." Karen gently pleaded. She was aware that the obliging Dr Riel was becoming increasingly home sick. However, she was feeling such a strong need to solve this mystery that she had to continue, but she might just suggest that Dr Riel head home without her.

"Oh, Dr Riel, don't worry about money. I've won a ton of the wet tee-shirt competitions this summer. Entered as a bit of a lark. Some people take it so seriously. I still have lots of winnings to see us through." John O helpfully added, and patted Dr Riel on the shoulder. He so wanted to meet the elusive and colourfully cursing Stan. Plus John O had a fantastic recipe for tulip bulb casserole that he so wanted to try.

"Stan said really, really local but he didn't think the Greek Islands would give up any more clues. The sudden demise of the helpful fish seemed really important, according to Stan.

So, I have an idea. Why not head directly to Falkirk and find a link to our laughing Jock? We know the town very well; it has our local pub down Graham's Road and there's a local newspaper. Why not start with the Falkirk Herald? I think it's been around for a while." Karen helpfully added, and stuck her favourite pencil behind her ear. She very nearly confessed that they had an entrance and exit to Hell number one in Falkirk. She'd have to be more careful in the future.

Plus, why was Dr Riel murmuring about how difficult it was to hang an adult swing?

CHAPTER TWENTY-THREE

In Scotland, with a rapidly fading tan...

Despite the weather, Karen was delighted to be nearly home. She did a quick internet search. *"The Falkirk Herald's been on the go since 1845 so it fits within our timeframe. Let's go guys. Hit that microfiche and see if we can strike gold or a bloody great big, missing wall."* Karen was trying to cheerlead her man into a happier mood and it was sorta working. Well the uniform was working...meow.

After some microfiche hitting...

"There's nothing here that meets Stans parameters of 'odd', in 1900. So I've moved onto the 1901 articles.

Queen Victoria, sadly, died in 1901. That was a major incident that was reported throughout the globe. The entire world went into mourning for her loss. Do you think that's linked to our city, the missing wall, the empty box and the tablet?" Karen bowed her head in sorrow. She had really respected the dignified Queen and her stoic ways. Karen was also a big fan of the Queen's favourite plum pudding drowned in thick, gooey custard.

"It was very, very sad but not what I'd consider odd. It doesn't fit with Stan's strange story suggestion and it doesn't fit with the Falkirk angle. We need to continue with the search." Dr Riel argued. He had vetoed Karen's suggestion regarding the whole him returning to Hell number one on his ownsome.

That usurper John O looked good in swimming trunks but even better in a zipped to the neck, navy blue padded anorak. And John O's hair was a lovely colour when it was drenched in the rain and plastered to his skull. Damn Scotland and it's perpetual, but beautifying, rainy seasons.

"I have sort of a weird one here and it's from 1901, so fits our dates perfectly. It says here that the steel workers, in Glasgow Central Train Station, were drinking too much beer whilst at work. In response, A.G. Barr made a tonic like drink to give them energy to help them keep working throughout the day. I've also checked other sources, as I can't believe that someone would think a tonic could ever replace an ice cold beer. But it's true. They gave up some of their beer for this newfangled drink.

It was original called Strachan's bru. The tonic has thirty-two ingredients and contains a small amount of iron hydroxide, but the exact recipe is a closely guarded secret. A secret! I think we're on to something now, my lovelies.

Oh this is funny. The distinctive colour is said to be due to the disproportionately high number of ginger people in Scotland. That's sort a true. Isn't it?

The other oddity is its taste. No one can accurately describe it. They use words like... 'elusive' and 'inconclusive'. Or more recently: tutti-fruity or bubble gum flavour. That is weird, don't you agree?

It was first made in Falkirk in ..." John O was interrupted by a very excited Karen.

"That's it. That's the story we're looking for. I'm sure of it. It's Irn Bru. The answer to the hidden treasure is... Irn Bru. The temple definitely had fruits and bubbles on the columns, and the factory may well have had the same emblems on their external columns. Maybe that was in honour of its unique flavour. It must have been so important to the ancient people that it was worth stealing for it.

Stan is a genius and John O, you're no slouch in that department either. What if the broken pottery jars contained the secret recipe? What if a bottle, with the letters AG Barr, sat on the podium? In a place of honour? And that troublemaker Jock

Mackay put the tablet on top ...in its place. As act of naughty vandalism. A way to be remembered after he'd gone? The missing wall could have had the cooking details: like how long to brew the concoction or how long it lasts before it goes off. Information that the makers required. Information that they had to hide from their competition. Information that their competitors then stole in 1900? That doesn't quite make sense and distorts the timeline, but let's celebrate one win.

That doesn't explain the damaged empty decorated box on the other podium but I think we've solved one big secret. The bigger building ***was*** *an ancient factory that made Irn Bru."* Karen was whirling a delighted Dr Riel around the quiet library.

CHAPTER TWENTY-FOUR

In a building that's not a quiet library...

"So, if and it's a big if, we agree that the broken pottery vase and the missing wall contained the secret recipe for Irn Bru then the next question or questions are: what was on the other podium and where is the rest of the sunken city? Oh yes, and is the item, that was in the box, still with the rest of the city?" Karen couldn't believe that the librarian had set her library card alight. Karen was only dancing, and she may have been singing the Irn Bru Christmas tune. She was only a little bit off tune and it was a difficult song, afterall. She was built as more of a miming baritone, and it was written for a testosterone free soprano.

"Falkirk is the key to this puzzle so where's large enough to hide a bloody great big city or maybe just a wall? And, as no one has discovered the city or the wall: what areas of Falkirk have been left relatively untouched since 1901 or 1902?" John O had never heard of Irn Bru but this seemed a big deal. As in BIG.

Dr Riel treated John O to a small bottle of Irn Bru, well it was John O's vast wet tee-shirt winnings they were all using to fund the expedition, afterall. So it was less of a treat and more on the lines of necessary piece of reluctantly provided research. John O could totally see why someone, called Devil Keith, thought it was his second favourite drink of all time as John O found it delicious. Sorry, my bad, it was Devil Keith's third favourite drink. It sat behind a shot or eight of tequila and a good old pint of grilled haggis laden Falkirk Sewer. John O still couldn't fathom the being they referred to as Devil Keith. Karen and Dr Riel seemed to love him, tolerate him, be fearful of him, and think Devil Keith was a complete idiot. And a hero. All at once.

Karen decided to chance her arm and enlist Stan's help in the search again. *"I tried to get Stan over lunchtime, but I only got his messaging service. He's away buying an escape proof playpen. It has to withstand a chorus line of nimble dancers who have the skills to distract nanny-type guards, and charm a bevy of theatre critics. Not sure what that's all about but I, for one, am very intrigued.*

And he can only be contacted if the world is ending. As in ending within twenty minutes or less. His message was surprisingly specific about that time detail. Dippit was shouting in the background that she'd come if the world was ending in twenty-five minutes or less. The pair of jokers.

Come on, chin up, we can work this one out. It's a beautiful Tuesday afternoon in Falkirk and I'm sure the world has more than twenty minutes before it explodes." Karen pulled out a map of Falkirk and a new packet of neon pink highlighters. She'd snuck them out of Harry's alphabetised stationery draw when she'd last visited Hell.

A couple of hours later…

"It's Callendar House and the surrounding park. It has to be. The Forbes family owned Callendar House in Falkirk at that time and they were running out of money, fast. So, they might have been open to a nefarious deal.

Also, there's been fishponds on the estate since 1707 so it's conceivable that they could have just extended the fishponds to create a lake big enough to hide the missing wall and just maybe, they were big enough for the lost city too. No one seems to have disturbed the ponds since 1901. Why would they? So I vote that we should grab our gear and look there." Dr Riel was delighted with his find. John O was leaning over Dr Riel's shoulder and manically pointing at a tiny blue patch in the middle of the crumpled map, but a triumphant Dr Riel had found it first. So there!

Could the grounds of Callendar House, in Falkirk, hold the secret to the location of the legendary Lost City of Atlantis? Should Dr Riel and Karen come clean and tell John O the name of the city and their link with it?

CHAPTER TWENTY-FIVE

In the dead of night and battling ferocious midgies...

After nipping past the fenced in children's playpark, passing the public toilets and resisting the urge to break into the ice-cream kiosk for a ninety nine cone, the team made it to the abandoned crazy golf course and the side of Callender House. As an aside: Callender House is worth a visit as they filmed some of the series Outlander there, and the house is free to the public. If you contact the authors they can provide you with the opening times.

Back to the dead of night...

The team slid behind trees, sneaked past the Faery doors, crouched under purple rhododendron bushes and swatted away some terribly curious grey squirrels. The three black clad treasure seekers began furiously paddling a fleet of white, swan pedalos across a small, Scottish fishpond.

They were very cold and hungry, having spent most of the evening diving into the freezing, cold water. But mostly they were chuffed. So, so chuffed. They had, with the use of some mighty strong torches, peered through the murky, weed chocked waters and located a few pieces of the sunken city. The city was crumbling but still recognisable as an impressive part of ancient history. They had found it. They had twitting well found it. Although the missing wall still remained annoyingly... missing.

John O had decided to do one last dive to see if he could find the elusive wall, or find some clue as to the identity of the item that use to reside in the empty decorative box. He took a fortifying breath then dived into the frigid water and sunk to the bottom of the pond. He pushed and pulled at some of the smaller underwater stones and boulders. He shifted an old bike to the side and found yet more oblong shaped boulders. He vigorously rubbed away some gloopy algae and, low and behold, he found some letters on the broken stone. Then some more. Although slightly worn the words were clear enough to read: *"Atlantis and Co, Ltd. Fine purveyors of the Elixir of the Gods".* They had found the Lost City of Atlantis. Atlantis! John O was bubbling with glee and nearly choked on a lead fishing lure. He ecstatically grabbed his camera to capture the life-changing moment.

Before having the opportunity to take his photograph John O was savagely grabbed and pulled to the slick surface of the pond. There he faced two heavily armed men wearing camouflage paint, stab-proof black commando gear, woolly scarves and striped mittens. Their teeth were noisily chattering as they clasped their machine guns and teetered in the centre of a small shabby fishing boat. A panic stricken John O looked over to the jetty only to find that Karen and Dr Riel had been similarly captured by fierce men who were jumping up and down and rubbing their arms to keep warm. They looked less intimidating whilst leaping around, so made up for this by snarling threats and brandishing blood encrusted machetes at Karen and Dr Riel.

A few minutes later...

On dry land, and shaking, the intrepid trio of treasure hunters faced their dastardly, but still jumping, captors.

"You think you're all so smart. Racing around Greece, plotting and dipping in and out of this vile duck pond. But you

failed to see what was in front of your face." The *"what"* that was in front of their collective faces was John O's *"mates"*. The hobnob stealing, volley ball players had returned and they were all tooled up.

"Why are you doing this? I thought we were pals. I always let you win at scrabble." Dr Rile blustered and stamped his feet. Not because he was huffing at the injustice of being held captive, but because it was damnably cold and he'd forgotten to pack his favourite Tigger onesie.

"I won those games of scrabble fair and square. And you know it. You're here because you're nosey. You wouldn't leave well alone. I pushed those rocks onto Karen and still you persisted in your games.

So we decided to let you continue. See what you found. We followed you down to the Ionian seabed, but we couldn't find a thing. There was no 'charming fish' for us to follow that day. So we thought we'd let you do all the hard work then jump in to scoop the winnings. Oh, John O thanks for all the sketches. We used Karen's pencil to rub over the drawing pad you were using, and voila it all came out as clear as day. We saw the pictures of the temple, the factory and all that gold, but you didn't take it. Not one net bag made it to the surface. So we knew you'd found something even more expensive. Rarer. So we held back until now." The truly terrible scrabble player boasted and pulled out another bloody great big knife. There was a snag on his toasty mittens, and it had been annoying him all-night. It had to go.

"Yeah, we don't have any of the treasure, we left it all behind. The diamonds, sapphires and all the gold's still there. It didn't belong to us. We had no right to steal it. Nor do you." John O clarified, shaking with rage. He had trusted these guys and made sure they always got home safely after a night in the pub. He made sure they had a glass of water and a couple of paracetamol on their bedside cabinet.

"We don't want the gold, platinum, silver or those measly trinkets. We want the treasure. The real treasure. The secret recipe for the Elixir of the Gods. That's what we want. Jock Mackay stole

it and hid it. Yeah, we found old Jock's diary a while back. He found the sunken city and described the treasures and the factory. The factory in your drawings. He wrote that he had chipped at the columns to hide the clues to the recipe, and to hide his thieving ways. He dumped the rest of the city here because he couldn't get planning permission for a garden gazebo. He didn't want to pay the council to dump the bricks and the Forbes family offered a highly completive disposal rate.

He was going to sell the secret recipe but he died of iron poisoning before he got that far. He had tried to give up smoking and he had made a cast iron vape. That was his downfall, the old idiot." The equally terrible Monopoly player added and pulled out his even bigger knife and a bayonet. There was no snag on his mittens. He was going to shish kebab the successful hunters.

"The wall? You wanted the wall? The recipe that was written on the wall? The Elixir you're seeking: it's Irn Bru. That's what was stored in the broken jars. On the wall." Karen smiled despite the immense danger. They had definitively solved the mystery. Well most of the mystery. What was in the temple podium box?

"So where is the famous wall? The recipe?" The dreadful Snakes and Ladder player asked. They had to fill their time between dives so they amused themselves with a variety of board games. John O's deceitful friends were all atrociously bad players and would throw the boards in the air if they didn't win. Babies, the lot of them.

"Hands up and no funny business." Oh, goody. Yet more armed men walloping about in the dark park and playing at being gangsters There were more folks waving pistols in Callendar Park than usually went to Falkirk Football Club home games.

"Oh, I can answer that for you. I have the wall secreted in my home office. A.G. Barr bought the valuable wall from Jock Mackay, just before the old reprobate died. By then Barr had already

researched and made the delicious tonic for the steel workers. When he saw Jock's grainy photographs of the wall he thought someone had committed industrial espionage and had stolen his recipe. He scooped up the wall and propped it up in his office, but he had no idea about its priceless link with the Gods. Its true commercial value.

Many years later I was trying to purchase the company for Poke. I had read all about Jock's fantastical claims. So, when I saw the wall and realised what it was. Its true potential. I was ecstatic.

The elusive Elixir. Its link with the Gods of Atlantis would have put us all out of business. Who wouldn't want the heavenly liquid? I couldn't let anyone know about its esteemed provenance so I 'collected' the wall and its history.

It's currently in my home. Where's it's safe, and no longer a threat to other soda makers. Oh yes, and the next time you make an earthshattering discovery don't sing and dance around Falkirk library...you can never tell when someone may have a spy hidden amongst the ancient tomes and day old newspapers. Now enough yapping and get in the vat." A distinguished grey-haired older man, in a brown Mac, barked. He then pointed a sawn-off shotgun at the trembling trio and the really, really bad board game players. What an out and out villain: it takes a truly dastardly crook to carry around his very own, customised boiling vat. Most bad folks just rent them by the hour or if they were really really busy, by the day.

Oh yes, he told everyone his background story and his plans so that his muscly minions had the necessary time to fill the deadly vat and let all the pesky bubbles escape. He had found that the soon to be departed often tried to drink the contents of the warming vat: in a vain attempt to thwart their horrific fate. It was so embarrassing when the smouldering people got a rousing case of the hiccups, especially before they slowly simmered and melted into an island of floating blubber. Plus, how **do** you stop their hiccups? Give your captives a fright? You feel that, by then, you've pretty much given them all the scares they can possibly handle.

Any more would be overkill: a villain joke that always gets a rousing round of applause at the Annual Assassin Summer Fete.

Karen, John O, Dr Riel and the bad board players reluctantly climbed into the huge, metal vat of low-calorie lemonade. Oh, the old villainous guy was still trying to hide his crimes and put the blame on another soda maker. The out and out baddie.

The damp wood beneath the vat was set alight and the flames gently licked the condensation on the sides of the metal death trap. They were a surefire goner. Well, technically Karen and Dr Riel would survive as only beheading would fully kill them, but they would feel every part of the torture, flames and sugary boiling. However, their friend John O was surely dead. What a waste of gorgeous muscly manliness and all those lush, golden locks. Oh, one of the authors may have had a small flush and needs a cold flannel applied to the back of the neck.

Dr Riel pulled a distressed Karen to his chest and hid her face against his shaking body. He didn't want his Karen to witness John O's cruel demise. Meanwhile John O had pulled the mittens from one of the terrible board game players and was soaking it in the lemonade, then wringing it out over the side of the vat. He was trying, unsuccessfully, to both empty the vat and dampen the growing flames. The board game players were trying, in vain, to contribute to his efforts by blowing on the warming soda but their tears were helping to fill the vat as quickly as John O was emptying it so they negated all of his actions.

A white tube plopped into the steaming vat of death. A grateful Dr Riel grabbed and unrolled the waterproof scroll.

To the voices of a Welsh male choir: singing to the tune of Twinkle, Twinkle Little Star.

"Congratulations, you have gained

a second horn to put on your shelf.
Come home, come home and celebrate
your wonderous achievement. You are great
You are a person without equal.
Well not quite as good the other Hells
They already have at least two horns.
But off you pop and collect your prize.
Congratulations, you have gained
a second horn to put on your shelf."

"Good old us? No, solving most of these clues wouldn't have given us another horn. Would it? No, surely not. And we still have issues with the timeline being off balance.

It can't be Stan and Dippit, they're sorting out their nursery and being terribly threatening to interlopers. Bub and Harry are on honeymoon in Italy and come to think of it...Devil Keith and Nora are all loved up too. Willing is cruising with Cesealia and searching for the Selkie's skin. And anyway, it's not her responsibility to look after our Hell. Gab and Fachance are living it up in the Renaissance period and probably causing mayhem. Gab must have the patience of a saint if he can stay with Fachance 24/7.

So, who is looking after Hell number one and who got the extra horn? Oh Dr Riel, this can't be good." and with that Karen and Dr Riel and dived onto the snorkelling cockroach's moving pavement. They grabbed a smouldering John O and paddled back to Hell number one.

CHAPTER TWENTY-SIX

So how did the team get the extra horn?

The barely clad Bub and Harry were the first of the team to race home and were warmly greeted by Willing, the Horsewoman of War and coincidentally Harry's delightful half-sister. They had expected to be greeted by an ecstatic Dr Riel or the industrious Karen. Karen with a large trophy tightly clutched in her bony fist. A trophy elaborately engraved with the details of the newly acquired horn. A trophy worthy of the central spot on any self-respecting fireplace mantle.

Although slightly disheartened Harry and Bub assumed that Karen and Dr Riel were off putting the final touches to the buffet, for the celebratory banquet, so they nipped off to ditch the semi-transparent shower curtain togas and change into their bestest finery.

An extremely harassed Devil Keith and Nora arrived a few minutes later. Devil Keith seized a canister of bug spray and assumed a crouched position in front of his Nora: in case the irksome Faeries had followed them to Hell number one and were going to continue with their revenge, cruelty and general extortion tactics. The animated bric-a-brac were also a bit of a pain in the butt and Devil Keith was more than happy to be away from the whingers. After a few minutes of Devil Keith's stiff forward rolls and arthritic star-jumps he took a relieved breath. However, there was still his rapid finger pointing gun sorta thingy that he loved to do and finally Devil Keith jerkily jumping into impossible action poses before it was clear that they were home...and safe. For the moment, anyway. However, the dastardly Faeries were still a force to be reckoned with. They had the memory of an elephant and wouldn't forget this slight upon their tricky finances.

They were quickly followed by a soggy Dr Riel, Karen and John O. They were trailing hot, steaming lemonade in their wake. Willing, not at all surprised by this development, threw a couple of towels over to the sodden trio as she had just buffed the floors to a high shine.

John O, wide eyed, looked around him. *"Eh, where are we? What happened there? Were they really going to put us on a slow simmer? Why didn't they just destroy the wall and write the recipe down on a piece of paper? Did you know that old Jock accidently lobbed the Lost City of Atlantis into that pond? Again, where exactly* ***are*** *we, my lovely? You know the timeline for these events is completely buggered, my lovely? Are those cockroaches for real?"* John O babbled away. He was in shock but still upright so that was good.

Karen assured him that she would explain it all later, but to be completely honest she didn't have a scooby as to why they all kept the wall. A souvenir per chance? Maybe? Devil Keith always kept a boat load of crap from his adventures. Could it just be a bad habit that guys had? An extension of their sock drawer debacles?

"The item in the broken box: where is that, my lovely? Do you know?" John O broke into Karen's train of thought. He appeared more concerned with the box's location than his own. Warmed lemonade can sometimes effect folks like that, or is that just a rumour perpetrated by Devil Keith? The authors may have to have a wee look at Wikipedia.

"No idea, and can I say you're taking all this really quite well? Really well. I'll have to think on your questions and get back to you. Have a wee nappy nap and it'll all be better in the morning."

And Karen bopped a startled John O on the head with Willing's awfully useful mallet. She wrapped him in a soft towel and Willing helped her to tuck him into a lovely toasty bed.

Harry, Bub, Devil Keith, Nora, Karen, Dr Riel and Willing waited on Stan and Dippit's arrival but after a few minutes they reasoned that the expectant pair hadn't, in fact, received a scroll. In truth, Dippit, Stan and their pregnancy brains had decided to completely disregarded this non-baby related request and within seconds had totally ejected it from their respective memories. The need to buy an elaborate, and robust baby gym taking its place.

As Devil Keith and Nora had, mainly, been based (aka hiding) in the Falkirk area they were able to do the honours and update the others on Stan and Dippit's pregnancy developments. They received some raised eyebrows and the occasional gasp but generally everyone agreed that Dippit was never going to have a normal pregnancy. Hence all the previous searching, time travelling, slapping of Roger the reprobate and the general tomfooleries that took place in book three, The Devil's a hunting by P and K Stoker. They all agreed that they couldn't wait until the opening night. Sorry, not opening night. The birth? That's a much more acceptable term, right?

Ah, Stan and Dippit's peculiar nursery requirements and terribly threatening answering machine message now made a little bit more sense, Karen thought. Although the twenty or twenty-five minute deadline to death continued to be persistent and slightly concerning. And worryingly short.

Then who had won the horn for Hell number one?

Harry, Bub, Devil Keith, Willing and Nora held their collective breaths and waited on Karen's speech. Karen just stood there; looking at them and their puffed up cheeks. She was mildly concerned by their expectant, oxygen starved, blue faces. Then Karen glanced over at a multiple shrugging and ear scratching Dr Riel, and she raised her shapely eyebrows. The teams couldn't wait a moment longer, as they were thrilled and close to swooning, so they shouted and congratulated Karen and Dr Riel on their sterling achievement. Karen broke the news that it wasn't them that had won the horn as they had been busy winning a wet tee-shirt contest then searching for the Lost City of Atlantis. That, by the way, was no longer lost. Hooray!

CHAPTER TWENTY-SEVEN

Again, who won that twitting horn…

The team turned, as one. The found Brownie Hilary vigorously sweeping, what appeared to be pieces of a greyish desiccated corpse, into one of the battered old filing cabinets. She then gave the ill-fitting drawer a good old, satisfied slamming.

"What ya doing over there, young Brownie?" Karen questioned the skinned knee hellion. Brownie Hilary stopped brushing and robustly re-adjusted her bunches. They were forever escaping her pretty garlands of cherries hair baubles. Brownie Rachel had helpfully offered to staple them to Hilary's head, but Brown Owl Mac had stepped in when Brownie Rachel began lovingly stroking her nail-gun and maniacally muttering, "*soon my stabby one, soon.*"

"Jo-than says, 'Brown-knee Hilary, yous has a biggest mouse tache and a goat on yous face so you's needs to gets a barbell badge so yous can luck after it'. Sos I prac-tass sweeps so I's cans get mys shavery badge. Lifts yous feet, or yous goes ins the ca-nets or undus the rug. I nos mind." With that very important announcement, a meticulous Brownie Hilary brushed a couple of fragile femurs under the loose muddy brown carpet tiles and she stubbornly stomped the squares back into place. She smiled and nodded, then gave herself a rousing round of applause.

Devil Keith was surprisingly good at interpreting *"Brownie speak"*, so he informed the others that Brownie

Hilary was working towards an especially tricky Brownie Barber Badge. This was because she was currently sporting a particularly handsome goatee and wanted some maintenance tips. Hence all the practicing of the sweeping up, and the clomping around that was currently occurring. Plus, she said they had to lift their feet or they too would end up in the cabinet or under a rug. She wasn't too bothered either way. Perfectly reasonable actions for a rather hirsute young'in, Devil Keith thought.

Karen was a little wary of the Brownies so she joined in with Brownie Hilary's enthusiastic clapping, and she added a hearty cheer for good measure. The industrious Brownie pulled back her lips and showed her white sharpened teeth. Karen thought she'd probably done the right thing when she'd cheered. And Karen really hoped she wouldn't find a partially skinned alligator in her bed. Again.

Speak of the Devil or the wannabe Devil…

Jonathan strutted down the metal staircase from Karen's room into the main, open plan office in Hell number one. He was wearing a shiny lilac and grey three-piece pinstriped suit that was topped off with a matching fedora. The hat had a spritely canary yellow feather plonked in the hatband. Devil Keith would have looked so much better in that get-up as he would have had the good taste to add an extra-large Blackwatch tartan pocket square and a fake, fox-brush beard to the ensemble. Jonathan was such an under-dresser; it was all so sad. Devil Keith slowly shook his head and grieved for Jonathan's poor tailor and his troubled milliner.

"Hairy Brownie, begone from my sight and do your pitiful sweeping in that oh so distant corner, over yonder…. there. Yes, I mean there. No, over there, ya muppet. Disgusting creature. I can barely keep my nausea at bay when I see the hairs on her chinny-chin-chin." Jonathan viciously pointed, and pointed again. He made a show of grimacing and gagging at the startled little

girl. He gave the obliging little Brownie a sharp shove to the floor, then promptly dusted off his manicured hands. Nora held a fuming Devil Keith back and whispered that they'd get their revenge later.

Two days before the Faery intimidation incident at the charity shop, Devil Keith had said that he urgently needed something green to hold or he'd faint dead away. So Nora, being the wonderful wife that she is, had gifted the upright Devil Keith with an extra firm, new cabbage. It was all she had in her cupboard and she didn't fancy changing out of her Grinch onesie to pop over to the supermarket. Once she put on her onesie there was nothing that could drag her from its cosiness. Well, apart from one of Devil Keith's appealing come hither looks. Meow!

Back to the cabbage and some much needed revenge. The useful cabbage was then fitted onto a mightily strong elastic band. A band that had previously held up a pair of Nora's big, big underpants. The band was mighty powerful and ever so brave. This cannot be emphasised enough and may be the basis for another book. That bouncing and re-bounding large Brassica yoyo would sort the Brownie pushing, rotter out. In no time at all he'd be eating his liquidised greens through a significant hole in his chest wall, Nora joyfully predicted.

"Ah, welcome home everyone, especially Devil Keith. My intrepid travellers, I see you are suitably impressed with all my improvements. It is I, Jonathan, who am responsible for the begetting of the extra horn." And Jonathon made a clumsy attempt at a bow and nearly tripped over Brownie Hilary's bent, rusty shovel. A shovel that Harry had edged closer to the Brownie hitting, silly cookie bun.

"You, you. How can it be you? You're meant to be all tubby and sad. And you're meant to be all tortured and crying in a dusty corner. You're in Hell because you're an out and out bad yin. You're a terrible gossip and cause trouble everywhere you go. You hate

everyone, and are jam packed full of piss, wind and spite.

You... you. You tried to ruin my delightful dates with my Nora. Bub, tell him to be all tortured and rocking in a dirty corner. Tell him." Devil Keith was equally flabbergasted, furious and alarmed. Jonathan was meant to be in nipple agony and unable to stomach fabric anywhere near his mutilated areoles. He was also meant to have multiple cigarette butts lodged in his teeth, and have empty beer bottles hanging out his pockets. Devil Keith had his thumb suspiciously close to his mouth as he urged his brother on.

"Gail, the spreadsheet if you please. Although why I'm uttering the word 'please' to any one of you is beyond my comprehension. You're so below me. You should be grateful I permit you to serve me. Breathe my air." Johnathan hissed at the gorgeous blonde standing to his left.

Jonathan made such a show of scanning the plump file that the Hell team managed six full eye-rolls, ten tuts each and put in a complex coffee order. It took so long that Devil Keith was seriously considering going for a nappy nap with his lovely Nora. He was just about to unpack his very bestest come hither look.

"Well according to my calculations. You all went off galivanting and left Hell number one with no means of feeding the Demons or the residents. I, as the Deadly Sin of Gluttony, found that to be a mere inconvenience but the other inhabitants of this pathetic hell-hole found it to be very much a big inconvenience. Ahhh, I'm such a wit and an absolute delight. Gail, take a note of my joke.

After all the fighting over the food scraps, the frequent eye-gougings, a session of nippy nut-kicking and a few random strangulations, the inhabitants just laid down and wasted away. Turned to finely milled dust. Poof and they were gone. Gail, take a note of this joke too. You'd think she'd just know to do that automatically as I make so many wonderful jests. You just can't get the staff.

Anyway, I, the mighty Johnathan carried on regardless.

I mastered the old Punishment Decider and reversed all the shameful punishments you unjustly heaped upon my innocent head. I no longer have cigarette butt infused drinks forced upon me every hour, and no more fleshy gashes appear upon my person. I have also banned Curly Wurlys as I cannot tolerate the flashbacks they induce, so don't go checking out the vending machines for that evil confectionery.

I kindly and magnanimously employed Brownie Hilary as my cleaner and, as you can plainly see, she is woefully attempting to earn her pitiful badge. Aren't you? You mop-headed dwarf." Jonathan sneered at the industrious Brownie and he tried to bounce the hefty spreadsheet file off her tiny head. He also sneered at Gail, his efficient assistant. A mistake. A big, big mistake.

"Who are you sneering at ya skinny aubergine wannabe?" And the sassy Gail sadistically kicked Jonathan in the shin for his twitting cheek, and poor fashion sense. Then she added a particularly brutal Chinese burn to the mix. That brought Jonathan, and his extremely tight trousers to his bony knees. She wasn't taking any of his snash. She only agreed to be his assistant due to her love of all things spreadsheet related. Her Christmas and birthday gift giving spreadsheet was a thing of true beauty. Patent pending, of course.

As an aside, if Nora had gotten to Jonathan first he would have had more than just a kick and a tortuous Chinese burn to worry about. He'd probably be talking out of his protruding bellybutton and wearing his ribcage as a sticky hat. Yes, our Nora was a big fan of the Brownies and their Brownish ways. She also hated that Jonathan was misogynistic, a homophobe, a racist and openly ridiculed anyone who had a disability. He was a general all-round horror of a man, a coward and a wannabee Brownies' assaulter to boot. The courageous cabbage yoyo might not be enough, Nora concluded.

During an early, *"getting to know each other"* date, Devil Keith had told Nora all about Jonathan. His role in their awful dates and the extra punishments Devil Keith had added to Jonathan's initial Hell tally. Nora thought it was horrendous that Devil Keith's Hell thought that being gay was a legitimate means of punishment, and she made sure that Devil Keith knew how barbaric and shortsighted that was. She had lots of friends and family from the LGBTQ community and they would be appalled by this antiquated notion. After some probing questions, and two bowls of tuna flavoured popcorn, Nora had surmised that Jonathan had been given the opportunity in Hell number one to have an allergy, and experience being gay. She reasoned that it was not a punishment, not at all. Rather it was seen as a means to promote some understanding of others and how his behaviours negatively impacted on a variety of different people. Plus, Johnathan's attempt at building his own Conversion Camp made Nora's blood boil so she was delighted that it wasn't successful, and caused Johnathan substantial financial woes. That was why, Nora thought, the Punishment Decider had chosen to make Johnathan gay and not to make him a woman. Ironic justice and a chance to redeem himself was the Decider's plan.

However, Nora, in all her wisdom and her very short-lived apprenticeship as a telephone engineer, knew that the gossiping, small-minded rodent would never learn. Never change. Nora felt that despite Devil Keith's age, and the many, many experiences of the Hell number one management team, they could be very cutely naïve at times. If she ruled Hell number one there would be an awful lot more naughty steps, skelped legs and fireside tartan on the menu. Come to think of it: that's probably why she's not allowed to rule Hell.

"Yesss, I's sweep and I's sweep but there's awas more dead thingies. They's messy They's are. I triez. I's really dos. I's sorry." Brownie Hilary blew her thick fringe out of her eyes, rubbed her freshly trimmed beard and noisily scrubbed her blocked nose with her uniform sleeve. Another lovely uniform for

Brown Owl Mac to launder. The last sentence should be read with a Scottish accent and a sarcastic eye-roll...go on then, have a go. You'll feel great!

"Shut up you offensive midget, and tidy yourself up. No one wants to hear your pathetic complaints. Where was I? Ah, yes. The addition of the ever so deliciously evil desiccation… then ***my*** *totally original idea of re-animation of the residents, to start once again, gave* ***me*** *the extra Hell horn. The management of Hell number one was both a guaranteed certainty and rightly mine. I am the King of all you survey. I will take your abject grovelling now. Line up and kiss my ring."* Jonathan said, with a tear in his eye. That burn was an absolute doozy. Jonathan decided to add Gail to his torture team. Her talents were sorely wasted as his mere assistant. Oh, she'll so get him if she reads this book, and sees the word "*mere*" anywhere near her name. One of the authors shivers in sheer delightful anticipation of all that wonderful carnage directed his way.

"Oy, you little liar. You stole the re-animation idea from the Beach Comber's Hell. I saw you read their manual. You giggled like a little girl and I saw you take some notes. You asked me how to spell re-animation even though it was written in the book. You can't take credit for that idea, ya skinny red onion." Gail helpfully clarified. She so enjoyed cooking and baking, so many of her observations were fiercely food related. She then waggled her index finger and mimed giving Jonathan a savage slap across the coupon (head). She finished her tirade with a curtsy and a sharply assertive nod. Jonathan tried to act casual but everyone could see that he had hastily backed away. And he was keeping the feisty blonde firmly in his line of sight.

"I'd ***like*** *to say that it's been lovely to see you, but what I'm* ***actually*** *saying is that I'd like you all to leave. I have the Office Manager Demons on standby with their sock garters and packs of A4 paper at the ready. They've been training to decapitate with a thousand papercuts and have gotten rather good at it. Chop, chop, now. You have one hour to pack your grungy things and do a thorough clean of your rooms. Or I'll be forced to fine you*

and you'll lose your cleaning deposits. Also, be warned, I will be checking your bags so no sneaking away with Hell number one property, you naughty band of incompetent minxes.

One last thing. Devil Keith, you handsome Devil, you're very welcome to stay and bunk with me. I always share my blankets and snuggles with my closest friends. And whenever did you change your fine clothes, you tempting hunk?" Jonathan moped his sweaty brow. He then batted his stubby eyelashes and pouted at the disinterested Devil. Nora tucked Devil Keith behind her back and put her clenched fists on her hips. Jonathan would have to come through her to get to her man.

Devil Keith had indeed changed into his saddest clothing regime: black PVC mid-thigh platform boots, semi-polished breast plate armour and grey budgie smuggler underpants adorned his grief-stricken personage. All bright orange and pale pink clothes were temporarily banned from his wardrobe. He was in mourning for his beloved Hell.

Jonathan, the pratt, had done a fair bit of whispering behind his hands, preening, fingertip clapping and theatrical eye rolling during his well-practised speech. He then dramatically pushed a sand filled hourglass timer into Bub's hand. Like they don't all have Smart watches and count their daily steps, sheesh.

CHAPTER TWENTY-EIGHT

In Karen's, sorry Jonathan's office...

"That silly cookie bun. He totally underestimated us. The solution's simple really. Get C.C. to turn back time so that one of us can volunteer to stay in Hell and look after the residents. Saving them from starvation, desiccation and re-animation. Or get one of us to stay in Hell number one and **we** *starve the residents then powder them so we get the credit for the extra horn. As I said. Simple really."* Harry helpfully suggested. She rubbed her hands together then plonked down on Bub's very comfortable knee. Stealing a slurp of his Falkirk Sewer and chewing the haggis flavoured maraschino cherries with gusto.

"I had already considered that, but I was waiting until you returned to summon him." Angel Gab shuddered at the thought of the delicious but potent Falkirk Sewer cocktail. He'd had many a hangover due to the intoxicating potion but he still went back for more, especially when he was dealing with the shenanigans of the Hell number one folks.

Angel Gab and Fachance or Fat Chance, the Horsewoman of Famine, had arrived back in Hell number one before the others. So they had already heard a version of Jonathan's spiteful speech and witnessed his fanciful gloating and endured his multiple air blown kisses. They also had a "*helpful*" hourglass timer and had heard the bizarre ultimatum. Well, to be fair it was less of an ultimatum and more of a straightforward threat to their neck region. However, Gab and Fachance's hourglass was more elegantly crafted as Jonathan so wanted the Angel to like him, despite the multiple eviction notices slathered about the place.

Gab promptly nipped off and returned with a slightly breathless C.C. by his side. C.C. was in mid costume change when the apologetic Angel broke into his flower strewn dressing room and requested the small, time reversal favour. The four foot high pixie that is C.C. or Cher Capade, as he is known in the business, was a Drag Queen extraordinaire. And it comes as no surprise that his chosen icon was the incomparable superstar that is Cher.

C.C.'s back story...

C.C. was also a truck driver, hailing from Bolton, England. He elegantly balanced out both of the jobs he loved by having a smoking hot body, for his nighttime activities, and he was totally covered in rather racy tattoos for his more subdued daytime job. When he was younger he had felt that the tattoos made him appear more manly and virile. This was because his fellow drivers, before getting to know him, had insisted on giving him the trucker handle of, *"Not so Sonny, ma lad"*. A rather pathetic nod at Cher's previous husband and singing partner. New drivers still occasionally ridiculed both his short appearance and his excellent after dinner cabaret routine. They felt that as he reached his dashboard by sitting on feather-filled, scarlet, velvet tasselled cushions and he reached the pedals by tying a bundle of books onto his large feet (at the moment, due to his preference for a muslin empire line cream dress decorated with white embroidered rose buds, he appeared to be in the middle of reading Jane Austen's superb Pride and Prejudice), he was an easy mark for their unrelenting jests and derogatory comments. They didn't realise that beneath those lacy frocks, fishnet tights, body stockings and tightly bound muscles, lay a man who was a black belt in Mixed Martial Arts. A man who could bend their jeering bodies into the shape of a soft pretzel and launch them onto the surface of the midday sun.

C.C.'s gorgeous wife was a calming influence in his life, and told him that revenge was a dish best served cold. So C.C. took that to heart and instead of giving his new colleagues a bit of much needed sunburn, he poisoned them. He poisoned them with anti-freeze and gleefully watched them die a slow and terribly painful death. Then C.C. would reverse time so that he could kill them again, and again, and again. That only happened if they said things about his darling wife not being good enough to get a real man, or if they said mean things about Cher. He also gave them an extra dose of anti-freeze if he wanted them to blow on his hot chips with their frozen breath, but they refused to do him that small favour. However, there was one tiny problem with this multiple killing lark as his victims could develop an aversion for Magnum white chocolate ice-cream lollies and they positively loathed the freezer aisle in Asda supermarkets. C.C. tried to stop before they got to that stage but some of them so deserved it.

C.C.'s wife was mighty pleased with her husband's reasonable compromise and frequently bought in bags of microwave popcorn. This was so they could both enjoy a Saturday night in, cuddled up under a blanket, with a good gasping death. And just above room temperature chips, followed by a lovely salty/sweet snack. She had simple needs.

C.C. wasn't sure why he had been selected to gain the skill to turn back time. One night he was dressed head to toe in black spandex and rhinestones belting out Cher's, *"If I could turn back time,"* when he did a particularly fast pirouette and whizzed back to the very beginning of his set. After a few minutes, to catch his breath, C.C. re-started his set and he used the opportunistic re-run to deal with an exceptionally annoying heckler. His quick and witty put downs were a thing of legend that night and resulted in the desolated heckler taking an unbreakable vow of silence. Devil Keith and Bub had caught the fantastic show so they knew what had happened although they didn't know why he was chosen for this superb gift. After the show they took the perplexed, but jubilant, C.C. out for a vindaloo curry and a couple of pints of foaming lager. The lager was probably on the turn. They then explained how this gift could benefit them all. Since then C.C. would bet on the greyhound racing and always come up with the winners. The poor confused dogs occasionally developed an overwhelming passion for eating raw salad potatoes, but C.C. would gladly adopt those mutts and kennel them on his large allotment. Giving them unfettered access to as many tiny potatoes as their slobbering chops could gulp down.

Back to present day Hell and the team's need for a re-do...

*"Alright there, my favourite Hell team. Heard you had a bit of ******* bother going on. So I did, like. ******* **** it comes to something when a person can't nip out for a pint without having his ******* home stolen from under his nose. Right, I'm in the middle of a ******* good chapter of ma book. They're about to kiss so will thirty ******* minutes turn around do it, ya ******s?"* C.C. could probably benefit from a thesaurus as he called friend and foe a ******. You had to pay attention to the tone behind the swearing, and surreptitiously check his pockets for the outline of a bottle of poison and a well-used funnel before you could completely relax in his company.

"Hi C.C. You're looking well. Sorry to interrupt, but we're looking for a few weeks of turn around this time." Karen asked and crossed her fingers. This was a big, big ask of the talented singer.

*"Weeks, ya *******s? Well, I'm speechless. I am. I spoke with Stan a fortnight ago about the ******* rules and even he couldn't help change them. No can do, lads and lassies. That's just too long. Those ******** Oracles would have my ***** *****s for trying that. Gab, ya ****** can you get me back for my last ******** number? Then I'm off for the night. There's some mouthy ****** due some numbing*

*in his ******* future. Doesn't rate Cher, he ******* said! The wife's got a family bag of popcorn all ready and waiting. Sorry folks I have to ******* go. Oye, Devil Keithie boy when are you gonna measure me for those **** off shoes you promised me? It's no joke dancing in these workman's steel toe-capped boots."* The tiny pixie did a couple of nifty tap-dance moves and the room shook to its very foundations. His feet were truly huge. When he walked he resembled two letter Ls held together by a long curly black wig, or a two legged spider, on stilts, scurrying towards a fly encrusted web. The authors will stop typing now as they don't want C.C. to take offense and insist on the consumption of some "*tasty*" ice-cubes in their near future. One of the authors is a big fan of white chocolate Magnums, hint, hint.

"I'll sort out your shoes tomorrow if you give it a try for us. I'd like my Nora to have a second home here. I think she'd like the ambience and my mannequins to shout at." Devil Keith was picturing his Nora in a pink frilly apron and nothing much else. She was cooking pancakes, sprinkled with fried, thinly sliced koala bear, in their kitchen. And he was imagining the gorgeous C.C. in red silk platforms with heels covered in phoenix feathers. That reminded Devil Keith... he needed to get more firelighters and petrol soaked bird seed for the fussy eaters. Who said men can't multitask? Devil Keith promptly fell off the sofa as he had forgotten to breathe.

C.C. agreed to try, but after his fourth attempt and two nose bleeds later they realised that the time reversal just wasn't going to work. They needed a new plan of action. However, C.C. did make it home in time for the show and the mouthy **** did learn to appreciate Cher.

Still problem solving in Hell...

"What about the Time Scavenger? One of us can go back in time and warn the rest of us. Stop us from leaving Hell in Jonathan's grubby little mitts. A bit of the old 'Back to the Future' vibe." Bub was exploring a tickly bit on Harry's neck

and not really wanting to understand the gravity of the whole situation. His brush with death, at the hands of the mafia, had made him realise how precious Harry, and his life with Harry was. He'd also decided to just keep turning the hourglass timer over so that the time limit was immaterial. Rule breaking Harry was, possibly, not the best influence on her usually conservative husband.

"Ah, there is a slight problem with that suggestion. Fachance and I arrived here precisely twenty-five minutes before the rest of you descended into Hell. In that time we listened to Jonathan's unmitigated drivel but only after we had happily dropped the Time Scavenger off at the Oracle's cluttered abode. That thing is an unmitigated menace. I shall illuminate, shall I?

We were forced to leave Florence when we realised that we were at risk of ruining the whole timeline. Purely by chance, the lovely Fachance and I were in a tavern one evening extoling the virtues and the sins of the rather wonderful music festival that was Woodstock. The atmosphere, the free love, the unwashed masses, the blocked toilets and the excessively liberal groupies bring back such sweet memories. Memories where I had to take charge and curtail the antics of some of the more colourful characters. I was full of joy at that blessed role. However, I am not sure if you are aware of this, but Fachance is a rather large fan of marijuana due to the ravenous munchies that it elicits. Her experiences, and hence her memories, of Woodstock were slightly different from mine own. Two sides of the same coin, as it were.

So, we may, as they so quaintly say, have 'over egged the old pudding' and talked the festival up to truly majestic proportions. The patrons were entranced with our tale of excess and debauchery.

As a result, the Florentines, in their exuberance, were going to knock down San Miniato al Monte. That is a rather large and prestigious building that was dedicated to the first martyr of Christian Florence. It had been there since 1018, so Fachance and I could not in good faith support that act of architectural vandalism. The Florentina's reasoning: they wanted to create a large enough space for their very own version of Woodstock. Complete with lutes, harps and many, many Hurdy-Gurdys. We could not endure that slur upon the musical and cultural world so Fachance and I used the Time Scavenger to warn our earlier selves about avoiding the whole Woodstock chatter. And voila. The timeline was left entirely intact. And, as Bub so eloquently put it, 'the old Back to the Future' vibe was successfully utilised.

So no others could be tempted to re-enact a thoughtless event we returned the Time Scavenger to the ever so grateful Oracles. The Oracles, recognising the potential risks, then shoved the Scavenger in the cupboard under the stairs. That cupboard was overwhelmed with Nile boxes and has expanded exponentially in order to enable their shopping addiction. I fear that you will not locate that object now or in the near future. Please accept my sincere apologises for your loss." Gab hung his head and righted Bub's hourglass. Fachance had nervously eaten their hourglass during the catch up. And the office vertical blinds were also being stored, purely for safe keeping, in her concave stomach.

"Don't the Oracles live in a 1960's bungalow? Why do they even have stairs?" Bub enquired and looked over at a sagely nodding Devil Keith.

"Oh, I asked them a wee while ago about that and they said they just fancied a set of stairs to slid up and down, so they scavenged them from some palace or other. They did tell me where. Give me a minute. I know this. Ah, got it. It was from some bird called Rapunzel. Seemingly she didn't need them anymore because she had grown her fringe out." Devil Keith had had a very productive day after his chatty, chat with the Oracles. He'd used their information wisely and only for good. Purely coincidentally and not at all connected to the stairs, one of his Neanderthal actors received a lovely long, blonde, plated toupee that very same night. Oh, and that Rapunzel *"bird"* went blind. Or some such thing...the Grimm brothers were

never one for happy endings.

"Enough about the twitting Oracles. Angel-Boy, I thought you weren't able to, 'over egged the old pudding' or to be precise... Be a big fat liar, due to your special honesty washing powder? The powder you're forever harping on about." Queried a pissed off Harry. She heartily disliked that powder as it meant that Angel-Boy knew all about her adventures, and she did so like a little mystery surrounding herself. Mystery and allure. She also liked to be surrounded by chicken and pineapple pizza boxes and many, many chocolate wrappers. Oh, and empty bottles of tequila. Well, not quite empty. When she was dealing with her hangover she was always pleased, and relieved, to see a worm or two curled up for a snooze in the bottom of the empty-ish bottles.

"Ah, yes. Fachance and I had to use the local products on our clothing. The animal fat soap, ash and all that banging of clothes on large stones did not have the same impact as my usual brand of washing powder. Hence the slight over-exaggeration we were caught up in." Angel- Boy, sorry Gab alluded. Devil Keith took a step away, then another from the "*fragrant*" Angel. Devil Keith thought he could smell goat.

"Well, that's not good news but at least we're quickly eliminating possible solutions rather than following our usual wild goose chases. So, any suggestions? Anyone?" Bub looked around for raised hands or a bit of welcome eye-contact.

When faced with a problem the Hell team would usually ramble on and on forever until they forgot what the problem was or the issue magically resolved itself. Devil Keith, invariably, would be leaving for a much needed nappy nap, and returning from his snooze in a preposterous but stylish new outfit. Karen would be writing unnecessarily threatening memos to the postal staff of Mississippi then adding hearts to the top of all her Is, in the vain hope that this would negate some of her more lively and descriptive threats. She would also be hoping that they didn't sue her sorry ass. Harry would be blowtorching something or other, then questioning why she could always smell burning. She would then check her much worn medical dictionary as she would be worried that she was having a stroke or suffering from epilepsy or whatever else she had recently watched on a sappy medical soap-opera.

Dr Riel would be practising his many and increasingly flamboyant, marriage proposals to his Karen. He would then chicken out after he'd paid the exorbitant deposit for the World Champion, Spoon Throwing team's deluxe wedding package. Part of the award winning team's proposal bundle included large soup spoons engraved with the words, *"Karen, will you spoon with me forever?"* The spoon chuckers critical injury insurance waiver was brutal hence the non-refundable and larger than usual booking deposits.

Then there would be Bub: stepping in when things had already gone wrong. Bolting in when the Hell team were no further forward in their quest for vengeance. Or there would be Bub having to mediate an argument when the Hell team's need to create the perfect, half-price grocery list had taken a sudden deadly turn. But this time Bub was taking charge now, and he just might be taking this whole losing Hell to Jonathan situation seriously afterall. Harry may have brought out his wilder, hoppering side but he was still steel to his very core. Another hooray moment in the making!

CHAPTER TWENTY-NINE

Tumbleweed was the response to Bub's very reasonable question...

"Willing, oh you look nice. Have you done something different with your hair? A wee dab of mascara and some lip balm going on there? Is that a new snazzy backpack you're sporting? Did you happen to get a scroll too? I didn't think you would, but how else would you know to return now? And who is the big guy skulking behind you? Eh?" Karen rambled on, whilst also stepping away from the unusually scented Angel. A few dozen pine scented car air-fresheners were going to be added to the shared shopping list. Even if they were all at full price. Hell's budget be dammed, she decided.

"Karen, you sure have a lot of questions ha, ha, ha. Erm, I'm trying out a new style just now. I thought I'd do something different with my hair. Just for a change. Yeah, I had to get a new back pack. I needed something a bit bigger than usual because of all the recent, international travelling I was doing. Plus, I felt a bit awkward leaving things unguarded in unfamiliar and dodgy hotel rooms. I couldn't always find more upmarket places to lay my head and, of course, do the obligatory pinching of all the lovely freebies. I so love a stolen dressing gown or flat screen TV tucked into my suitcase. Fachance normally just eats them all before I have a chance. So it was easier to just carry everything with me. To be honest, Cesealia and her trust issues have kinda rubbed off on me. I think that I just need some time around people I love then I'll dump

the bag in the back of the wardrobe. Where it belongs.

Oh, and this is Vinnie. I acquired him around about the same time that I found Cesealia's seal skin stealer. I must say that his skills of gentle persuasion were a very useful negotiating tool.

Oh, Cesealia says 'hi'. She was every so grateful that you could spare me and my extensive skills from Hell, to assist her in her furry quest. She's now very happily frolicking in the India ocean currents, and she's joined the dating site 'Waveder'. It's an aquatic version of the dating site Tinder. There are an awful lot of sharks, pretending to be dolphins, on the site but she's devised a full-proof list to weed out the more teethy matches. She's doing good and she's already asked me to be her maid of honour. But enough about me and my wild adventures. As I said, this great big hulk of a brute is Vinnie." Willing introduced the colossal Vinnie to the team.

Vinnie was a six foot-ten inches tall man and he was wearing a pair of lemon coloured, teddy-bear themed pyjamas. He reasoned that the cuddly pyjamas made him appear soft and vulnerable: all the better to rip off an unsuspecting man's leg and beat him with the blood-clot dripping femur. His purple nylon bum-bag was bulging with brass knuckle-dusters and a myriad of different cheeses and salty crackers. So were his distended, scarlet veined cheeks. They were filled with snacks not knuckle-dusters, although you can never be certain in Hell. It's a brutish kind of a place. Vinnie sort of smiled at the mildly intimidated team and a lump of blue cheese fell onto his black-bristled chin. He used the very tip of his mammoth pinkie finger to pick up the smear of cheese. He removed his sunglasses then lifted the eyepatch covering his left eye-ball and stared angrily at the morsel. He then looked accusingly at the team as if they had the audacity to chuck the dairy item at him. He was rhythmically grunting and no longer attempting any form of smiling. Nor were the team, they were all stepping back and checking for the nearest exit. Except Devil Keith, he had his Nora over his shoulder and he was tightly holding onto her bum cheeks: kinda firefighter style with a side order of sexual harassment thrown in for good measure. The fire hose, tightly clasped in his right hand as a makeshift club, was probably a bit of an over-kill.

Vinnie then slurped down some coffee. He made the usually innocent act look so threatening that Bub grabbed his Harry and began looking for his very own fire hose to clobber the giant menace.

Willing realised that Vinnie, and his famous hair-trigger temper, probably wasn't going to be staying in Hell number one very long. *"So, who do we have here?"* Willing was pointing at Nora's chubby posterior: relieved to change the subject.

"This irresistibly woman. This Kissable Kumquat, with a gorgeous arse, is my Nora. My wife. My reason for getting up in the afternoon." And Devil Keith whirled the giggling Nora in front of him and chuckled excitedly. He still couldn't believe his luck at bagging his Nora. And he was ever so grateful for Christopher Columbus' bobbing boats that led to his opportunity to hold back Nora's hair whilst she projectile vomited over the side of the ship. Carrotless barf that sealed Nora's place in his heart. That's not right! I'm sure it was the other way around, an author huffed indignantly.

"Married? When? Why weren't we invited? I wasn't in a maniac's prison cell this time. Plus, I'm sure no one would have objected to the match. Well, I certainly wouldn't have. And, that's the third wedding I've missed. The third! Can't you lot keep it in your pants long enough to invite your family to the celebrations? Anyway, none of this, I'm sure, is poor Nora's fault. So, Nora. Erm, you look familiar. Very familiar. In fact, you have an uncanny likeness to Leonardo Da Vinci's painting of the mysterious Mona Lisa. Has anyone else commented on this?" Willing looked around the others for confirmation. The rest of the team nodded. She was delighted to hear the news about her close friend and half brother-in-law's (?) recent nuptials. There

really needs to be a bit of new blood in Hell number one as it's all very difficult to remember where folks were hanging in the old family tree.

"Ohhhh, the more accurate question is: why does the artist's model, in the famous painting, look just like my adorable Nora? Now that's a story of biblical proportions, (The Devil's a hunting, by P and K Stoker, just in case you need any ideas for a truly brilliant birthday gift for your very discerning friends or relatives). But I'm sorry Willing, a full catch up will have to wait as I think we're in a spot of bother." Devil Keith looked at Bub for confirmation. Bub slowly nodded. He was truly amazed at Devil Keith's ability to focus on the disturbing issue.

And with Devil Keith's understatement out there for debate and hopefully some action. Bub added, *"so to quote an old Scottish saying 'Oor arse is oot the windae.' Or, our bottom appears to be hanging out of a glass aperture. There's only one thing for it..."*

CHAPTER THIRTY

The team cast their faces upwards and shouted *"God."*

"Yes dearies, what can I do for you? Well done on achieving the extra horn. I bet young Karen and Dr Riel are cock-a-hoop with their triumph." God appeared in a yellow flowery apron with a large wooden spoon clasped in her hand. A smear of flour on her nose and the remains of a pint of milk dripping from her skirt completed her domesticated look. She had been trying one of Mary Berry's recipes for a summer, lemon drizzle cake. It was proving to be a touch tricky.

The team then explained that Karen and Dr Riel were very much not cock-a-hoop, and the rest of the team were also without a single hoop to cock. God listened and nodded and then offered round a packet of stale ginger nuts. Devil Keith cheekily dipped his biscuit in his cup of pungent, pilchard tea and smiled. He was home and life was exceedingly good.

God looked increasingly distressed as she digested their terrible news. Shaking her head: she snatched back her packet of ginger nuts as she realised that they probably didn't deserve to celebrate their extra horn. She stuffed the biscuits in her pinny's patch pockets. The numpties! The complete and utter numpties. God sunk, despondently, into the corner sofa. *"Well dearies, your life is not good. Not good at all. You really do not have a hoop to cock, now do you dearies?*

Even though I'm a great believer in free will, you should have set out a rota so that you each took a turn looking after Hell number one. As you were absentee landlords Jonathan has stepped up and usurped you. Based on your previous actions, I suppose it was just a matter of time before something like that happened here.

Oh dearies, I'll get our Sarah from HR, she'll explain it better than I can. Sarah, dearie, can you come down for a minute? I think we have a small problem." God sighed and shook her recently tinted hair. She was trying out new colours at the moment and quite liked the Sun on the Serengeti look mixed with Dead Gazelle mauled by a hyena, highlights. Blonde with some red bits to the uninitiated.

The ever so dainty Sarah appeared with a dazzlingly white smile, ruby red lipstick and wearing a purple and grey toned kilt. She had been practising her highland and belly dancing fusion routine when God made her wonderfully, wonderful request for Sarah's expertise. Sarah was absolutely delighted to help, and listened to the team's tales of woe. She was asking probing questions and suitably gasping at all the appropriate points. She was also taking copious scribbled notes in her small lined jotter, as it all had to be done strictly by the book. She was a consummate professional, although she wasn't always taken as seriously as she would have liked. This may have been due to her deep, husky and quite frankly sexy tones. There is no doubt that she would make a killing if she ever wanted to be a, "*There are gorgeous women in your area just waiting to speak with you*". This was always followed by, "*for the princely sum of £10 a minute,*" and this was all advertised at one o'clock in the morning. That type of gal.

"This is all highly irregular and contravenes many, many Demon employment laws. As managers you have a duty of care to provide food, water and comfort breaks to Hell number one employees. As well as remuneration in the form of a living wage.

And according, to the Descriptor Manual for Hell number one, you should also provide basic nourishment to your residents. Prescribed torture, scratchy woolly jumpers and vitals are the bare minimum requirements in order to fulfil your custodial Hell duties.

As I see it, you will have to make amends, and really rather quickly. I would suggest some self-motivation, self-reflection and urgent re-training are in order. According to the highly secretive HR manual you have two quite difficult choices. So, you either undertake an apprenticeship at Falkirk's 'What is that in your spoon?' or you undertake an episode of work experience in one of the other Hells. Work experience that ***must*** *result in a useful and applicable learning opportunity. Otherwise, you forfeit your Hell forever and Jonathan becomes the permanent manager."* Sarah gave them a copy of their two choices and asked one of the team to sign and date a copy for their file. She so enjoyed a burgeoning filing cabinet.

"Just as I thought, dearies. A possible, no make that a probably, disaster in the making. One last thing. You only have an hour to decide on your course of action. So, tick, tock and for goodness sake stop turning over the hourglass. You'll break it and have to pay for it. Good luck dearies." With that threat hanging in the air God re-lit her joint, adjusted her magnet laden menopause knickers and nipped off to watch a re-run of the Neanderthal games. The drizzle cake would keep for another day. The saucy, primitive racers would not.

Sarah thought she'd just pop back home for an hour to put her feet up and watch her highland dancing championships. She had a particularly busy day planned as Dancer Angela was leading a belly dancing Hafla that night and HR Sarah was delighted to be helping with the choreography. She had incorporated Dancer Joanne's very difficult kitten push move to the routine. HR Sarah thought her little kitties, Ash and Bradley, would so enjoy that furry treat.

CHAPTER THIRTY-ONE

Still in Karen's, sorry Jonathan's office...

They all agreed that an apprenticeship at Falkirk's *"What's in your spoon?"* Was too much work. All those early mornings and late nights, with endless toilet cleaning in-between, was a chore too far.

After some imaginative swearing, and a fair bit of scrambling around, Devil Keith picked up the stolen Hell Descriptor list from Hell number eight's employment manual. The very same manual that Jonathan had hotly denied that he copied his ideas from. That one. Devil Keith began reading aloud and only needed to be told off six times for using a heavy, and oddly insulting, Dutch accent. Insulting to the people of the Netherlands, just to be clear. *"Cough, cough. Pay attention minions we're on the clock here. So, to begin...*

'Hell, number one

One Horn

The Office

This Hell will leave you cold and bored. The decor is dreary, the food combinations are the work of a buffoon, and the punishments are sloppy and lack imagination. The management are permanently out to lunch. It's blah, blah.'

That sounds interesting, eh? Any takers?" Devil Keith stopped and beamed at the team. *"That sounds easy and vaguely familiar. Where have I heard that before? It's on the tip of my delightful tongue. Nora, please tell them it's a delightful tongue. Bags that boring Hell for my Nautically Starved Nora and I. We'll be off then. Nora don't forget to pack my spare giraffe. His breathing soothes me."*

"Devil Keith, wait. That's us. Our Hell." Harry huffed out and brought both her hands to her cheeks. She was exasperated and mightily glad that she was not the Nautically Starved Nora. Harry had seen what Devil Keith's tongue could do to an innocent pencil sharpener and she wasn't keen to ever, ever experience that.

"Oopsie. My bad. I was just checking that you were listening, you ginger mop-headed numbskull. Nora, please take note that we aren't going there. No matter how much the management want us in that hellish office. So back to the Hell list, my termite infested team."

The team in question were now plotting to remove the Hell Descriptor list from Devil Keith's sweaty mitts. They were also stealthily checking their armpits for tunnelling termites as Devil Keith did, occasionally, notice unusual occurrences before the rest of the team did. Chick the dastardly, spying Mouse being one such occasion. And, although they would strenuously deny it: they were also mildly interested in Devil Keith's tongue. Only mildly interested mind you, as they had all heard and gasped at the epic pencil sharper tale. Although neither Harry nor Bub were interested in Devil Keith's tongue acrobatics. No siree, Bub was not interested in that appendage. He knew that he had a magnificent probiscis all of his own, and Harry...

Oh, this has the potential of becoming a totally different kind of book. The authors have gone off for a wee lemonade and an essential cool down.

"Cough, cough. Pay attention you lot and stop checking on the length of your armpit hairs. No smelling each other either. Now where was I? Ah, yes.

'Hell, number two and three
Two Horns each
Meet the Brownies and Medieval Chivalry at its Best.'

Well, what do we think? Are either of these two a possibility for our little, old adventure? Our very own Homer's Iliad? Although what the Simpson's have to do with our current predicament is beyond me." Devil Keith looked around hopefully. He quite fancied being a gallant knight and going on a mighty quest. A quest to find the Holy Grail, or to find ripe oranges that really are truly seedless. He also made a mental note to try out some yellow foundation as the Simpson's may be onto something.

"Nope we can't go there either, because we've caused enough headaches for Brown Owl Mac and the Brownies. She sent me a newsletter, via Chick the Mouse's spy-network. It's quite a complicated system. Useful tool to have access to, by the way.

Anyway, the cockroaches, that the Knightly triplets were training to replace their unreliable tricycle, are openly revolting. They're either refusing to work or being suspended for being intimidating and overly aggressive. A few of the cockroaches have permanently moved in with the Brownies, and now won't answer to the name 'Mary'. They found out that Periwinkle use to be called John so they all want to be called... Periwinkle. Based on how Mac's feeling: I think the Brownie Hell may be heading for another horn too.

Plus, the rest of the Knights are smack-bang in the middle of re-decorating. They're finding it very difficult to get rid of King Adrian's horrifically, graphic arthouse paintings. No Devil Keith, not even you can do something with the ex-king's nauseating nudes so please put your hand down. Nora, believe me. You don't want them in your house." Bub shuddered, then impatiently rolled his hand to indicate that Devil Keith should continue with his painful narrative.

Nora noted how Bub spoke to her darling Devil Keith, and she wasn't having it. Not at all. She decided that her and her new brother-in-law needed to have a sit down and discuss Bub's lack of understanding and respect for Devil Keith, his older brother. She reasoned that as she had cured Devil Keith, and his obsession with poorly used air-quotes, by treating him with kindness and love. Oh yes, and by repeatedly pinging an elastic band at his stubbornly beautiful head, then surely Bub could come up with a better way of interacting with his charmingly odd brother. She reflected on this for a moment and decided that she might just need to bring a bloody big spanner to that sit down, powwow. Afterall, the seats in this Hell were very shoddily built.

"Cough, cough. I'm still here you know. Nora, I did tell you that I'm so quiet, shy and retiring that they often forget all about me but on this one occasion and in your honour, I won't allow it. So...

'Hell, number four, five and six

Three Horns each

The Health Inspectors Non-recommendations, The Nursing Home Mystery Tour and the Gambler goes Large.'

They all sound exceedingly charming but I shall, of course, continue with my descriptions as you all look thoroughly captivated by my dulcet tones." Devil Keith actually stopped and waited for his well-deserved applause. Then waited some more until he realised that he would get a standing ovation when he was finished. He wondered how he could still be so endearingly naïve and obliging when dealing with these ruffians.

"Cough, cough. Testing, testing. Johnathan is a pratt. I say, Jonathan is a pratt. And so say all of us. A delightful song but enough frivolity.

'Hell, number seven and eight

Four Horns each

The Midnight Gardeners go a Cutting, and the hardy Beach Comber's Delight..."

Nora interrupted Devil Keith's majestic speech. (Devil

Keith made the authors write that). *"I know I don't really count in all of this, but I'd really like to go to the seaside. I'm currently blindingly white. Well, that's how Brownie Mary Jo described me."* Muttered Nora as she stared at her ghostly forearm. A forearm that was less blindingly white and more a delightful shade of pale, veiny blue. That little lady definitely needed a wee touch of sunshine on her Smurf like body.

"Oh no. No, no, no," bellowed a terrified Bub. *"No, I can't do that one again. The squirrels. Nora, the squirrels. The sharks and their hairy legs... No, no, no. Surely Devil Keith told you about the heavily muscled mermaids, the come hither looks and all those fish hooks?"* Shouted an alarmed Bub as he lifted Harry into his arms and backed towards the open doorway. Harry could get used to a frightened Bub and his unique transportation skills. Although his elevated heart rate was giving her a headache.

"Cough, cough. Enough of the squealing. 'Hell, number nine and ten..."

"No, no." Bub was now yelling from the corridor and patting himself down in case there was a mysterious resurgence of sudden sunburn or a barrage of gobbling gerbils on the loose. He still had the occasional nightmare when he ate a coconut Bounty bar or drank a few pints of pina colada.

"Please stop with all of the interrupting and dramatics. Sheesh, the dancing red squirrels were positively delightful. Now where was I? Ah, yes.

'Hell, number nine and ten

Five Horns each

The Cruise Ship/love boat and the Va-Va, Voom Volcano not to be mistaken for the Va Voom Volcano. The additional lava makes all the difference to the volume of screams hence the extra Va.

Hell, number eleven, twelve and thirteen.

Ten Horns each

For the connoisseur otherwise leave well alone. You have been warned.'

Now those last ones sound so mysterious and ever so sexy. So, what do you think? A visit to the ten horns Hells? Oh, you're all shaking your heads. Quite violently shaking your heads, I might add. Do you all have earwigs in your ears? The earwigs will pop their little brown heads out of you tempt them with Brownie Mary Jo's tacos. No? No earwigs? Try the ear tacos anyway, they're ever so delicious." Devil Keith mimed pulling an earwig out of his ear then giving it a good scolding for not paying enough rent. His manicured index finger was going ten to the dozen: my if there had been an actual earwig nipped in Devil Keith's fingertips it would have immediately paid any arrears due.

"Devil Keith, don't you remember the Occulites stones? The fire, the billowing smoke, the coughing and all those bandages? G.O.D. was absolutely furious with us." Harry whispered, anxiously looked to the ceiling and soothingly rubbed Bub's trembling arm. That was a horrendous incident that neither of them wished to experience ever again.

"Ah, yes, the 'nippy time Hell', as I like to call it. Not too keen on anyone doing that again. Completely ruined the midnight blue, fake sheep-skin rugs and my Iron Age doll collection. I was only one doll off having the full set. We need to replace them ***Stat****. My scrumptious Nora, would you please make a note of our needs? We can add those to our wedding list. Just below the Kangaroo boxing gloves, framed photograph of Colonel Gaddafi and the ridiculously useful melon ballers. We need five full sets of those ballers for my new plan.*

Well then, it looks like it's the five horns Lava Hell? Or the five horns Cruise Ship Hell? My Nora and I really, really, really deserve a honeymoon after all our heroic crime busting, so the Lava would be absolutely perfect." Devil Keith grabbed Nora's hand and made for the door, in order to pack his essentials into his first eighteen suitcases. The other eighteen suitcases could be forwarded on later: along with Nora's rucksack of thongs. They needed to hustle as no one was pinching his deliciously warm honeymoon and his insatiable need for smoky smores.

"Stop, just stop. Devil Keith, step away from the luggage tags and stop looking up travel insurance quotes. You know we always

go to the same guy for our insurance needs.

We have eight minutes to decide where we're going. That's still enough time to think this through. Right. Right. Let's take a moment to think about this. We have to make the right decision because we have to get our Hell back. We also have to survive this and learn something in the process. It can't be too many horns away from us or we'll never survive it, but it must have some real-life application here." Karen thankfully had stepped in to stop Devil Keith and ensure some level of success.

She also wondered when Devil Keith had changed into a chocolate brown pinstriped suit that cut off at the elbow so that he could show off his fuchsia pink satin gloves, and he had a ravenous Venus's fly trap corsage adorning each of his wrists. The suit trousers stopped at the knee, only the one knee mind you, and it was all finished off with live lobster nipple rings. What was more stunning was the addition of tennis shoes. Just plain old white tennis shoes. Karen decided, there and then, that Nora had quite a bit of positive influence on good old Devil Keithie-boy.

CHAPTER THIRTY-TWO

Time was up...

God and the sumptuous HR Sarah appeared and looked hopefully at the vulnerable Hell team.

"Your time is up. So, dearies, what have you decided?" God sneaked in a bite of an oatcake heaped with mature cheddar cheese and topped with apple and fig chutney. She had missed lunch as she was receiving a disturbing number of portents of doom at the moment. Many more than was usual. They exceeded the number she usually saw round about the Black Friday sales, and man's insatiable need for table saws at a knock down price. She concluded that something really bad was a coming.

"After much debate. Well, eight minutes of debate and a bit of Devil Keith wrangling, we've decided on 'The Gambler goes Large' Hell. We all enjoy a bit of a flutter and it's not too far away from us...horn wise. It's not going to be as bad as the Beach Combers Hell as that was a four horn Hell and the Gamblers goes Large only has three horns. Well, that's the hope anyway. Either Harry and I will go, or Karen and Dr Riel will do the honours. We just need a moment to sort that out." Bub felt that was the best decision regarding learning location and hoped he could take charge as the expedition lead. That meant that Karen and Dr Riel could check out Jonathan's Hell number one changes and see if they could derail his takeover bid. That was their back-

up plan in case the learning opportunity didn't pan out. Bub had already decided on the list of essentials he would require to take with him in order to survive the Gambler's Hell. Loaded dice, marked cards, a jar of olives stuffed with peppers and an expresso martini were a must on this quest. There was no way he was going in there unprepared. The horrific experience in the Beach Comber's Hell had taught him that.

"Sarah, dearie, can you check the rules? I want to make sure that I'm not at risk of being accused of favouritism, as that would void this whole learning experience. The pen pusher's upstairs are very picky. Very picky indeed." God was scowling at the ceiling and deeply regretting her decision to establish a limited company and float all those shares. It was so much easier when she was all powerful with no one to answer to. But now anyone could set up a religion and add any rules that they wanted.

She was particularly concerned about a group of Pastafarian's who were monopolising the colander market: to use as compulsory, religious headwear. The Pastafarians recently won the right to wear their silvery, hole ridden helmets in their UK driving licence photographs. That was the thin edge of the wedge, as far as God was concerned. She feared that the group of tagliatelle eating zealots would substantially increase the price of that specific item of kitchenware and if the colanders go up in price then the sieves were sure to follow. Oh, she shuddered to think about the response of the pasta loving Italian's. They were at risk of revolting if they were pushed into being hungry then hangry.

"Mmm. Good idea regarding the location but the rules only allow you to choose the Hell, but not the participants. The participants are decided by a method devised by the one and only Mr Michael Edward Thomas. He did extensive research on conflict management and concluded that there is only one fool-proof method to eradicate conflict, fairly share a bar of chocolate and avoid fatal hair pulling incidents. The participants will be chosen via the infallible Rock, Paper, Scissors method. Before you object. I don't make the rules. Erm. No, that's not right. Is it? I do make

some of the rules but I have to make sure they're ***all*** *absolutely fair. So, please Rock away.*

One last thing: before you start. It says here, that if you received a scroll linking you to any part of the proceedings then you have to take part. Devil Keith, sir and Mrs Nora Mr-Hyphenated-Apocalypse: you're part of this too." HR Sarah helpfully added and closed her binder with a decisive snap. She popped her pen behind her ear and secured it with a silky ringlet.

"No need for the Mr-Hyphenated-Apocalypse. Please, call me Nora, no need for formalities here. It's not your fault that you're having to pass on this news. You're only doing your rather wonderful job." Nora was patting HR Sarah's hand and smiling reassuringly. Nora was also trying to sneak a look at the binder but HR Sarah promptly tucked it under her arm.

"If Devil Keith is chosen then I'll go with him. It would be an honour to help save this Hell and save Nora." Willing produced a noteworthy salute then stood at ease. Back straight and shoulders pulled back.

"Sorry Willing you didn't receive a scroll. However, Nora responded to the scroll so technically and, come to think of it, factually she has become part of the Hell team There are no substitutes permitted." And with that, HR Sarah extracted her panties from her red sequined catsuit. Giving out bad news always made her a bit squirrely in the old knicker department.

Bub looked at Karen then subtlety shook his head. He wanted to make sure that she knew that he was going to take this risk on his broad shoulders. He didn't check with Devil Keith as Devil Keith had never, ever, ever beaten him at Rock, Paper, Scissors.

Devil Keith beat Bub at Rock, Paper, Scissors and was loudly crowing over his win.

CHAPTER THIRTY-THREE

Devil Keith's room in Hell number one...

Nora and Devil Keith had ninety minutes to say their goodbyes and get ready for their big adventure. Devil Keith was still going on about how he, the master of all the known gaming universe, beat everyone at the hugely complex Rock, Paper, Scissors game. He was going to write his 250,000 page autobiography based on this event alone. He was going to call it "*Papering for success*" or "*All you need is Salt and Paper to be tasty and successful*". All the authors can say is...it's just as well that Devil Keith can sew a straight seam and has a lovely wee pert bum to get by on.

Nora was sat on the corner of a cluttered dressmaking table, absentmindedly playing with a very up-market, hotel sewing kit. There was a finely etched picture of flowing rosebuds, orchids and lotus flowers intertwined with delicate vines on the glass lid of the heavy, expensive souvenir. The resort group was subtly stamped on the bottom of the weighty object. Nora thought it looked exceedingly special and made a mental note to ask Harry what she thought of the accommodation, food, spa and overall service. If Harry liked it, then Nora was going to book it. She thought that her Devil Keith might appreciate a nice wee surprise when they returned from the Gambler's Hell. Devil Keith was always organising thoughtful little treats for his Nora, so she wanted a chance to pay him back for all his kindness and all those pre-chewed Curly Wurley's she would find floating in her morning coffee. Although, to be fair, Nora would prefer all her chocolate to come in their original wrappers sans bite marks and all that Devil saliva was a bit off-putting.

Plus, Nora wanted to spoil Devil Keith as she felt guilty about previously being so jealous of Devil Keith and Harry's close and very, very lengthy relationship. When Nora first started dating Devil Keith he would animatedly talk about all the places he'd seen, the people they'd successfully mentored (Nora wasn't entirely convinced of this) and the adventures he'd had with the wildly chaotic Harry. Nora found Devil Keith's admiration of Harry difficult to accept. After a few dates with Nora, Devil Keith then finished his fantastical tales by saying that it would have been much better if he had been with his Nora instead. He told her that he loved his Nora, and he reassured her that there would have been a lot more belly laughs, and more snuggles, if she had been there with him. Oh yes, and significantly less prison time and all that tedious tunnelling under federal basketball fields, if Nora had been there to strategize their escapes. And he predicted that there would have been an awful lot less above-knee amputations and fatalities, if his Nora had led their escapades and negotiated their scandalous bail conditions. Devil Keith had been forced to re-mortgage the moon to pay for a particularly wild free-love party bail-out in the 1960's, but he assured Nora that she probably would have got him off with handing over Australia and the sole rights to kangaroo onesies instead.

So, booking this little break would help Nora too, as it would help her see if Devil Keith truly was happier being with her instead of the superbly skilled Harry. Admittedly a bit of a stupid test but Nora, in the wee sma' hours of the night, sometimes worried that her lack of sophistication and experience would eventually bore Devil Keith and make him regret vigorously pursuing her. Nora would be gobsmacked to know that the super assured Harry had a similar lack of confidence with her husband, Bub.

Nora wrinkled her nose and pondered that despite Devil Keith saying that there would be less time in jail, he always made prison activities sound so much fun. All the contraband pigeon catapults he'd constructed, the ever so stabby gang initiations he always led, the well-constructed bunk-bed forts that Devil Keith declared were a prison necessity, and finally the retrieval of the soap-on-a-rope games sounded hilarious. Nora wondered if Devil Keith occasionally missed his orange clad incarceration and decided a bit of forced strip searching role-play was required. Stat. Well not quite Stat as they had a weird-ish Hell related job to do first.

Devil Keith was now humming and rummaging in his closet as he was looking for the absolutely perfect outfit for his quest. He was giddy with excitement: uninterrupted time with his Nora and the opportunity to be a hero again. He paused and thought for a full ten minutes, but he just couldn't imagine a more perfect scenario. He really couldn't. He tried but still…no. Nothing came to mind. Devil Keith's wiggling, and deliciously pert bottom was in the air as he dug around for his correctly toned "*touring sandals*". So Nora did what any self-respecting wife would do. She rubbed his favourite butt cheek then gave it a playful pinch and a cheeky slap. She then ran when Devil Keith chased her and ever so conveniently caught her near a box of beige top-hats.

Forty-eight minutes later…

A glowing and very satisfied Nora was back sitting on the sewing table but she was now unsuccessfully trying to distract herself with a delicate silver thimble. Despite their lovely, lovely interlude she was deeply troubled about a number of other things. This whole married into Hell was complicated, although HR Sarah promised her a personalised and fully functioning orientation folder. That's if HR Sarah could get the Hell gang to sit down and agree on the size of the font and the colour of the spacers, and then agree whether the folder should be written in the first or third person. Nora couldn't understand what the big deal was but Karen gave her a hard stare, so Nora decided to leave that one well alone. Then HR Sarah would start the infinitely simpler task of getting them to actually write the contents of the book.

The only thing Nora knew for definite was that she now had cockroach calling rights so she could request transportation around the world and, more disturbingly, through it. Devil Keith said it was positively ruinously expensive to keep the cockroaches waiting at the kerbside, but he'd rather that than have his Nora having to wait for common buses to arrive or unreliable trains to depart on time or a North Sea oil drilling platform to become available. He assured Nora that the drilling platforms would only do in a pinch, if the cockroaches were being particularly *"squirrely"* that day. To be fair, the cockroaches were only difficult if they had been to the hairdresser's and didn't fancy doing a backstroke through the earth's molten core. They strenuously stated that it did terrible things to a shampoo and set, although their perms and highlights always survived the ordeal. Nora couldn't image a scenario whereby the cockroaches **would** want to dive around in liquid rock, but Devil Keith just rubbed the side of his nose and gave her a rather salacious wink.

Putting the cockroaches' bathing habits and Devil Keith's gift of a very practical titanium rubber ring to the side, Nora had more pressing matters to consider. The lack of clarification regarding the *"learning experience"* was all very concerning.

The guidelines…ish.

Devil Keith and Nora had to learn something whilst in the Gambler goes Large Hell but no one knew what it was. Sarah raked through the HR manual but there were absolutely no clues as what the *"learning"* was. There didn't appear to be any other instances of this activity happening before, so no one was any the wiser. However, HR Sarah did stress that although this was a Gambling Hell the resident's weren't necessarily gamblers and they weren't simply in that Hell for reasons linked with gambling. The residents had committed atrocious acts of evil and were placed there in accordance with the severity of their crimes and their need for punishment.

Nora and Devil Keith were urged, then urged again, not to forget that essential piece of information. They were also informed that they could **not** get involved in the politics, policies or procedures of the other Hell. HR Sarah said that the annual HR inter-Hell conference had become somewhat of a bloodbath when someone had innocently suggested that another Hell might want to use multicoloured highlighter pens in their presentation. HR Sarah was extremely pale and continuously glancing over her shoulder when she recounted that tale.

Devil Keith and Nora weren't permitted to carry a mobile phone, walkie-talkies or any other means of communication into the Gambler's Hell. So, they were entirely alone with no means of requesting assistance, support or further guidance. Even smoke signals were banned: Devil Keith had asked about them a number of times and was going to sneak in a thick red and black stripy blanket, on the off-chance, he could blag a suitable campfire. Nora asked what a "*suitable campfire*" was, but Devil Keith just wiggled his shapely eyebrows and impersonated a cow. A surprisingly common Devil Keith response, so Nora just patted his powdered cheek and kissed the end of his gorgeous nose.

The Hell number one cockroach moving pavement service was temporarily suspended and the Interdimensional Drill was being confiscated for the duration of the quest. Although the Drill's current location was unknown so that was a moot point. Nora thought that the Hell team should maybe keep a list of their more important artifacts, but no one else was bothered so she assumed that they must have a few things safely hanging around and about.

There was no time limit on their stint in the other Hell. Devil Keith had mentioned a researcher, called Bowie, who was still wandering around Hell number one: slurping pee infused tea, speaking Spanish and telling folks that she really needed to go home to wash her long blonde hair. Karen was going to deal with that whilst Nora was away.

Nora and Devil Keith could only take one non-clothing item with them. The item had to fit in their hand and weigh less than 20 ounces. The item couldn't have any additions. Nora was puzzled by that, until a footnote explained that meant no bullets. So, no guns allowed although it probably wouldn't have been of much use anyway. The only way to ensure a Demon or Devil death was through complete decapitation. In response to this rule, Willing had happily given Devil Keith her trusty, prized mallet. The mallet she frequently uses to curtail the actions of the perpetually starving Fachance. Willing had added that so long as Devil Keith made it back safely, that was all that mattered. She could always replace her cherished mallet.

Other little bits of worry...

Nora's cat, Hercules, had gone walkabout and no matter how many tins of condensed milk Nora left on her doorstep he hadn't returned. However, forty-eight bluebottles and seventeen pounds of maggots had taken up residency on the catless step. So, despite the local cut-throat fishing and tackle competition, Nora was considering setting up her own bait shop. She just had to work out how to pick up the seventeen pounds of maggots, whilst completely covering her hand with the sleeve of her jumper, and manipulating a pair of eyebrow tweezers. Again, another task for a later date.

Lastly, and this was really of no consequence but it did annoy Nora a little bit. There appeared to be trails of fine sand in their bedroom. The sand certainly wasn't there during their previous visit to Hell as Nora had done a bit of very basic dusting and a quick run around with the hoover. Also, their bed was very precisely made up and that never happens as Devil Keith was forever constructing elaborate forts with the duvet cover. Using his extended leg as the central tent pole, then bitterly complaining when he got fatal cramps (that were easily as painful as childbirth... Devil Keith asked nicely for this fact to be added to this paragraph).

So, who had been in their room? Devil Keith had previously told Nora that Gab used a washing powder that was imbued with a truth telling serum. Devil Keith said it really ruined a good game of "*Truth or Dare or Pet a tame-ish gnome*". As the washing powder wasn't currently working, due to the shoddy Florentine laundry, Nora decided to have a chat with Gab when she returned from the Gambler's Hell and get to the bottom of the intrusion. In the meantime Devil Keith had added additional door locks, that he assured Nora could only be accessed by a top code breaker, to their abode.

CHAPTER THIRTY-FOUR

Nora stood basking in the warm summer sunshine...

"I thought, that as we were doing the whole Gambling Hell, we'd be in Las Vegas: with all the neon lights, incessant noise, long legged dancing girls and extraordinary Casinos. I always wanted to go there. Visit the Bellagio Casino and wash my smalls in the dancing fountains. So, where exactly are we?" a giggling Nora turned to Devil Keith and squinted against the bright daylight. She hadn't thought to bring her sunhat, sunglasses and her sunscreen with her. She could already feel the smattering of caramel coloured freckles, on her nose, poking out to say *"hiya"*. Devil Keith thought her freckles were adorable and would use them to form dot to dot pictures across her face. Nora just wished he'd use a crayon rather than permanent markers. The local butcher had asked some pretty awkward questions when she'd gone in to buy half a pound of corned beef, whilst sporting a detailed copy of Leonardo Da Vincis' Last Supper on her forehead and across her cheeks.

Devil Keith looked around, then looked some more. He did a quick handstand, as he'd heard that it was always good to look at things from a different perspective. He promptly fell over, skinned his knee and Nora rubbed it all better. He then created a viewing square with his thumbs and index fingers. He peered through the aperture.

"Oh, I've been here before. It's St Louis, in Missouri, in the

good old U.S. of A. And it has a bloody great big arch in the middle of it. Yes, it does." Devil Keith nodded, slapped his thigh and gave a wild whoop: immensely satisfied with himself and his ability to provide for his Nora. He wasn't sure what he was providing but he was immeasurable pleased that he was doing it.

He then looked around again: he was decidedly perplexed. *"Where's the arch gone? It's totally fantastic: you can use an elevator capsule to ride all the way up to the top of it and look out the windows. See all of the city going about its business. I can't believe I can't find it."* Devil Keith looked under a tiny rock, patted down a particularly guilty looking daffodil and scuffed a bit of the lime green grass, in his search for the elusive arch. Then he looked up again.

"It's gone. Completely gone. Not a sign of it anywhere. I can't believe this Hell would pinch and hide the arch. Philistines, the lot of them." Devil Keith pouted then decided that he'd write an absolutely blistering letter of complaint to the managing directors of the Gambler's Hell.

Nora gently nudged Devil Keith in the side and pointed up. Then pointed again.

"Oh, there is it. I thought I'd never find it." Devil Keith exclaimed. Ever so pleased with his fabulously clever detective skills.

The *"it"* was a six-hundred-and-thirty-foot monster of an arch. An arch that crossed the winding Mississippi river and dominated the vista: framing a delightfully serene picture. An arch that went soaring into the brilliant blue sky. A sky studded with soft fluffy, puffy white clouds. Clouds depicting leaping plump bunny rabbits, frisky lambs a frolicking and hippos eating their young whilst pirouetting across the clear expanse of the most perfectly, perfect azure blue sky.

The stunning silver arch was situated in the Gateway Arch National Park, St Louis. A small but beautifully formed garden where quaint, rambling stone paths cut across the daisy dotted, lush green grass and then wandered over a gentle mound of earth. The splendid arch museum was nestled under the grass covered mound and was flanked by two brightly coloured ice cream trucks.

"A little known fact. St Louis is famous for making ice cream cones. To be clear. Not for making ice cream, but well-known for making the cones that made ice-cream portable. Imagine not having ice-cream outside. Having to always eat it in your home. In your kitchen. In a bowl. At your kitchen table where anyone could steal a lick or add an unsolicited maraschino cherry.

Or having to hold the creamy treat in your hands where it would get all melty and sticky. And you'd nearly always be attacked by voracious butterflies. Outdoor butterflies, no less. Butterflies that you just couldn't fight off because your hands would be full. It was grim. Nora, you're so lucky that you've never had to endure that. You've always had the luxury of cones and non-violent butterflies.

Plus, before the invention of the majestic cone the ice-cream would quickly melt on your hands, so even if you had brain freeze you had to power through that agony. Agony that's easily as bad as childbirth.

The world would be completely unbearable without a cone. They should have won a Nobel Prize for that invention. How can maths ever be better than a cone with a lovely chocolaty flake stuck in the middle of it? They were robbed, I tell you." Nora let Devil Keith ramble on for a further forty minutes about the benefits of wafer cones and the limitations of Einstein's unprovable theories.

Nora loved her Devil Keith's little eccentricities and one of his more frequently expressed oddities was his absolute conviction that any number of things were as painful as childbirth. Nora had removed a small splinter from Devil Keith's thumb the week before. He had declared that it was as bad as childbirth and thanked Nora profusely for her kindness and expertise. Nora caught him as he popped on his coat, so that he could nip into town and take out a full page advert in the Falkirk Herald. An advert that would promote his heroism and bravery whilst he faced and defeated a dastardly (and large) impaling wooden plank.

Unfortunately, Dippit was in the room at the time of his comparison and wasn't quite as forgiving as his Nora. There may have been an expletive that indicated that Devil Keith should fornicate then leave the room. This was followed by the invitation that Dippit should visit again the following week.

Dippit did indeed pop in the following Tuesday, just before Devil Keith and Nora received their saving scroll. Stan and Dippit had told them all about the scan, the disgraceful lack of horse parking spaces and all the superb womb dancing. Devil Keith was sceptical and told Dippit that she should fornicate then leave the room. My, that Dippit has a mighty powerful left hook for a lady who is massively obscene. Stan knew Dippit was still carrying a massively obscene grudge!

Still in the Gambler's Hell...

Nora was blissfully content, as she had never, ever felt so at peace in her surroundings. So centred. So, utterly Zen. The whole park was enveloped in an inviting blanket of calm, love and gentle tenderness. Nora placed her hand in Devil Keith's and coaxed him onto a smooth, cool path. They began a leisurely walk where they stopped for stolen kisses and admired the bright pops of colour from the petite wild flowers. The flower's faces were sporting huge smiles as they danced and swayed in the soft, summer breeze. The murmuring bees and tiny humming birds happily darting from perfect bud to even more perfect bud: collecting sweet, golden nectar and giving the flowers a wee nuzzle of affection.

The majestic orange Baltimore Orioles sang their merry tunes as they glided across the still sky. A touch of fiery-feathered perfection soaring in the heavens and getting in the way of the flighty hungry, hungry hippos.

Nora sniffed the air and licked her pink chapped lips. There was the very faint scent of famous Kansas barbeque on the warm breeze. The tantalising first barbeque of summer that makes you reach into the back of your cupboard for the margarita glasses, a bag of limes and a salt pot. Smoky, saucy comfort food at its very finest.

"What's hidden at the back of the wee hill? Do you think that it might be food? A little nibble or two for the brave explorers?" She grinned then smacked her lips together. She was the very tiniest bit hungry. Not ravenous but she could manage a small snack drowning in rich, brown silky sauce.

"It's the river, but it smells a lot like lunch. Come on." Laughing and holding hands they raced up the gentle hillock and stopped.

CHAPTER THIRTY-FIVE

There, that hit the mark...ahhh...

It was a truly picturesque landscape that laid tantalisingly before them. A view that evoked a blissful childhood memory of laying back on a pile of comfortably fat, tasselled cushions in a small bobbing rowing boat. The boat slowly floating down a meandering river whilst you're trailing your fingertips in the cool, clean water. Water that was crystal clear with silky ripples that make the surface sleepy... almost hypnotic. Soft, dappled light dancing over the water and painting delightful pictures of hazy summer days: drinking tall icy glasses of minty Pimm's cocktails and scoffing ripe, fat, glistening strawberries topped with towering dollops of decadent clotted cream.

Nora had never actually experienced that memory as most of the rivers she encountered were hoatching with greedy black flies, choked with dying Tesco shopping trolleys and littered with bits of rusty bikes but she had seen this type of scene on a battered chocolate box. And she could always dream whilst, in reality, she had scratched her hordes of insect bites, gone for a needle in the bum tetanus jag and put gallons of soothing calamine lotion on her lumpy, red hives. Come to think of it...Nora just then realised that the tetanus vaccine should have gone in her arm: those bloody student doctors were forever playing body-part darts with their unsuspecting friends.

Back to the Gambler's Hell and the lovely scene...

An enormous paddle boat was moored on the lavish, verdant river bank. The charming vessel came complete with a huge, churning wheel and tall black and white striped chimneys: popping out little balls of pale grey and misty white smoke. The stately steamer was all decked out in its Sunday best of pristine white, red and blue glossy paintwork. Flamboyantly decorated emerald green bunting and multi-coloured flags fluttering in the mild breeze, whilst long garlands of subtly scented violet flowers intertwined with the sturdy hemp ropes.

Nora and Devil Keith just knew that was where the delectable cooking smells were wafting from.

Nora and Devil Keith ran down the small incline and joined the long queue of exquisitely dressed and perfectly coifed animated people waiting to climb onto the wooden gangplank and gain entry to the spectacular boat. The waiting passengers were all chatting and amicably sharing trays of watermelon flavoured, vodka jelly shots as they queued. They were giggling when taking selfies with the highly skilled jugglers and repeatedly asking the (very patient) stilt-walkers how they managed to get through the toilet doorways to "*do their business*". The elegantly attired guests were laughing and engaging in spurts of uncoordinated dance moves as they listened to the gentle chug of the swaying boat and the tinkling of entrancing music.

Nora was struggling to process her feelings as there was a curious mixture of excitement and joy in amongst the serenity: a beautiful but slightly overwhelming song to the senses. Plus, how can this possibly be a Hell? She wondered, but she knew that Devil Keith would never put her in any form of danger. He would risk his life to save hers. The feeling was entirely mutual.

Nora glanced at her Devil Keith and his attire: admiring his innate self-confidence. And his dark-red leather gladiator sandals, lime green Bermuda shorts held up with sparkling pink braces and a beaded crop top that complemented his ruby-encrusted poppy, belly-ring. She worried that her lacy, black cocktail dress, red suede kitten heels and smear of lip balm weren't up to the mark. Devil Keith assured her that she was stunning, as always, and only needed a little pop of colour. He pulled off his belly-ring, and a good chunk of his bellybutton fluff, then clipped it on the shoulder of her dress. Pure Perfection!

CHAPTER THIRTY-SIX

Gambler's go Large Hell and an hour later...

As a mildly reflective Nora gingerly stepped onto the crowded gangplank she checked in with Devil Keith. She was still slightly concerned that everything was *"too good"* and she was fearful that they were due to experience a big bad shock. Devil Keith tried to alleviate her concerns and explained that this Hell wouldn't be nearly as bad as the Beach Combers Hell, as that particular Hell had more horns. And, what's more, the Gambler's Hell flowers were particularly annoying. He concluded that the smug flora fulfilled all of this Hell's horn evilness requirements. Nora wasn't completely convinced, but thought she'd give Devil Keith the benefit of the doubt as he always had her best interests at heart and he had more experience to draw from.

After finishing a particularly rowdy game of couple's only eye-spy, where Devil Keith flagrantly cheated and won because of his incessant eye poking. Then a robust game of leap frogging over the King's Coronation themed crocheted bollards, Devil Keith also went onto explain that the Beach Comber's Hell wasn't nearly as bad as Bub, the wimpy, wimp made out.

However, Devil Keith admitted that he had burnt off all the skin on his back in the Beach Hell, but he regarded that as a bonus as he could then show off his skin-free muscles. He'd only excavated his sinew once before, for the illustrations in the first edition of the comical Grey's Anatomy textbook. He planned on doing it again for the newest edition of the much-admired, and highly amusing medical text book. It was on Devil Keith's ever-expanding to do list. Just below learning how to ride a bike sans stabilisers, evenly applying false eyelashes during a force eight gale and teaching dolphins correct dinning etiquette. They refused to use monogrammed linen napkins, the cute seafaring savages.

"Erm, didn't that hurt a bit? It must have been so raw, slippery and ever so gooey when the skin slid off." Nora enquired. She swallowed down her gag reaction and winced as she tentatively wiggled her shoulder blades. She could only imagine how sore that would be. She'd scraped her back going down a slide once and it was tender for days. Now, when they went to the playpark she stuck with the swings, seesaws and roundabouts whilst Devil Keith clambered over the monkey bars and requested bags of pre-broken peanut brittle to throw at the small scruffy people, aka little children. He then threw boxes of anti-histamines at the cowering kiddies, just in case they had a nut allergy. He had tried throwing epi-pens at the toddlers but seemingly that's deemed an assault with a deadly weapon, or so the scores of unflattering Wanted Posters said.

"A little bit achy but I was immortalised in print. So it was soooo worth it. I even signed a few of the special copies. Give back to the masses and all that tosh. You know?" Devil Keith tried to look at his gorgeous back and lick his magnificent elbow. He managed to give the elusive elbow a good old saliva soaking but he couldn't quite see his hunky, chunky back. He instantly regretted giving his extra neck vertebrae to that duplicitous old owl. The deceitful owl had duplicated the bone pattern and now all owls had a copy of Devil Keith's deliciously sexy spine upon their personage. The neck twirling, feathery despots.

"Are you sure you want to do it again? It sounds so agonizingly painful and I bet you got lots of spots of blood on your sheets. You hate anything hurting your luxurious Egyptian sheets. I heard you singing them, and your plush silky towels, a lullaby last Thursday night. It was oh so sweet." Nora was having less success licking her elbow so Devil Keith gave it a good old tongue

lashing for her. Very reminiscent of the previously mentioned tongue and the pencil sharpener scenario.

"I absolutely must do it for my scores and scores of fans. My Surefooted wee Sugar Lump, don't you worry. I'll be incredible and utterly gorgeous with all that sinew on show. Maybe not as gorgeous as you in your new cute pigeon onesie, but I'll try." Devil Keith had decided to track down every last cunning owl and rip out their treacherously rotating necks then re-fit them to his spine. Easy. Like de-boning a feathery and untrustworthy fish. Oh, that reminded him... those smug stingrays needed a bit of a telling off too.

"I'd prefer if you didn't rip open your lovely back but I understand your overwhelming need to participate in the arts, so please, just don't tell me you're doing it and I'll care for you afterwards." Nora wiped her sodden elbow on the hem of her frock then tidied up her hair. Her hair appeared thicker and healthier in this Hell. In fact, everything seemed so much better in this Hell.

"Okidoki, that sounds like a really good plan. Can I have some of your Power Puff Girl plasters? But only if I really need them. Afterall, I am a hero of the first water and I don't want those girlie gobshites to get any of the credit for my artistry." Devil Keith wiped away a melodramatic tear and wrinkled his nose. Nora gave it a wee peck. His nose not his eye. She wasn't some type of weirdo.

"Of course you can. Love you more today than I did yesterday, ya beautiful big lummox." And Nora gave Devil Keith's arm a reassuring squeeze. They'll be alright she thought. They were a solid unit. They'd survived bathing reluctant elephants; Hannibal's highly lascivious suggestions and they'd just cracked a ring of international jewel thieves. Nothing could break them. Nothing at all.

CHAPTER THIRTY-SEVEN

Something might just be able to break them…

As the carefree, canoodling couple strolled up, and nearing the end of the wooden gang plank, they began noticing a few of the steel nails tugging at their shoes. The irritants were barely poking through the soles but they were ever so slightly scratching at Devil Keith and Nora's exposed skin. Not a drop of blood was drawn but it was a slight annoyance, although quickly forgotten as the atmosphere was such a delight. It could easily be described as beautifully buoyant and jammed packed full of relentless cheer. Following Devil Keith's reassurances Nora had decided just to go with the flow and enjoy herself. To hell with the consequences, she thought. Fake it till you make it.

Just before stepping onboard the deck of the cheerful boat, Nora and Devil Keith were each handed a brand-new pair of green wellington boots by a perpetually smiling and enthusiastic young sailor. The awfully handsome, and extremely helpful seafarer was in a spotlessly white linen uniform. Starched, crisply ironed and generally, pretty spruced up. Devil Keith was thoroughly impressed and thought he might sneak his laundry onto the efficiently managed boat. Is this what they were to learn? How to get their whites back to dazzling white? Devil Keith closed his eyes and waited, but he wasn't whizzed back home so he decided to just enjoy the uneventful break with his gorgeous Nora.

Nora and Devil Keith grinned as they held onto each other and ungainly changed their shoes for the crisp, new wellies. The deck must be a little bit wet with all that relentless scrubbing and rubbing. And positively swimming in sweat from all the dancing, sea-shanty singing sailors, Devil Keith happily decided. A smiling Devil Keith took his Nora's small hand and they began their step onto the pleasure, paddle steamer. Time for a spot of lunch for two, he thought. Mmm, juicy sticky barbeque and a snifter of brandy was in order. Just the ticket. Just in case you're wondering...Devil Keith sounds remarkably like a mixture of Prince William and the actor, Hugh Grant.

CHAPTER THIRTY-EIGHT

Nearly on the boat...

They merrily finished stepping onto the deck and violently lurched into the real Gambler goes Large Hell. The abrupt change from the playful festivities to a living nightmare was extraordinary. Breathtakingly evil. Blunt to the point of extreme, gasping pain.

The terrified people in front of Devil Keith and Nora had turned around and were frantically trying to push, tug and pull their way back off the huge dilapidated boat. They in turn were also being angrily forced forward and off the boat by people further down the listing deck. Multiple squashing's, scuffles and fights were breaking out throughout the ramshackle ship. Bits of broken teeth were flying through the air and the remains of a viciously ripped out tongue whipped a stunned Devil Keith in the eye. The sheer volume of the noise was nauseating and physically overwhelming. There was pleading, wailing and crying being drowned out by threats of violence and skreiches of abject terror. A frail elderly woman was leaning into bevelled railing and holding her wrinkled face against the side of a door. Trying to seek refuge and comfort from the agonising stimuli. She slid from view as another person took her place and shattered her prone body with the sheer mass of a screaming mob.

The previously young and attractive young sailor lifted his grossly misshapen head, opened his elongated maw and screamed. *"Roll up, roll up, roll up. Check you lottery ticket. Everyone's a winner. There's nowhere to go but up."* He used his red talon tipped claw to point to the dark, angry and thunderous sky. Grabbing his skeletal sides and laughing uproariously at the fear he evoked in the startled masses. Devil Keith noted that the sailor's whites were no longer quite so white. They we covered in rivulets of dried blood and snot... flagrant false advertising Devil Keith fumed and cancelled his future laundry service.

The startled Nora and Devil Keith covered their ears and screwed up their eyes. They then looked up and up some more, through their rapidly blinking lashes, and into the darkened skies. There was a huge wooden and steel catapult bolted to the top of the ramshackle paddle boat. There were lines of petrified, sobbing people reluctantly handing over sweat-stained crumpled slips of paper before being roughly grabbed by demonic, slavering sailors and unceremoniously loaded into the deep bucket. The huge lever was drawn back, stopped abruptly, before hurling the "*winners*" out of the bucket and into the boiling black clouds.

The shrieking people went sailing through the cannibalistic hippos and the rabid lambs who, incidentally, had now eaten all the innocent bunnies. Devil Keith and Nora watched as a young female "*winner*" finished the first leg of her traumatic journey by smashing into the huge arch. After momentarily sticking, the pulverised woman then began sluggishly sliding down the arch's steep sides. As she gradually rolled down the vast mirrored monolith the smell of bacon intensified. She was slowly being grilled on the hot, mirrored surface. Losing her brittle hair; then her seared skin was exposed. Her patchy red skin bubbled as the yellow fat beneath liquified and distorted the woman's body into a sludgy ball of pain. The browned sinew, beneath the creamy fat, sloughed off and roughly stuck to the arch's blistering surface. Finally her charred blackened bones, wrapped in raw nerve endings, fell in a heap on the ground at the far side of the river. The young woman and her fellow winners were no longer screaming but they were, somehow, still able to whimper and softly moan. The grotesque sailors chortled as they took souvenir photos of the "*ride*" so that the participants could remember their fun and re-live it. Yes, the bones and nerves had already started to lay down new spongey organs, re-string muscles and regrow their doomed humans. Ready for the next barbaric ballot. The young woman dizzily lifted her battered skull... and a new set of terror filled eyeballs popped into her recently gouged sockets.

The sailors used huge sharpened rakes to drag the fleshy corpses onto flat barges so the "*winners*" could be hauled back onto the paddle steamer and start the process all over again.

The usually stoic (the authors aren't entirely sure about the stoic description, but Devil Keith insisted on its use and he threatened to go off in the huff if the authors didn't comply) Devil Keith was no longer hungry and thought that if he ever experienced hunger again it would surely be for a salad type of dish. Going vegan was looking mighty attractive, to the Devil, at that particular moment.

A horrified Nora stepped forward and tried to pull people back from participating in the lottery and the human barbeque. Devil Keith grabbed his brave Nora, slung her over his left shoulder and rapidly patted her rather delightful left bum cheek. He then patted her right bum check as he didn't want to be accused of favouritism. He noticed that her previously spotless green wellies were now pre-worn: broken, ripped and heavily scuffed. Full of bits of torn verrucas, damp moulting skin and congealed, lumpy blood clots. There weren't going to be a lot of dancing or sea shanty's, he surmised and tucked his highly polished, patten leather tap-shoes back in his short's pocket. He **may** have swapped the useful mallet for the delightful dancing shoes. However, he will **definitely** have to explain his choice to his baffled wife.

The thick, sticky air was clogging up windpipes and causing the Hell residents to claw at their constricted throats and hack up small pieces of their air-starved lungs. The suffocating clammy heat was also encouraging mosquitoes, the size of vultures, to dive bomb the unprepared winners. Piercing through the winners eye sockets, slicing into their moist brains and pinning their victims, by the skull, to the mush strewn deck. Actually, as an aside, what **would** prepare you for mosquitoes that size? Answers on a postcard to P and K Stoker, please.

This brutal assault to the senses continued unabated. The boat appeared to be a living creature or to be more accurate: a sentient being painfully and tragically dying. There were deafening sounds of sloshing, ripping, whimpering, shredding, tearing, cracking, grinding and squealing as the injured boat shuffled off its mortal coil. The majestic Mississippi Hell river, instead of cradling and comforting the dying, wooden creature, was no more than a puddle of death. Instead of opaque blue water, in its place was a heaving, squirming, moving scab of bodily fluids, crawfish and alligators. The ten foot long crawfish were peeling then sucking out the inners of any resident unlucky enough to fall into the oily, contaminated sludge. The alligators were rolling the remaining human skin bags into loose balls and playing a very competitive game of racket ball. They were into extra time so the alligator game was especially brutal that day.

Devil Keith and Nora turned to each other and blinked in total astonishment and fear. The need to run away was crushingly intoxicating but cruel, as there was nowhere to go but further into the boat and the horrors it would gaily reveal.

CHAPTER THIRTY-NINE

The Hellish deck…

Devil Keith and Nora tried to push their way through the field of impaled skulls and the barrage of screaming, heaving people. People who were gagging due to the smell of old rusty blood, bitter sweat, concentrated acidic urine and nose-hair burning salty air. Nora had visited a slaughterhouse, as part of a primary two school trip. The six year old Nora wrote a poem describing the unusual day-out and she gleefully won a highly coveted abattoir sticker. It was the best sonnet ever she was happily told: she had found twenty-two words that rhymed with gore and forty-three words that rhymed with viscera. This boat was smelling very much like that prized slaughterhouse visit.

Nora was sadistically yanked from her pleasant school days' reminiscence when she and Devil Keith were viciously dragged into one of three misshapen lines, and violently pushed towards a towering pair of peeling doors. The doors bounced opened to reveal a sensory blitzing Casino. Nora cowered against Devil Keith's side as she knew that the deck was merely an aperitif as the chaos and madness had only really just begun.

The sobbing people in front of Nora and Devil Keith were simultaneously snivelling and stepping back plus eagerly stretching forward. It was a truly bizarre and deeply disturbing sight: the need to save themselves from the new terrors that awaited them in the Casino versus the overwhelming compulsion to enter the room so they could gamble and then gamble some more.

There was a large, shiny banner hanging overhead at the entrance of the Casino that read *"Congratulations Gambler goes Large Hell. You have earned two extra horns. Let the celebrations and random flayings begin. Proceed and pull up a chair".*

Nora tugged on Devil Keith's arm and shouted into his ear. *"Devil Keith, I think we may have made a mistake. We chose the wrong Hell to visit. Those extra two horns mean that this Hell is going to be so much worse than the four horn Beach Comber's Hell. This is now a five horner Hell. A full five horner.*

We could be here forever and get repeatedly brutally tortured if we don't get a chance to learn something. We have to get outta here and make some room for ourselves so we can search. Come. Now." Nora was trying to be brave but she was quietly crying and pushing into Devil Keith for comfort. Devil Keith was trying to offer that comfort but he was starting to struggle as well. He had genuinely believed that the arrogantly smiling flowers were the worst thing that could happen in this Hell.

Devil Keith and Nora entered the Casino...

It was clear that instead of the piped oxygen, that Casino's normally depend upon to keep their customers awake, this Gambling Hell had been a shade more creative. The room was drenched in feelings of blissful hope followed by unmitigated failure and ending with a hefty dose of utter doom. It's always good to give the punters hope then snatch it away, appeared to be the devastating Hell theme. Nora was all too aware of its effects as she'd been experiencing this roller-coaster of emotions since first stepping foot in this Hell. Even on the quay she had felt slightly uneasy and couldn't quite embrace all the forced gaiety.

Ahh, all the usually brave and unflinching Nora's requests for reassurance make sense now.

CHAPTER FORTY

The crafty Casino and its naughty ways...

Devil Keith stared at his Nora. He slowly blinked as he realised that he had, in deed, made a terrible mistake. They couldn't get back out of the crushing room as the only direction of travel appeared to be forward. This could be too much for even him to handle. Why was he so good at that damn Rock game? At every game? He mused.

"Right, I'm all here. You're all here. We're still in love, so that's good. We don't have a lottery ticket, also good. So, erm, read everything. We need to learn something. Anything. Scan the room for anything you don't know and I'll do the same." Devil Keith quickly turned and viewed the colossal room. He snatched up the nearest cowering person and shouted *"Tell me something I don't know."*

The terrified person responded. *"My name is Colin."*

Devil Keith closed his eyes and waited. He slowly opened one eye and looked around. They were still in the Gambler's Hell. Still surrounded by a devilishly evil Casino. Devil Keith now knew that getting his whites even whiter than usual, and the possibility of making a new friend called Colin was not considered enough of a learning experience to appease the HR manual. Damn this pernickety Hell and it's sly, sly ways.

Devil Keith and his Nora looked around again, in the vain hope that they could plan a route out of the crushing carnage and the headache inducing noise. They were abruptly interrupted by one of the slick fedora wearing Hell demon

Dealers. The oily Dealer flashed his gold and diamond encrusted teeth at a startled Devil Keith and Nora.

"Would you care to pick a card? Any card? They're only a little bit marked in my favour so have a try. You'll like it. I promise." The Dealer smoothed out his waxed, pencil thin moustache and pulled a pack of blatantly marked playing cards from his snug trouser pocket. Trousers that were so tight that it was possible to see the pattern of the Dealer's hairy legs through the shiny fabric. Devil Keith was very impressed with the dexterity of the conman and took a moment to admire the rest of his unique ensemble. The Dealer's indecently fitted trousers were matched with a purple and yellow striped shiny satin and brocade waistcoat. The waistcoat was strung with a mass of gold chains and hung with noisy, chunky pocket watches. Watches that displayed a variety of different times: to confuse and bemuse the strung-out gamblers and ensure that the gamblers didn't realise that it was now past their bedtime. Between each pocket watch was a series of tiny, crunchy shrunken brown heads. Heads that were merrily singing the infinitely talented Ms Kylie Minogue's *"I can't get you out of my head,"* and Kenny Rodger's *"The Gambler."* Two great songs utterly ruined by the dehydrated warblers failed attempt at a mash-up.

Devil Keith absentmindedly reached for a card but Nora punched the pack out of the shady Dealers hands and onto to floor. The Dealer laughed then deliberately plucked a Queen of Pitchforks' from the top of his red and black Spatz shoes.

"Those Spatz would look really good if you teamed them with navy blue polka dot laces. I'd lose all the sovereign rings if I were you. No criminal worth his salt wears them now, and that Oxford University tie is a dead give-away that you're up to no good." Devil Keith was still entranced with the Dealer's look, but he did so enjoy a bit of fashion critiquing. Devil Keith decided that he needed to buy a couple of yards of the waistcoat fabric. He thought that Nora's plastic garden gorillas would appreciate a new summer wardrobe and the Hounds of Hell would slobber

over new yellow and purple leashes.

The polished thief of hopes and dreams smiled. His rubbery lips drawing up into his chubby, apple cheeks. *"Thanks buddy I'll pass on your suggestions or you can do that yourself. There's a feedback box somewhere over there. Just past the live Roulette table and right at the spinning Wheel of Misfortune. If you reach the hurling random body parts slot machines then you've gone too far."* The merry, whistling Dealer wandered off to fleece another unsuspecting punter. He was due to work at the Black Jack table where the aim of the game was to get 666 points, not the usual 21 points a person would expect of the game. It was an unwinnable task as each player was only dealt one card and the buy-in for that specific game was particularly gruesome.

I don't know if you are aware of this, but being a Gambler goes Large demon Dealer is serious business and a hotly contested employment opportunity. Everyone loves the tins of moustache wax and the unlimited personalised mugs are an unmitigated hit with all the ladies. So the demon Dealers undergo extensive training, where the ultimate test is to peel a seedless purple grape. A grape that is lodged deep in their left, front trouser pocket. The test is scrupulously timed and the scoreboard is constantly being updated as Dealers race to complete their dexterity defying ordeal. Each month the Dealer with the longest time is unceremoniously keelhauled, then made to wear the puce waistcoat of shame. The disgraced waistcoat's shrunken heads sing *"He's got a lovely bunch of coconuts,"* by the talented Merv Giffin.

No one knows why this particular song was chosen but only one or two notes of the dreaded ditty causes the Dealers to burst out in hives and crave copious amounts of banana bread pudding.

CHAPTER FORTY-ONE

No closer to the feedback box...

There was an old, wooden upright piano against one of the garishly decorated Casino walls. The dreadful instrument was bouncing and banging from one peddle to another: gaily clattering away as it loudly spewed out bits and pieces of summer "*one hit wonder*" songs, and tinny elevator muzak. Tunes that stick in your head and are still loitering there when you wake up in the morning. Those kinds of frustrating, brain stealing bits of rubbish. The piano never completely finishing one ditty before starting another. And never, ever truly in tune but just off-key enough to grate the nerves and produce a dull headache behind the eye. There were missing ivory keys so the spiteful instrument used lengths of punishing piano wire to lasso people's teeth. Dragging them over and using the molars as crumbling, yellowed piano keys. Perpetuating the piano's hatred of music and all things remotely cultured.

This music was accompanied by shrill screams as the enormous crystal chandeliers casually dropped their glistening diamond tips. The sparkling shards plummeting downwards and cleanly slicing through the delicate skin webs between the fingers and the thumb. Effectively and painfully impaling the "*winner's*" hands to, and through, the green baize poker tables. Removing the razor sharp glass shards would cost the gambler their fingertips, their fleshy finger pads and at least half of the palm of their hand. The demon Dealers would casually sweep the plump debris under the table and carry on.

There were massive, steel poker chips also randomly falling from the high, ornate ceiling. The humongous discs crashing down on the gambling addicted people and flattening them into the swirling patterned Casino carpets. Splattering blood, chunks of grey brain matter and milky spinal fluid up the decorative, panelled walls. Devil Keith pushed Nora to the side as they narrowly missed being crushed by the terribly destructive saucers. Devil Keith thought this was bang out of order. They had come here to learn and not to have his outfit savagely ironed. Ironed without the necessary and highly specialised starch, too. Learning to wear poorly ironed garments: was that the learning they sought? Devil Keith waited and waited some more but they remained in the Casino. So no, it bloody well wasn't. This Hell was just being rude and inhospitable, he huffed.

The sensory overload was painful in the extreme, and Nora was flagging under the weight of it. The screaming winners, the hardy piano playing and the flashing lights were only a small part of the torture. The games, in the centre of the room, appeared to be the main attraction. If you scrunched up your eyes you could nearly, maybe, sort of recognise the games being played.

Let the fun and games commence..

The central Poker tables were surrounded by heavily maimed players and random, shredded body parts. Devil Keith and Nora watched in sickening awe as a curly haired young man smiled then nervously pulled out a chair and joined the rowdy game. He tentatively paid his game buy-in by using a small sliver of bamboo to gouge out the nail on his left index finger. After panting and vomiting over the side of the table, he tossed the splintered nail onto the gruesome pile of body parts residing in the centre of the table. He then looked at the scowling Dealer and reached over so he could heavily salt the raw, sticky red nail-bed. His agonising shriek was so powerful that Nora nearly threw up herself. He cradled his aching hand to his chest and only stopped bawling when he received his first marked card. He frowned then hesitantly lifted the smallest pair of pliers from the table. The Dealer nodded in agreement. The young guy was violently shaking as he roughly pushed the pliers into his quivering mouth. He gagged and grabbed the edge of the table. There was a sickening crunch and the young man pulled out a tooth: the bloody root hanging over the edge of the plier jaws. He held his mouth closed, swallowed the searing pain and tossed the tooth onto the greenish table top. He then slowly nodded for another card. Nora covered Devil Keith's eyes and tried to pull him in for a hug. She had noticed that all of the tables had packs of playing cards plus thin slices of sharpened bamboo, heavy salt shakers, well-oiled pliers, blunt machetes, ice-cream scoopers, sharpened screwdrivers, drills and a range of very pointy pencils. All held at the ready to "*assist*" the player into the rigged games.

Once hooked the game quickly progressed or deteriorated, depending on your point of view. The lost man picked up the dulled machete and held it to his clammy forehead. He began slowly sawing the knife back and forth. He fainted but picked himself up from the sticky floor. He continued the cut then threw his mushy scalp onto the centre of the table. He was losing, badly, but he just couldn't stop his own piece by piece destruction. More cards followed and his debt mounted. He painstakingly flayed the skin from his wrist to his elbow and raised the impossibly high stakes, again. Another card appeared on the table. The profusely sweating man scrapped away the layer of forearm fat then picked at the exposed muscle. He pinched out a long thin nerve and coiled it onto the table. This was not enough to satisfy the grinning Dealer so the juddering man grabbed a pencil and painstakingly rolled his stiff white tendons onto the handy pencil. A card was turned over and the Dealer slid the drill and ice-cream scoop at the rocking man.

Nora, despite her revulsion, could feel herself being drawn to the compulsive poker table. With considerable effort she made herself look away before the marrow drilling and all the sludgy organ scooping started. As Nora turned she realised that the disembowelled players, who were moaning on the floor, were starting to re-grow their nails. And their teeth were descending through their bumpy pink gums. She shed a tear as she now understood that the house always wins so the person will forever regenerate and start the grisly process again. The gamblers wore truly horrified facial expressions as their bodies reformed, so she also knew that the gamblers realised their gory predestined fate only too well.

Nora had let go of Devil Keith's hand but quickly recognised her error in judgment. Devil Keith had moved away and was captivated by the flashing, addictive slot machines. Noise filled beasts that required a person to slowly tear their own arm from its socket to use as a crank. A well-dressed woman had tied her left arm to the machine and was using an ice-pick to split open the shoulder joint and free the offending limb from its fleshy mooring. It was an agonisingly laborious process. Full of squelches followed by moans and self-pleading. She was begging and imploring herself to stop. Just stop. She could not.

The pulverised joint gave way with a lurch and her left arm hung free. The bloody end scrapping along the ground. She untied the limb from its anchor, carefully picked it up with her right hand and pushed the ravaged end into the waiting machine. She pulled the macabre limb lever and expectantly held her breath.

The flashing lights raced around the contraption: giving a sense of winning. The woman held her breath. She did, indeed, win but the appealing coins were edged with razors, and these flying missiles embedded themselves into her exposed chest and throat. She collapsed into a gurgling mess of blood bubbles: bursting on her grimacing lips. Nora was staring at the woman and recognised her from the quayside eye-spy game. Her make-up was no longer pristine. Now it appeared to be a caricature of her former self. A face smothered in thick foundation, dusty concealer and gaudy lipstick. All applied by a highly enthusiastic but poorly skilled mortician's assistant.

Nora pulled Devil Keith away just as he was reaching over to the apparatus and eyeing the leather, restraining straps. He was less immune that he thought. Nora saw a beleaguered server approaching. She grabbed a sherry glass from his burgeoning tray and threw its contents into Devil Keith's slack face. Belatedly realising that the glass was full of warm, salty bone marrow. She slapped Devil Keith, apologised then slapped him again. Then another couple of times just to make sure he was listening to her. Married no more than ten minutes and she already knew the difference between man listening and real listening. She was a whiz at this old marriage malarkey.

"Nora, not here. Save it for the bedroom." Devil Keith saucily whispered and pulled Nora in for a lengthy snog. She could taste the salty, viscous marrow on his lips but didn't care one whit. Her Devil Keith was back and he still had all four limbs. And they were all attached to where they should be.

Nora, and a very much awake Devil Keith, skirted around the noisy Roulette wheel. That was more challenging, and took more time, than you would think. The Roulette wheel was a gigantic beast of a thing because rather than black and red numbers around its circumference it had to accommodate a circle of numbered cages. Cages containing dozens of frightened, tightly bound people. The colossal roulette wheel was reversed, held for a second, then set off to do its dastardly job. It was rotating clockwise at approximately a hundred miles per hour. Well, the screaming players flapping jowls were certainly going at a hellava rate so Nora thought that a hundred miles an hour was a reasonable guess. A solid white ball, the size of a large baseball, was carefully loaded into a cannon by an exhausted, panting Dealer. The Dealer happily lit the short fuse and fired the ball into the centre of the wheel. The ball started wildly bouncing within the rapidly spinning roulette wheel. The speed of the wheel meant that within seconds the sphere was displaying centrifugal force and slamming into the caged players: breaking delicate shin bones, dislocating shrieking jaws, exploding through eye sockets and pulverising skulls.

Nora gasped as the wrecking ball slammed into an old man's chest and ploughed through a large Y shaped scar. The cuts ran from his collar bones down through his sternum and were held together by large black, uneven stitches. The previously white ball was covered in pieces of the elderly man's pale pink lungs as it made its escape via his ruptured ribs and mangled spinal vertebrae. Nora was going to ask Devil Keith what had made the intrusive scar when she realised that it was due to the pathologist's scalpel, bone-saw and clamps. The autopsy that had explored the elderly man's body, after his death. Well Nora hoped the autopsy was after his death or the pathologist was less of doctor and more of a murderer.

Devil Keith wasn't paying attention to the mutilating wheel as he was sniffing quite loudly and often. *"Nora, can you smell that? I think that beneath all the cloying iron scent of blood and the stinging acidic urine, I can smell a garden of blooming roses. Their yellow and cream petals touched with morning dew. Are you catching that scent? It's not just me, is it?"*

Nora was reluctant to take in a full breath, but Devil Keith gave her a second prompt so Nora filled her lungs and expected the worst. *"Oh yeah, definitely something sweet. Could it be an exit?"* Nora excitedly turned towards the lovely scent and began searching for a doorway back into the serene garden and the tinkling ice-cream vans.

There was no lovely doorway but there was a gargantuan,

multicoloured octopus taking up a full corner of the vast Casino. A glittering overhead banner proclaimed him to be the *"The one and only Magnificent Octopus of Hell".* Devil Keith had already encountered a few Peacocks of Hell, residing in the Medieval Hell, so he wasn't entirely happy with this new, and frankly, scary discovery. Although, he had found some of the Hounds of Hell, from Hell number one, to be a Spanish speaking delight.

The Octopus' white gloved tentacles were whizzing through the air as he was shouting. *"Find the lady, find the lady. The Queen's under one of these cups. Or she will be. You!"*

Nora and Devil Keith watched as the overly confident Octopus yanked the head from one of the mesmerised players and stuffed it under a large blue and white China cup. The would-be gambler's body trembling then falling lifelessly to the grubby floor. The full decapitation meant that the gambler's time in this Hell was now over, as there was no recovering from that injury. A blessed relief Nora decided. The other players paid no attention to the mounds of headless corpses that surrounded the speedy cephalopod's folding table. The gambling compulsion was a visceral, living thing that had captured their will and corrupted the tattered remnants of their black souls.

The player's agonising and bloody buy-ins began and the swift cup shuffling commenced. The players used the handy "*assisting*" tools to remove their skin, teeth, eyes and bones but the crooked Octopus of Hell wasn't satisfied with the quality, or the grossness, of the body bets. The cunning Octopus added to the obscene betting pool by shooting out random streams of highly corrosive acid, instead of the usual black ink, during his double and triple dealing. The horrific chemical burns, bubbling skin and melting tissue adding an additional frisson of risk to the whole procedure. The putrid smells, viscous drips and ragged moans didn't stop the urge to continue gambling. Nora feared that nothing could.

"I think that cheeky, bloody Octopus is cheating. There

are eight tentacles and I think there's a couple of white gloved prosthetic hands mixed in there as well. Are you seeing this too?" Devil Keith started a quick hand count and his Nora was correct. The Octopus was, indeed, shady. He clocked Devil Keith's lips moving through the escalating numbers and quickly threw a distracting mini hand at the numerating Devil.

"Oy, I was counting there. I'll have to start from the beginning again." Devil Keith stamped his welly clad foot and started following the speeding, blurry Octopus' movements.

"You'll do no such thing so stop with all the counting. You'll come here...to me." The Octopus hypnotically murmured. He slowly removed a white cotton glove and softly curled a tentacle, in invitation, at the heroic Devil. Devil Keith was not enticed by the cheating Dealer although he respected the Octopus' sheer nerve... and his lovely manicure. The frustrated, and probably psychotic, Octopus pulled himself up and coiled his muscular tentacles: ready to blast Devil Keith with eight jets of his dissolving acidic mix.

Nora tried to push in front of her Devil Keith and offer a small shield. Devil Keith shoved Nora behind him and told her to stay still. Devil Keith used a fair amount of expletives during that instruction, but the authors are trying to market the book as children's bedtime reading so are cleaning up their act.

The strangest thing happened. The astonished, and definitely psychotic, Octopus rapidly floated up to the high, nicotine stained ceiling. His gigantic body was swiftly flashing through the colours grey, brown, pink and blue as he tried to grasp at some swagged curtains in order to cover himself. Whilst rhythmically bobbing off the yellowed ceiling the Octopus did a great deal of panicked gasping and repeated the myriad of colours, finally settling on a bright, startling red. He was desperately trying to camouflage his spectacular bulk from Devil Keith, Nora and the maimed gamblers, but to no avail. Plus, there was no hiding from the almighty explosion of wind and gas that erupted from the blushing beast's portly posterior. The G force was speedily rippling across the gambler's cheeks, lifting full bodies out of ill-fitting wellies and blowing off entire pony tails. Whole pony tails! A goner.

The large Roulette buckled and groaned in the wind. The massive wheel tipped: squashing its human cages and discharging its destructive ball. There was utter carnage in its tsunami wake.

Devil Keith and Nora tightly grasped each other. They held their breath, scrunched up their respective eyes and waited on the pungent methane fart to melt their, and their neighbours, eyeballs. The naive duo were under the impression that their eyelids would somehow save their sight.

Ohhh. Ohhh, something's happening. The entire room was bathed in the most delightful scent of blooming, summer roses. Yellow roses? The flatulent Octopus was to blame for the gorgeous sweet smell and he was obviously very embarrassed by his beauteous bottom burps. He shamefully sank back to the floor and began glaring at the laughing Devil Keith and Nora. The raging Octopus quickly brushed off his shame and rapidly assumed his bad ass (sorry, not the time for jokes) persona. He was unceremoniously ripping off people's heads and furiously pitching them at the giggling gamblers. When that didn't work the Octopus started spitting out clouds of red, hot ink and mimed slitting Devil Keith's throat. Devil Keith wondered if learning the Octopus' secret scent was the learning required to get them outta Hell. Devil Keith held Nora's hand and waited. Nope that wasn't it either, but it was extremely entertaining to see how far the obnoxious Octopus would fall.

Nora grabbed Devil Keith's hand and hid behind the upturned Roulette wheel, hoping the Octopus would run out of destructive ink. Well the pen **is** mightier than the sword, although one of the author's did try that theory out when requesting mole removal surgery and the attending doctor asked for a mental health consultation. Stat.

CHAPTER FORTY-TWO

Still trapped in the crafty Casino and squatting behind a conveniently tipped Roulette wheel…

"Devil Keith, this place isn't getting any better. In fact I think it's getting worse. I can't concentrate enough to see any learning opportunities and I can feel some of the gambling cravings rearing their ugly heads. I didn't really care about those last mutilated players. I only needed and I mean NEEDED, to know who was going to win. I'm scared that I'm losing some of my humanity and compassion. Do you have any ideas on how we move this forward?" Nora put both her hands on Devil Keith's cheeks and pulled him down to the floor. She had to ensure that he was listening and able to function. She had tried channelling her inner swan: calm on the surface whilst her legs paddled like buggery and her heart was a pumping, but it was a difficult act to maintain. Luckily, after the marrow dowsing episode, Devil Keith appeared relatively immune to the compulsions: he was an old hand at this whole gambling lark. Afterall, he had won many a late night shopping channel from God.

"Right. Give me a minute to think." Devil Keith poked his head up. The Octopus was back to enticing the gamblers to find the Lady. Devil Keith helped Nora up and brushed her down. Lingering on her curvy bottom: he was scared but he wasn't dead…yet.

He put his index finger against his cheek and pursed his

glossy lips. He then pointed to the left, thought a moment then shook his head. He did the movements again but pointed to the right and shook his head. He finished this off with an aggressive point down the centre of the room and a violent shake of his head. He may have been relatively immune to the need to gamble but he couldn't fathom a way out. He was failing his Nora and he was getting mad.

"*Maybe I can be of some assistance.*" A small wizen man queried. The voice coming from somewhere around Devil Keith's manly knees.

"*Where on earth did you come from?*" Devil Keith looked back and forth then picked the grizzled man up by his patchy brown beard and turned the startled man upside down. Devil Keith was searching for an on/off switch for the talking garden gnome. Afterall, discovering the location of the switch may have been just what they needed to learn in order to return home. Devil Keith gave the astonished man a sound jiggle and put his ear to the old guy's rounded tummy: there was no sound of rattling batteries so Devil Keith unceremoniously dunked the shaken man on the floor. Not the Gambling Hell learning experience afterall, Devil Keith defeatedly mused.

"*Oh, that was exciting. I've not had a free judder for quite some time. Normally it costs extra. A lot extra. There was this one time…*

Oh, your question. Not earth, no, no, not at all. Hell, that's the place my Sonny-Jim. I'm always here. And I'm always known as 'Helpful Man'. So I am." And with that the diminutive man saluted and re-adjusted his ruffled zebra print leotard, then he smiled. A grin that would have looked a bit more friendly if he had possessed more than just the one humungous yellow tooth in his balding head.

"*You look slightly familiar.*" Now that Devil Keith no longer had the poor man doing unsolicited acrobatics he was able to look at the smiling creature and wonder if the big tooth made a wild pinging sound. Best not check that out just now, Devil Keith thought, as the man could prove to be helpful. Devil

Keith wouldn't be at all surprised to find that his Nora had the exact same idea, but she thought the flicked tooth would sound quite deep in tone. Like a church bell on a Sunday morning. A Sunday morning when her mouth would be full of a fried egg roll. Mmm soft yoked, fried egg with a pinch of salt. Lovely.

"Ah, I get that a lot. You're thinking of my big cousin. He was on a sabbatical to Hell number three. The Medieval Hell. You heard of it? Oh, the stories he had. He was such a joker. He told us such a tall tale about an utter dimwit that answered 'trifle' to the riddle.. 'what cheese is made backwards?' None of the other cousins believed our big cousin and his odd story so he was permanently ostracised to the other Hell. Last I heard he was engaged to a very demanding polar bear. A bit of a drama queen, by all accounts. Keeps fainting all the time and draping herself around couches. A shame really, our cousin was such a minx.

Come to think of it. He said that the strange, idiot fella wore some mighty unusually clothes. Was it you by any chance?" the old guy looked Devil Keith up and down, and not in an admiring way. Not at all. He then picked a lump of old, grey lung out of his patchy beard and lobbed it over his left shoulder.

Devil Keith stumbled and mumbled a denial but the old guy remained suspicious and gave him the stink eye.

"Oh, please forgive him. He's just a harmless old man looking to make some friends in this dreadful place. He talks a little bit of nonsense now and again, but he wouldn't hurt a fly. He's one of the good 'uns. I like him immensely and we often share a hidey hole when it all gets too much to bear.

I, however can help you. Well, I think I can. The name's Marsh and I might be able to lead you through to the engine room and out to freedom. I can't guarantee your safety though, as there might be some risks and dangers we have to face." A tall, handsome man gently moved the older guy out of the way and softly patted his head, before handing the hoary geezer a couple of jammy dodgers. Marsh awkwardly bowed at Nora then shyly held out his hand to the relieved Devil Keith.

"You can? And why would you do that for us? Wait, please. First things first: can we borrow your mobile phone?" Nora questioned. She looked pointedly at the open pack of biscuits and held out her hand for the phone. Nora knew that Devil Keith could be too friendly and far too trusting for his own good so she took it upon herself to protect him. So far she'd saved him from three feral beavers who wanted to add Devil Keith to the foundations of their newest dam, two thieving clowns who did not have magical shoes no matter how good their power point presentation was and a horny Santa Clause. Well that one's self-explanatory... but suffice to say that Santa wants several icepacks for his Christmas as he was not a nice boy.

"Ahh, the mobile phones only work on the dock. Apparently they help with the whole carnival vibe this terrible Hell initially portrays. It helps put the prospective gamblers in a good mood so they're easier to manipulate and herd onto the boat.

Sorry, where are my manners? Please have a biscuit or two, or as many as you want. It's awful here. And I'm just like you. I'm not a gambler and I can see that you aren't one either. The awful games hold no sway over me. I think there's been some sort of admin error and I really shouldn't be here, but I don't know who to turn to for help. The feedback box is just an illusion: no one gets back to you to help. I've been waiting to find someone just like me so that we can escape this hellhole together." The man was well dressed with no evidence of the pathologist's knife or the undertaker's thickly applied make-up. He didn't look or dress like a Dealer either, so that was a definite plus.

"Ok. Ok. You don't look like you belong here, I'll give you that, but how do we know we can trust you? You could be lying through your straight, white teeth. All this could be your game and that, in turn, would make your overly generous offer our gamble. We'd be betting our life on your sincerity." Nora said between biscuit crumbs.

"An understandable accusation. You don't know me and I

can understand your suspicions, especially in this terrible place. I can only say that I have nothing to gain, except my potential freedom. And possibly your freedom too. I can't promise anything but I've done the run to the engine room a few times but I just can't get past the final Dealer. He's cunning and unmoveable. I think that the three of us stand a much better chance together. Working together. Even if only two of us make it, isn't it worth the risk?" Marsh was handing out pieces of sweet biscuits to the shocked and injured gamblers. He began ripping up his clean white shirt and tearing it into strips for much needed bandages. He then began using his belt to make torniquets: he was trying to stanch the blood flowing from the mewing *"winners"*. He was obviously distressed by the suffering surrounding him but his valiant efforts were futile. The gaseous Octopus' antics and aftermath were truly deadly.

"I agree with my beautiful Nora. I too am suspicious, but I can't think of anything else that we can do. So, I'll help so long as my Nora can get out of here. I don't care about myself." Devil Keith pressed a fingertip against Nora's pursed lips: to stop her protests. *"And Nora, you know I'm such a good judge of character, afterall I pursued you. And don't forget I am such a snappy dresser and a fashion aficionado...extraordinaire. Nora, his waistcoat is disgusting. Only a truly good person would have the confidence to wear such a disgraceful, repulsive rag.*

Plus, he ***is****, willy-nilly, handing out the very best of biscuits. Well second best biscuits. Tunnock's caramel wafers are the very best biscuit, but I don't think he'd be so keen to give them away. Do you?"* Devil Keith shook Marsh's muscular hand then wiped off some gooey entrails that the distraught, amateur first aider had scrapped off a concussed gambler. This Hell could really do with a decent set of cleaners Devil Keith thought.

Nora removed Devil Keith's manicured index finger from her anxiety, bitten lips. Nora reiterated her objections and, after a stage-whispered argument, eventually said she would go but only if they **all** agreed to leave the boat. She wasn't leaving without her Devil Keith. Devil Keith tucked a wayward curl behind her ear then gave her a quick cuddle. Marsh assured her that they would all try to leave. He went onto explain that they had to go as soon as possible because the gambling addiction would only get stronger, and they would quickly lose the will to leave. Nora knew this to be true as the flashing lights were luring her towards the slot machines and the horrific ice picks.

CHAPTER FORTY-THREE

The engine room...

Devil Keith and Nora had silently followed the skilled but slightly apprehensive Marsh as he slowly navigated the maze, that was the underbelly of the huge floating Casino. Marsh had kindly helped all of the maimed gamblers they happened to come across: rolling up his drab waistcoat to provide a soft pillow for a piteously sobbing man and using his silk necktie to secure a gurgling man's mangled jaw onto his pitted skull. He also gently placed a wailing woman's roughly amputated fingers in his shoe, for safe-keeping, and possible re-attachment at a later date. She had softly smiled and tightly hugged Marsh to her chest. Reluctant to release her humble saviour and part from her only experience of kindness since she descended into the Hell.

The intrepid trio had travelled along extremely narrow corridors and. when told, they anxiously hid behind crooked oval doors in their efforts to hide their escape from the Casino. They easily avoided the dandified Dealers. Dealers who were practising honing their fine motor dexterity by plucking lazy and flesh engorged bluebottles from the fetid air. The journey, although long, was thankfully completed without too many issues. Marsh's endless whispers of encouragement and silly stories helping Nora cope with her slight claustrophobia. The unlimited access to some rather fine biscuits helped too.

The roar of the engine room became incrementally louder and the heat in the corridor had moved from spa sauna pleasant and was now suffocatingly hot. They had reached their final destination but Marsh warned them that they still had a last barrier to overcome. He covered his hand with the remains of his shirt and grabbed the blisteringly hot doorhandle. He flung open the robust steel and iron door then ushered his relieved charges into the stifling room. A fearsome soot stained Dealer spun around and brandished a well-worn shovel at the shocked intruders.

"About bloody time you got here. The furnace needs a feeding. This boat doesn't run itself; you know." The filthy Chief Dealer snapped and gave Marsh a dirty look. A look that was boiling over with contempt, disdain and disgust. The Dealer pushed back his strands of limp sweaty hair, adjusted his battered tweed cap and straightened his string vest. His grey matted chest hair was poking through the holes in the vest and the ends of the hair were clogged with lumps of damp coal dust. The Dealer went back to his task and threw a couple of violently twitching limbs into the greedy bright, white flames.

"Patience, patience, oh chief dirty one. All in good time." Marsh sneered and made an insulting, half-hearted salute at the engine room boss. He suddenly grabbed Nora's hair and painfully pulled her head back against his chest. Clapping a beefy hand on her forehead whilst exposing her vulnerable and pale throat to a lethally sharpened tiepin. The unnatural position making her cry out in absolute agony and stopping her from stamping on the traitor's toes.

"Stay still you big ignorant mongrel, or I'll slice into her jugular then rip her ugly head clean off her flabby body. And I'll enjoy doing it. Oh, I will. I still haven't forgiven you for the insulting waistcoat comments you made earlier. You absolute imbecile. Everyone can see that I have sublime taste in all things. Unlike you and your revolting, screeching wife. You should be thanking me...afterall I plan on getting rid of this mumping,

female carbuncle. For good.

And as for you, you dirty wretched being. You only have this job because no one else would lower themselves to do it. A boss? Ha! Don't make me laugh. And you can stop with all the moaning and bitching. You should be kissing my feet. It's getting harder and harder to find gamblers who can resist the pull. And I found you not one, but two toadies today so the fire with be well satisfied with all the lovely new emotions it gets to gobble up.

You pair of pathetic clowns are so full of hope, fear, anger, shame and the need for revenge, it nearly makes me sick. Sick with happiness. I'm positively giddy with joy. Those 'feelings', you probably whisper about in the dark and love so much, make such lovely colours in the flames. That's what helps keep this place afloat. The games on the Casino floor are mere child's play." Marsh laughed as he made the air quotes with one hand. He abruptly stopped his twisted merriment and viciously smacked the furious Devil Keith across the head with a thick plank of wood. My that Marsh is mighty strong, and able to effortlessly multitask. A dazed Devil Keith fell into a warm puddle of yellowish, rancid human fat and was held down by eight, sweat-stained minor Dealers.

"As if I care what you think, Marsh. There'll be no kissing your cloven feet, you deceiving, two-faced cur. And as for you two bumbling, simpletons. Bloody idiots the pair of you. Who does something for nothing in a place like this? ***Who*** *would believe someone would do something just through the goodness of their heart? Arses, that's who. Anyway, I have a tight schedule to keep. I have a couple of things to do, then I'll see to you pair of naïve morons."* The Chief Dealer grinned then scoured the manky, black floor for prey. He calmly picked up a wriggling lump of whimpering flesh and casually threw it into the blazing fire. Nora gasped at the nonchalant savagery of the brutal act.

"I saw that look you gave me. Don't give that evil thing any pity. That use to be the infamous Eva Braun. She deserves everything she gets here. She moved up to Hell number one, then tried to unite Hitler's grated, cloned body. They were planning

on starting another world war. But just so you don't think we're completely heartless here, ***I'll*** *re-unite her with her cowardly lover."* The Chief Dealer opened a cavernous cupboard, rummaged around, swore a little bit and pulled out a rusty clothes hanger. A sliver of a barely recognisable Hitler limply hung from the worn hanger. The Chief Dealer happily crumpled up the piece of pitifully crying, and pleading, tissue into a pathetic ball.

"He tried to bite me, the swine. Cheerio. In you go, you lousy murderer. You have millions and millions of deaths and acts of torture to atone for, so I'll be seeing you again later today. Then again tomorrow, and the day after, for an eternity. You and I will become bosom buddies by the time I'm finished with you. You yellow-bellied beast. And no bloody biting the next time." The Chief Dealer closed the belching furnace doors and crossed his massive arms over his chest. Neither Devil Keith nor Nora could argue with that logic. That murderous tyrant deserved that and much, much more. An eternity of flames didn't seem nearly long enough to pay for his crimes.

"So, what's your story missy? What have you done to deserve this Hell? Was it juicy? A hormonal fuelled rampage or the unleashing of a deadly plague? Do tell. It can get a bit monotonous here, so entertain away while I eat my beef and tomato Pot Noodle." The Chief Dealer plonked himself down on a mound of peat. He slurped up a forkful of slippery noodles then stopped. He squinted his eyes, pursed his lips and looked Nora up and down.

"Whoa, wait a cotton picking minute. Aren't you that famous sulky model? The one with the really strange smile? The gal that legendary painter used for the Mona Lisa? Your eye's a bit wonky: a bit squint, but I'd recognise you anywhere. That's you, isn't it? Can I have your autograph for my collection? Eh?" The Chief Dealer clicked his rather grimy and sauce covered fingers together, then smugly pointed to his wall of fame.

A soot blackened wall, where an autographed picture, of a grimacing Genghis Khan, hung. Genghis had an abacus clasped in his hand and appeared to be calculating his exorbitant monthly child support payments. There was also a photograph of an indignant Napolean caught in mid strut as he narrowly avoided a battlefield cesspit. In the centre of the wall there was an oil painting of an obscenely massive King Henry the Eighth proudly displayed. The murderous king was eating the roasted, rosemary studded leg of a hefty stag, whilst perusing a large stack of divorce paperwork. The Chief Dealer was making the best of his smoky situation and trying to make the place a bit more homely. He had lost the grape peeling contest for four consecutive months, so after his third painful keelhauling and barnacle removal, he had reluctantly realised that he probably wasn't cut out to be a top shelf Dealer. So, until he could get a transfer to another Hell he was in charge of the sweltering engine room and all its pleading inmates.

"We're both innocent of all crimes. And no, I wasn't just the model. I was the inspiration. And no you can't have an autograph. No autograph for you, you utter horror." Nora stubbornly stated and tried to pull out of Marsh's punishing headlock. She so wanted to check on her Devil Keith as he was turning a funny, orangish colour and he had a bony lump forming on his forehead. Plus, and most worryingly, he appeared to be swelling up. Despite her noble struggles she couldn't break free of Marsh's gruelling hold. She tried to distract herself from the terrors engulfing and freezing her into inaction, so that she could formulate a plan of escape. To that end, she subtlety checked out the Chief Dealer's wall of fame. She quite liked the Abba song *"Waterloo,"* so was surprised to see a fuming Napolean up there on the wall. She thought he'd want to be captured, on celluloid, mid dance and possible shaking a beribboned tambourine. Nora was just about to offer the Chief Dealer an autograph as a bribe when...

"Oh, Marsh they're so pure and innocent. So good and wholesome and far too good for my measly wall. Better just apologise and let them go then. Make them some hot, sweet tea and crustless strawberry jam sandwiches as they go on their merry way.

How could we be so wrong? Oh, we are such silly billies." The Chief Dealer sarcastically stated and belched out a braying laugh. He whipped out his calloused hand and brutishly slapped Nora across the face then pointed to the sooty floor.

"The big guy goes first so she can watch...and learn her place. The snooty madam won't be so mean with her photos after I've finished with her." He kicked Devil Keith in the head and stood on his throat.

He was really annoyed by the lack of autograph, as the other Dealers never believed him when he told them about his famous burnings. And they called him such awful names. It was so hurtful to be bullied and known as the *"Pocket fumbler"* or the *"No peeler Dealer."*

Nora and the stupefied Devil Keith stopped struggling, and swelling, then closed their eyes for a second. They tentatively opened their eyes and looked around, but they stubbornly remained in the Gambler goes Large Hell. So the conceited Chief Dealer was wrong about Nora needing to learn her place, although completely correct about the need to punish the wicked and the cruel. Blast it!

The eight harassed minor Dealers lifted the violently struggling Devil from the mucky floor and pushed, then pushed him some more. Eventually getting some of him into the white hot furnace. Devil Keith held onto the door of the oven as his skin blistered, popped and peeled away. The fraught Dealers received kicks, punches and bites but they steadfastly completed their gruesome task and the Devil was fully ensconced in the greedy fire. Devil Keith, with all his polyester clothing and gallons of colour tinted hairspray, quickly caught ablaze and he started screeching in agony.

Nora pulled away from a giggling Marsh and rushed towards her Devil Keith. She couldn't possibly save him, so she wanted to join him. She couldn't have him dying all alone. Not her Devil Keith.

Marsh viciously yanked her back by her hair and obviously enjoyed painfully re-tilting her head. He was tearing out clumps of Nora's crisping, heat-frazzled hair whilst chuckling and flicking the end of her nose with his middle finger. There was no way he was permitting Nora to close her eyes and miss the spectacle. He painfully cracked her rigid back in his need to ensure her complete compliance and to assert his sadistic dominance.

"Don't be too hasty, ugly, ugly girl. You're too late to save your love from his roasting. And you ***are*** *most assuredly next. But first, let's watch all the pretty colours his fatty bits make as they melt, ooze and drip. Just imagine it's Christmas morning and you're watching the old balled-up wrapping paper make all those delightful colours in the fireplace. That's a lovely memory, don't you think? Although all the revolting cooking smells his body is making sort of ruin the mood. Don't you agree?*

Minions, keep the door open so she gets the full show. We don't want her to miss a moment. Then she's frying tonight...and tomorrow night too and probably the one after. What a delightful thought." He smirked then giggled. Then giggled some more as he held the tortured, grief swamped Nora still.

Devil Keith's screams and roars died down until there was barely a whimper emitting from the blistering oven. Nora collapsed to the ground. Broken, howling with grief and utterly defeated she curled up on the grubby, fat soaked floor. Marsh kicked her exposed back: making sure he bruised her vulnerable kidneys and making her yelp in pain.

CHAPTER FORTY-FOUR

In the Hell engine room with Devil Keith's charred and flaking body…

Nora was now quietly weeping and rocking as she looked into the glowing furnace and the crumbling remains of the man she loved. She took a steadying breath.

"I won't resist you. Just get it over with. I want to be gone from here. To be with my courageous man." She sobbed a hiccup and slightly stumbled as she staunchly rose from the floor. Refusing assistance, she dragged herself forward and with her head held as high as she could, she passed the Chief Dealer. The Chief Dealer was quietly surprised by her bravery, her dignity and her apparent love for her crispy husband. The smug, dishonest Marsh winked at her and cackled with delight. He was so much closer to earning an undisclosed favour from the Chief Dealer. Marsh was shaking with sheer anticipation. His mouth salivating and his hands damp with sweat.

An explosion of naked male flesh erupted from the furnace and knocked the desolate Nora to the ground. She was stunned for a mere moment then jumped to her feet and ran her hands over Devil Keith's unblemished, golden skin. She promptly turned and soundly punched the Chief Dealer in his awestruck face. Loosening one tooth and belting another tooth down his throat.

"One I owed you; I think. I told you my husband was

courageous and innocent. You're so gonna get it now, and nothing is going to save you. I know you have to punish the guilty but can't you show some compassion to the gamblers. They might not have done what they were accused of. We didn't, but you just wouldn't listen. Too busy with all your crappy decorating, hob-nobing with the infamous and noodle scoffing to care." Nora screamed in the face of the gobsmacked Chief Dealer.

"My Nora never lies. We are completely innocent, you fiend. Well she is and I'm sort of trying to be." Devil Keith tightly hugged his glorious Nora, then grabbed the dirty, startled Chief Dealer. Devil Keith tossed him over his shoulder into the roaring furnace. The Dealer deserved that for hitting and scaring his Nora. Although Devil Keith instantly regretted making it too quick a death as he fancied tying the Chief Dealer to the highly imaginative Wheel of Misfortune. Just for a couple of spins... or ten. The next seven frightened and cowering minor Dealers disappeared into the fiery depths just as quickly. Nora reasoned that the Chief Dealer, and the other minor Dealers, would eventually re-animate, but she did so enjoy their temporary discomfort. And she reasoned that this experience may teach them some much needed empathy towards the gamblers. It's worth noting that Nora, in her grief, anger and panic, appeared to have forgotten HR Sarah's sound advice regarding the Hell's residents. They are not just guilty of gambling. All of the residents, in the Gambler's goes Large Hell, have committed truly atrocious acts. Hence the number of Hell horns and the singularly destructive punishments on offer.

A gorgeously nude Devil Keith evilly smiled at Marsh and beckoned him forward. *"Now, what will I do with you my deceitful friend? Erm? Who's ugly now? You vile pile of excrement."*

Marsh smiled and gave another of his famous saucy winks. *"Not so quick my trusting friend. The alligators and crawfish are always hungry and your Nora is a tasty little number. Well, not to my taste. Of course. I have slightly more exotic tastebuds.*

You still need me to get you outta here so back off, you

animal. What **are** *you anyway? How did you do that? I've led countless people to this room and not one of them has survived the burning. You can't possibly be innocent, so what's the scam?"* Marsh wasn't concerned in the slightest, but he was intrigued. He wondered how he could profit from Devil Keith's heatproof hide.

"He's right. You do need him. He's the only gambler that's made it to the custodial level in this Hell. He might be able to help you, but he's a tricky one. I've never trusted him." Whispered the poorly hidden, eighth minor Dealer.

Devil Keith was going to show the cowering Dealer some mercy but thought, *"Nah, best leave the place tidy and I'm sure he was the one that pummelled my liver"*. So he quickly chucked the minor demon into the furnace as well, and brushed off his dusty hands. A shocked Nora didn't have time to put a stop to Devil Keith's *"housekeeping"*, so she hoped that the minor Dealer was only mildly singed. The Dealer's screams of, *"I'm burning in here,"* put paid to that hope-filled delusion.

"So here's what I want in order to aid your escape." Gloated the despicable Marsh. He whispered in Devil Keith's ear, chortled and confidently held out his hand in order to shake on the deal.

Devil Keith slapped a surprised Marsh to the dusty floor and ground his bare foot into Marsh's rapidly cracking ribs. *"No, I won't do that. No way. Not even to save my Nora. She wouldn't allow it either, so get that filthy thought outta your head. It's not happening. Not now, not ever. You disgust me."*

"What does he want? I'll give him anything he wants to get you outta here. Anything." Nora stated and pulled Devil Keith away from the wheezing, blue lipped beast.

"Ahhh the price is always the same. I prefer an open ended vow. A redeemable promise. A swapsy no backsy type of deal. A show of good faith, if you will." Marsh softly giggled then gasped at the end of his statement. Holding his escaping intestines in his abdominal cavity.

"No. That's not gonna happen, and I don't think that's what you said to my Devil Keith. Devil Keith, can you stop belting him about the head for a moment? I have to know what he wants." Nora stood over the heavily panting man. Devil Keith had smashed Marsh's ribs and Nora could see his evil heart struggling to beat through his heavily bruised skin.

Devil Keith dropped the piece of human garbage to the floor and reluctantly leaned into Nora. He whispered Marsh's horrendous request into her ear. Nora gagged and jumped onto Marsh's remaining ribs. *"No. We won't do that you pervert. You make me sick. No we won't smuggle that into this Hell for you. That's disgusting.*

Are there more of you here? If there are then they deserve everything they get and more. So much more. It's so, so wrong. Devil Keith we can't do that to an innocent. No matter what we have to go through. I'd rather face the alligators and be their lunch. I'd rather burn every single day. I love you more than life itself but I'd give you up rather than agree to his demands." Nora was crying, shouting and shaking Marsh. She slammed his head off the floor. Then did it again. It made a sickening gloopy sound as his brain leaked out of his ears.

"No, my Nora. I agree. We can't do that. We're just going to have to learn our lesson another way. I think we just need to go back the way we came and see if we can find 'Helpful Man' again. He might know something that could be of use, or his batteries might be somewhere else. I'll conduct a more thorough search and give him a bigger shakedown." Devil Keith tried to pull Nora away from Marsh. He feared that this adventure may have broken his tender Nora and corrupted her innocence.

"His demands. It's just so wrong." Despite Devil Keith's pleas and attempts to give her a cuddle, Nora refused to be distracted from her task. She was angry sobbing and had gone back to jumping on the pulverised pervert. She grabbed a dulled machete from the floor and began hacking, slicing and chopping at the disgusting beast. Not content with that she picked up bits and pieces of the repulsive Marsh and slapped

them around. Nora hummed as she happily shoved the minced monster into the burning furnace and watched the bloody, torn fragments melt into ash. He was gone and she was glad.

"I'm going back for more of those supposed gamblers. Those Casino games aren't bad enough. No, not nearly bad enough, not for what they've done or thought or wanted to do." Nora had accepted a small hug from Devil Keith but she was spitting mad at the gamblers. And she was more than a little bit furious with herself and her own naivety. She needed to vent, then vent some more then go killing. Or slapping. Or killing. Or maiming. Or killing.

Nora planned on introducing a Craps table with giant dung beetle Dealers who could squash the gamblers with humungous balls of excrement. She then decided to add a Killer Darts game where swordfish were hurtled through the air and pinned the players to the barbwire board. The swordfish would be supplied with full safety gear as she didn't want them to be hurt while they did their gloriously, justified work. She was warming to her crafty ideas and began searching for pen and paper so she could capture her wonderful designs...

And she was so going to change the embarrassed Octopus' diet so that the smell he emitted was truly diabolical. So wicked that the burgundy flocked wallpaper would curl from the walls and go on their holidays. Plus, there wouldn't be a dry eye socket in the room: not after that heroic Octopus did his floaty, melty thing. Actually, she decided she'd ban eyes all together. Then she re-thought that poor, eye-gouging, decision. She decided that she'd give the gamblers more eyes, but no eyelids, so they could clearly see the fishy points flying towards them and the poo spheres gathering crushing speeds and all those lovely acidy streams coming a calling.

Then there was the whole Marsh problem and his re-animation to contend with. Nora promised that he was never ever going to have the opportunity to garner any more favours **again**, as he wasn't going to leave the Casino floor ever **again**.

His new role would be to test all of the games. Every day for an eternity. Nora felt slightly better now that she had a plan brewing although she wasn't sure how she'd make it happen. She was mindful that HR Sarah had warned them to stay out of other Hells politics or face the consequences.

"Nora, you're high on adrenaline and you'll crash soon my wee scone. You did a good thing, just keep that in mind when you realise you mutilated then killed someone. So, try not to breathe too deeply and keep your eyes down and stay away from the lights. I think we're about to go on one hellava mission to clean up this joint." A weary Devil Keith kissed Nora on her bruised forehead and took her shaking hand. He had forgotten HR Sarah's helpful advice. He warily opened the engine room's heavy iron door and held his breath. He just hoped that he remembered the way back to the Casino, and he prayed that the flatulent Octopus had a very short memory. Devil Keith brightened up when he reasoned that octopus were just big, lanky legged fish and fish, like a goldfish, only had a five second memory. With that in mind he thought that the Octopus wasn't a threat. Not at all. Oh dear, Devil Keith may be getting an encyclopaedias for his next birthday.

As an aside…Devil Keith was also plotting a series of new games. He decided that hedgehogs weren't feared nearly as much as they should be, and with that in mind he decided that he'd do something truly despicable with the wild hogs. He'd work out the details later but it was going to be bad. Really BAD. Epically bad.

CHAPTER FORTY-FIVE

A physically and emotionally exhausted Nora and Devil Keith stepped into Hell…

"Get him some clothes. Arggg, my poor eyes. I'm gonna puke." Harry gagged then turned away. Seeking comfort in a bloody big cushion, and a quick grab of her husband's taut bottom helped too.

"Wow, wow, wow. We're home." Devil Keith grabbed his Nora and gaily swung her around the room. Dancing, cartwheeling and wiggling his rather pert behind to a bizarre tune that resided solely, and thankfully, in his rather fine head. Nora requested the last sentence be added to the chapter, and after her harrowing journey the authors thought she deserved a wee treat.

After Devil Keith was bundled into an oversized, pink furry dressing gown. He, understandably, objected to the cut of the dressing gown and changed a further sixteen times before grumpily accepting the first gown. He had reluctantly agreed that it was big enough to snuggle both him and his exceedingly bloodthirsty wifey. Nora and Devil Keith squashed themselves into the corner of the sofa and proceeded to drink a bucket load of sweet tea, but they refused the heaped plate of delicious jammy dodgers. It was just too soon.

The excited and exasperated Hell team sat down for a much needed debrief. No Devil Keith did not take off his briefs because Harry had sneakily superglued them to his fussy personage.

Devil Keith and Nora began by returning Willing's

prized mallet and explaining that they had stored it away for safekeeping. The trusty adventurers then recounted their bizarre and frankly, horrific, learning experience. The relieved duo explained that the learning was to understand that it's an honour and a privilege to adequately and fairly punish the wicked. Also, cheating the system and cutting corners just doesn't work as it always comes back to bite you on the bum. Ahhh, that's the real reason why Devil Keith burned the eighth minor Dealer: the foolhardy Dealer had taken a bite out of Devil Keith's pert bum on the way into the furnace. Pummelled his liver? Ha! The authors aren't sure that Devil Keith knows where his liver is. His very own Live Organs Pictionary game invariably produced diagrams that looked remarkably like Ben Nevis, in autumn.

At the end of their tale Nora nervously suggested that they should consider giving back the second horn as they hadn't actually earned it, and it might have a hidden catch. A white elephant type of deal that might, again, bite them on the bum. Devil Keith was still smarting over that teethy insult to his personage so Nora gave his lush bottom a reassuring pat and applied a Power Puff Girl plaster to the teeny, tiny bruise. He briefly considered returning to the Gambling Hell so he could get that cowardly minor Dealer and make him pay some more. Nora whispered a much more appealing suggestion to Devil Keith. He stayed put on the sofa and there was some wriggling under the dressing gown. Devil Keith's hand emerged and he was happily holding a warm cottage pie with a side of green beans, a mound of cauliflower florets and suspicious looking grey fluff. It's really amazing what gets stuffed down the sides of cushions.

Nora also put forward the notion that the more horns the Hell had then the more corrupt the residents were likely to be: so it was inevitable that the Devils and demons were much more likely to lose the last remnants of their humanity due to proximity to that evil. She suggested that Hell number one was very likely to become a more dangerous, and disturbing, place for everyone if they decided to keep the extra horn. The team decided to ask HR Sarah about that as they weren't too keen on giving back the winnings and all those lovely boasting rights. Plus, Karen had commissioned an elaborate commemorative cup to mark the occasion...and an equally big display cabinet. Budget be damned. They'd live off baked beans on toast for the next month or two, plus there must be more cottage pie and veggies lurking under the sagging couch. Right?

After reading the room, Dr Riel decided to change the subject and asked where the residents, who only deserved one horn punishment, were now going. A surprisingly good question so it was added to the *"to do"* list. Just below *"need to set up some policies and procedures,"* and directly above, *"stop adding random punishments to residents just because we don't like them."* The last item contained some question marks and a badly drawn sketch of Jonathan. Jonathan in a bathtub full of irate porcupines and fluffy skunks. The whole random punishment manifesto was currently up for a much contested vote, but Harry had bought an extra-large bath tub in case she won. Her speech was awesome. A thing of true beauty.

Other items on the to do list included, *"we maybe shouldn't take big baddies in our Hell as we don't have the equipment or the expertise to deal with them".* However, this was followed by, *"urgently need to get some new equipment and some expertise to deal with the big baddies in our Hell."* The very last item on the list was, *"stop adding odd things to the to do list, and get someone who can actually draw to do our diagrams of Jonathan (they look a bit pathetic and not at all threatening just now)".*

The very, very top item on the to do list was *"let's celebrate, with a big, silly cookie bun party, when Nora and Devil Keith stop swanning around and raking under the couch."* Devil Keith scored out swanning around and wrote a huge list of things they had done. Things like: saving Hell, learning loads, saving Hell, avoiding alligators, saving Hell, locating Lord Lucan, saving Hell, searching for batteries, saving Hell, locating Jimmy Hoffa's luxury pad, saving Hell and correctly answering ridiculously difficult riddles. He stopped writing when his pen ran out of ink and Harry steadfastly refused to give him some of her precious blood to refill the pen. She'd learned the hard way that Devil Keith frequently created secret blood oaths that way, and she was still working off the last one. She'd spent years, unsuccessfully, teaching a troupe of wild boar exemplary table manners and the correct use of a fish-knife, only to find that the naughty pigs preferred sushi.

CHAPTER FORTY-SIX

A big, silly cookie bun party, because Nora and Devil Keith had stopped swanning around…

The Hell number one Oracles had been invited to the party but they were unable to attend as they were, excitedly, helping out at the exclusive Nile Headquarters. The resident Nile Oracles were usually excellent at predicting buying trends, but they had recently come across a puzzling and persistent issue. Their most recent Nile prophesies were saturated with dire warnings of doom and imminent world destruction. Plus, there were all the projections of mass sales of rubber rings, umbrellas, cattle prods and earplugs. The Hell number one Oracles were drafted in to see if they could help out. Karen wasn't convinced that their Oracles could find their arses whilst using both their hands, but she had joyously waved them off on their merry way.

The day before the party Devil Keith had taken control of Hell number one's kitchen and was planning on producing a deconstructed menu that heavily featured bales of damp mouldy straw, hessian sacks packed full of dust and lightly steamed turnip tops. He very quickly suffered a debilitating injury, due to a mysterious rolling-pin to the head incident. So he was dizzily re-assigned to the bunting making table. An essential task that Devil Keith knew would earn him many, many medals and was sure to be a page turner in his highly anticipated autobiography.

Willing was rushing around with piles of fresh laundry

then hiding them in cupboards and bracing her body against the bulging doors. She then began warning people to avoid opening the doors in case there was a crop of catastrophic linen avalanches. She only had to dig Devil Keith out twice from a load of souvenir dishtowels, so her warnings were obviously working.

John O and Vinnie valiantly, and occasionally grumpily, moved all the heavy furniture out of Karen's office. This was in order to create a spacious dance floor and a glitzy karaoke stage. Ten minutes later, after cracking their aching joints, John O and Vinnie moved it all back because the buffet table was going in that precise spot. The chocolate fountain urgently needed access to an electrical socket. Plus, the unfortunate karaoke machine had suffered a mysterious rolling-pin to the deck, a whack to the microphone and a belt to the speaker, so the stage and dance floor were no longer required. Harry so loved her new, portable, problem-solving wooden kitchen tool.

Harry took over in the kitchen and immediately barred the perpetually starving Bub from the unsolicited tasting table. Despite ruining the line of his rather dapper suits he had taken to carrying his very own folding testing table so that he could adequately critique any, and all menus. She had also confiscated a large box of coconut snowballs and three tins of pineapple rings in syrup, as they gave her Bub terrible nightmares and she couldn't afford to keep replacing her shredded goonies (Scottish word for nighties).

Gab and Bub were tasked with dusting down the antique cobwebs and chasing away the fist-sized spiders. Fachance was supposed to be in charge of the music, but she was mostly just eating the more spritely arachnids. Afterall, they were full of protein and she had a new spool of minty dental floss, so the long hairy legs were relatively easy to pluck from between her sparkling teeth.

Karen and Dr Riel hid away in order to complete a complex Party Risk Assessment, and catalogue the gumminess of their orange sticking plasters. This activity seemed to comprise of noises that sounded remarkably like a very long adult-swing testing session was in progress.

Meanwhile, the unusually subdued Nora filled dinosaur party bags with bottles of bubbles, finger puppets and slinkies. She also helped Devil Keith gulp down the gas in the helium balloons as she enjoyed a squeaky wee chat with her guy. Dr Riel encouraged this as he felt that anything that made her smile was positive and should be enthusiastically embraced by the team. Nora had gone through such a harrowing ordeal in the Gambling Hell. An ordeal that still had her whimpering during the night and clasping onto Devil Keith for support and reassurance. Her adrenal rush had quickly evaporated and she could still smell Devil Keith's roasting flesh in her nightmares. So Devil Keith had vowed to do anything to bring back the smile on the face of his feisty wee Scottish wife.

HR Sarah was genuinely delighted with the learning experience and very impressed that Hell number one was back to full working order. She had suffered many a doubt about the whole escapade especially as Nora was an unknown entity and Devil Keith was... well Devil Keith. As a special treat she had spoken with her dancer friend Angela, and requested that the "*Treubh Dannsa Performance Petals of Falkirk*" provide the entertainment for the much-discussed party. As Dancer Angela and HR Sarah were the Belly dancing choreographers they talked up Hell number one and persuaded the troupe into undertaking the unconventional performance. Vinnie and John O were creating a dancefloor and back on furniture moving detail. Oh joy! Yet more moaning from the lads.

CHAPTER FORTY-SEVEN

The day of the party and the dancers arrive…

The heroes entered the party and awaited their applause. Devil Keith then turned tail and entered the party again, and yet again. He decided that his lemon and white striped shirt teamed with a black bowtie just wasn't creating the correct first impression, hence the lack of snivelling gratitude and cheering from the Hell team. He nipped off to change into his midnight blue shirt that was decorated with illuminous jellyfish, a pair of orange crocs that were sporting larger than usual headlights and a pair of candy pink pantaloons. He then sprang into the room and yelled "ta ra". There was a gasp and someone may have fainted. Still got it, he thought. Nora wore a classic 1950's swing dress in aubergine and pale yellow, that was paired with a string of freshwater pearls. She was a stylish hit and did deserve her delighted gasp and round of applause.

The entertainment arrived…

Harry was equally surprised and delighted to see Brownie Mirka descend into Hell number one. He had no idea that the Brownie Biker Chick was part of the Falkirk dancers. After a wee cuddle from Devil Keith and Nora, Brownie Mirka was busy picking at an awesome knee scab, widely smiling at the team and reassuring them all that she was still on the wagon. Well that's what Devil Keith said Brownie Mirka was saying. No one was able to confirm this so they just nodded and admired Brownie Mirka's latest badge: blindfolded jigsaw puzzle completing, first class. Harry's laughing friend, Amanda, was quizzing the Brownie as she was very impressed with the achievement. Amanda is an avid jigsawer and wanted to make sure that the Brownie had completed the outside edges first before adding pieces to the middle. They were completed first ...yahoo!

The rest of the dancers...

Beautiful Dancer Junko was practicing her hip isolations by carefully carrying a glass of delicious rhubarb and ginger gin on her head, whilst shaking her money maker. She was equally reassuring the Hell management team that she was **not**, in fact, on the wagon and that she doesn't actually make money by jiggling in that way. She finished her speech with a complicated shimmy and threw a handful of delightful origami frogs in the air. Her shimmy was especially complicated because she was expertly folding the trickly paper amphibians at the exact same time as she was executing the sexy move.

As a dancing inducement, Dancer Lorraine had been promised an audience with a real, live Angel. In preparation for the meeting she had humphed in a large painting of an Angel, that she had completed a few months before. After catching her breath, she then compared her stunning painting to an expectant and excited Gab. Holding it against his face then loudly tutting, holding it against his muscle-packed chest and repeatedly shaking her head. She confidently told him that his eyes did not match the ones in her painting, therefore he could not be a real, live Angel. She sent the perplexed Gab off to check his face in the over-mantle mirror. Fachance, in her role as Horsewoman of Famine, gallantly offered to eat the offending painting but Gab refused to take her up on her wonderfully kind suggestion. He quite liked the thought of finally being captured in acrylics or oils: he wasn't fussy. Gab had planned on auditioning for the Sistine Chapel, Angel-model rollcall in 1483. However, he slept in that morning and lost out to Angel Raphael. Ever since that lengthy, and unfortunate napping incident, he had deeply regretted not being on the exalted ceiling. Gab also secretly thought that he, rather than Raphael, would have made it into the Teenage Mutant Hero Turtles franchise if not for that blasted nap. So Angel Gab reassured Fachance that he'd take to wearing coloured contact lenses if that helped make the new painting happen. However, he steadfastly refused to give up his camouflage gear in order to don a mini toga and shave his shapely legs, but Dancer Lorraine was quietly confident that she could change his mind.

Curvaceous Dancer Julie was in one of the corners. She was wriggling her way into her black fishnet stockings, silky French knickers and red lacy Basque. She was also repeatedly telling Devil Keith that she didn't need him or his devices to make it any easier to get into her costume. After a few stinging hand slappings, a poke in the chest (Devil Keith's manly chest) and a good old-fashioned telling off, Devil Keith with his head hanging low hurried away from the naughty Julie. He was going to tell his Nora on her. So there!

Dancer Gayle was frowning at her glittering headdress and furiously tugging a brush through her short blonde hair. She was desperately trying to dislodge some mighty resistant, dried in glue from her tousled tresses. The glue was from her Christmas wreath making class: despite it now being the middle of May. Devil Keith decided to magnanimously assist Gayle as he was full of, ever so, helpful suggestions and gadgets. She too has just been reported to Nora for being "*unreasonable*" and being a heartless chest poker.

"Erm, could someone have a wee word with Dancer Joanne and ask her to keep her Arbroath Smokies earrings in the fridge

until she really, really, really needs them?" Dancer Gail was dragging in her biggest blackboard, a huge box of white chalk, a bushel of apples and several school rulers. She could never find enough of those pesky rulers. It was as if someone was eating them. Dancer Gail then got to work scribbling convoluted equations on the previously pristine board. She was busy formulating a plan that ensured that there was adequate space for the dance performance and all the intricate moves that entailed. She was also rapidly calculating how far people had to stay away from the glamorous Dancer Joanne and her less than glamorous fishy jewellery.

There were fears that Dancer Lindsay wouldn't be fit to dance as she had a pronounced limp and was tilting dangerously to the side. Dancer Joanne reassured everyone that Dancer Lindsay was fine. She was just a little off balance due to her bizarre handbag fetish. Apparently, Dancer Lindsay was a big Mary Poppins fan and as such there was everything you could ever need stored in her large tartan clutch bag. Dancer Lindsay proved that point by pulling out eleven sets of turquoise beaded bikinis, a broken flare gun, a twelve foot blowup orca and a fully waxed surf board. Well they hoped the orca was a blowup or there was something mighty fishing going on over in Dancer Julie's corner. Ah, an update. Julie was just wrestling with a smaller than average live killer whale... and she was winning. My that's a relief: Dancer Joanne's flavoursome earrings were safe from whale mastication for another night.

"Now, wee Dancer Morgan may not be able to dance tonight. She has a bad back as she's just moved house and needs a surprisingly big bed for someone so tiny." HR/Dancer Sarah asked Julie and Lorraine to send Morgan some warm healing and kind thoughts. And some king-size fitted bed sheets.

There was someone missing from the limber gang. *"Hmm, Dancer Karolyn's not here tonight. She left an odd message* *on my phone saying that her pet dragon had drank some of her French Kiss cocktail and had choked on the rubber tongue. I think Karolyn was a little bit tipsy and meant to say her pet **cat**. Although I'm not sure what the tongue was all about."* Dancer Joanne innocently smiled and shrugged her narrow shoulders. HR/Dancer Sarah thought that Dancer Karolyn probably wasn't all that tipsy as she had previously noticed a bit of singeing on Karolyn's blonde eyebrows. Plus, there was that strange and lingering scent of horse that Karolyn was struggling with.

The performance...

The belly-dancers all lined up and the hypnotic music started. There were whirls, turns and leaps aplenty. Followed by hip swivels, skip-steps and shimmies galore as the purple and grey tartan clad, talented women commanded the Hell dance floor. The final pose and the mystical music faded. The applause was deafening and long. Very long. Devil Keith decided that he needed to add a few dance steps to his wardrobe.

Dancer Angela shyly asked the Hell management to join her and the troupe for an impromptu dance lesson. The appreciative audience readily agreed and the place was in an uproar with traditional Camel dance moves being swapped for the infinitely easier Dying Giraffe Gyrations.

Disclaimer: No animals were injured during the writing of this rather smashing book.

CHAPTER FORTY-EIGHT

The festivities, fun and food for afters...

"Fantastic dancing and bobbing and twirling. I liked that thing you did with your left buttock, but I think my Nora did it better than you did. She's such a natural at bottom jiggles. Her bum cheeks can wobble for over five minutes after she finishes climbing the stairs. She's adorably jelly like. Anyway, enough of my cherub's talents. You must be famished. Help yourself to the buffet. There's lots." Devil Keith swept his open palm magnanimously over the heavily laden table and stepped away with a flourishing bow.

"Oh I meant to tell you that I'm a vegan so I doubt you'll have anything there for Dancer Joanne and I, but it's totally all right. These things happen. I usually bring my own Tupperware box but it slipped my mind. I think it was the 'fireman lifts' and robust bottom pats that the cockroaches insisted we all needed that put me off. Is all of Hell obsessed with posteriors?" Dancer Angela smiled brightly and checked her handbag for a stray polo mint. She picked off the fluff and popped, what she hoped was a mint sweetie, into her mouth. The day before she had found what she thought was a brownish coloured Fisherman's Friend menthol lozenge in her coat pocket. Unfortunately, once it was on her tongue she belatedly realised that it was just a buffed up, brownish stained indigestion tablet. She ate it anyway: waste not want not.

"Posteriors? I have no idea what you mean. Wait. You could

be right. The authors never seem to spell check the word bum or the word bottom as they use it so often. Maybe we are all obsessed. Is that a bad thing? Text me later with your answer. We need to eat just now. Fachance is prowling.

Well, following a rather harrowing adventure I too have decided to adopt a vegan diet so everything here should meet your needs. But I'd steer clear of the big blue bowl in the centre of the table...it's full of chicken pate and buttered elephant tusk toast. Oh, and the big red flowery plate has a full side of Scottish salmon under all that yucky thinly sliced cucumber. Ah yes, whilst we're on the topic of fish...the red flowery bowl and come to think of it, the green dish over there, are jampacked with flaked tuna lips and chicken breast salad. There might be a bit of poached whale tucked down the side too.

Oh, in case you're in any doubt: that ostrich is very much dead but the woman chewing on its scrawny leg is very much alive. I'd avoid her when she's eating. Mind you, that's nearly all of the time. Isn't it my munchy friend?" Devil Keith hesitantly waved at a growling Fachance then counted his fingers. And toes.

"Ah, back to you and the bountiful vegan choices. There's a couple of dozen devilled eggs in the bottom of that salad bowl and that salad, over there, is just a plain old side of rare topside beef smothered in suet pastry. The small glass dishes are full of Beluga caviar and not black peppercorns. I found to my infinite surprise. And the rather large chicken shaped tray... well that's just a great big roast chicken full of sausage and onion stuffing. You could pick out the onions and blow on them, if you like. Your hands look clean enough."

"So the small dish of cherry tomatoes? Are they ok?" Dancer Angela was looking at Devil Keith rather oddly. Devil Keith had expected quite a bit of gratitude by that point in the culinary conversation.

"Well yes, if you like them tossed in a bit of melted lard and tripled cooked they'd do nicely." Devil Keith looked around the heaving table.

"The chocolate fountain in the centre of the table. Well

someone with divine tastebuds dropped a tiny bit of chorizo in there earlier, so that might or might not work for you. Do you like sweet and salty vegan delights? I can tell you that they're simply heavenly.

Oh, I can see from your face that the buffet may be too sophisticated for your Falkirkanian basic palate." Devil Keith tutted and fluffed his hair. He looked over the table then pointed, and huffily added. *"Ah, there it is. See that glass bowl hanging over the far edge of the table?"*

"The bowl with the brown edged, curling lettuce and weird lumpy bits? That bowl?" Dancer Angela politely enquired and tried to talk over the noise of her rumbling tummy.

"Yes, that's the ticket. Although, come to think of it, the salad dressing might be a wee bitty meaty. And a touch fishy. And have a hint of cheesiness. I do enjoy playing with a grater or two in Harry's kitchen. Head injury be damned, I always say. That is a widely used Scottish saying, right?" Devil Keith enquired and nodded enthusiastically at the softly giggling dancer.

Dancer Angela shook her head and burst into peals of laughter. *"I've never heard of it before but I did hear that I should avoid falling rolling pins while I'm here. I'll bring my own food the next time. Shall I?"*

"Jolly good. You don't mind if I tuck into the vegan buffet then?" Devil Keith said, through a mouthful of partridge stuffed swan. He'd go chorizo divining in the melted chocolate later. His last attempt had been less than successful, and the grumpy garden gnome wanted his fishing rod back first thing in the morning so Devil Keith needed to get a bit of a move on.

The wildly popular night finished with lots of warm cuddles and promises of jugs of icy cocktails and multiple coffee morning dates. The dancers left with pockets full of lasagne and Lindsay's bag was chock-a-block full with warm minestrone soup. HR/Dancer Sarah, a chortling Amanda and Brownie Mirka nipped off home to put their feet up. The satisfied Hell team settled down with a few pints of Falkirk

Sewer and a family pack of cheese and onion crisps. Life was good.

CHAPTER FORTY-NINE

The party was winding down...

"I'm heading to bed. I'm all done in. Karen, I'll help with the cleaning in the morning. No Devil Keith, please, you stay. Have some time to catch up with your bro and the wild team. I know you've been looking at those Spacehoppers and positively salivating. And I know you're desperate for a race around the office tonight. Consider tonight a practice run and I'll beat you all, tomorrow.

I'll clean my teeth and snuggle in with a good book. I'll save all the naughty bits to read to you later. Meow my lover." Nora kissed her Devil Keith. He tucked a curl behind her tiny ear and she shyly smiled. Then, with a tonsil displaying yawn, she headed off to a soft warm bed. Dr Riel made a mental note to contact Brownie Arlene for advice, as he felt that Nora needed some professional assistance to help with adjusting to Hell and its many foibles. Well, anyone would...they're all bonkers down here.

Karen looked around at the mess, shook her head and decided that she just couldn't wait until the morning. Her OCD was giving her awful hives and a rampant case of the burps. It all needed sorted before the cocoa, whisky and box of dominoes came out to play. Plus, she just knew that Nora wouldn't wait for help and would do all the cleaning up, on her own, before they woke up. So Jonathan was called from his prison cell and informed that he would be doing the tidying up for them. This, along with serving at the party, was his punishment for trying to steal Hell and lodging those insulting evictions notices all over the place. Sticking them to the lid of the gents toilets was just plain crass.

Thirty minutes later...

Dr Riel couldn't take it any longer and he was gently fuming. Jonathan was reluctantly carrying one small item from the cluttered table and slowly trudging over to the office doorway. Dragging his feet and hunching his rounded shoulders the whole way. At the door he would drop the item: making sure that he made as much noise as possible before he dramatically slid down the wall and onto the floor. Sighing and groaning all the way down. After a few exclamations and threats from Karen, he slowly crawled from the floor and leisurely slouched back to the burgeoning table. Looking over his shoulder and sneering at the exasperated team the whole time. He then repeated the entire moody process verbatim. Although he did add some colourful, if mumbled, threats of his own to the routine so there was some entertainment to be had. Although his much repeated misogyny ideology and homophobic comments, and his general hatred of all people was now getting a bit tiresome.

After a particularly well-acted teenage strop and drop, Dr Riel leapt to his feet and grabbed handfuls of his hair. *"No, no. I just can't watch this drama any longer. He's doing it deliberately so we'll get fed-up and let him off with it. I'm not having it. I'll deal with this. Karen, please get one of Stan's kidnap proof glasses and some rope."* Karen whispered that all their rope was currently spoken for. Dr Riel raised his brows and gave her a wide cheeky grin.

Jonathan stood in the middle of the room and threw a filthy scowl at the mighty satisfied Dr Riel. Jonathan was wearing a large, floppy straw hat tied under the chin with a wide cream and green polka dot ribbon. There was a pint glass, tied with the same ribbon, attached to the hat's brim. The pint glass was kidnap proof and was designed so that it would shout, *"help, help me…I'm being robbed,"* when it was removed from a pub, bar or restaurant. Dr Riel had cleverly set the permitted perimeter to the size of Karen's office, but that wasn't stopping the Hell team from making Jonathan step across the office threshold and into the adjoining corridor. Jonathan was nearly deafened every time the glass started to squeal and seek assistance from the giggling team.

After a great deal of laughter and gentle ribbing, the Hell team decided that Jonathan was going to drag the cleaning on all night so they all pitched in to finish the onerous job. Scrapping plates, wiping down tables, collecting rubbish, vacuuming up invasive pink confetti, sweeping floors and trundling the kitchen trollies out to the waiting lifts. All completed whilst practising their newly acquired belly dancing moves, laughing at each other's hip breaking gyrations and generally gossiping about nonsense.

Devil Keith and Bub were briefly banished up a couple of ladders to bunting removal duties. This was in response to their highly competitive spicy sausage fishing expeditions in the chocolate fountain and their side of salmon wrestling bouts. Harry's lavish side bets were making her an absolute mint although she didn't make the money she expected on the Spacehopper racing: Karen was a fiend at the old bouncing.

As a final punishment Jonathan, and his exuberantly complaining hat, were sent off to Devil Keith's room with a huge pile of slippery bunting. He was warned, on pain of death, not to disturb the sleeping Nora and he was instructed to leave the bundle outside the bedroom door. Devil Keith would move it later. The Hell team listened to the complaining glass as it was "*stolen*" up the corridor. They reached for the whisky decanters, poured a liberal measure of the amber nectar and put their dance achy feet on a comfy foot stool. Life was now very good.

A couple of minutes later and Jonathan lazily sauntered back into the tidy room. Whistling a merry tune and stopping every few steps to do a quick cha-cha-cha move. *"Devil Keith, Devil Keith. Nora no longer has a squint in her eye. In fact, she won't have to worry about that ever again."* Jonathan giggled and sipped some creamy egg nog before promptly stepping to the right and pointing to the door. *"Although you might have to get your carpets cleaned. Afterall, getting blood out of lilac shag pile is a pure bitch."*

CHAPTER FIFTY

Chaos ensued...

Crystal glasses, shot glasses, antique decanters and padded foot stools were thrown in the air as the team shouted, scrambled and raced from Karen's office, up the short corridor and towards Devil Keith's room. Bub was in front of the baying team: he could smell the overwhelming, and unmistakable, warmed iron scent of blood and the raw stench of death. He stopped in the corridor: at the bedroom doorway and staunchly braced his hands against the doorframe. He was attempting to bar a panicked and howling Devil Keith from entering the bloody scene. To stop his brother seeing the heart wrenching sight, so they could all pretend that this just wasn't happening.

Devil Keith's Nora was lying just inside the doorway of their shared bedroom. Still and pale in a pool of rapidly congealing blood. A look of utter dread captured on her slightly imperfect face.

Devil Keith didn't stop. Not for one moment. He savagely grabbed Bub by the throat and bodily shoved him into the dimly lit room. Devil Keith swiftly followed his partially throttled brother. Barging into the room and collapsing, on his knees, onto the red soaked floor. Nora's slender throat was splayed open. Sliced from ear to ear and so deep was the cut that her previously white spinal column was exposed for all to see. The assailant meant to behead his beautiful wife. His Nora.

Devil Keith was on his knees and gently shaking his Nora

by her slim shoulders. *"Wake up, Wake up my Dozy Dumpling. You've spilled something all over your lovely dress. Please Nora, wake the fuck up. We'll use a bucket of cold water to soak it and it will all come out. You love this dress and I can make it all better again."* Devil Keith had lifted Nora's head and shoulders off the floor. He began shaking his Nora some more and trying to scoop the sticky blood back into the gash in her neck. Her neck was floppy and her head was lolling towards the floor.

Devil Keith pressed his ear against her stilled heart. He looked up at Gab and whispered. *"Angel. She'll be alright. Her head's still attached. It's only a flesh wound. I'll just buy my Nora a fancy choker so she can hide the cut, until it's all better."* Devil Keith lovingly gazed at his Nora and lightly pushed back her unruly brown hair. *"I can't believe you scared me like that, you silly cookie bun. Now open your eyes and I'll get some yellow ribbon for your new necklace. You like yellow. You can choose your own pendant. Anything you want, and we can add that tomorrow. Now come on, now. You're scaring me, now. No, more kidding around or I'm going to get so angry with you. You've never seen me really angry, but you will."* Devil Keith went back to roughly shaking his limp Nora, then hugging her to his heaving chest. Tears, blood and snot was drenching Devil Keith's shirt and trailing over Nora's still, breathless body.

"Devil Keith, Devil Keith. She has gone, my friend. I am so sorry to have to say this. It is not a mere scratch. She is only human so she cannot survive an injury like that. Devil Keith, let Bub and I lift Nora onto the sofa so Dr Riel can start cleaning her up. She would want to look nice for you. Wouldn't she? We can then help clean you up and sort out the floor." Gab reached down past Devil Keith and tenderly placed his hand on Nora's pale, cooling arm. Devil Keith grabbed Gab's outstretched hand and ripped it clean off at the wrist. The Angel yelled out in sudden, blistering pain.

"Liar. You liar. You're not sorry. Not sorry at all. No one touches my beautiful Nora. No one. She's just sleeping and doesn't like to be disturbed when she's sleeping. It makes her grouchy and if

my Nora is grouchy then so am I. You're nothing but a big fat liar. All of you. Liars." Devil Keith growled then gave a small yelp. He bared his rapidly sharpening teeth and barked, then snapped at the Angel. He pulled Nora more firmly onto his wide lap. Enclosing her frail, dead body in his ridged arms. Devil Keith flicked his long blackened tongue over his thinning, chapped lips. He finished his accusation by sniggering then contemptuously curling his purple lips at the weeping team. He was rapidly descending into full demon.

Angel Gab held his dripping, bloody stump against his body and gently slid the dangling tendons, ligaments and scraps of muscle back into the ragged hole that use to be his wrist. He subtly shook his head at the confused Hell team: a warning to stay back from imminent danger. He held his uninjured hand out to Fachance, as he was concerned about how she would react to his wound. He was anxious that she might take a chunk or two out of the despairing, sobbing man. He feared that would cause the room to descend into utter carnage and they were facing enough problems at the moment.

Fachance gave him a small reassuring smile and softly rubbed Gab's glistening cheek. She tore off a length of her dress to use as a bandage and looked over at Dr Riel. She pointed at Devil Keith then mouthed. "*Can you do something? Gab will heal pretty quickly but I'm not so sure about Devil Keith. Is he going demon, do you think? Or full Devil?*" Fachance had heard about Devil Keith's ability to transform into a demonic beast, but that hadn't prepared her for the rapid changes she was currently witnessing. Devil Keith was turning into a snarling, spitting monster before their eyes.

Dr Riel mournfully shook his head and pulled a sobbing Karen into his comforting arms. Drawing comfort from each other, they subtly rocked and cried.

"Please Gab can you help? Can you bring Nora back? Can you ask God for some help?" Harry pleaded and softly stroked Devil

Keith's hair. Worryingly she felt a small horn bursting through his scalp. Devil Keith grunted and hissed at a startled Harry. Bub was rhythmically rubbing Willing's back and holding Harry's other hand. Aware that he may have to quickly pull Harry away from danger: to a safe distance from his distraught brother. If there even was a safe distance.

John O and Vinnie were silently standing against the wall and keeping away from the anguish ridden scene. They were helpless and felt they were invading the grief-stricken scene.

A pale Gab gravely nodded at Harry and left them in order to speak to God. He appeared extremely stressed when he returned to the sorrowfully stunned group: less than an hour later.

"I spoke with God but she is in a bit of a tizzy just now as the world appears to be tilting off its axis. She knew that a significant tragedy had transpired but she was not sure what it was.

I told her about Nora and the murder. She began gasping and breathing via a paper bag. The bag did not help. Not at all. I have never seen God like that. Her whole face collapsed in inconsolable grief. She told me that she was afraid that something unspeakable had happened, but Devil Keith and Nora's situation never occurred to her.

She then told me that she had reasoned that, as Nora was human, they would have a full sixty years before Devil Keith lost his true love and started the Apocalypse. It turns out your baffling Oracles were correct when they could not define the precise outcome of the apocalyptic prophesy. They had surmised that Devil Keith loving Nora might, or might not cause, the Apocalypse. In a round about way that is accurate. As we have witnessed: loving Nora made him a better person so the world could improve but, on the flip side, losing her would be catastrophic. Hence their confusion and hedging their bets. Your Oracles are not very good at their job and should be replaced. I would suggest placing a job advert as soon as possible.

With that in mind God tried her best to bring Nora back

but no matter how hard she strained there seemed to be an impregnable barrier blocking the difficult process. It was as if Nora, herself, did not want to return. It makes no sense. No sense at all.

After leaving a baffled God, I spoke with C.C. He immediately agreed to help but when he tried to turn back time he developed acute laryngitis and went into violent muscle spasms. He could neither speak nor move. Not even his panic stricken eyes could blink. I have never heard of anything quite like that either. His wife is beside herself with worry and when I left she was in the middle of ordering a two ton box of caramel flavoured popcorn. For express delivery, no less. I think we may have to be careful what we eat and drink from now on. Absolutely no ice cubes, I would say." Tears were rolling freely down Gab's cheeks as he knew that Nora had a pure, innocent soul and he feared that Devil Keith would not recover from her loss.

"I know this is of little comfort but I have brought some washing powder with me and I will find out the truth. Just give me a few minutes to wash out my shirt and I shall begin the tricky process." Gab patted the pocket on his camouflage jacket then grabbed the edge of his shirt and made to pull it over his head.

The lights went out and the room was plunged into thick, impenetrable darkness. There was a faint brr-ing sound then the lights came back on. Gab and his truth inducing powder were gone and a small mound of sawdust rested on the floor.

"Where is my Gab?" Fachance started shouting, wailing and throwing heavy furniture against the wall, where Gab had so recently stood. Devil Keith hunched over his Nora: trying to protect his wife from injury whilst plotting how to destroy Fachance, the unhinged lunatic. If he didn't stop her soon then Fachance could hurt his Nora, his brain screamed at him.

Devil Keith rose to his feet. His unkempt toenails snagging on the crispy carpet. He lunged at the distressed and startled Fachance. Bub, Dr Riel, Vinnie, John O and Willing leapt at Devil Keith and held him back from the skreiching Fachance. Bub spotted a familiar green, canvas rucksack propped up in the far corner. Breathing heavily he frantically nodded at Harry. Harry grabbed the weighty bag, dragged it across the floor and rummaged inside. With some difficulty and an undamaged chair to stand on, Harry threw a heavy iron net over the powerful Devil Keith. Harry pulled the shaken Fachance to safety and hugged her tightly. Whilst the exhausted team pegged the net, and a thrashing Devil Keith, to a blood free area of the floor.

Meanwhile Karen crouched over. Trying to shield Nora's cooling body and preserve the remaining evidence. They had a murderer to catch.

CHAPTER FIFTY-ONE

The diabolical story begins…

A sniffling Karen reluctantly left Nora's vulnerable body and exited Devil Keith's crowded room. She promptly returned with a camera, a measuring tape and a couple of yellow note books. She had quickly realised that, even though they were all distraught, they needed to capture as much information as possible from the crime scene. It appeared that with every second some vital clue was disappearing. Everyone had trampled through the blood and left bloody footprints over the floor, so trying to follow a blood trail to the culprit was already lost. Plus the chairs, that Fachance, imbedded in the walls needed to be carefully removed as there may have been evidence caught in the flying objects. And lastly, Harry had just dragged a bloody great big bag through the crime scene and the Hell team had scrambled over the scene whilst attempting to restrain Devil Keith.

Devil Keith was thrashing against the sturdy net whilst making vile and anatomically improbable threats against the Hell team. Well everyone hoped they were improbable and impossible otherwise things were going to go downhill very fast.

Harry was gently stroking Fachance's hair whilst studiously avoiding her razor sharp incisors. She was also trying to come up with a viable plan of action. A highly complex and dangerous task at the best of times, but adding Harry's tears and copious snot to the scenario made it even more perilous. *"Fachance, we don't know what's going on just now. All I can say is that Gab is a fighter and a survivor. If he was taken, or if he was pushed into another dimension then he will survive."*

"I'll strip the meat from the bones of the unlucky person who harms him. I'll suck out their marrow and slurp up their liquified organs." Fachance was baring her straight, white teeth and licking her pale pink lips. Imagining Bub topped with a golden puff pastry lid and drowning in rich gravy.

"Fachance, I'm not sure that's helpful at the moment. And will you stop looking at Bub and rubbing your portable cutlery set? He didn't do it and it's really quite off putting. Especially with everything else that's going on just now." Harry sniffled and gently patted Bub's outstretched hand.

"Fachance I didn't touch the lights or Gab. However, there are a few scenarios we need to consider. Number one: someone used the missing Dimensional Drill to remove Gab before he could use the truth serum washing powder to disclose their identity. Number two: Gab used the Drill to escape after killing our Nora. Number three: we have a murderer in this room with us. Number four: someone else snuck into Hell to do this and they may still be on the premises. Number five: someone snuck into Hell to kill Nora and left with Gab and the Drill. Are we all in agreement that those are ***all*** *the possible explanations? If you've any other suggestions please feel free to speak up. Fachance, I know you don't want to even think about this, but please stop threatening us and sharpening your teeth on Devil Keith's sewing machine foot-pedal. We need you to think, not eat."* All heads reluctantly nodded at Bub and they looked at each with equal measures of fear, anger and suspicion in their eyes.

"We can't use God to aid us as she is so busy just now and I don't think there's anything she can actually do for us. We can't contact the police as well... we don't have a police force and we don't have time to recruit and train one. So that leaves us. We have to bring the criminal to justice, find Gab and care for our Devil Keith." Karen scrubbed her eyes. She opened her note book and placed the nib of the pen on the paper. She knew they had to

start but she just wasn't sure how to do that. How could this have happened? Especially after how well things were going.

Bub looked down at Devil Keith and wiped away a stray tear. His brother was tortured with sorrow and rage. He took a calming breath. "*Right. Let's begin. We need to divide our limited resources in order to find the killer.*

I propose that Willing and Fachance look after Hell number one. Hell is still in a very precarious management position and we can't spare anyone if we have to do some sort of learning debacle again. Plus, they can monitor Jonathan, as we can't trust him. Not at all. He could be in league with the killer. Unfortunately, Willing and Fachance, your first management act is to find that snivelling ratbag and pass him onto the investigators. I'll come to all that in a moment.

I don't think that we should tell Stan and Dippit about Nora. They have enough going on just now what with the pregnancy and Dippit's continued risk of fainting. Plus Stan's made it clear that he's only contactable if the world is ending in twenty minutes or less and we aren't anywhere close to that. Well not just yet. Fingers crossed.

John O and Vinnie are proven, successful hunters so I propose that we dispatch them to help find the Time Scavenger that's stored in the Oracles under-stair cupboard. If we can warn one of us from the past they can then protect Nora from the killer so none of this can happen. Well, that's the thought anyway. I'm not sure if that will work but it's worth a shot. To be honest I think we should try anything and everything to resolve this horrible incident including potentially wrecking some of the Oracle's precious timeline.

Myself and Dr Riel will look after Devil Keith and keep him safe. We might not be quite so lucky but again, it's worth the risk. Karen told me that there is an icehouse situated in Callendar Park, in Falkirk. They're old but well-built structures with limited access and the walls are so thick that all sounds should be safely muffled from the humans. Plus, with the way Devil Keith's crying and letting loose other bodily fluids the ice drain with come in really handy.

That leaves Karen and Harry to conduct the investigation. They have the most experience in this area and I trust their judgement. Explicitly.

You'll have noticed that I've paired you all up. This isn't like a cheesy horror movie where we all act alone and put ourselves in perpetual and stupid danger. This is real life so be careful and keep in constant contact with one another. I'll have new mobile phones and chargers ready for us all as soon as possible. Please use them for more than catching up with the latest soap opera gossip." Bub added the last comment in a failed bid to lighten the sombre mood.

"Are we all in agreement?" Bub gave everyone a hard stare. He left the room to raid Karen's secret supply of phones.

The Hell team solemnly nodded and shuffled off to fulfil their tasks. Fachance was leaning heavily on Willing for support as she sniffed and quietly sobbed, then left the room. Only pausing to look down at Nora and quietly whisper goodbye. They also kept their more valuable body parts away from a highly imaginative Devil Keith.

CHAPTER FIFTY-TWO

Karen's office...

Bub hugged a worried Harry and assured her that he would be safe as he had faced worse dangers and succeeded. Harry didn't want him to go but she couldn't come up with a good enough reason for Bub to stay. Karen and Dr Riel were having a similar conversation although Karen had thoughtfully packed a Tupperware box of cheese and pickle sandwiches and a two gallon thermos of coffee for the darling doctor. Karen had heroically fought off a scowling Vinnie for the rights to the hot brew: such was her love for Dr Riel.

Dr Riel and Bub had reluctantly and tearfully left Hell number one with the heaving, whimpering and snarling mass that was their desolated Devil Keith. The unusually obliging cockroaches had already delivered seventeen large trunks of clothing and other essentials to the Falkirk icehouse. After Devil Keith's last brush with the Deadly Sins he had made the strangely sane decision to pack sixteen "*go bags*" or "*go trunks*" in case it all happened again. They were similar to hospital bags, although they did appear to carry more bedazzled clothing items than was strictly necessary for any possible occasion. Plus, some mighty sharp weapons were warmly tucked into the trunk's false bottoms and there were boxes upon boxes of full-size luxury toiletries (no mere samples for good old Devil Keithie-boy). There was a trunk solely crammed with lurid Bodice Ripper novels sandwiched in between tomes of first edition romantic poetry. The poems were signed by

Lord Byron, no less. Lastly, there was a truly astounding number of packets of butterscotch Angel Delight pudding tucked into Devil Keith's eighteen pairs of kitten-heeled shoes: for safekeeping.

So, in retrospect maybe there wasn't quite so much in common with a hospital bag as first thought. Afterall, there was a distinct lack of Victorian styled flannelette pyjamas, no packs of fragile paper underpants and no dog-eared trashy magazines. Magazines that featured articles about how a person's cat was the reincarnation of Marilyn Monroe and that's why they were snogging the face off the ginger pussy in the middle of the busy Waitrose carpark. Honest, your Honour... Marilyn, the frisky cat, was well up for it the defendant would exclaim!

The one remaining non-Devil Keith trunk that was delivered to the ice-house was full of iron chains, reinforced hand cuffs, aloe vera tissues, boxes of Magnum white chocolate ice-cream lollies and pints of potent sleeping draughts. Dr Riel and Bub had hastily packed those and hoped the links were strong enough to withstand Devil Keith's epic rages and horrific transformations.

CHAPTER FIFTY-THREE

An hour later and after a good cry…

A blotchy faced Harry and Karen were standing in Karen's office and staring at the starkly empty whiteboard. They didn't know where to start their emotional investigation. They were held immobile by their bubbling grief and their own perceived lack of skills.

"We have to start somewhere but I can't seem to put pen to board. Is that cowardly? If I don't write on it…I can pretend it's not happened." Harry was rubbing the warmth back into her arms. Sorrow is so penetratingly cold and unforgiving she thought and tucked the remains of her soggy tissue up the cuff of her old jumper.

"I know how you feel. I mostly just want to curl up into a ball and wait on an adult dealing with this. Then I have episodes where I get so angry with everyone that I want to tear the board apart and start beating the answers out of everybody. But we can do this. Look at how you solved the whole Eva Braun and the evil French loaf mystery. We ***must*** *do this. We owe it to Devil Keith and Nora to do the very best that we can. We are doing this, so let's just start. Ok?"* Karen confidently wrote the word *"Investigation"*, in big red letters, in the middle of the board then stood back and looked at Harry for some inspiration.

"Well according to Google, and every Agatha Christie novel I've read, there are three parts of the investigation process, 'Means,

motive and opportunity'. I suggest that we look at opportunity first. I think it's the simplest and it might help clarify who our suspects are." And with that pronouncement Harry blew an annoying white feather away from her face then started writing.

Twenty minutes later...

The previously pristine board was now surrounded by crumpled up used tissues and covered in multiple scribbles. There was writing in an array of bright colours and many, many expletives at the beginning, middle and end of each sentence. There were also horizontal, vertical and squiggly arrows dispersed throughout the crowded board. But the most noticeable addition was the many, many question marks that littered the packed surface. The authors would have attached a photograph here, as it was the easiest way to show the board, but they're not sure about all that formatting nonsense so here it goes...

Opportunity

It was a closed party so everyone invited was a potential suspect. Nora's body was still warm when she was found so Dr Riel, via liver temperature analysis, was able to provide a tight time frame for her murder. That didn't really help as from the time of Nora leaving the party and Jonathan finding her, the whole team were in and out of Karen's office. Plus, there wasn't really all that much time when Nora was alone, in her and Devil Keith's bedroom, that night anyway.

Karen and Harry then surmised that as the previously missing Dimensional Drill was used to silence Gab or to help him escape, then the murder must have been pre-planned rather than opportunistic. With that in mind they decided to expand their search to include the time before Nora left the celebration. That meant there were more suspects as the criminal or criminals may not have been working in isolation.

The Alibis

The belly dancer troupe and Amanda were immediately eliminated from the suspect list. The investigators were positive that they weren't in Hell during the time of the murder. They had no way of entering Hell number one without assistance from the Hell team, as neither the jiggling, coin wearing, noisy belly dancers nor Amanda, and her loud laugh, knew about the hidden Falkirk entrance. They had all been transported to and from Hell number one via the cockroach walking pavements.

The cockroaches confirmed their alibis. They also happily handed over their autograph books, with the dancer's signatures and phone numbers incapsulated in purple hearts and in pride of place at the front of their much prized books. The roaches had merrily discarded a lock of Brad Pitt's armpit hair, a swatch of Queen Victoria's racy acid green petticoat and a highly personal DNA sample of James Dean's, in favour of the dancer's monograms. The starstruck roaches had also demanded a signed photograph from Amanda: to tape up on their bunkbeds so they could blow her a kiss before bedtime each night. They were less willing to hand over that treasured item to the investigators.

And the lovely Brownie Mirka hadn't earned her interdimensional badge yet so she had no means of entrance or exit to their Hell. She, too, was transported in and out of Hell by the cockroaches. Plus, the belly dancers, Brownie Mirka and Amanda had had no discernible motive to hurt either Devil Keith or Nora.

The Oracles were still at the Nile Headquarters and, as Karen had predicted, they were being less than useful. A comment about being as useful as a chocolate teapot was banded about willy-nilly. Although, on a positive note the Oracles **had** promised to bring back goodie bags from their trip. Karen predicted that it would be umbrellas yet again, but she would be wrong as umbrellas were about to be in very short supply.

The Hell number one residents were still in mid reanimation and none of them had the muscle mass to climb up the stairs to get to the first floor offices and bedrooms, so they were all ruled out too.

Assistant Gail's name was briefly mentioned but was quickly disregarded for a number of reasons. Reason one: she hadn't made it to the party as, even though it was only the month of May, she was busy cataloguing her Halloween costumes. The second reason was that fact that she didn't know Nora and the third reason was the most compelling... neither Harry nor Karen wanted to get on Gail's bad side as that Chinese burn was legendary.

Callum, the Comedian, provided the warm up act for the belly dancer's terrific show but he was so awful, and ridiculously unfunny, that he hadn't deserved a mention in the previous chapter. His jokes were less Dad jokes and more great, great grandad jokes. In fact they were old when Adam was a lad. Callum was briefly added to the suspect list, as Devil Keith had taken great delight in eating the comics post-performance feedback forms. Karen had checked his whereabouts and alibi with his harassed booking agent. After a slightly strange conversation with the manager she assured Harry that Callum was utterly delighted that Devil Keith had eaten the form. The agent told Karen, in graphic detail, what audiences normally did with Callum's form. That made Karen gag and she refused to tell Harry the specifics, but suffice to say Callum was permanently removed from the suspect list. He was also permanently removed from Hell number one's visiting and entertainment list. Although, if Callum kept repeating those same jokes it would be considered both criminal and a sin so he might make it back to Hell all on his ownsome.

Seven potential sets of suspects down, many more to go. Karen and Harry sighed, gave each other a comforting hug and rubbed their bloodshot eyes. They then continued with their mammoth task.

More alibis...

The investigators were confident that Fachance was eating all night long. She may have been hidden behind a sage and onion stuffed ostrich, for most of the meal, but she ate all night. No one could make that much of a dent in the food without constantly chewing, crunching, slurping, belching and gurgling. Well not just the food but also the silver platters the food was served on, the cutlery, the serving spoons and the highly polished mahogany dining table. Not without eating **all** night long, that is. She was also constantly busy after the party, again eating, rather than tidying up. And she didn't really know Nora and was too busy gorging to pay any attention to the honeymooners stories. In fact they were confident that Fachance had never met Nora before.

Karen and Harry were horrified at the quantity of food consumed but happy that they could confidently cross Fachance off their list. Plus, Fachance was completely devastated when Gab went missing. Maybe too devastated, and she used that as an excuse to mess up the room? Hide the evidence? Fachance was re-added to the suspect list with a large question mark affixed to the side of her name.

Willing and Vinnie each gave the other an airtight alibi. They maintained that they were inseparable that night. Karen found that hard to believe because Vinnie was essentially mute and when he did speak it was always very threatening and extraordinarily grunty. Neither of the investigators could fathom how they managed to hold a coherent conversation for that amount of time but Willing and Vinnie were tentatively removed from the suspect list. Then re-added with a large question mark at the side of their names to indicate that they were highly unlikely suspects.

Apart from watching the superb dancing, John O was by the office window most of the night. This was noticed because he appeared to be talking to himself or talking to a pair of rather engrossing, nicotine stained, brown stripy curtains. Karen blew her blotchy nose then confessed that this was not nearly as strange as his other bizarre habits.

"John O has a favourite dishcloth. I kid you not. A favourite dishcloth! He goes mad when it's being washed and it's his turn to do the dishes. He stomps about the kitchen and gets all grumpy with the washing machine. He shouts at the innocent machine and tells it to hurry up. It's quite funny really. What's not so funny is that he uses the kitchen scissors to cut his nasty toe nails. That's so gross. He also hides his midget gems and wine gums so he doesn't have to share them. He got quite a fright when your Bub sniffed them out.

This is a really odd one though. John O flushes the toilet when he's in mid pee. No idea why. You only find out that type of thing when you're all crammed in a small boat together. Plus, you can nearly always track where he's been as he's always eating bags of chips instead of eating his dinner. Just follow the scent of warm vinegar and you'll find him. Weird. Alas, none of that really helps us with our current problem.

However, he's not as odd as Vinnie. Have you noticed how often he falls over and his eyepatch keeps moving from one eye to the other? I swear it's haunted. And all that coffee he slurps. He should be a bit more lively and less sulky by now." Karen shuddered whilst discussing Vinnie's odd behaviours.

A tearful Harry agreed that there was something decidedly fishy about the newcomers so kept John O's and Vinnie's names on the suspect list. Their question mark was average sized.

Back to the alibis...

Bub and Harry had spent a lot of time together that evening although Harry grudgingly admitted that she was frequently distracted with Nora and Devil Keith's stories so couldn't account for all of their time. Unfortunately they didn't have an airtight alibi for one another. Karen and Harry agreed they all were equally entranced and flabbergasted by the newlywed's tales. Devil Keith and Nora were the *"learning heroes"* afterall, and they could spin a mighty fine yarn.

"I know that when a wife is murdered it's nearly always the husband that did it but I just can't see it. Not at all. He's besotted with his Nora and he doesn't care who knows that. He was so happy that night. Kissing and hugging each other. It was quite nauseating...but nice.

He was practically purring when he was sitting on her knee. Willing kept laughing and trying to pull Devil Keith off Nora, because she said he'd do Nora's kneecaps in and he'd have to carry Nora around like some sort of Gone with the Wind tragic character. Devil Keith and Nora were ok with that weird notion but he pulled out the scales to prove Willing wrong. It was so funny when they whirred, burped and died when he stood on them. The look on his face... I thought that was the high point of the whole night. I think I peed myself, a little bit, I was laughing so hard.

Plus, he was delighted to share the praise he received with his Nora. He's normally so mean with the limelight. I heard him boast about Nora's smashing right hook, her machete hacking technique and her incomparable sleuthing skills. I've never, ever heard him doing anything even remotely like that before. I was gobsmacked a few times, I tell you. I vote that we don't even consider Devil Keith as a potential suspect. What do you think?" Harry looked expectably at Karen, but although Karen did agree with Harry's reasoning she argued that they couldn't discount anyone so essential, so early in the investigation. Harry responded by making Devil Keith's name, on the suspect board, as small as possible so as to indicate that his guilt was a teeny, tiny possibility. Karen had to use a magnifying glass to check his name was still there.

Karen and Dr Riel also spent a great deal of time together that evening, but again they were distracted by Devil Keith and Nora's tall tales so couldn't provide a watertight alibi for each other. Although Karen assured Harry that she and Dr Riel were entirely innocent. Harry kept Karen and Dr Riel's name on the board so Karen, on principle, kept Bub and Harry's name on the board. Harry used a measuring tape to check that the letters in the names and the question marks were all the same size. This wasn't her first rodeo.

Jonathan was another likely suspect. He was kept busy at the beginning of the night as he was constantly having to top up the table for Fachance and her insatiable appetite. *"I can't believe Jonathan found another three ostriches in the freezer and they were microwaveable in less than five minutes.*

However and much as it pains me, but I don't think he did it. We knew where he was all the time both during and after the party. Stan and his kidnap proof glass is infallible. And Jonathan's a lily-livered coward. Big on brave words and hurtful gossip but small when it comes to action." Karen agreed with Harry, and Jonathan's cursed name was also written, in small letters, on the suspect list but there were many, many knives drawn around the cursive script.

Karen added Kitty and Fifi, "*The Falkirk Grannies*", to the suspect list. Harry nipped away to check with her many prison contacts and get an update on the felonious thieves.

When Harry returned she clarified that, "*the Grannies were put into seclusion for making so many shivs. The rumour is that they're making more money dealing in prison arms than they ever made when stealing diamonds. They brazenly swapped their commissary Mars bar supplies for wire wool, and both cast on earlier today. Plus, they had no idea that Nora was already dead. I could hear them wildly cheering, from the gatehouse, when they heard the sad news."*

"Absolute Rotters, the pair of them. As an aside. Why do the

Grannies knit the shivs when they could just use their sharpened crochet hooks and knitting needles as shives? Surely that would be simpler and more effective than all that incessant knitting, casting off and darning." Karen queried. Those emotionally inept Grannies were never getting a file or a bulldozer in a cake. Not while Karen could provide a cute Hound of Hell as a sniffer dog. The darling doggies so enjoyed a moist Victoria sponge and a file, or a piece of heavy machinery, just added to the jammy flavour.

"I asked the helpful Prison Officers the same thing but they couldn't answer that. Although, they did say that the knitted shivs make fantastic steak knives and the knitted spoons make great mini sieves. Also, they're an excellent conversational piece at any respectable dinner party."

The cruel Grannies were removed from the suspect list but added to a *"to do"* list under, *"people who need knots added to their wool"* and *"people who deserve their cream cakes to be eaten by a slavering but adorable hound".* Their names were also surrounded by poorly drawn weapons. Sawn-off shot guns were the weapon of choice.

Karen and Harry had avoided this discussion for as long as possible. However, Gab's name **was** on the suspect list but as he wasn't to be found, despite reaching out to the other Hells, the investigators decided to start up a new whiteboard titled, *"Where is Gab and what happened to him?"* Underneath the title was one question. *"Who used the Drill?"* They had checked out his story with God, and a recovering C.C. The distraught entities both supported Gab's version of that night's events, but Karen and Harry knew that they couldn't remove Gab's name from the board as his disappearance was just too important to their case. However, they kept his board covered in case Fachance broke into Karen's office and started chucking things about again. No one wanted that. Plus, Karen and Harry had made the decision to eat and sleep in Karen's main-room so that no one could interfere with their boards and undermine their investigation.

Whilst they had access to the deeply distressed God they had requested a box of the truth telling washing powder to help with their enquiries. Unfortunately God didn't have any as the formula was one of Gab's closely guarded secrets, although he did share small amounts of the miracle compound with the other Angels. However, the fortunate Angels had used their coveted and meagre shares whilst searching for Gab, so there was none to be had at that time.

Lastly, Harry added the Faeries to the suspect list despite neither Harry nor Karen having seen the bodacious Queen, and her entourage, either before, during or after the party. So they had no idea if the winged ones had an alibi, but they certainly had a significant motive. On reflection...this was the investigator's only real, solid motive. Harry was astounded when she heard about the successful Neanderthal racing and miffed that she hadn't been asked to come in as a founding partner. When she said this to Karen she realised that she may have just given herself a motive for Nora's murder, so she shut and locked her lips up tight. The Faeries, however, were kept on the suspect list until more information was provided.

In summary...

There were no definitively viable suspects to report to God, and the Hell team. No arrests yet, as there just wasn't enough evidence and it was all circumstantial anyway. Although the Faeries were looking mighty dodgy at the moment so their names were circled in red permanent ink. Gab's name was also circled, but in semi-permanent ink, and his board was draped in a cloth.

"This is no use. It's getting us nowhere. While we're at it we should just add Stan and Dippit to the suspect list. They're just as likely to have killed poor Nora. And Falkirk has an access point to this Hell so they could get in and out completely undetected.

Afterall, maybe Nora refused to buy the baby a new rattle so deserved her throat cut." Karen sarcastically finished and threw her hands up in the air. Then, in utter frustration, she punched an innocent clipboard.

Harry ducked out of Karen's way but refused to add Dippit and Stan to the suspect pool as she believed that they would be too clever to get caught and they would have been much more creative killers. Although heartbroken, Harry was secretly proud of how devious her sisters could be.

CHAPTER FIFTY-FOUR

In the icehouse…

Devil Keith had stopped using highly imaginative language to threaten Bub and Dr Riel's respective manhoods. He was now sitting, with a wide grin plastered on his face, in the corner of the perishingly cold building. He appeared impervious to the chill and the tense atmosphere surrounding him. The only sensible comment he had uttered in the last hour was to ask Bub to hang up his peach linen hotpants as they creased something awful. Bub felt so helpless that he was willing to do anything to make his brother more comfortable. Even leave Dr Riel to manage Devil Keith on his own for a short period of time.

So Bub nipped into town to buy some more padded coat hangers for the grieving man. He briefly smiled as he remembered a lengthy discussion he'd had with Devil Keith about stealing hotel coat hangers, and Devil Keith's unwavering need to reinstate the death penalty for that particular crime. Devil Keith had been incensed that people never packed enough of the essential tools when going on holiday. Those poor garments were locked away in a dark cramped suitcase then, due to the lack of coat hangers in the hotel, they were left in an untidy pile on a poorly vacuumed wardrobe floor. A travesty! He eloquently and frequently stated.

Bub argued that hanging petty criminals was probably a bit extreme, but Devil Keith provided an astoundingly convincing argument for a bit of much needed neck stretching for the thieves. Devil Keith was relieved that hotels had finally caught onto folks stealing the useful items and had taken the matter in hand. It pleased Devil Keith no end when he heard a rumour that the hangers were going to be alarmed soon, in order to prevent the despicable thefts. Bub thought that Stan probably had a hand in the alarm patent and envisaged a coat hanger screaming *"help, I'm being unwillingly adopted by a thief who has too many shirts, I say too many shirts,"* or some such nonsense. Bub produced a ghost of a smile at that fanciful image.

That aside, Bub was relieved to have the opportunity to take a break as he desperately needed to shed some of his own tears in private. He feared that he'd lose his brother if they couldn't offer him some solace, and a means to grieve and hopefully heal.

Back at the icehouse and the clawing silence is broken...

"Bub, do you think my Nora would like to go to Venice for a small honeymoon? You made it sound so warm and romantic but, admittedly, a wee bit boring. Nora would certainly liven it up, and we could try to Spacehopper all over the city. I bet we'd be so much better at it than you and that twit Harry. We'd never get caught by those jumped up janitors. We've got form with avoiding janitors.

What do you think Nora? Does a wee trip to Venice sound good to you? Oh, you're so naughty. Of course we'll do that, you vixen. I'll add it to our list, shall I?" Devil Keith scratched his lengthy list into the dripping wet granite walls. He looked at his nails: mildly surprised to see that they were long, curling at the ends and exceedingly sharp. He shook his head, paused and briefly searched for his usual shell pink manicure and pedicure. He then tilted his head to listen to a silent voice. He started rhythmically rocking his body, nodding his head and smiling again. Another odd item was added to the extensive list scraped into the dripping wall.

A puzzled Bub looked at Dr Riel. Dr Riel shrugged his despondent shoulders and whispered, *"I think poor Devil Keith is trapped in the midst of denial just now. He's been planning Nora's wedding and honeymoon trousseau for the last twenty-five minutes. And just before that he was asking if she wanted him to organise her bikini wax? He seems to think that she'd prefer a Brazilian over a Porn-star wax. I'd go with the Brazilian too. My Karen loves it. Especially when it's growing back in and all itchy.*

Sorry Bub, I'm inclined to use humour and over-sharing as a coping mechanism in situations like this. Please don't tell Karen I told you about the intimate scratching."

"That's ok. I've never had to deal with death before so I don't know what I'm doing or what's normal. Anything you do is fine by me. And, yes, I won't say a word to Karen." Bub admitted although he wasn't entirely convinced about the pleasures of the Brazilian grow-in.

"Never? Really? You've never had to do this before?" Dr Riel raised his eyebrows in astonishment.

"No, folks appear in Hell and they're already dead. We just sort out the paperwork and start punishing them according to their ticket. It's pretty simple really. This is tough. It's messy...dealing with grief. I don't like it. It's sore...so, so sore." Bub's beautiful eyes filled with shining tears that slowly overflowed and trickled down his cheeks. Dr Riel quietly nodded in agreement.

"My Nora just said yes. Isn't she just the best person ever? And so, so clever. And brave. Did I tell you about her magnificent punch? That Chief Dealer didn't know what hit him. Oh, Nora just laughed at my excellent joke. The punch...it was legendary. I think I might write a love song about it. You two must be so jealous of us and our ageless love.

Oh. My Nora, just told me not to be so mean to you. It's not your fault. Not everyone can be loved so completely as us. She's such a sweet Angel." Devil Keith was rubbing Nora's cardigan against his stubbly jaw and sweetly humming. Oblivious to the concern and bewilderment he was causing.

Bub was finding this all very disturbing and very confusing. He'd expected, and tried to prepare himself, for tears and snot or even extreme violence, but this was just too much to bear. His brother appeared pleasantly delusional, and Bub didn't know how to help the devastated man. Bub didn't know whether to be relieved that Devil Keith was currently deliriously happy, so he should just accept Devil Keith's imaginary conversations. Or should he keep telling Devil Keith that Nora was dead? Jolt Devil Keith back to reality? He'd previously tried to tell Devil Keith the truth and bring him back to his awful situation, but he'd received half a brick to the face for his troubles.

Bub was so out of his comfort zone and wanted to talk this through with the ever practical, and occasionally scathing Harry. She had gone through her own harrowing death and managed to carve out a meaningful afterlife, so she might offer some useful insights. At the very least she'd cuddle him, then make him some cocoa with tiny marshmallows and a slug of forty year old aged whisky on the side.

Dr Riel took the perplexed Bub aside and explained that there were widely accepted stages to the grief process. These included denial, anger, bargaining, depression or extreme sadness and finally acceptance with the ability to re-start their life. Although, Dr Riel clarified, that people didn't necessarily go through them in that order and they can move back and forth through the phases as they heal. Dr Riel also broke the news that some people never make it to the acceptance stage and they can wither away then die. Die either emotionally or physically, he sadly stated. Bub started sobbing in earnest at that news and Dr Riel pulled him in for a hug and a soothing rub across his back. Bub was breaking apart.

After a few minutes of respite, and a couple of awkward manly back pats, Bub responded to this distressing news by rubbing some warmth back into his frozen limbs. It was going to be a long night so Bub and Dr Riel got on with the job of re-oiling their restraints and re-testing the brickwork for any weaknesses.

Bub and Dr Riel were also struggling with processing the whole grief process and they couldn't image how much harder is was going to be for Devil Keith, but they'd learn.

CHAPTER FIFTY-FIVE

After Karen's strop...

"Sorry about all that. I just feel that we're no further forward and I'm struggling without Dr Riel to lean on. I realise that you feel the same so I need to grow a pair and get on with this." Harry accepted Karen's tearful apology and wheeled out a board titled "*Motive*".

"I've taken our suspect list and added possible motives. The internet provided some useful headings and I thought it might help us hone in on our murderer. Unfortunately it's not really helped with the suspect list so I would really appreciate your input." Harry started going through the board and adding Karen's observations and comments.

Motive: vengeance or revenge

Bub's reason for revenge: Devil Keith has been stealing Harry's affections for years. So, he now wants to ruin Devil Keith's relationship with Nora. Both Harry and Karen thought that was pretty flimsy as Bub was quite relieved that Devil Keith helps to defuse Harry's more outlandish notions. Well that's not quite right, but Bub's pleased that he doesn't **always** need to get into bother to appease Harry's wilder side. Bub's other reason for revenge: Devil Keith stole his hair. Another flimsy reason as Bub thinks the Neanderthal racing and Devil Keith's method of cheating is a hoot. Bub's last reason for revenge: Devil Keith says terrible things to Harry. Harry clarified that she gives as good as she gets and Bub finds the whole thing hilarious.

Harry's reason for revenge: Devil Keith says terrible things to her. Harry had to admit that she secretly loves it, and she stated that she always gets her own back. Plus Nora helps to distract Devil Keith, so Bub and Harry can have some much needed alone time. So Harry has no revenge motive to hurt either Devil Keith or Nora.

Jonathan's reason for revenge: he fancies Devil Keith, but would he kill Nora so he could have Devil Keith all to himself? Possibly, but he must realise that Devil Keith would never forgive him. And Devil Keith would definitely, indisputably kill him **Dead**. Really dead. Headless dead or torture him for an eternity...dead. Karen concluded that Jonathan just didn't fit this profile and Harry agreed.

Willing and Fachance's reasons for revenge: not being invited to two of their sisters weddings, then missing Devil Keith and Nora's wedding as well. Harry could nearly see Fachance being mildly upset at missing the weddings as she loves the opportunity to don a pretty dress and strut her stuff. She also proudly holds the Guiness World Record for demolishing a five tier wedding cake in less than seven seconds. She also ate the plastic decorations, and the statue of the bride and groom despite the panicked officials reminding her that they were not part of the challenge.

However, Willing, despite being a bit of a romantic, would have been relieved to have been kept out of the spotlight. Plus, she hated anything remotely girly as she preferred her biker leathers and the open road. She was an adventurer not a lover. Even on a bad day Karen agreed that the missed wedding reason was very unlikely to support a viable motive, but they added Fachance's name in small letters to the board...with a large question mark beside it. This was just in case she was miffed about missing the opportunity to shave a few seconds off her cake scoffing record.

Karen and Dr Riel's reason for revenge: nothing came to mind despite Harry racking her brain. Then racking them some more: if her sister's name was on the board then she wanted Karen or Dr Riel's name there too. Alas, it was not to be.

Gab's reason for revenge: he was unhappy with the Italian and Greek stunts that Harry and Devil Keith had initiated. Karen stated, and Harry reluctantly agreed, that Gab was more likely to bump off Harry than either Devil Keith or Nora. Although, Fachance might have mistakenly thought that Gab was unhappy with Devil Keith so she killed Nora. Again, a flimsy reason that neither Harry nor Karen could fully support. Gab's name was not making the board. Not at all.

Chick the mouse's reason for revenge. Again this was another stretch as he was definitely dead. Unlike a cat with nine lives, a mouse has, at best, three lives to play with. Chick used them all up and some more when he unwisely spied on the Hell management team. Plus, his sticky remains were still stuck in the bottom of the hoover bag. That was Harry's reason for not emptying the distended bag. Well that's what she told everyone.

The evil Eva Braun and Hitler's reason for revenge. Harry admitted she was stretching it with these suspects. Those two monsters were utterly cowardly and totally messed up now. And incidentally, they completely deserved to be tortured for an eternity and more. They didn't have the ability to act in any way, other than to burn to ash so their names were permanently removed from the board. That prompted Karen to add Marsh's name to the board. However, after consulting with HR Sarah they were assured that Marsh was very well occupied in the Gambler's Hell and would never darken their doors, unless he too was in the bottom of a hoover bag. HR Sarah was pleasantly surprised to find that the Gambler goes Large Hell was open to suggestions regarding Marsh's behaviour and punishments. She had been prepared to engage in some mighty tricky negotiations, in a politically charged meeting, and had brought a box of Mars's Celebrations to sweeten the deal. Well, HR Sarah had eaten all the Galaxy and Malteser chocolates first, as she wasn't that worried about the Gambler's Hell.

The Faeries reason for revenge: the Faeries were tricked by Devil Keith so killed Nora as retribution so that Devil Keith was in pain and easier to manipulate. A plausible reason, but they agreed that it was a bit farfetched as they both knew that Devil Keith could be distracted by as little as a shiny button or a dancing ant. However, the Faeries might want revenge as they had lost face during the Neanderthal gambling debacle, so their names were added to the board and a large-ish question mark appeared at the side of their name.

Motive: love

"All of the mystery books quote misguided or unrequited love as a major motivating factor in murder or murder/suicide. Jealousy is another key factor." Harry looked up from her internet search and gave a small smile then sniffed back a tear.

As Dr Riel's name hadn't appeared on the motive board yet, they decided to test this theory. So they argued that Dr Riel was jealous of the depth of Nora and Devil Keiths relationship so killed Nora to break them up. Harry and Karen agreed that was tenuous at best as the same could be said of Angel Gab and Fachance or Bub and Harry. Dr Riel's name was removed from the board and Karen gave an audible sigh.

"I'm not sure that this is getting us any closer but can you stick Willing's name here? We really should put her name somewhere even if it's just so we can cross it off later. Plus, she likes Devil Keith as he saved her and Fachance in Hell number three. Maybe she wants Devil Keith for herself," Karen laughed a lot at that notion but she added Willing's name. But again, she thought they were over reaching so a large question mark was added to the board.

Motive: power

They reasoned that as Bub is the younger twin, he might want Hell for himself. Karen and Harry agreed that Bub could take over Hell at any time he wanted and Devil Keith probably wouldn't notice. The same is true of Karen, Dr Riel, Stan, Dippit, Willing, Fachance, Gab and Harry. Basically, anyone including a random person on Falkirk High Street, could take over Hell number one and Devil Keith would be none the wiser. He only noticed the previous takeover because Jonathan was so mean to Brownie Hilary. The investigators agreed that the only person not competent to take over Hell was Jonathan. He'd had his chance and had royally blown it. Plus, they got the strong impression that God doesn't like him so the attainment of power was not in his immediate future. He was removed from the motive board.

After a few minutes of reflection...

Karen tapped a finger against her chin and launched a possible motive. *"I'm not sure about this, but what if someone killed Nora because of the new horn? She suggested that we give the horn back but we weren't keen on doing that."*

"Karen, I think you probably were the least keen of all of us to give it back, so do you have a confession to make? Ah, I can see by the fist you're trying not to make that you don't have a convenient confession in the making.

Ok, let's think this through. What if someone was concerned that instead of giving the horn back we'd lose the horn? Can we lose the horn if we have too much kindness and compassion in this Hell? Dr Riel was worried about how Nora was coping and encouraged us to be more sensitive to her needs. So, would his empathy be enough of a catalyst for the loss of a horn? Would the loss of the horn really be a reason to kill? Is it a big enough motivator?" Harry pondered this question and was slightly annoyed that she hadn't thought of it all on her own. Karen was sure to take some of the credit if this proved to be the case. Harry slapped herself, hard, in the face and reminded herself that catching the killer was all that mattered. Bub and his competitive spirit really was catching.

"We'll ask HR Sarah. Be back soon." Karen slipped away

to consult with HR Sarah then returned looking a tiny bit sheepishly. *"HR Sarah listened, asked some rather pointed questions and took some notes. She then heavily implied that we were both idiots as there wasn't enough compassion in the world to eradicate a Hell horn. So I'm presuming that* **our** *idea was a bit of a daft one."*

"Whose idea?" Harry taunted and ducked. Narrowly avoiding another innocent clipboard incident.

Motive: money

Another great motive for murder, but this was quickly discounted as Nora didn't have any money as she kept anonymously giving it all away. She hadn't even bought herself a new duffle coat with her winnings and her old coat was currently being held together by dryer fluff and a pint of school glue. And with his extensive collection of zippers to maintain, Devil Keith wasn't much better, financially speaking, either. So again, there was no motive to kill Nora and therefore no suspects.

Karen stopped Harry and excitedly pointed to the board… at the Faeries. They had been swindled by Devil Keith, so they did, indeed, have a motive under the heading of Money. They probably thought they could get Nora's life insurance out of a bereaved Devil Keith. They just had to find out if Nora had Life Insurance and whether Devil Keith was the beneficiary.

Karen and Harry surveyed their updated board with sadness and a touch of guilt. They felt guilty that they were happy that they had now solved their case. *"Well I think we know who murdered poor Nora. Those evil Faeries did it. They have several motives, and they're ever so crafty. Plus, you have to admit that they're small so they could have snuck into Hell without our knowledge and nipped back out again. Their ogres would have been happy to subdue poor Nora whilst Faery Ritamay did the despicable deed. The ogres could have pushed Gab through the Dimensional opening and jumped through behind him. It would have been difficult but not entirely impossible as the mannequin's would have provided excellent camouflage for the oafs."* Karen said this with both relief and anger. She couldn't believe that those uppity moths would sink to such a despicable low. Nora was an innocent and didn't deserve any of this.

Is it time to call the team back from their missions?

CHAPTER FIFTY-SIX

In the icehouse...

"Ah, yes. You will need a new suitcase, my Peculiar Pumpkin. Good idea." Devil Keith nodded his head in agreement and put his finger nail against the algae covered wall. He suddenly slumped to the freezing floor. Bub jumped up from his camping chair: grabbed his brother and pulled his limp body into his trembling arms.

Devil Keith snuggled into his brother, seeking warmth and comfort. *"Bub, someone killed my Nora. What am I going to do? How can I survive without her? She's perfect and so, so wonderful. My chest hurts so much. My heart is so heavy that I can't take a breath. Please help me. I'm suffocating."* Devil Keith was softly mewing and drowning in the depths of his misery.

"I've got you, bro. I've got you, now. How can I help? What do you want me to do?" a sobbing Bub cradled Devil Keith's head and stroked his hair back from his face. Devil Keith gazed up at his brother and coughed a broken tooth into his fist. Bub gasped but tried to hide his alarm.

Devil Keith's gleaming white teeth were black, rotten and tumbling out of his open mouth. The usual minty freshness overwhelmed with the putrefying scent of sweet decay and bitter, bitter disease. Devil Keith's cheeky dimple was no more as his cheeks were now pale, hollow and gaunt. His skin so white that his blue veins provided a road map to his rapidly wasting muscles and dissolving fat. His few remaining teeth were clearly visible through the fabric of his translucent cheeks. His blonde hair was streaked with black highlights and coated with lumps of dandruff and grease. His sparkling green eyes were now huge, deep black pits boring into his face, and surrounded by entrenched, dark purple bruises.

"Please, Bub. Please kill me. I want to die. I can't go on without my wonderful Nora. Take pity on me. Please." Devil Keith whispered through quivering, peeling lips. He was pining for his beautiful Nora and melting away. His skeletal shoulders were shaking as he cried soft tears of heartache. Bub could feel every rib and ridge of Devil Keith's spine through his paper thin skin. Delicate skin that was splitting and torn; dissolving like wet tissue paper. Tears silently streaming down his cheeks, Bub looked at Dr Riel for guidance and reassurance.

Dr Riel looked away as his shoulder gently heaved too. Hiding his own blubbering and sorrowful moans in his rounded shoulders. *"Devil Keith, I'm going to help Bub get you up from that damp floor. Make you more comfortable. Come on. We've got you."*

Bub accepted Dr Riel's help but didn't really need it as the shaking, angst ridden Devil Keith barely weighed more than a small, battered child. Devil Keith's body was shrinking as his sorrow increased. His anguish burning his meat from his very bones.

"Dr Riel, I don't think I can do this anymore. I'll get someone else. Someone who knows what they're doing. I'm scared that I'll hurt him. Say the wrong thing and do him harm. Dr Riel, what should I do?" Bub slowly backed away from his crying brother whilst tightly holding his chest and stomach. Holding in the raw pain of worthlessness. Devil Keith's tears had soaked through his clothing and were rapidly filling the icehouse's central drain and creating a puddle on the floor. This was a worrying development that Dr Riel decided to deal with later.

*"You **will** stay and you **can** do this. You're the only person that can do this."* Dr Riel abruptly slapped Bub and roughly grabbed him by the shoulders. *"Look at him. LOOK AT HIM. He won't survive without you. He can't lose you too. Please, don't abandon him. Not now."*

Devil Keith was moaning as he lay on his side, in the foetal position, guarding the remains of his ravaged heart. Bub could barely look at the suffering and torment his brother was enduring. Bub would rather have taken the pain on his own shoulders than watch someone he loved going through this relentless agony.

"I am going out for some air, and to see if there's been any updates on the Apocalypse. You will be here when I return and you will manage this. I have faith in you. I really do." Dr Riel warned the deeply distressed Bub then gave him another awkward man cuddle and a pat on the back.

Bub clung onto Dr Riel and whispered into his shoulder. *"I'll try my very best, but he's suffering so much, Dr Riel. He's overflowing with woe and I'm useless. Completely useless. I think I'm broken. There's something wrong with me."* Bub punched himself in the face and dislodged a tooth. He preferred the physical pain to the psychological pain he was currently enduring.

"How will I cope if I lose him? My twin. My womb buddy. He made me my first baby bib to cover and protect my pinstriped navy blue baby-grows. He knew I couldn't resist curried goat, and the mess it made, so he stayed up all night sewing that bib. His tiny hands were cramping and sore but he persevered. He commissioned my first architectural project. I was so proud of that playpen and Devil Keith, went all out, pretending that he couldn't escape from it. I later found out that he wasn't really pretending but that wasn't the point. He had faith in me and my teeny baby hands. He gave me confidence in myself even when he was stealing my dummy and I was clobbering him about the head with his bottle of milk.

When we were toddlers we played hide and seek behind the vats of acid, and Devil Keith hardly ever allowed me to retrieve our ball from the toxic chemicals. He nearly always made a Hell resident do it for us. Then we'd laugh at their screwed up faces and melting thumbs. We're a pair. We've always been a pair. Please Dr Riel, I can't lose him. Not now."

Dr Riel paused and looked at a trembling Bub. Finally seeing how badly this was impacting on the normally calm, cool and confident man. It was easy to forget that Bub and Devil Keith were twins. Their characters were so different from one another but in this they were one soul…torn asunder. He assured the devasted Bub that no matter what, no one is truly prepared for death and the ensuing grief. But the fact that Bub was feeling so awful meant that he cared for his brother so deeply that he couldn't possibly get it wrong. Bub was the right man for the job. Dr Riel finished by telling Bub to listen to his heart as this would help keep him centred. Keep him focused. Keep him sane. Bub took a breath and tried to focus.

Dr Riel didn't want to alarm Bub, but he was also going out to find a plunger. He needed to clear the drains, as the water was quickly rising with no means of escape.

A few minutes later…

"What was that horrendous noise? There are lots of birds squawking then falling from the sky. A fat seagull hit me and I think it broke my collar bone. And what is that awful smell?" Dr Riel entered the building at a pace and abruptly stopped. He was holding his hands over his ears and narrowly avoiding tumbling over a stack of cloth covered, open books. He gagged then gagged again and the third time was a charm. He spat stomach acid into a tissue and held it over his nose and mouth. The gut-wrenching stench was rolling through the normally un-fazable doctor and burning through his nasal hairs.

A scrawny Devil Keith was manically pacing around the small, domed building with a book held open in his claw like hand. He pushed back his lank, greasy hair and growled at Dr Riel. *"Do not interrupt me in mid flow. I'm expounding great wisdom and poetry here, you serf."* Devil Keith sneered then scratched his concave, flea bitten chest.

Devil Keith was wearing a white muslin shirt that was open to the waist and hanging over shabby black breeches. The tattered shirt had been white at some point in its miserable life but its many lacy ruffles were now heavily stained with dirt. The shirt's underarms bore witness to months of fever induced, sweat soaked nights.

Devil Keith pointed a long, grimy finger to the ceiling and wailed then wailed again. His sunken cheeks collapsing into his face. His many infected mouth ulcers bursting and bleeding onto his pale retreating gums. Devil Keith was the cause of the gut emptying stink that was seeping into the old stone structure.

"The wailing... it's pure Banshee screaming. I can't get him to stop and have some rest. He's exhausting himself with all his pacing. Is your shoulder ok? I heard the dead birds slamming off the roof of the building. If Devil Keith gets any louder I fear that it'll take out a satellite or an airplane. Killing someone or lots of someones in the process." Bub held his head in his hands and tried to avoid breathing in the repulsive odours. They reminded him of an eviscerated dead rat he'd once found smouldering on a mid-summer barbeque grill.

"I'm fine. Just give me a minute. Did we happen to pack any earplugs and menthol vapour for under our nose?" Dr Riel made a simple sling to immobilise his injured shoulder. He feared that might be the first of many wounds they were about to endure.

Devil Keith dropped his first edition of Lord Byron's poetry and rushed to his brother. *"What's wrong Bub? Are you Ok? You're a peculiar green colour. Do you need a seat or a lie down? Do you want a sweetie to suck? Chocolate or a blueberry lollipop? You might be hypoglycaemic. That's a thing, right? I've got some jelly babies somewhere."* Devil Keith rummaged in his filthy trousers for a sugary treat. He stopped mid fumble and stepped back. Stunned.

"Bub, what's wrong with me? Bub, I think I'm sad. Really sad. Bub, why am I so sad? What can I do to stop feeling like this? Make it go away, Bub. If you love me then make it all stop." Devil Keith had adopted the voice of a scared little boy and his lips began quivering.

Bub pulled the ravished man into his arms and rubbed Devil Keith's frail back. *"I've got you bro. I'll make it all go away."*

"Thank you." Devil Keith whispered and put his thumb in his mouth. He leaned into Bub and fell into a deep, healing sleep. Well Bub really hoped it was healing as he didn't think Devil Keith could take much more, either physically or mentally.

Dr Riel helped to tuck Devil Keith into his camp bed and smoothed back his hair. *"I don't think you can make this all better, Bub, but you're definitely helping. I'm so proud of you.*

I don't want to add to your burden, but I think Devil Keith's tears are having a major impact on the world. There's been reports, on the news, that there's been a significant rise in sea levels throughout the globe. Locally the Forth and Clyde canal has burst its banks despite careful control of the locks. There were swans gracefully gliding along Falkirk High Street earlier today, and that can't be good." Bub was taking notes as Dr Riel gave the disturbing update.

There was a waterproof map hanging on the wall. Bub added the notes to its glossy surface: plotting the rapid climate changes and the kamikaze birds. Things were escalating at a terrifying rate and they could only hope that God could cool things down.

A little while later Bub stopped wandering around the small icehouse. He smiled and gently pushed Devil Keith's tangled hair from his forehead. A large clump of hair came away in Bub's hand. He worried that they were heading for yet another stage in the complex grief process.

CHAPTER FIFTY-SEVEN

Karen's office and the investigation...

There was a gentle knock at the office door. The tiny but beautifully formed, Faery Lynn (also known as Faery Hammy to her many, many friends) popped her head round the door. *"Is this a bad time? Well, of course it is, but are you busy? Well of course you're busy. Silly me."* The pretty red-headed Faery, who usually had the biggest smile imaginable, went to leave the room. Her smile gone and her head hanging low in embarrassment and grief.

"No, no. I was going to speak with you anyway. How do we get in touch with the Queen of the Faeries? On the quiet, like." Harry enquired of the sweet Faery. The exhausted investigators weren't sure who they could trust and Faery Lynn just happening to arrive at the very moment they had boldly added the Faeries to the suspect list was...fishy.

Faery Lynn flew into the room. Whilst flying she was doing martial arts moves. Chopping the air, kicking the floating dust mites and ha-cha-ing for all she was worth. The authors aren't sure if ha-cha-ing is even a word but it definitely was the noise that Faery Lynn was making. The Faery's bizarre antics were still not the strangest thing the investigators had seen or heard that day.

Faery Lynn patiently explained that all of the otherworldly messages went through her as she was the Faery

Liaison officer, Postmistress extraordinaire and Hell's official photographer. A new designation instigated by Jonathan, but currently still in place, that is until someone gave her the sack. She really hoped she didn't get fired as she absolutely loved bringing good news to people. The assorted gift baskets and delivering the surprisingly large number of crates of baby alligators were nice too.

"Sorry but if you're one of Jonathan's lackeys then I don't trust you. Not one bit. We'll find another way to communicate with the Faery Queen and bring her, and her unruly squad, in for questioning." Harry abruptly pointed at the door then turned back to their cluttered big board. She really needed some sleep and a special Bub cuddle. Just a glimpse of his pinstriped suit and pocket square would help curb her need to cry.

Faery Lynn's small smile faded, and she started karate chopping to the door. She stopped, turned and put her little fists on her curvy hips. *"I know you don't like the Faeries. You don't like our festivals, and our bizarre treasure hunts for the right to purchase the much prized music tickets for our Faer Days. You hate our ability to turn the plainest flower into a stunning hat but I can be trusted. I care about Devil Keith and I want to help find out what happened to his Nora. Devil Keith's always been a friend to me. I don't know if he told you this, but he saved me. I was stuck under a shuttlecock for three days. Three full days. I was crying out for help but those rude beetles just stuck up their snooty antennae and waddled off to watch the Great British Bake off. It was pie week, so I suppose that was a justifiable waddle.*

Anyway, Devil Keith was practising his very, very difficult hoola-hooping and heard my woeful cries. He was the only one that stopped and lifted off that dreadful cock. He got mud on the knees of his splendid burgundy plus fours. They were nearly ruined and he only complained for three hours about it. He is a true hero. He is my hero." Faery Lynn was furtively wiping away an angry tear and softly patting her heart. She was clearly in awe of the big galoot.

"Really? I can't believe he did that for you. He really doesn't like the whole Faery hat business that you lot endlessly boast about, and he loved those odd trouser things. Plus, you lot have been threatening the loveable Brownies. Devil Keith loves all those skint kneed wee hellions." Harry scoffed, and furtively stole a spare gas cannister for her flamethrower whilst Karen wasn't looking. Old habits die hard. Harry was still not believing the panting and slightly flushed Faery act. Although Devil Keith moaning about a small grass stain for three hours sounded about right.

Faery Lynn slammed her small, balled fists on her hips. *"The 'loveable' Brownies were throwing stones at our front doors! Brownie Anne is an unmitigated menace. She was throwing bricks. Actual bricks at us! And she never apologised for breaking our letter boxes. The postman couldn't get the letters and parcels though the Queen's letter box, so he piled them up outside her door. Queen Lucy was trapped in her house for three weeks and she nearly starved. The manky fishfingers, caught in the back of the freezer drawer, were the only thing that saved our precious Queen. That's why we're not so keen on the Brownies and their chucking ways.*

Plus, I can prove that I care for Devil Keith and that he ***did*** *save me. The shuttlecock is still in one of his China cabinets. It's a souvenir of his heroics and bravery. He told me he has lots of them. More than you have."* The Faery asserted and stuck out her teeny, pink tongue. She had her hand over her mouth when said tongue appeared, as Devil Keith had told her all about Harry's bullying ways. Poor, poor malnourished Devil Keith couldn't eat without Harry stealing all his chips, and his many slices of perfectly grilled blackpudding were forever being hidden by the loathsome thief.

◆ ◆ ◆

CHAPTER FIFTY-EIGHT

Devil Keith and Nora's bedroom...

Before moving into the icehouse Bub had draped a couple of large blankets over Devil Keith's bedroom floor in order to hide the dried blood stains from the distraught Hell team, and to try to preserve the scene of the crime. Not that there was much to preserve by then. Bub, then Devil Keith, followed by the rest of the team had run to and around Nora's body with little thought to solving the crime. Walking through the entire scene and the blood, then wrestling and fighting over Nora's mutilated body had pretty much eradicated all possible evidence. Plus, there had been the throwing of the furniture and the less than pristine removal of the furniture and parts of the crumbling wall. The final nail in the evidence coffin was when the team had scattered throughout the room looking for a hidden culprit. The team, the room and Nora had been splattered with Nora's still warm blood. The physical evidence irretrievably lost.

During this visit Harry and Karen decided to avoid that part of the room and pretend everything was fine. Just fine. They could do this. Afterall, this was too important to be sentimental or squeamish they repeatedly told each other. They kept to one side of the doorway then carefully skirted around the blankets.

"I'm never allowed in Devil Keith's room, alone. Well, I know

I'm not alone just now as you two are with me. I mean I'm never allowed in here without Devil Keith peering over my shoulder and telling me to step away from his treasures. He's very protective of his privacy and his stuff. I think Nora was the only person I know that was allowed to just saunter in and out of here. Even Bub had to make an appointment and sign the visitor's book when he popped in." Harry was whispering as if she was in one of Venice's many churches.

"Isn't that because you tried to break into one of his China cabinets and go rummaging in his stuff. Remember? It was just before you left to go to Italy with Bub. You were looking for hair products or hairclips. I remember you blethering on about plastic heads, wigs and Bub's hair going missing." Karen helpfully responded and re-arranged Devil Keith's gas cannisters so he wouldn't know that they had been in his room.

"That was a totally justified burglary and I was caught before I got the goods on Devil Keith. He turned me upside down and kept hitting my head of the floor. He called me a rusty old screw that needed banged to rights. I didn't find out about what he was doing with all the hair then...you know? About his toupee's, Neanderthal racing and gambling until recently. The devious wee dog.

Oh, I miss him and his naughty ways so much. I'd give any and everything to be hit off the floor again." Harry sniffed and coughed into her fist. She rubbed her forehead and tried to push away her stress headache. Harry turned away and knocked off one of Devil Keith's twelve, long dressmaking tables. A small glass jar fell off the table and would have landed on the floor if not for Karen's swift reflexes.

"That was close. He'd go mad if we broke anything. Oh, that looks swanky." Karen was trying to distract Harry by holding a hotel sewing kit up to the light. There was a finely etched picture of some flowers and leaves on the glass lid of the expensive souvenir.

"It does. Devil Keith must have really adored his Nora. He

would never have taken me to somewhere like that. Not that we'd have been allowed in there anyway. Imagine the carnage we'd have caused if we had access to room service, and unlimited hot mud baths to play in. I'm surprised that Devil Keith bothered with that small kit, though. He always use to bring a massive portable sewing kit everywhere he went. I know because it was yet another thing that I was never allowed to touch. He used to, grudgingly, do my repairs for me but most of the time he just burned my clothes and made me a new outfit out of one of his old towels. Have you felt his towels? I'm sure they're at least severity-five percent silk." Harry stuffed her soggy, tattered tissue back up the sleeve of her cardigan. A small tear escaped and slowly trickled down her cheek.

"Harry, you don't have to talk about Devil Keith in the past tense... as if he's gone. We'll get him back, I promise. You'll be getting hit off that floor and ridiculed again, in no time. Now help me find that twitting shuttlecock, and keep an eye on that Faery. I still don't trust her and her mischievous Faery ways." Karen began rattling the glass fronted cabinets and causing the small keys to fall out of the locks. Then scrambling under the cabinets to find the keys. Why couldn't Devil Keith just use a steel safe like a normal Devil?

They found the twitting shuttlecock after searching through four cluttered, but recently well dusted cupboards. If it wasn't such a sad time Harry would have spent hours raking through Devil Keith's jealously guarded possessions. The Moon landing negatives, alone, would have taken up a full afternoon of conspiracy theorising. While the fully illustrated Children's Books, penned by Genghis Khan no less, promised to be a hoot. If a little raw and dismember-y and generally not for folks under the age of thirty-seven and a half.

After checking the hateful shuttlecock and finding three, shaky lines scored into the underside of the rubber. And Faery Lynn giving the offending feathered prison a good sharp kick and a telling off, they agreed that Faery Lynn's incredulous story was, in fact, quite genuine. Devil Keith was indeed her hero and deserving of her gushing praise. Karen and Harry concluded that she could contact her daughter, Faery Eve, and start a dialogue with the Faery Queen.

Faery Eve was famous for her ability to rattle up a divine chocolate sponge with little more than a small cuckoo's egg and a wilted buttercup petal, but she was also a master spy. Her particular skill was sending complex, hidden messages on a single fingernail. She once copied the renowned novel War and Peace onto a thumb nail and she still found enough space to add a synopsis, in case no one could be bothered reading the full book. If you too can't be bothered reading War and Peace: there's snow, lots of chatting, a bit of fighting, soulful looks and people die. The end.

Harry and Karen decided that Faery Eve would send a coded message via Faery Layla's manicure. Faery Layla was no longer doing her own nails as they keep breaking due to the ill-tempered, damnable charity shop tin opener. This important message would then be transferred to Lucy the Faery Queen. It all sounded overly complicated, but as they didn't know who to trust this was the only surefire way that the message would get through without external or internal interference.

CHAPTER FIFTY-NINE

Back in Karen's office...

Lucy, the Faery Queen slowly entered with her downcast Faery henchwomen and a cloud of very subdued bees. The bees were humming a recognisable rendition of, *"My Immortal"* by Evanescense.

"My condolences for your tragic loss. Thank you for using the coded network to contact me. I'm presuming you suspect you have a mole in your Hell, for sure. How can we be of help at this truly dreadful time?" Queen Lucy presented Harry and Karen with a single, perfect white lily and solemnly bowed her head.

Faery Jax was out of breath as she dragged in a large wicker basket of Bodyshop samples and plonked it in front of Harry and Karen. *"I wasn't sure what you would need in your time of sorrow so I brought a selection for you to try."* The cowed Faery murmured and respectfully tipped her pansy hat at the distraught investigators.

"Queen Lucy, Karen and I are leading the investigation into our Nora's death..." Harry started sobbing and noisily rubbed her nose on the hem of her holey jumper.

Karen took a steadying breath then took over the difficult and potentially fatal conversation. *"We're compiling a list of suspects and possible motives. You've made it onto both lists. Actually you made the lists a couple of times. Where were you..."* Karen didn't get to finish as a furious Faery Ritamay dive bombed the startled investigator and pulled out her well-oiled pistol.

"Enough Faery Ritamay. Enough. Put away the gun and stop

scowling. Under the circumstances, it's a reasonable question. I was at the Neanderthal Games that night. All night. There are hundreds of spectators who can confirm that I was there all evening long." The Queen was patting Faery Ritamay's arm and murmuring reassurances that she could puff gun the next person who accused the Faery Queen of murder. Or accused the Queen of eating the last custard cream. Both were equally heinous in the Fairytale assassin world, and their secretive rule book. The rule book included the best way to hide a body. Hint: those Faery toadstool circles that look so cute, are probably hiding at least one mafia boss and a cheeky, overcharging lollipop man.

"And your henchwomen? Where were those frightening Faeries and torturing ogres during the timeframe?" Karen cast a dirty look at Faery Ritamay. A look that promised a largish fly-swatter in that death-hungry Faery's near future.

"They were with me, and yes, the same creatures can confirm this, for sure. I know you think I have the means to influence their memories and testimonies. Money does, indeed talk and bribe, but I did not do this. Not this time, anyway.

I'm having the devil of a time with Ralph, the Neanderthal Chieftain. His demands are getting way out of hand. They started with a season ticket for Falkirk Football club, and have now escalated to me having to clear his bar tab at the Colonial Inn. And the bills for his jars of pickled eggs, and twice daily meat paste and Branson pickle sandwiches are nearly bankrupting me. Faery Ritamay is taking on more kill contracts than she can safely handle in order to keep us all afloat. It's making her very tetchy, as she does not love this development to the moon and back. Do you my loyal friend?

Mmm, now there's a thought, for sure. I have a question for you. Did you happen to smell warmed coconut oil when you found our Nora's body?" the Faery Queen was now reassuring Faery Ritamay that there wasn't a fly swatter brave enough to do her any harm.

Neither Karen nor Harry had noticed that particular

scent. The only smell they could recall, from the horrible night, was the overwhelming smell of iron. Warmed bloody iron, salty tears and now that they thought about it... a hint of shoe polish.

"Lastly, I can assure you that I have no motive. The rest of the Real Neanderthal's are proving to be difficult as well, for sure. They're no longer willing to race until they receive written assurances that Devil Keith will still re-decorate their cave kitchenette at the end of the racing season.

Plus, most of the Fake Neanderthals have raging headlice and are blaming the ogres, for sure. The ogres readily admitted that they farmed the greedy headlice and set them free, but it was only in retaliation for the Fake Neanderthals stealing their tile cutters and new grout sponges. Seemingly the grout sponges are ideal for applying the Fake Neanderthal's beige foundation, and a touch of blusher. I'm not sure what they were using the tile cutters for, but they needed a lot of them, for sure.

The only positive thing in this whole debacle is the hearty Mr Havel and his delicious craft beer. I originally thought he said crap beer, and I thought he was being unduly critical of himself and his skills. However Faery Jax cleared up the misunderstanding and syringed my delicate ears. Mr Havel's pints of creamy brew have nearly mellowed out the ogres and the Fake Neanderthals are using it in their shampoo. It gives such a lovely shine, and their hair is nearly tangle free. Or so I was told at the obscene time of 4.30am this morning.

And, although I'm assuming a caretaker role, Devil Keith hasn't actually signed over my rightful shares in the race business yet. And he won't be able to do that in his current condition. So, you see, I have no motive to kill Nora and nobble Devil Keith. I need him to function and create an acceptable decorator's mood board to get those guys running again. My credit card bill is due soon and the interest rates they charge are cripplingly sore, for sure.

Lastly, and this is the absolute and unquestionable reason why I did not harm your Nora. I happen to like Nora. She lacks a little confidence and needs to stop second-guessing Devil Keith's affections but she's a real asset to our world, for sure. I heard all about disgusting Marsh in the Gambler's Hell, and it was all I could do to stop my Faeries, ogres and I from going in there to do a bit of punching and gouging ourselves." The Faery Queen's reasoning, and obvious blood lust, lacked any guile and the investigators unequivocally believed her.

"I like your Nora too. She's uncommonly brave and stands her ground when she believes she's in the right. Although I didn't want it, she gave me some really good advice. Those pesky charity items couldn't afford my Life Coaching services afterall. They would have bankrupted my business and I would've had to re-enlist in the Marine Corps. I'd have had to cut my nails short and give up all my metallic polishes, the military philistines.

So I'll give you some free advice: I'd look at the forensics again if I were you. You obviously missed the importance of the lack of coconut scent at the scene. What else did you miss?" Added Faery Layla with a flick of her long, shiny brunette hair and a glance at her gleaming manicure. Faery Eve was a genius with an emery board and a buffer.

CHAPTER SIXTY

Meanwhile in the icehouse…

Bub looked at the short blonde hairs coating his fingers. Devil Keith was still sleeping but that didn't seem to stop him from transitioning into another phase in the grief process. Dr Riel was unable to predict what he and Bub were due to face next. Devil Keith's Devil physiology was interfering with the natural order of things and appeared to be speeding up and exaggerating the grieving process.

Dr Riel and Bub had been nearly relieved when Devil Keith had moved from the bizarre conversations of the denial stage, straight to grief and sorrow. That they could nearly understand, although they could barely watch his suffering and torment. They now feared that they were due to manage the much dreaded anger and bargaining phases. These were less predictable as they thought God might be pulled into the mix, and they weren't at all sure how she'd feel about that.

Bub and Dr Riel had another worry as, despite the coating of thick tar, they were seriously concerned about the integrity of their handcuffs and chains. Devil Keith's salty tears had caused the iron links to rust and crumble into ginger dust.

"Nora! My Nora. I want my Nora. Where have you put her?" Was the first indication that Devil Keith had awoken and was writhing in emotional pain. Devil Keith leapt from his sweat soaked bed and shredded sheets and fell into cold, salty water. His tears had formed a three foot deep pond on the watery icehouse floor. He tipped back his head and screamed at the

trembling domed icehouse ceiling.

"God, you pathetic creature, come to me now. Now, I say. We have a mutually beneficial bargain to discuss, you evil hypocrite." He finished his less than polite invite with a lengthy Banshee scream. Then another and another. The icehouse roof shuddered and skreiched with the force of his torment. Bub also feared that another light airplane had fallen and had skimmed the buckled structure. The icehouse was becoming increasingly unstable and they'd have to move soon. Find higher ground to escape the flood waters, and some thick tree cover to reduce the bird bombs.

"Yes Dearie. How can I help you?" God appeared looking haggard and poorly dressed. Her normally starched, red and white gingham apron was in complete disarray and covered in a multitude of suspicious looking, fleshy stains. Her American Tan stockings had multiple runs and appeared to be badly repaired with bright red nail polish. She ran a shaky hand through her messy hair and two dead, baby rabbits fell to the flooded floor.

Bub carefully picked up the warm rabbits and their bones crumbled to dust in his large hands. God shook her head and gently stroked their downy, grey fur. *"I'm afraid that is one of the next stages of the Apocalypse that you're witnessing. The sea water, lakes, lochs and rivers were rising to an alarming level, but now the waters are all falling away. There isn't enough fresh water to hydrate the animals or the people in some areas of the world just now. However, there's a few tsunamis brewing so the vicious droughts won't last long. I fear the new flooding they bring will be devastating and terribly cruel. So cruel.*

There's chaos coming and it's due to arrive very soon, my dearies. I'm not sure what to do. I don't think an ark, or a fleet of arks will hit the mark this time around. Do you?

However, these poor bunnies were shouted to death by their maddened, bellowing parents. The decibels vibrating through the bodies of the poor babes, and shaking them to death from the inside out. I'm afraid these babies won't be the last innocent casualties of this abomination. By my reckoning there are still fires, earthquakes and explosions on the horizon." God shuddered and rubbed her left eye. Her sore eyes were dry and gritty. She had no more tears left to shed. She felt totally hollow and bereft. She pulled out a can of full sugar irn bru. She offered a slug to Dr Riel and Bub but they politely declined the treat.

"Now Devil Keith, how can I help you today sweetheart?" God sighed and cupped his thinning cheek. She pushed a stray foam curler behind her ear and blew a white feather from in front of her strained face.

"You can start by parking that terrible attitude, you bitch. I want one more day with my Nora, and you are going to give it to me. Or suffer the consequences." Devil Keith managed to sneer and whine at the same time.

"I'm sorry but I can't. I tried. I really..." God tried to pull Devil Keith into her arms but he slapped her away then growled. He stuffed one of her curlers into his mouth and bit down. Hard.

"Yes, you can. Of course you can help. You're God. All seeing but not doing. You can bring my Nora back. What will it take? My hair? Have at it. I don't need it anymore. My gorgeous Nora isn't here to stroke and plait it." Devil Keith sarcastically shouted. He furiously grabbed at his remaining patchy hair. His white knuckles tightly gripping, as he ripped out his fringe. This was followed by a wild scourge on his remaining straggly hair and raw scalp.

A few bloody hair follicles were resisting his torment and clinging to Devil Keith's bald, bruised pate. Devil Keith abruptly bent over, whilst gasping for breath, and rubbed his aching heart. He was in utter agony.

"Not enough you hard-faced bitch? What about my hands? You want them too? I don't need them if I can't stroke my Nora's soft, pink cheeks and pinch her deliciously pert bottom." Devil Keith panted, and roughly dislocated the fingers on his left hand. He callously ripped them from their swollen joints. The snapping, popping and tearing sounds were revolting. Bub

gagged and covered his mouth.

Wildly throwing the mutilated fingers to the saturated floor Devil Keith screamed, *"are you satisfied yet? Are you happy now? Or do you want my right hand. The right hand of God is a prized place, or so I've heard. Do you want another one for you collection, you condescending cow?"*

"Devil Keith, dearie you don't und..." God tried to intervene but failed to stop the dismemberment.

"Not my right hand then? Not enough? You want the rest of my arm or my kidneys? I can't cuddle my Nora anymore or enjoy a wine spritzer with her at the end of the day. So take the useless things. Enjoy!" Devil Keith tightly grabbed his left elbow and viciously yanked it down. He pulled a second time and loudly grunted. Tearing the limb from it's fleshy, shoulder mooring and chucking it at God's feet. God made to step forward and put a stop to Devil Keith's self-mutilation but Bub and Dr Riel gently held her back. They had to let Devil Keith do this and then, hopefully, he could move on.

Devil Keith didn't flinch or register any surprise as he watched his nails lengthen and sharpen into lethal ten gage, steel scalpels. He dragged his terrifyingly elongated nails across his exposed abdomen and split open his skin, fat and muscles. He dug his remaining hand and scalpels into the newly formed cavity. Throwing out pieces of wet, sticky bowel and slippery muscle until he located the offending organ. He threw his viscous kidney at the far wall. Watching, in fascination, as it ruptured and slid to the mossy, wet floor.

"Is that enough? Or do you want more? There's still plenty of me to sell for my Nora's soul. For one more day. One more smile. What about my beating heart? I don't want it anymore. No one wants it. I'm unlovable. I'm obscene. I'm disgusting." Devil Keith was choking as he tore open his filthy shirt and roughly pushed his fingers through his rib cage. Fingertips touching the beating organ, he stopped and glanced at his trunk of poetry books.

"It hurts too much to go on. I can't find the words to describe

how bad it is. The poetry isn't helping me." Devil Keith whispered. He burst into sore, heaving tears and sank into God's open embrace. Defeated and completely broken, the Devil was seeking kindness, comfort and a true death.

God watched in wonder and horror and despair as Devil Keith's clothes changed. From those worn by a Victorian poet, into sackcloth, and his skin turned grey due to fresh ashes. God looked at the puzzled Bub and Dr Riel for an explanation, but they were unable to rationalise the changes they were witnessing. God wiped away a tear as she hummed a beautiful lullaby and Devil Keith sank into a peaceful slumber. She laid him on his rumpled bed and tucked in his sheets. Producing a brown fluffy teddy bear, from her apron pocket, to cuddle into the exhausted Devil. That was the only comfort she could freely give.

Bub and Dr Riel sat on the soggy floor and rubbed their weary eyes. They looked at God in amazement and awe. She was their absolute hero. They could finally breathe and think, and hand over their caring responsibilities for a short time. She quickly disabused them of that notion. She was very apologetic and empathetic towards Bub and Dr Riel, but she was adamant that she had to leave immediately. Too many people currently needed her assistance, and she was down her most trusted Angel and helper. She had also sent one of her most trustworthy Angels to track down Gab and prove his innocence.

She softly hugged Dr Riel and Bub and chucked their respective chins, then wished them well. She feared they would need it. She promised to call in later, although she couldn't specify when as the first tsunami alarm had been raised and the wave was heading for a crowded beach bar.

Dr Riel and Bub now knew that they were due to face the full force of Devil Keith's wrath completely alone. Those chains needed replacing and soon.

CHAPTER SIXTY-ONE

Devil Keith and Nora's bedroom...

Harry and Karen hesitantly peeled back the blankets from the bedroom floor and looked at the blood drenched scene. They stifled a couple of sobs and each told the other that they had to be objective and calm their emotions. The opinionated Faery was correct. They had to analyse the scene and gather clues. No matter how small they were.

"So we're looking for forensic evidence such as DNA samples, ballistics, blood pattern analysis and fingerprints." Karen took out a spiral notebook and waited on Harry finding the essential data. Harry had used the cockroaches to slip into the local Falkirk police station and she'd pinched a forensic kit and a box of extra-small rubber gloves. And the remains of a Chinese take away, that was innocently lying about minding its own business. The investigators had forgotten to eat that day and the deliciously warm Chinese food might have gone to waste.

An hour later...

"Karen, there's too much of everything here except ballistics. Thank goodness there were no guns involved. There are fingerprints everywhere, there's so much blood everywhere and there's DNA everywhere. It's just...everywhere. We all rushed in and scattered it ***everywhere.****"* Harry held her head in her hands and stared at the clouds of fingerprint dust peppering the entire room. This was a waste of their time. The Faeries were

wrong. There was nothing useful to be found in here.

"Right. Ok. Right. Take a minute. The blood should be here, but what's here that shouldn't be? You know Devil Keith better than anyone else. What's here that shouldn't be? Think." Karen stared at Harry and impatiently rolled her hands. She knew they were onto something. Her varicose veins were throbbing.

Harry sighed heavily but she closed her eyes, opened them and slowly turned around. *"The towels. Why are there so many towels in here?"*

Karen tentatively picked up a towel: crispy with dried, rust coloured blood. *"They were used to mop up Nora's blood? I think that's why they're here."*

"No. They were here when we ran in. I'm sure of it. I nearly tripped over one of them. They were already here! Let me see that one." Harry was excited and playing the scene over in her head. She knew she had grabbed Bub's arm to steady herself when she'd ran into the room.

Karen handed over a large bundle. *"It's big. It's one of those huge bath sheets. Nora or Devil Keith must have used it before the party. It probably got blood on it during the murder, or someone used it clean up the blood afterwards."*

"No, no it isn't. Devil Keith's towels are flimsy and delicate and very silky. Barely able to dry a damp hamster on a warm summer day. Plus, his towels all smell of lavender and saffron oils. He told me that he won't let his Nora use anything else. Nora told me she sneaks in tea towels as they're more effective than his luxury towels. She slips them in because she can't stand watching her Devil Keith cry over her deceit and lack of taste. Well she use to sneak them in." Harry sniffed and a tear fell.

She took a calming breath. *"This is a heavy duty. A really thick towel and it smells of dried blood. And I think that's sea salt I can smell under the blood. He would never lower his standards to either buy or steal a towel like this. He says that he has a strict code of thievery: no towels or coat hangers are secreted in his luggage or on his personage. He wants to bring back hanging for folks who do that. He made me sign a petition supporting his ideals, but I can't see it going anywhere.*

So, if I'm right, then the killer must have brought these towels with them." Harry could have kissed the bossy Faery.

"To protect their clothes? Just as we thought. This was meticulously planned." Karen was livid at the audacity of the evil criminal. They divided the towels into two piles. Devil Keith's and Nora's highly scented ones on the right and the other two towels on the left.

The investigators examined one of the offending towels. They laid it on the dress-making table. *"This end of the towel has very little blood on it. Then there's blood splatted in this area below the cleanish section. Then there's a solid band of blood where I'm sure the awful cut took place. Below that is blood that is flowing downwards until it pools to the floor. What does that tell us?"* Harry queried.

Karen looked again and suggested they hang the towel over a handy mannequin. They adjusted the towel until the clear area was hanging over the mannequin's head and down the statues back. There was a lot of the towel laying on the floor in front of the model's feet. Karen pushed a book under the mannequin's feet but there was still quite a lot of towel remaining on the floor. She added a second, third and fourth book to the pile. They were beginning to get an approximation of the person's height. The killer was really tall. That excluded Harry from the suspect list, and unless Nora was willing to walk over and wait until Karen stood on a small stool then Karen was also eliminated from the suspect list.

"The killer is tall. Taller than either of us. They used this towel to completely cover themselves. From their upper back, over their head, down their front and to the floor." Harry confirmed.

"Ok, well that eliminates us but Bub, Devil Keith, Dr Riel, Willing, Vinnie, John O and Jonathan are still on the suspect list as they're tall enough. And the ogres, although I can't see them going against the Faery Queen. Plus, they're all brawn no brains. Their fur would be all over the place and they would have used

a DIY tool, like a screwdriver or a chisel, not a simple knife." Karen removed the ogres from her list. She then scored her and Harry's name from the notebook. That was a relief as Karen, after speaking with the Faeries, had secretly circled Harry's name as the prime suspect. Karen had reasoned that Harry was overcome with jealousy over Nora usurping her place in Devil Keith's affections. She hadn't been entirely convinced of Harry's relief at having Nora around to distract Devil Keith and his antics.

"Yes, that eliminates us. Thank goodness we can categorically rule people out. Not that I suspected you for a minute." Harry nervously smiled and pushed her handy rolling pin into her baggy trouser pocket.

"So why didn't Nora run away when she saw a towel walking towards her?" Harry queried.

"I think I can explain that. Dr Riel said that the cut was deeper on the left side of Nora's throat than right side. That made no sense because we are all right-handed so we'd go across the body from right to left. The cut should have been deeper on the right, unless..." Karen stood in front of Harry, facing her and made the slicing move. From right to left.

"What if the person was behind Nora?" Harry turned away from Karen. The cut worked. Nora was attacked from behind by a shrouded, cowardly figure.

"Dr Riel also said that there were no hesitation marks. It was just one lethal cut. I'm sure that we're looking for a seasoned killer." Karen gulped and glanced behind her into the shadows hiding the corners of the room.

Harry nodded. *"I think that completely eliminates Jonathan from our suspect list. He's a coward. He loves inflicting pain but he gossips and hides from the consequences. If he was able to pluck up the courage, and that's a big if, he'd want to watch the hurt and grief. I can't imagine him risking himself to do this.*

Let's look at those towels again."

Karen and Harry cracked open the hardened towels. They

tugged them flat and pulled out a small, round magnifying glass. The towels were thick but plain: utilitarian in nature. Harry picked at the washing instruction tab and found a small label underneath it. The smaller label was obscured with thick, clotted blood. She asked Karen to confirm her findings and they both concentrated on the washing instructions and the label. Could they wash the blood off the partially hidden label and get more information?

Karen and Harry gently, and nervously, held the end of the stained towel in cold water. The blood separated from the towel in a bloom of red. The label read *"From Spring to Winter"*.

"From Spring to Winter? Hold on. I've seen that recently. Give me a minute. I need to think. The sewing kit over there. What did it say on the lid?" Harry grabbed the fancy glass and held it tightly. She peered at the lid and ran her finger over it. *"No, there's no name on the lid, but wait a minute. There is a company name here on the bottom. Yes, it says the same name. I think we know where the two towels and the sewing kit came from. It was one of those fancy hotel resorts. They have lots of hotels in that group, so how do we find out which one it's from?*

Oh Karen, they might have seen the killer. Be able to identify him." Harry hugged Karen tightly, and could feel some of their tension seep away.

"I think I might have another clue to add to that one. Nora said that when they returned to Hell, after their wedding, there was sand in their room. She was adamant that they hadn't left any. She also thought that someone had been using their bed. Their room. Nora was planning on speaking with Gab about it, but with all the celebrating going on she never got a chance. So, I think that we only need to check the hotels that are on, or near a beach." Karen smiled her first genuine smile since they had found Nora's broken body.

"There must be more clues hiding in here. So what about the shoe polish we both could smell that terrible night?" Harry queried and looked around for a tin of the substance. She couldn't find any in the bedroom as Devil Keith had recently added a

specially built, airtight room just for his shoes, sandals and boots. This was in response to his recurrent difficulties, when categorising his bountiful clothing collections.

"I have Nora's dress, here, in an evidence bag. Luckily it was bagged and tagged, by Dr Riel, before it got any more damaged. Let's check it out and see what we can find." Karen tentatively pulled out the crushed dress and awkwardly draped the crispy fabric over an obliging mannequin. Karen and Harry were tearful as they thoroughly checked every inch of the beloved garment. As they searched they recounted how delighted Nora was with the party dress and how hard she found walking in the tiny heels, but she had persisted as she wanted her Devil Keith to be proud of her and her achievement. They concluded that Nora and Devil Keith had been so good for each other.

Karen and Harry breathed a sigh of relief when they found a largish smudge of thick shoe polish near the hem of the dress. After laying the mannequin on the floor they surmised that the killer had ferociously kicked Nora whilst she was on the floor dying. The spiteful assassin had unwittingly left that important piece of evidence behind. Karen and Harry angrily concluded that the murderer wasn't content with just taking an innocent life, they had also wanted to harm Nora in a very personal and unnecessary way. Her death wasn't about hurting Devil Keith. It was all about Nora. Punishing Nora for something.

"Faery Layla will never have to buy a drink again." Karen gave a half-heated laugh. She sighed and gratefully sunk to the floor.

CHAPTER SIXTY-TWO

Meanwhile in the icehouse…

Bub and Dr Riel held their breath as Devil Keith stirred and softly moaned. Devil Keith's hair had grown back in, but as they gazed at the distraught man it changed from golden blonde to lengthy black, greasy locks. They were probably dealing with a sad, poetic Devil Keith again.

Devil Keith slowly sat up and rubbed his sore, red rimmed eyes. "*My Nora was too trusting. If she had just ignored me and my stupid ways she would be alive just now. I did this. Me and my idiotic adventures. I must have upset so many people, and they rightly took their revenge in the most cruel way possible. This is all down to me. I did this to a beautiful person. An innocent.*

Did you know that she thought she wasn't exciting enough for me? Not experienced enough? I'd hear her during the night talking to her mirror. She say 'he chose you and he's wonderful, so deep inside I'm worth it'. Imagine my brave, fearless girl thinking that she was less than me. I'm nothing really. A jumped up fashion designer who thinks the right colour of bowtie can save the endangered Siberian tigers or the cut of your jacket can stop a tsunami. I'm useless. A joke." Devil Keith produced a wry laugh and collected a single tear on his finger tip.

Devil Keith punched himself in the face and fell back onto his creaking bed. He then leapt into the air. "*God, please, I'll give you everything I have for one more smile from my Nora. Please, please just one smile. Not even a smile: a glimpse of her lovely face and I'll give up Hell. You can have it all. Please, please help me. I need my Nora so, so much. It hurts so bad."* Devil Keith croaked and curled up into a small crying ball of pain. God did not appear as she was busy with a busload of children.

Bub stepped towards Devil Keith but Dr Riel put out a hand and pulled him back. *"We don't know what we're dealing with. It could be sorrow but he's changing so quickly. He could cycle into anger just as quickly. Best to be safe just now."*

"You're right to ignore me, God. Nora should have known better than to be with me. It's really all her fault. She did this to me. I was content to love myself and sort of care for other folks. I mean you pair of pathetic toads, over there. But she went and made me love her. Completely and totally love her. She's the one that's making me hurt. I hate her. I hate her so much. I tell you. I may be the Devil but she's pure evil. A trickster. A fraud. A liar. She said she'd never leave me and the first chance she gets she's off. She's evil to the core." A furious Devil Keith screamed. He burst up from the watery floor. His pale skin erupting into green and grey weeping pustules. A ten inch scally horn flew out of his forehead and imbedded in the stones above Bub's head. Devil Keith's arms lengthened and his thick knuckles glanced off the floor. Bub and Dr Riel braced themselves for the fight of their life.

"No, no I didn't mean it. Nora. Nora. Nora. Please come back to me. I'm sorry. You're the best thing that's ever happened to me." Devil Keith pleaded and whimpered. Devil Keith's skin peeled away and his dirty Lord Byron outfit materialised again. He dived at his trunk of books. *"There must be something in here to help me understand. Bub, don't just stand there help me look. I have to look. Nora needs me."*

Bub took a small step towards the frantic man. The sturdy trunk and Devil Keith went up in a whoosh of white hot flames. Bub and Dr Riel jumped back from the blistering heat and threw themselves into the water covering the floor. Less than a second later Bub and Dr Riel were on their feet. They were splashing the human torch with water, whilst frantically screaming and pleading for Devil Keith to calm his fury.

An unblemished Devil Keith stepped out of the tower of flames. *"I'm so tired and I feel unwell. What's wrong with me? Why are you all wet? Where's my Nora? I want to start planning our honeymoon. Nora, do you fancy going to Venice to a nice bit of 'relations' in the sun? You mysterious minx."* Devil Keith winked and looked around for his saucy wife. He looked under his torn blanket then collapsed in a heap of sorrow: pulling the blanket over his head. The flames puffed out and the incinerated trunk crumbled into the flooded floor.

"The poor, tormented soul. He can't take much more of this." Bub wrung his hands as he paced around the cramped icehouse. He looked over at the map. It was covered in frantic writing and sticky labels. He rubbed his face and yawned. He was exhausted and fearful and sad and angry. All at once and all equally awful. He couldn't begin to comprehend how much worse Devil Keith was feeling.

"He's rapidly cycling and he's so unpredictable. I know you don't want to do this but we need to use the chains and restraints now. The new titanium handcuffs that the Faeries loaned us should be able to contain him for a short spell while we get more help. Well that's the hope anyway.

I saw you look over at the map. The world isn't doing too well either. There's been reports of earthquakes and volcanic reactions in regions that are normally considered quite stable and safe. One of the tabloid newspapers have reported incidents of water going up in flames but everyone is denying that as being trashy fake news. However, I think it may be true. I've checked the Apocalypse prophecies and we're due rivers of tears and blood emitting from plants and trees any day now. That's going to be a lot harder to hide, and it's going to cause mass panic and evacuations. Then the final destructive stage is huge explosions and the world will split apart. It feels so close. Too close."

"What can we do about it?" Bub rubbed his face and blew out his thinning cheeks. He rolled his shoulders then flexed his back: trying to avoid the inevitable. He could delay no more: he consulted the disintegrating wall map and traced the fragile

tectonic plates with his index finger. There were going to be catastrophic casualties if this continued.

"The only solution I can find is if Devil Keith moves onto acceptance and learns to live again." Dr Riel signed and shrugged his weary shoulders.

"Unlikely. Very unlikely." Bub looked over at the shell of his quivering brother.

"Yes, unlikely. Can you pass over the restraints and the gallon of sleeping potion? Let's get this over with." Bub handed Dr Riel the heavy chains and a funnel. He sent up a silent prayer.

CHAPTER SIXTY-THREE

Karen's office...

The bolstered investigators started the next phase of their lengthy inquiry. They interviewed the cockroach Union Representative, but he was clear that neither him nor his card carrying brothers and sisters had provided transportation to or from any of the Spring to Winter resorts. He was indignant that Karen and Harry were implying that any of his law-abiding members would aid and abet a felon.

Harry appeased him by offering him un-fettered access to her cloud storage and all the photos of her friend Amanda that they could squash on to their crowded walls. She was sure Amanda would agree with the compromise, but if not she was going to offer her a basket of Galaxy chocolate bars and a dozen packs of Quavers as a wee bribe. The delighted cockroach negotiator left the room with a song in his heart and a large packet of Blu-tac in his back pocket. Well not his back pocket per say, rather a convenient storage crack in his back shell-type thingy. His exoskeleton: one of the authors just did a Wikipedia search on cockroach anatomy whilst the other author hoped no one checked their unique, some would call it bizarre, search history.

Karen and Harry then, unsuccessfully, tried calling the Spring to Winter resorts and asking them for assistance in identifying the killer or towel stealer. They figured that the hotel staff might have more of an invested interest in the linen thefts. No luck was the response. They even offered to send photographs and bios of the Hell team, but the hotel staff were polite but insistent that they had to respect their guests privacy.

The investigators then tried a *"good cop bad cop routine"* but they quickly realised that they were both, *"bad cops"* when the reception staff informed them that threatening to expose the hotel staff's entrails to the midday sun was not the way to make friends and influence people. Karen and Harry were frustrated with this block to their investigation, but they were also impressed with the professionalism of the reception staff. Not many people could withstand a good Harry bollocking and still ask if she wanted to be added to their resort mailing list.

An hour later...

"I don't trust you but I don't trust anyone, so you're the best of a bad bunch. And you're tall. So tall." Karen snarled and threw a dirty look at Harry. The fifth such look in the last five minutes.

"Erm, thanks? I think." Bub replied and ducked down to minimise his offending height. Difficult to do as he was also firmly holding Harry away from the maniac that was an enraged Karen. Harry and Karen had discussed this development at length. Well they mainly swore and called each other rather nasty names. Karen had learned a lot of colourful adjectives and uses for ropes whilst playing board games on the high seas. So she had.

Harry and Karen had both agreed that they needed someone they could trust to go around the Spring to Winter hotels and resorts to look for clues as to the killer's identity. Karen had stubbornly voted for Dr Riel to take on this vital task and Harry, equally stubbornly, voted for Bub to do the honours. After some particularly vicious hairpulling, Bub was chosen as they needed someone skilled to stay behind in the icehouse to take care of poor Devil Keith. Harry and Karen were initially going to do the searching of the hotels themselves but they reasoned that the killer may still be in, or near Hell number one so others could be at risk of death or intimidation. Plus, they still didn't have enough evidence to identify the disgusting culprit, so they had to continue with the onerous job of gathering and shifting through the clues. Lastly, they were allocating time each day to look after Fachance as she was struggling to cope with Gab's absence and his possible guilt. Willing was also looking a bit frazzled around the edges and needed some support too.

As a reluctantly agreed compromise, to allowing Bub to search, Harry had made another cockroach excursion to Falkirk police station. They really needed some additional security and a better standard of biscuits there, Harry concluded. So Bub was now fitted with a low to midrange police issue body camera that he had rigged up to Karen's mobile phone.

"This stays on. No matter what. I don't care what you're doing. If this is turned off then I will not hesitate to de-capitate Harry." Karen tossed her gleaming battle axe in the air then swung it over her back to rest in her leather holster. She normally used the axe to chop her carrots, celery and horse chestnuts for her and Dr Riel's Friday night stir-fry, so this was a nice little change of pace for the death dealing object.

"Oy. I never agreed to that. I'm not putting my Harry at risk. What if this gizmo goes on the blink, and you lose contact? What if I need to visit the little boy's room and I need to turn it off? What then?" Bub slipped a mini toolkit and set of spare batteries in his breast pocket. He wasn't convinced that the police were issued with the best of equipment. He'd seen too many episodes of Crimewatch and their grainy videos. He had previously argued with Devil Keith that no one, not even a despicable criminal, was that particular colour and still breathing.

"Take it or leave it, tall boy. You just better hope that

everything works. And the camera stays on." Karen growled and reached behind her back for her trusty slicer.

Bub did take it, and he promptly left to search the hotels. Well, he tried to promptly leave but Harry repeatedly told him to take care and be vigilant as they didn't know what Bub might find or what danger he was walking into. She also needed to be pried away from a truly humungous Bub cuddle that was going on for many, many minutes.

However, Harry was reassured that Bub recognised how serious the situation was as he hadn't hesitated in shucking off his expensive tailored suit then donning neon yellow board shorts and a puce tee-shirt advertising a bar that provided unlimited shrimp cocktail if you could lick your own elbow. Bub had clearly received that as a gift from Devil Keith. He topped this off with a wide-brimmed straw hat and large mirrored sunglasses. He was also carrying a baseball bat with retractable spikes and a bowling ball heavily disguised as a beach ball. He was amazed at the things Harry had hidden in the bottom of her pink, flowery toiletry bag.

He was obviously desperate for results, and willing to do whatever it took to blend in with the holiday makers and catch the murderer.

In preparation for Bub's quest Harry had checked the internet and luckily there were only three luxury hotels that were situated on, or near a beach, so that narrowed the search criteria. A good thing as Bub wasn't keen on leaving Dr Riel on his own, for a prolonged period of time, with the increasingly erratic and violent Devil Keith. Another reason for Karen's growling, snarling and general anger directed towards Harry and Bub. She didn't want her doctor harmed, and removing Bub from Devil Keith's care duties definitely rated as increasing the risk of harm to her guy.

A tearful but slightly hopeful Harry and Karen went back to the tedious job of searching for clues. Bub left to identify and/or apprehend a killer. A killer that may very well be called Gab.

CHAPTER SIXTY-FOUR

Karen's office…

There was a heavy knock at the office door. *"Are you expecting anyone? Did we organise more interviews? Quick, throw a sheet over the board and I'll get the door before they knock it in."* Harry hastily threw the sheet at Karen and answered the shaking door.

Vinnie and John O stood in the middle of Karen's office and appeared both disappointed and embarrassed. They explained, well John O explained as Vinnie just grunted and scratched at his robust beard. So, John O stated that despite an extensive under-stair cupboard search at the Oracles house they were unable to find the Time Scavenger. However, they had found something else lurking in the back of the hairy spider and ventriloquist's dummies infested cupboard. John O wiggled his shoulders when he mentioned the invasive spiders. He wriggled a lot more than just his shoulders when he pictured the gruesome papier-mâché dolls and their nightmare grimaces.

"I know it doesn't look great but I think it will help. We just need to fix it up a bit. Get it working." The item that didn't look "*great*" was pieces of a heavy iron cage. A cage that was big enough to hold a ferocious, demented Devil. For a little while anyway.

"Do you think it's really come to this? A cage? Devil Keith

needs a cage? I don't know. It seems too much." Harry whispered. She hiccupped then blew her sore, red nose.

"I know you've been busy but I think you need to check the news regularly and put on the radio. The whole world's falling apart and we're pretty sure that Devil Keith's grief is causing it. And it's getting worse. We also thought that you might appreciate having Bub and Dr Riel back home so that you can all help look after Devil Keith. Going by the state of things, Bub and Dr Riel are probably having a hard time of it too. We wouldn't want to manage Devil Keith on our own. No, not at all." Vinnie said this whilst slurping his thermos of hot coffee and chewing on a raisin and chocolate breakfast bar. He softly dabbed his lips with a cream linen napkin. The big guy can speak in full and non-threatening sentences? So Willing had been able to converse with him during the party. That was a relief. Harry was also touched by their thoughtfulness regarding bringing their men home, where they belonged. She needed a Bub cuddle so much.

John O and Vinnie blushed as they shrugged off some very enthusiastic praise, then they stripped off. They got to work greasing the metal bars with heavy motor oil and checking the locking mechanism. They arranged the bolts and washers in order and finally wrestled the sides of the cage into place. The thing was colossal but they all agreed that it was very necessary precaution during these erratic times. Devil Keith so needed to come on home.

CHAPTER SIXTY-FIVE

Karen's office...

There was another knock at the door but rather than waiting for an invite to enter the room, the door was thrown open and the doorhandle hit off the wall. Dislodging some plaster board and a prized, signed photograph of Elvis Presley, from the nicotine stained wall in the process. Karen sighed, it would take forever to re-fill that hole and match up the brownish stain.

"We're back. Bet you've missed us. What a time we've had of it. It's chaos out there. Stop staring and get the kettle on. We've brought buns." Marjorie, the Oracle declared and plonked a paper bag stuffed full of iced treats on Karen's cluttered desk.

"Oh, that's a nice cage. We have one just like it at home. Don't we Marjorie? They're so alike. Like peas in a pod, eh Marjorie? Are you redecorating then, Karen? About time. You might want to start by filling in that hole in the wall over there and clearing up those bits of broken glass. Shocking workmanship in this place." Gilbert, the other Oracle ran his hands over the cage then wiped his greasy digits on Karen's newish curtains.

"No, not redecorating. It's for Devil Keith and the Apocalypse that's going on. You might have noticed it." Karen sarcastically stated. She subtly tried to manoeuvre the insensitive Oracles out of her office before she skelped them about their empty heads.

"Oh, it all makes sense now. An Apocalypse. We did wonder why everyone was ordering umbrellas, sandbags and luxury yachts

from Nile. I was just saying that it was odd. Wasn't I Marjorie? It was odd? We really should go back to Nile and help out. They said our assistance was indescribable. Didn't they Marjorie?" Gilbert was busy stuffing his pockets with Karen's best stationery items. Karen doubted that Nile wanted them back. She could just imagine their relief at getting shot of the clueless Oracles. Angel Gab was right, Hell number one needed a new set of Oracles as soon as possible. She began composing the job advert in her head. Number one, no orthopaedic sandals or polyester clothing as they are a red flag and a fire risk. Number two, no hoarding or thieving allowed. Number three, no misplacing important artefacts and using Ryan Reynolds greasy marks to foretell the future. Number four, no evil French bread storing debacles. Number five, no nonsense of any kind. Number six, no...

"Wait a minute. You look familiar. I think I know you." John O pointed an accusing finger at Marjorie and Gilbert.

"No, lad I don't think we've ever had the pleasure." Gilbert guiltily slid towards the door. Marjorie gulped then gulped again. She grabbed the warm buns and stuffed them back into her yellow net bag. Ready for a quick getaway and a tasty snack for the road.

Vinnie's large body blocked the doorway and only means of escape. *"I know you too. I think you two have some explaining to do. Don't you? Sit your arses down, now. Don't try to get around me. I ain't moving other than to pound you into the floor. So try me...I dare you."* Vinnie cracked his knuckles and gave a demonic smile. He had quickly slid back into the grunting and intimidating stage of his social skills training.

"Yes, sit down you murderous beasts, or don't. Up to you. I'd really like to see Vinnie turn you into a sludgy stain on the carpet. Oh, you're taking us serious now... I'll get some rope." The normally sunny dispositioned John O was sporting a thunderous frown. In the blink of an eye he liberated Karen's axe from its cosy, knitted holster. He was tossing the axe from hand to hand and hard staring at the frightened Oracle. He

clearly knew how to use the lethal weapon, and he had every intention of doing so. Their heads were going on a spike. Stat. The wary Oracles did sit their padded arses down, but John O couldn't locate any rope

CHAPTER SIXTY-SIX

Vinnie, John O and how they know the murdering Oracles...

"I'm not sure you should be treating our Oracles like this." Karen queried and patted Gilbert's head.

"Oh, you'll think we're being kindness itself when we tell you what they did. Vinnie, can you do the honours?" John O responded and removed Karen's hand.

"I was a palace guard on the breathtaking island of Atlantis. You know? The famous one that's in all those awful B movies that people inexplicably like. I can't believe how badly they portray my home in those films. Don't you worry, I'm going to deal with that later. I have a plan and a need to audition, but that as I said is a job for later.

Anyway, part of my job was to take the young ones out into the world to be fostered and nurtured by wise and kind families. This was an old tradition going back centuries that allowed the island to flourish and gain knowledge from other cultures. The children of Atlantis would return when they were about twenty or twenty-five years old. Some people would bring new skills such as medicine, architecture, music or art. Some would bring their spouses and, if we were lucky, some would bring their offspring with them. It was also a way of spreading our knowledge, history and stories with others too. We were welcoming, enlightened and the centre of all known civilisation. Sadly, it turns out we were also naïve and foolish.

I was scheduled to leave port and make a delivery of our treasured children, but we had to bring that journey forward by a few weeks as Atlantis started to sink. In all the panic and chaos I had to leave everything behind and just go. Poorly prepared, and with only half the crew required, I was piloting the boat towards what you now call South America, when we ran into a raging storm. The boat was badly damaged and it began taking on water. On that boat was young John O here, although he was called Adonis III then."

"I have no memory of that event as I was only about three or four years old. Oh, please don't ever repeat that name, or my brother will never stop teasing me about it." John O pleaded, in jest, although he really would get a right roasting from his bro and the local rugby team if it ever came out.

"You would have been three or four. That was when Atlantean young went out on their first of many adventures." Vinnie clarified, with every intention of passing on the name, and the ribbing it would cause.

"Thanks. I was found wandering around the streets of Rio De Janeiro, in Brazil, nearly thirty years ago by a holidaying family. I was rummaging through a pile of rubbish looking for food and shelter. And, according to my less than flattering big brother, I was semi-feral, when they found and rescued me. I was also filthy, crying and confused, with no memory of my past or even my name. I was lucky as I was fostered, then adopted by that amazing family. I was wearing a ragged piece of torn sheet so there were no clues as to my identity, so my parents thought I'd wandered away from a nearby orphanage. They contacted the local authorities and spent months looking for my biological parents but they had no success. By then, they tell me, they had fallen in love with my naughty ways and brilliant smile so they decided I'd be the perfect addition to their growing family. My brother still says it was pity, rather than love as they had just lost their pet dog, but that's what brothers are for.

They were, and still are amazingly supportive and loving people. Seemingly, and I know you'll find this hard to believe, but I was a bit of a wild child. Always getting into mischief and when I got older this transformed into my need to travel and look for adventures. I always felt a calling to the waters and, with the help of my folks, it just made sense to set up a small salvaging business.

It wasn't until a few weeks ago, when I kept having the most vivid dreams, that I knew I needed go to Greece. I'd wake up and just know I had to go there. It was also then that I knew that Vinnie had woken up. Even though I had no recollection of ever meeting someone called Vinnie, I knew he was important to me."

Vinnie smiled over at John O. *"When the ill-fated boat sunk I was lucky and floated to land. I was bereft at my loss of my charges so I searched and searched for the lost children of Atlantis. My responsibility and my greatest failure, that even to this day I cannot atone for. For years I kept moving North, through South America, and hunting for the special children. I had no luck and they remained lost to me. Eventually I reached mosquito ridden marshes then swamps. I was very unfortunate and sank into a large sinkhole and there I remained for many, many centuries. Asleep with no awareness of the passage of time.*

I slept deeply until I abruptly woke up and had the overwhelming urge to travel. It was a compulsion that I just couldn't shake. I had no money but luckily I met Willing at the docks, and she offered me a job acting as her hired muscle. She doesn't know my history as I was so grumpy, and needed many weeks' worth of coffee to awaken fully and chat. I'm not sure if you noticed that I was less than pleasant to you all?" Vinnie smiled again and raised his bushy eyebrows at the investigators. He had a lovely smile when he hid some of his gnashing teeth.

"Ahem. We did wonder about all the growling, muttering and the thermos flasks scattered about the place. Well, the flasks were a little bit puzzling. We just kinda thought you were leaving them out as snacks for Fachance to find. A weird support sorta thing during her time of need." Karen tentatively added. Although now that she looked at him, Vinnie did appear much more approachable and nearly welcoming. The bruising brass knuckle duster had been replaced with a recently plaited, rather fetching, green and sea blue Friendship Bracelet.

"So, as Vinnie here travelled the globe with Willing I went to

Corfu, for what I thought was no more than a holiday with some lads I had recently met at a bar. They came on as my temporary crew, and you know how well that turned out. Sorry about that, by the way.

Well, I met you. Karen, I couldn't believe what we found, my lovely. I never for one minute thought that fortunate fall on the beach would lead me to a sunken city, to Scotland and eventually discovering Atlantis. An adventure of a lifetime. I genuinely had no idea what was going on, my lovely. I have so much to thank you for my wonderful friend." John O patted Karen's hand then spontaneously pulled her in for an appreciative hug.

"When we escaped Falkirk and arrived in Hell number one I met Vinnie. We had an instant, blinding connection, and although Vinnie's social skills were poor, we started to talk. And talk some more. Well I talked and he listened. I told him my story about being fostered, my need to travel and the tale of finding Atlantis. And, not putting too fine a point on it, Vinnie was gobsmacked. He explained that due to our instant bond he knew that I was a child of Atlantis and, as such, I had slept through adversity. Hence the reason I had stayed dormant for many centuries until the right people had appeared to care for me. I wasn't even sceptical when I heard Vinnie's story as I just knew that everything now made so much more sense. I felt tethered to something solid and just. It reminded me of how close I feel to you, Karen.

Vinnie asked me to describe Atlantis now, and the destruction I had found on the seabed and in the duckpond. He cried and cried for the loss of all that beauty and culture."

"I did." Vinnie sniffed and wiped his nose. He smiled at John O and John O rubbed Vinnie's cheek.

CHAPTER SIXTY-SEVEN

Why Atlantis sank...

"These two murdering barbarians sank Atlantis. No don't try to justify your actions. You two did it and need to be punished. So sit yourself backdown." Vinnie barked and lunged at the guilty pair. Although they didn't really look all that guilty. Not guilty at all.

"We only meant to sink it a little bit." Gilbert pouted and tossed his short curly hair. He sneaked out a bun and nibbled off an end.

"How do you sink an island just a little?" Harry was horrified and knocked the bun out of Gilbert's undeserving hand.

"You don't. You absolutely don't sink it 'a little bit'. These folks you call your Oracles were visiting Atlantis when they discovered our Time Gatherers. Well one tool viewed time and the other allowed us to select essential items that could save lives or develop our civilisation further. We had strict rules that we followed. We only took what we absolutely needed from the future and we only viewed the past to learn from our mistakes. No more, no less was our ethos. We were proud of our laws; our achievements and we naively shared the magical items with our visitors. As I said before: we were so innocent and naive.

They were sly and lavished us with extravagant praise and compliments. We lapped this up and looked for more. They methodically corrupted our beliefs with the aim of using our tools for their own twisted agenda. They went 'scavenging' for anything and everything they wanted. They brought back things we didn't need and talked us into needing and wanting them. Craving them. They convinced us to build a temple to their collections and hoarding ways. A temple decorated in beaten panels of gold, silver and platinum, then carefully etched with pictures of their 'essential finds'. They called those things precious when we all knew knowledge, love and kindness were the only truly precious things in the world... but we were caught up in the hype and glamour.

When the Atlantean people questioned them and their crimes, they confused us with dinosaur hunts and glass ceilings. They encouraged us to ridicule our ancestors for their simpler, gentler ways and embrace the finds of the future. They built a lavishly decorated box to hold their thieving tools and put it on a podium in the centre of the temple. They told us we'd eventually worship them and the tools ***they*** *used to their 'full potential'.*

However, they went too far when they stole the recipe for Irn Bru, from the future. A.G. Barr had worked really hard on developing that tonic, and they stole his knowledge to make it their own. They turned us away from farming the land, exploring medicine and building our future. And, worst of all, they banished our need for learning and growing, so they could make us work in their factory. Focus only on producing the wonderful tonic. Then they made the tonic too expensive for us to purchase.

They said we couldn't take the children from the island as they were needed to work for them. Meet quotas, they said. That was when we realised our mistake. We'd had enough and secretly planned on banning your Oracles from our island paradise and taking back our sacred, but corrupted tools. Somehow they found out about our plans. They devised a terrible revenge on our island, and they wanted to keep us busy while they stole our Time Viewer and Scavenger.

So, they put all the bathplugs into our sunken baths and turned on the taps. With overflowing baths and sinks, and blocked toilets our idyllic island began slowly sinking. The elders instructed us to remove the bathplugs but those beasts kept putting them back in, until all was lost. The island was lost." Vinnie was crying tears of sorrow and rage. The Oracles were beginning to look slightly upset, but not upset enough to stop them from requesting a cup of tea to go with their iced buns.

"Vinnie explained all of this to me, and I was initially sceptical, as I couldn't believe a whole civilisation could be fooled so easily. However, the more I thought about the more I realised that it all made sense. Old Jock and the Oracles created a time loop with their thieving ways. A.G. Barr definitely created Irn Bru in 1901 and the Oracles went forward in time to steal it for their evil ways. They stole the elixir of the Gods and put the revered recipe on the wall. They used the wall because they wanted everyone to see it and fear their all-consuming confidence. They thought the Atlantean's were too cowed and brow beaten to revolt." John O added. He handed the distressed Vinnie a damp, used tissue then rubbed his arm.

"John O told me all about the grotesque statues that were added to the outside of the Atlantis factory. So, not content with destroying an enlightened people and their home, those philistines over there created statues of themselves to decorate their folly. A permanent memorial to their cold, calamitous ways. A shrine to their obscene plans, actions and ambitions. They are monsters. In the true sense of the meaning of monsters." Vinnie stuffed the soggy tissue up his sleeve. The time for tears was over and some much needed axing was due to begin.

"Hey, we only added the statues to hide the location of Atlantis and preserve its secrets and legends. We did it all for your people. We made you famous. Plus, it was a bit of a laugh to have caricatures of ourselves gracing its holier than thou walls. We're just surprised the Blu-tack held so well, aren't we Gilbert?" Marjorie giggled as she admitted their awful crimes.

"Lies and deceit. Even now you can't, or won't take responsibility for your heinous crimes." Vinnie bellowed and lunged at the reckless pair. Karen was so relieved when John O just managed to hold him back. Although there was a scuffle

and many, many desks lamps were lost in the process.

Still in Karen's office and the desk-tidies are upright again…

"Wait a cotton-picking minute. So all this time you've told us we have to maintain the time line no matter what. Or, as you recently said, you'd 'wear my skin as a scarf', if we didn't. You've been blithely causing mayhem for centuries. And you created one of the biggest mysteries ever. Look at yourselves. You aren't even ashamed of your actions. How can you just sit there and nibble on cake like you accidently left the milk sitting out? You destroyed an entire civilisation. You cretins." An exhausted and exasperated Harry plonked down on a cushion and rubbed her forehead. Karen had said she sort of recognised the models used for the statues, but Harry would never had believed it was those two vain nincompoops. She didn't think they had the brainpower to pull off, and successfully hide, such an audacious and horrific crime.

"Now, now boys. You're making us sound so bad in front of the girls. So uncaring. We did ***want*** *to use the Time Scavenger to send ourselves back to warn our earlier selves not to do it, but we realised that if we did that then we wouldn't have the Scavenger for ourselves. And we so wanted that device. So what if we sank an island and its people for the tool? It was such a long time ago and we made them famous. They became legends due to us.*

And they were going to stop us from using the Scavenger and by then it was our addiction. We couldn't help ourselves. It was an illness. You should have some compassion for us, lad." Gilbert rhythmically nodded and agreed with Marjorie's horrific argument. He stretched his arms out to the side then spread his palms and gave a shrug. He genuinely expected some sympathy. And possibly a hug.

"Come, come. There must be something we can do to turn that frown upside down." Gilbert inappropriately joked then jumped to avoid a downward stroke of the lethal looking axe. He really was not reading the room.

"Wait. Wait. Before you dice them up, and incidentally I don't blame you for wanting to do that, I have a couple of questions for the Oracles. Did you really go to Nile to help them out or is that a fake alibi? A rouse? Did you kill Nora to hide you're secret from coming out?" Karen stepped in to get much needed information, and to stop the Atlantean's from chopping up her room. She already had an Elvis original to replace, and Johnathan had made a few disastrous changes of his own whilst she was away.

"Yes... and no." Gilber answered with a grin. Again, not reading the room and still hinting for a cuddle.

"What do you mean 'yes and no'? Did you murder our Nora? And stop with all the smiling. It's making me nauseous." Harry pointedly stared at the axe then pointed at the unperturbed Oracles.

"Yes we went to Nile, and no we did not kill Nora. Even though we only met her a couple of times, we liked Nora. She was feisty and brought us shortbread rounds for our tea breaks. We had no reason to harm her or Devil Keith. Neither of them knew our secret. **We** *hardly remember what we did as it was so long ago.*

So, is there anything small and easy that can make this all better? Something to stop the axe throwing and all the unnecessary threats?" Marjorie sighed then pulled a 24 carat gold pen and an ostrich skin diary from her Chanel handbag. She crossed her stubby legs and impatiently waited for instructions.

Harry and Karen knew the Oracles were probably telling the truth as it had always been highly unlikely that they had killed Nora. And the Oracles never ever polished their sandals as they just bought, or Scavenged new ones when their shoes got scuffed. So they wouldn't have deposited the polish on Nora's dress.

"You thieving, murderous animals. Yes, there's things you can do. You can give us the Time Viewer and the Time Scavenger back for starters. Then we can go back in time and warn the people of Atlantis not to trust you and your devious ways. We can slap you in irons the moment you open your deceitful mouths and sling

you in the ocean." Vinnie barked. He then sweetly smiled as he recalled the fabulous island and the close friends he had been forced to leave behind. He so wanted to go home and get out of his jeans and itchy jumper. A toga was so much more forgiving and comfortable for the larger man.

"We're animals? Really? Young Harry, here, broke the Time Viewer. The Time Scavenger...well if you can find it, you can have it, lad. Gab and Fachance gave it to us and we tossed it in the cupboard under the stairs. We don't need it because Nile has refused to let us use their company to buy and sell our treasures. They said we were 'unreliable' and had too many poor reviews. Or they told some other lie about us, so we're going to look into finding another hobby to keep us busy." Gilbert brushed his hands together. He was going to have a look at their Big Bang runes and see what they were capable of doing. He quite fancied doing a bit of diamond fishing at the earth's core or a bit of mermaid wrestling. Something water related he decided, with a sneaky smile and a pinch of Marjorie's rapidly spreading bottom.

"Harry, how could you break such a wonderful item? No, no. You can explain yourself later, and if you have the pieces I'll see if I can fix it. You do still have the pieces? Right?

However, the Time Scavenger is a different matter entirely. We've been looking in your under-stair cupboard for days and days. We can't find it anywhere but we're never gonna stop searching. On the bright side, we did find a cage that you might find comfortable." John O shouted and kicked a chair across the room in sheer frustration.

"Ah, well that's that then, lad. There's nothing we can do, so bye, bye then. Marjorie?" Gilbert indicated that Marjorie should precede him and he made to leave the room. He was grabbed by John O and slammed against the nearest wall. Gilbert's false teeth tumbled to the floor. By the looks of them he had recently been eating broccoli quiche and steamed turnip tops with a side order of extra sticky raspberry seeds.

"Stop, stop. You can't really hurt them, much as they deserve

it and we'd like to see you do it. I know it sounds highly unlikely, but we may need them to find Nora's killer, heal Devil Keith and stop the Apocalypse. Harming the Oracles might impact on these things. We can't risk them or the world just now." Karen reluctantly pleaded for mercy for the disgusting, gloating pair.

"She's right. We're crucial to all your futures." A smug Gilbert crossed his arms under his ever expanding man boobs.

"No, Karen didn't say that. She said you might be useful. Vinnie, John O, you've been through such a harrowing time. Can you give us a few days then you can do whatever you want with those two horrors? We need to sort things out here, but we'll throw them in a prison cell in the meantime." Harry called in a couple of minor demons to remove and guard the protesting criminals, whilst Karen placated the distressed and quietly seething Atlanteans.

Just in case you're interested: the demons in Hell number one look less demonic than you'd think. They all resemble office mid-managers of the 1970's era, complete with fawn brown trousers, scuffed loafers and a beige jumper that has a number of suspicious looking stains trailing down the front. Stains that indicate that they had bravely tried a trailblazing Coronation chicken sandwich or a scandalously unfamiliar prawn cocktail for their lunch.

Still in Karen's office...

"The Time Viewer is broken and, according to Stan, it can't be mended. He and Bub tried to fix it a few months ago. If it had worked we would have used it to view the night of Nora's murder, and found the killer straight away. I'm so, so sorry.

I know you probably hate us all just now, and you don't have to answer my questions, but why did you need me to find Atlantis? Surely you could have found it on your own. Wouldn't your dreams have guided you?" Karen quietly enquired and patted John O's hand.

"I think I can answer that. I think ***you*** *were the catalyst that*

woke me up, and called John O here, to the island of Corfu. When you stepped onto the Greek Island you must have unconsciously pulled us to you. I'm positive that you're an Atlantean Princess and as such, you are very precious to our people. Your varicose veins and amber chip mean that you will always be able to find Atlantis. It's the equivalent of making small children memorise their full name and address in case they get lost. The elders had just started the useful practice when Atlantis began sinking. You're probably the only person in the world with that piece of remarkable body art, although quite a few Atlanteans have those varicose veins.

This next theory I have is a bit of guesswork. Unfortunately, I think that because Old Jock took pieces of Atlantis away with him, your homing beacon wasn't as strong as it was meant to be. That meant that instead of you finding the island straight away, you needed to go on multiple dives and do some research to locate it. The friendly fish also really helped your quest, and I highly doubt that it would have responded to anyone but you. You really did find Atlantis. All of it. Now you have to decide what you want to do with it, Princess.

As to the rest of your history. John O and I think that the Oracles may have taken pity on you when the island was sinking and brought you with them. You probably want to ask them for details, but don't expect the full truth. I'm not sure that they're capable of telling the truth. Unless it benefits them." Vinnie was making plans to bribe the demon guards with his famous tuna pasta salad and triple chocolate cheesecake. Those Oracles were going to be freed from their cell so they could suffer… and soon. He just needed to locate some cream cheese and ginger nut biscuits.

"That's quite some story. So, you're sure I'm a real princess? Positive? Harry did you hear that? Dr Riel will be so happy. He always said I was special." Karen was delighted and ever so slightly smug. She'd always wondered about her past and could never get a straight answer from the devious Oracles.

"Yep, that's what he meant." Harry teased. She gently

pushed her friend on the shoulder and wondered if she could get a knighthood from the newly appointed Princess Karen. Harry also wondered if Karen could score her some gold panelling for her bathroom shower cubicle. It had never been the same since the Roberto chomping incident.

"Sorry, you're both probably exhausted and very emotional, but I have more questions. Why didn't you just tell us all this? Let us help you? Ok, we would have struggled to believe you and the role of our Oracles played in your calamity. They always seemed so harmless, but we could have helped you. I thought we were friends. We went through a lot together." A disappointed Karen patted John O's hand again, and he pulled her in for a comforting hug.

"We are friends, my lovely, but we weren't sure if you'd believe us. It's all very farfetched and incredible. And, we genuinely didn't know that your Oracles were to blame for our misery. We were truly shocked when we saw them here.

Plus, we didn't know how open you were to new ideas, and our lifestyle. We didn't think you'd like us when you got to know us better. We were worried that you were... well..., homophobic as you are so horrible to Jonathan. Brace yourselves. Yes, Vinnie and I are together, but we'll make sure we keep it under wraps so we don't offend you. Embarrass you, and make you uncomfortable." John O took Vinnie's hand then quickly dropped it. He gave Vinnie an apologetic look and went to hug him but stopped.

"Oh, no. No, no. We hate Jonathan because he's an awful, spiteful person. He gossips and causes trouble all the time. When he was alive he hated everyone that wasn't him or his inflated idea of himself. When he came here he was turned gay, but not as a punishment. Not at all. It was to give him some insight and help his development. We initially had high hopes that he'd change and understand other people and their journey. Their bravery, and their struggles to be accepted. Then he'd get outta here, but his nastiness just got worse. We don't care about your gender or your sexual identity. You could have sex with that table over there, for all we care." Karen indicated a small occasional table with her thumb.

"Please don't." A very high pitched voice whispered. Bulbs began shattering and crystals fell from Karen's new glass windchime. Mr Hamhands removed his large tray hat and waddled over to the startled team. He pushed his pound of square sausage into his cheek pouch then explained that he was hiding from Judy, his wife. She likes to holiday in Egypt but he wasn't so keen on going there as he had developed a deep distrust of olives and their slippery ways. Harry was extremely empathetic and could see his point of view. They bonded further when she told him all about her skint knee and nearly being hit by a moped in Venice.

"I wanted to go to the Canary Islands, just off Africa. I so like budgerigars and parrots. They're like little flying rainbows. So they are." Mr Hamhands pronounced with obvious longing. Karen didn't enlighten the wee chappy as she couldn't handle his disappointment. She decided to leave some travel brochures on his hat/tray and let him find out about the islands and their wildlife on his own.

"I hate to ask you this, Mr Hamhands...but do you know anything about Nora's death?" Karen was standing at the cloth covered whiteboard and hoping that Mr Hamhands could provide the break they so desperately needed. They still hadn't found a motive to connect Gab to the murder. Mr Hamhands, hoping to avoid any more glass related injuries, grabbed a pen and wrote on a corner of the board. He explained that he had been playing an online dominoes and scrabble tournament until the internet went down. Consequently, he hadn't left Karen's room for the last few days and could easily prove that he had played non-stop during the time of the murder. Harry and Karen were disheartened, but at least they didn't have another suspect to add to the board. Karen then subtly asked about Mr Hamhands bathroom breaks. The wee guy just smiled and wrote that he had his ways. Karen made a mental note to ask someone else to empty her bins.

Vinnie was entranced by Mr Hamhands and announced that he was just the cutest little guy he'd ever met.

Harry couldn't believe the change in Vinnie's demeanour. He explained that he was always grumpy in the morning and, due to the length of his sleep, this was still technically his morning. He was still amazed that Willing had put up with his silent treatment for so long.

Vinnie, John O and a famished Mr Hamhands left Karen's office to go rummaging for some snacks. Vinnie had a cheesecake to make and some Oracles to slice, dice and splice.

CHAPTER SIXTY-EIGHT

Karen's office...

"We need to check up on Fachance again. The poor wee scone. She's really struggling and her appetite's worryingly declined. Although, I hope she hasn't eaten the stairs, the carpets and all the banisters again. I'm not sure I can manage balancing on those stepladders, whilst having to shout at everyone to stop looking up my skirt... again. It's at times like this that I regret having all our offices on the first floor." An exhausted Harry sighed and tucked an emergency seventeen pound sack of potatoes in a rucksack. It was always handy to have something to entice and distract Fachance with, especially as they had to tell her that they still hadn't located Gab, and found him to be innocent.

"You're luck, I had to ask the residents to look up my skirt. They'd rather write flat-pack furniture instruction manuals than harass me. I bet they'll take a look now that I'm a genuine Princess." Karen grumbled and added a box of highly decorative Christmas baubles to her bulging rucksack. Fachance liked to end a meal with something shiny to nibble on, or someone's thumbs to chew. She usually wasn't that bothered either way.

"Honey, that's less to do with what they think about you, and more to do with how much harm you can cause them. No matter how often we tell them they still think you could be Eva Braun coming back to get them. It's really quite sweet when you think

about it." Harry added the battered Angel from the top of the Christmas tree to Karen's bag, then decided that was probably not the wisest choice. She compromised by tucking twelve feet of tinsel in the side pocket of the rucksack. They humphed the bags on their backs and headed for the office door.

"Sweet? Really? I'm not sure what goes on in that head of yours sometimes." Karen managed a small smile and a small shoulder bump. A rarity during these difficult times.

There was a loud bang and a few very bad sweary words flooded the room. Words that your folks warn you about, and threaten you with a mouth full of soap. Those kinda words.

A panting and beaten-up Bub burst into the centre of the room carrying, or nearly carrying, a struggling person wrapped in a blood stained, cream canvas blanket.

"Step back. Please, step back. Watch yourself. They're a biter." Bub dropped the wriggling bundle and spryly jumped away. He did a quick count of his fingers and checked his hair for bald spots. He swiftly nodded then blew out a long breath. His left shoulder was sloping downwards and his arm was hanging uselessly by his side. It was well and truly dislocated, so he banged it against the wall. It popped back into place and he accompanied this painful adjustment with a loud moan.

Another original Evis photograph fell from the wall. Karen sighed and reached for the flowery dustpan and brush. She decided to just leave the pan and brush out as it wasn't worth tidying it away in the back of the stationery cupboard. She seemed to be needing it willy-nilly these days.

Harry rushed to Bub's side and checked him for any additional injuries as he appeared a bit unsteady on his feet. She gave him a quick cuddle, an embarrassingly long snog-a-rooney and she finished with groping his gorgeous bum. Yep, bottoms are mentioned a lot in these books.

Who's under the blanket…

"Let me go. I have to go back. You can't keep he here." The wiggling blanket hotly declared and began wriggling even more energetically.

"Nora? Nora, is that you? Oh, Nora." Harry gasped and ran forward to embrace the writhing bundle. She narrowly avoided standing on the cockroach moving pavement. The roaches bill was going to include danger money and a request for a life-sized, but fully clothed model, of Amanda. They had voted and all decided that they deserved a big treat after the trauma they had just endured. Their statue of the esteemed baby Yoda just wasn't cutting it any longer.

Bub pulled Harry back and stood in front of her. *"She's a bloody savage. I nearly lost an eye, and I think my testicles are hiding somewhere around my throat."* Bub checked his neck for lumps.

Nora abruptly pulled the sheet from her head and lunged at Bub. *"I told you. I bloody told you I can't be here. They'll kill Devil Keith, you interfering shit. Oh, what have you done? You've killed him. You've bloody killed him. I hope you're proud of yourself."* She fell into a chair with a bump. Nora started rocking her body and wailing into her cupped hands.

"What? Why are you here? You're dead. We saw your body. It was all dead-like and glassy eyed. There was blood everywhere." A startled Karen stopped sweeping up the glass shards, dropped her brush and took notice of the surprising event.

"I bloody know I was dead. I was there. I felt the pain. However, I don't know why I'm not dead now. What did you do? What did you do to me? I can't be here." Nora pushed her oily hands through her tangled hair and openly wept.

"We didn't do anything. We were looking for your killer, and we sent Bub to some hotels to find clues or find the culprit. We never, in a million years, thought he'd return with you. Your dead body's in the fridge next to the three gallon drums of cottage cheese. The ones with the pineapple chunks. You know the ones? Even when the Hell residents were starving they left them well

alone." Karen explained and shudder at the thought of the pale vomit-y looking chunks on toast.

"That's understandable. No one ever chooses to eat that so called cheese. What am I saying? You're distracting me and I'm crazy enough just now. Please, let me go back, and just pretend you never found me. I have to go." Nora pleaded and climbed back into the blood stained canvas blanket. She cooed and tried to entice the cockroaches back over to her so that they could return her to the hotel They looked back and forth, from Nora to Harry, but quickly realised where their bread was buttered. Plus, they knew Harry was friends with Amanda, but they weren't so sure about Nora and her bed-headed ways.

"Oh Nora, sweetie. We missed you and I'm not sure we can do that. There's some mighty strange forces at work here. Can you tell us what happened?" Karen tried to calm the distraught woman...from a safe distance.

Whatever happened to our Nora...

"Alright." Nora sighed. *"Try not to interrupt me with questions. I want to tell you my story as quickly as possible, then get away from here before I'm found and something really bad happens. Promise me you'll let me go when I'm finished?*

So, the night of the belly dancing party. I had a great night... we all did. But, as I said at the time, I was tired. Bone weary and still struggling with the idea that I'd killed a man. Yes, I know he was already technically dead, and evil to the core. And barely a man, and justifiably in Hell, but it was still difficult. I don't regret doing it, but I still haven't fully processed it. I never thought I had it in me to end a life. To enjoy ending a life as much as I did. Plus, there were all the nightmares. Night, after night.

Anyway, I went to my bedroom and within minutes of crossing the threshold I was ambushed. A black hood, that smelled of dried blood and stale vomit was tossed over my head. It was pulled hard against my face and I could barely breath. I panicked. They had a hand clamped on my forehead and one held tightly across my chest. I couldn't fight back but I tried. I really tried. A heavily muffled voice said…" Nora gulped back a sob and breathed into a cushion. Harry sat beside her and put her arm around Nora's heaving shoulders. Nora took a calming breath.

"The voice said 'it's either you or him. One of you is going to die tonight'. I couldn't let it be Devil Keith. I just couldn't. I only had a split second to decide, but I thought that Devil Keith was more important than me. He'd be missed by so many people. So many of you would be hurt by his loss. And, I thought he might have a better chance of getting over me as he always knew I'd have to die someday. Have to leave him eventually. I knew that was his biggest concern, and his biggest weakness. He told me that most nights. Plus, I always knew that there was a risk that his enemies could use that against him. Dying…that was the only way I could protect him. You have to understand that I had no choice. It had to be me. It just couldn't be him." Nora screamed the last two sentences and gripped Harry's hand.

"We understand. Honestly we do. You were so brave. I would have done the same thing. Nora, I don't want to interrupt your flow, but can I ask some more about the hood?" Harry whispered and tenderly stroked Nora's arm.

"Please, no questions. I'm not brave. Not at all. I'm a coward. A big fat coward. You don't understand… I saw Devil Keith die before… and it broke something in me. I couldn't do that again. I couldn't face it again. Please, it's so painful to re-live this. I need to finish this quickly and go." Nora took a deep steadying breath and tried to calm her quivering chin and her shaking body.

"The disgusting person giggled and seemed really excited by my answer. They told me I'd made the right decision. The only decision. They held me so, so tightly then tilted up my head and slit my throat. I wasn't prepared for the pain of the attack. Oh, the pain was terrible. So raw. I felt all this wet heat pouring down me. I didn't really understand, but it was my blood pouring from my burst throat. Then I went cold. So cold.

By then I was laying on the floor and I'm sure they kicked me. There was a sharp thump in my side. They laughed again. They laughed so hard as I lay in a pool of my own blood. My hood slipped a little bit, and as I was dying I saw something fall to the floor. It was a large piece of fabric with tiny writing on it. I can't believe that I read that label rather than look at my killer. As I took, what I thought was my last breath, I felt like I was floating then there was an almighty whoosh of air. The air pushed through and over me. It was indescribable... and strangely invigorating.

I woke up a couple of days ago on a sandy beach. I was covered in lumps of sand, seaweed and broken sea shells. I was also badly sunburnt and my blistered skin was peeling. I think I had been laying there since I died. Exhausted, distraught and dehydrated I looked for help but the whole place was deserted. Luckily, I found some discarded coconut shells at the side of a couple of sunbeds and I drank them down. Instead of juice, it turned out that it was dregs of cocktails and booze soaked maraschino cherries that I'd gulped down. I must have passed out. I woke up later feeling worse... so miserable, alone and terribly hungover. I drank a whole lot more and unfortunately I woke again.

The pain just wouldn't go away. I didn't really expect it to, but in my drunken state I'd hoped it would have dulled a little bit. I was, and still am completely heartbroken over this terrible thing. I could hardly take a breath without choking and holding my chest. There's a heavy weight pressing on my heart and crushing it. I felt terrible and so scared and so alone. The pain was so much worse than having my throat cut.

Alcohol poisoning didn't work, so I tried to drown myself. Unfortunately I floated to the surface of the sea and stayed there. I tied heavy rocks to my waist but still I floated. I jumped off a high cliff but again I sort of floated until I landed on some sharp boulders. I was hurt but unfortunately not dead. My back's still aching something awful. I tried a few other increasingly horrible things but nothing worked. I felt that I was doomed to live with this agony growing in my chest. The only positive thing about my situation was knowing that Devil Keith was safe. You've taken that from me and I won't ever forgive you for that." Nora was shaking with anger and viciously shoved Harry away from her.

"I found Nora in one of the hotels…" Bub mumbled.

"Yes, wonder boy over there really saved me. Not. Today I decided to explore the full length of the beach and look for some help as I just couldn't die, no matter how hard I tried. I stumbled into the local hotel and due to staffing issues…some of the locals had gone home to be with their families as there were portents of doom on the horizon. I was initially employed as a chamber maid. By 2 o'clock this afternoon I was relocated to the spa, and as of fifteen minutes ago I was promoted to full-time spa manager.

I took the job as I just needed some food, and drink that wasn't rum based, then I was going to think through my problems. Find a better way to end it all. So, I was elbows deep in a complex bum massage, and I never for one moment thought I'd see Bub march through the French doors."

"Nora screamed then ducked behind a palm plant when she saw me. And then she ran out onto the beach. I found her huddled inside a cabana. I used the tent to corral the tigress. My, you're a fighter." Bub showed Harry the teeth marks and multiple scratches gouged into his arms.

Nora sobbed and pleaded. *"Please, you have to believe me. I didn't mean to hurt you, Bub. I had to run. I didn't know if you were the killer. Please, please. I'm begging you. Please, you have to take me back to the spa. I'm putting you all, and Devil Keith in terrible danger. I can't be here. I just can't. I can't take that responsibility. I'm barely managing as it is. If you don't take me back then kill me, but this time make sure I'm dead."*

Harry pulled Nora in for a tight hug but Nora wriggled away and slapped at Harry's hands. Nora lay on the floor and cuddled into the canvas sheet. *"Nora, honey. Please get up off the floor. You have to listen to us. You have to be here. Those portents of doom that frightened the locals? Well… they're Devil Keith's grief at losing you, and they're getting worse. We'll protect you and keep you hidden; I promise. I think you're right. You and Devil Keith are still in danger until we find the culprit. But you can help us. You can help Devil Keith."*

"No, no, no. Just pretend you never found me. No one has to know that I survived. Let me go. Please I have to go. They'll come back and kill Devil Keith if they know that I'm alive..." Nora's face was drenched in tears and she raised her hands in supplication.

"Nora I would if I could but if we stopped the investigation now it would look suspicious. No one would believe that we just stopped and gave up. It would raise too many questions. I think... no I believe it would put you at more risk of being found out. And we're so glad you're back. We've missed you and don't want to lose you again. We've been grieving too.

Plus, and this is really important. More important that any of our individual lives or any danger we might face. You're the only one that can calm Devil Keith. ***You are*** *the only thing that can stop the Apocalypse from going any further. Stop billions of people and animals from dying. You're our only hope."* Karen placed an empty bin next to Nora as she thought she might be sick.

"Oh, no. I didn't know I was to blame for all the strange things that are happening. Oh, my poor Devil Keith. He must be in so much agony. So much pain. You have to believe me...I never thought he'd suffer that much. Go that far. But, I don't know if I can do it. What if I can't comfort him? What if I can't stop it? What if he hates me? Despises me for taking the coward's way out? What if I make it worse?" Nora was on her knees, rocking and holding her crossed arms tightly against her trembling body.

"Nora, he loves you more than I ever thought he was capable of loving anyone or anything. You have to believe me when I say that you aren't to blame. Not at all. Not one little bit. The evil person who killed you did this. They should be feeling guilty and ashamed of their actions. If they had come forward and confessed, this might not have gone this far. We might have found you earlier, or Devil Keith might have felt better if he'd gotten revenge or justice. They are the criminal and you're the innocent victim in all this. Please, help us." Karen draped a soft woollen blanket across Nora's trembling shoulders.

"I'll try. I'll do as much as I can. I'm sorry I'm not as brave as

you but I'll do what I can." Nora stood up and took an unsteady step towards Harry's outstretched arms.

"Bub, can you go get Devil Keith please? Can you ask Dr Riel to bring the extra chains and the stronger sleeping draft? I think we'll need it. Nora, you have to prepare yourself. Bub's described Devil Keith condition and it's grim. It's going to be difficult for you to see." Karen checked the structural integrity of the cage and placed a couple of soft blankets and pillows on the floor. Bub reassured her that they would probably have to sedate Devil Keith to move him, so they'd definitely bring the extras with them.

"I'll send a guard to get the rest of the Hell team, and everyone else who made it onto the evidence boards. I'll ask them to meet us here in an hour or so. That will give Nora time to review the boards and see if she can spot anything that we've missed. Nora this is going to be so difficult for you, but it will be invaluable to see how folks respond to you. They will be surprised and delighted to know you're alive, but someone will definitely be more shocked and I suspect they'll be very, very angry. Don't worry too much, as we'll put a few safeguards in place to protect and guard you." Harry, full of dread, went to order the collection the suspects and organise the additional safety measures.

CHAPTER SIXTY-NINE

Karen's office and the uncovered investigation boards...

"My, you've been busy. I can't believe how much trouble I've put you through." Nora tentatively touched the board and traced a large question mark with her fingertip.

"It was hard work but it wasn't your fault. None of this is your fault. We used the highly recommended Means, Motive and Opportunity method to help find your killer. The Opportunity board was probably the least helpful as everyone seemed to have an alibi for that horrible night. The Motive board was just as bad as everyone had a fairly sound reason to harm Devil Keith. Sorry, but it's true. He can be a little bit 'challenging' at times but we all love him. Well... I tolerate him. The big galoot. But the Means board proved to be really helpful. That's the reason Bub found you." Harry more than tolerated the galoot. She was his wingman and was cast adrift without him and his capers.

"Not so helpful for me though. Anyway, I noticed that you circled the Faeries a few times. Was it them that did this? They were very annoyed with us and the whole cheating scam. And they're scary little buggers." Nora looked over her shoulder at the investigators.

"No, we're nearly 100% convinced it wasn't them. In fact they helped us to find you. Faery Layla was particularly helpful as she led us to the glass souvenir and the label on the towel. Led us to finding you." Karen tried to rub the Faeries from the boards. Easier said than done as the red permanent marker was living up to its name.

"I know this is difficult but can you add anything? Gab's

board is nearly completely empty and he's still unaccounted for." Harry hopefully asked. She was crossing her fingers and holding her breath in anticipation.

"Yes, I think I can. I don't know if you know this, but Devil Keith had an elaborate locking system added to our door just before we left to go to the Gambler's Hell. Don't worry Harry, it wasn't because you kept trying to break into his room. It was because I found sand in our room and the whole place was tidier than when we left it to go to Falkirk. I didn't like the thought of someone sleeping in our bed and touching our stuff. Whoever killed me had the skills to break into that system because I know I locked the door behind me when I came into the bedroom. I can't give you anything specific for Gab's board but I'd be so hurt if it was him. How evil am I if it was an Angel that killed me?" Nora added and burst into sore tears.

"You're not evil and if it was Gab that did this terrible thing then we'll find him and drag the reason outta him. He'll be punished and it'll be horrible. For him. You're being so brave and helpful. Your information is handy to know. Essential. Right, we'll add that to the other clues." Karen patted Nora on the back. She wrote on the board and stepped back to review the clues.

The clues consisted of:

The killer was tall, strong and was a seasoned killer, as was evidenced by the lack of hesitation in the act of murder and the ease with which they completely subdued Nora. Nora was more of a scrapper than they would ever have guessed. Bub and his many boo-boos could attest to that.

The killer most likely had a personal motive for killing Nora, hence the maniacal laughter and the totally unnecessary kick that was delivered after the killer knew Nora was dying.

The killer was tidy...possibly obsessively so as was evidenced by the precisely made up bed and the carefully dusted China cabinets. Leaving the sand on the floor may have been due to the killer being fearful of being caught in Devil Keith's room. So, the investigators surmised that it was someone who really shouldn't have been in there in the first place.

The killer was probably fastidious regarding their appearance hence the recently, highly polished shoes.

The killer has some technical skills as they easily disarmed a sophisticated locking system.

The killer had access to the Drill and they knew how to use it. Gab was still missing, so they were very skilled at using the tool but that didn't prove Gab was innocent of the crime.

The killer has successfully hidden the murder weapon and the Drill, so they know the layout of Hell number one.

The use of the black hood was significant, as after its use the killer had removed it, but interestingly they hadn't bothered removing the incriminating towels. That one was a bit of a puzzle.

Another puzzle was the glitzy sewing kit. It helped the team find Nora but why was it in Nora and Devil Keith's room?

Nora took a steadying breath and studied the boards. *"This probably sounds stupid, but I just can't shake this feeling. Do you think the killer likes Devil Keith? I'm asking because the killer used our room when we were away, but they also took care of it. Left it neat and tidy? It was really creepy but maybe they thought they were doing a good thing for Devil Keith. Plus, the sewing kit souvenir was probably left as a gift for Devil Keith. I'm sure they wouldn't have thought that it would have proved to be useful for you two. Are you sure you have a full list of suspects up there?"* Nora looked at the investigators for confirmation.

Harry and Karen solemnly nodded then stopped for a moment. They both moved over to the Opportunity and Motive boards. Maybe those boards were going to prove to be useful afterall.

CHAPTER SEVENTY

Karen's office and a mighty big cage...

"Noooooo. Get away. You liar. I'm going to kill you. I'm going to enjoy tearing off your limbs and sucking out your marrow. You're a liar. An evil liar." A snarling beast bounced off the shuddering wall of the impressive cage. He thrust his arms through the bars and caught Nora by the hair. Bub grabbed Karen's handy axe and sliced through Nora's hair before Devil Keith tore her head clean from her body. The sedatives, used to transport Devil Keith, had quickly worn off and he was raging behind the shaking bars.

"My poor, poor Devil Keith. What have I done to you? I thought I was saving you. Protecting you." Nora lay on the floor at the side of the cage. Desperately trying to stop herself from stroking Devil Keith's malformed head and offering him much needed solace. He had very nearly ripped off her arm when she had previously put it too near the cage, so she was a little bit wary of the man she loved.

*"I am **not** your Devil Keith. I'm **Nora's** Devil Keith. She's all mine and I'm all hers. You're some kind of abomination sent to trick me and torture me. You don't even smell like my Nora. You're a poorly formed fraud of useless flesh. I hate you. I'm gonna enjoy tearing you apart. Just come a little closer my lying little tease. I want to see what makes you tick."* Devil Keith loudly barked before his voice reduced to a phlegmy gurgle. His tongue split down the middle and he began hissing and spitting. His eyes elongated and his pupils also split into black slits. His skin ruptured as his limbs grew and twisted. A horn tore through

his forehead and splintered his buckled skull. A demon was erupting from his grieving flesh.

"I can't help him. He won't listen to me. My poor man is tormented and I did that to him. I'm useless. So useless. I'm so sorry, my love. You should have let me go back." Nora sobbed and accepted some comfort from Harry.

"You've been through such a lot and you're trying your best. No one could do more. Truly, no one. Go. Get some rest and freshen up. Your face is covered in dried blood and you need to get those head wounds tended. Plus, you do smell a little bit rank." Karen gently suggested and helped Nora rise from the messy floor.

"Eh... that's my blood on her face. Nora headbutted me twice and broke my nose. It was a real gusher." Bub braced himself then re-aligned his squint nose. The crunch and gasp was really quite nauseating. Harry mopped up his stinging tears and kissed him on the cheek.

A despondent Nora headed off to Karen's bathroom for a much needed shower and a change of clothes. A few seconds later there was a piercing scream and a loud splintering of glass. Harry bolted to the bathroom. The shower screen had shattered into tiny pieces. The tiled floor was soaked in water and bubbles, and covered in fragments of broken glass.

"I'm an..." A stunned Nora was holding a towel in front of herself and looking in the full-length mirror.

"You're an Angel!" Harry shouted. She grabbed Nora and turned her around a few times. *"An Angel. Look at your skin. It's glistening. When did that happen? I didn't notice it before. Do you think that it was hidden underneath all that blood and your sunburn? Your wings. Look at your wings. Your wings are awesome."*

"They broke the shower screen when they ripped outta my back. It wasn't even sore. Not one bit, but it was a bit of a shock. Sorry I screamed and scared you all." Nora tried to look at her back in the mirror. To look at the twelve foot wingspan that touched the bathroom walls. To look at the pure white feathers

tipped with pale golden down. To look at her silly cookie bun wings!

"Well that explains the constant back pain you spoke about. Oh, Nora. You're an Angel. That's absolutely brilliant. I was at the birth of a twitting Angel." Harry pulled out her phone and took a photo. She then danced around the cramped bathroom and did a particularly unappealing bottom wiggle against the cistern. She stopped celebrating and carefully stroked Nora's wings. Harry gave them a big sniff. Yes, they were the genuine article. They smelled like artichoke hearts and mint chocolate chip ice cream, but in a nice way. A really nice way. Their Nora was an Angel!

The team were hammering at the door and shouting in alarm. Bub dislocated his shoulder again as he slammed against the obstacle. Harry poked her head out of the bathroom door and reassured everyone that Nora was safe and they weren't to come it.

"Can you apologise to Karen for me? I think I've completely wreaked her bathroom." Nora shyly requested and looked around the sodden room. The room was in bits as Nora kept banging her majestic, and surprisingly strong, wings off the tiles and taps. Mesmerised, she plucked at one of her delicate feathers. They really were rather beautiful and not at all pigeon like.

"I'm sure she won't mind. She's been talking a lot recently about needing to redecorate. Jonathan did a number on her offices when he was in charge. She can just add this to the list." Harry was still dancing and crunching through the glass. She decided that Princess Karen could shove her knighthood and her varicose veins: Nora, the Angel, could probably get her all kinds of lovely goodies. Harry predicted that her birthday gifts would be awesome that coming year. That's if they could keep the world in one, solid and non-burny piece until then.

"I'll just get dressed and be out in a minute." Nora looked at the pile of clothes and realised that she wasn't sure what she could put on. How do you cover your modesty and still

boast about your bodacious wings? A question she never, ever, ever thought she'd ever have to answer. She then gazed in the mirror, leaned forward and checked her illuminous skin. She really was gleaming with health and vitality. Plus, just look at her hair. Her hair was tumbling, in soft ringlets, down her slender back. Her squint was gone and the only distinctive thing about her eyes were her exceeding long eyelashes. Nora thought she was a babe now. An unmitigated ten out of ten stunner. Devil Keith would love it. Nora's mood sobered at that thought. What if he still didn't recognise her? Nora could barely recognise herself.

CHAPTER SEVENTY-ONE

Karen's very crowded office...

"Don't worry about all the screaming and banging you just heard. There's been a big development." Harry could barely contain her grin and her hip shimmies.

"Have you found Gab? Please tell me you found him." Fachance excitedly enquired. Her, HR Sarah and Willing were just entering Karen's office, as they had been delayed due to a clerical error. Well, not so much a clerical error as Assistant Gail threatening to skelp Jonathan if she ever got her hands on him again. Seemingly, just before he lost Hell he'd spitefully deleted one of Gail's essential anniversary reminder files. She was not amused. Plus, they were in the middle of negotiating payment on a particularly tricky account with the bickering cockroaches. Vinnie and John O were a mere fraction of a second behind them, and dragging in a heavily bound Marjorie, Gilbert and Johnathan. The Faeries, ogres and Hell's own Faery Lynn had already claimed the more comfortable chairs and were waiting patiently for the update.

"No, I'm so, so sorry for getting your hopes up, Fachance. We still can't locate him but we're going to try again tomorrow. I promise." Harry gave the bad news to Fachance, and Willing comforted their distressed sister.

"So what's the development?" Faery Layla enquired and popped a pack of *"acquired"* magic markers in her daisy

handbag.

Nora half walked: half floated through the open bathroom door. She wasn't very graceful as she banged off the doorframe and hit her funny-bone off the broken door handle. It wasn't at all funny so she produced a few colourful expletives and her feet thudded to the floor. Everyone gasped and jumped to their feet. Fachance fainted and hit the floor with a resounding thud. Stan walked through the office door and someone might have given him a distracted wave, or not. Nora was alive! Nora was an Angel! Nora's massive wings had just buckled the architrave around Karen's bathroom door!

"What? How? Are they real? How is Nora alive? Are you Ok? Are you alive? Who's gonna pay for the doors? You were dead. Can I have something to eat? My blood sugar's a bit low and seemingly I'm not allowed near the banisters? Are those wings real? Can you whoosh now? This isn't right. How are you still alive? Are you an Angel? You should be dead. Can I give you my birthday wish list? Are you real? What's happening?" the questions all came at once. Harry and Karen didn't have a chance to look at the stunned faces surrounding them, nor were they able to track the questions or statements that were directed at Nora. An opportunity missed.

After a few minutes of hugs, laughter and stroking of wings, Nora hesitantly made her way over to Devil Keith's cage.

"There she is...my Nora. She's back. I can die peacefully now. Love you always." Devil Keith's misshapen mouth pulled up at one corner as he struggled to smile at his lovely wee wife. He hissed in pain and grimaced.

"Devil Keith. Devil Keith, I'm so sorry. I didn't know this would hurt you so much. Can you forgive me? Please, talk to me. You're not going to die. We're going to go to Venice and cause mayhem. You promised." Nora whispered and pushed her arm through the cage so she could stroke his sore, battered flesh.

"It's all alright now. You're back. I can go now. You're safe." Devil Keith collapsed into the blankets. His skin bubbling and

melting through the fabric and into the floor of the cage.

"Do something? Help. Help him." Nora screamed at the stunned audience.

Dr Riel peered through the bars and shook his head. *"I'm not sure if it has been just too much for him to deal with. He's been cycling through so many emotions and changing so much. I've made him as comfortable as possible and we just have to wait. See if he makes it."* Dr Riel placed a blanket over the dying Devil. Nora crawled into the cage. She cuddled against Devil Keith and tenderly covered them both with her stunning wings.

CHAPTER SEVENTY-TWO

Karen's office, and the outlook is bleak...

The walls of their Hell were shaking, and tumbling. Above them the world was exploding and erupting. The earth's molten core was boiling over and shooting lava through volcanoes and the sliding tectonic plates.

"I want the person who's done this to Devil Keith. And I want them now. They need to pay." Bub bellowed. He threw another office desk across the room. That made a total of six tables and eight chairs impaled in the plasterboard wall now.

"Bub, we've been trying. Honestly we have." Karen tried to placate the furious man.

"Get away from me. I don't want to accidentally hurt you. It's not enough. Not nearly enough. And why is Stan here? Why are you bothering now? The damage is done. My poor, tormented brother's nearly gone. The world's beyond repair." Bub snarled and angrily shrugged Harry off. Dr Riel made to stop the distraught man but Karen gently waved him away.

"It's horrific out there. I've been dealing with the carnage above, and Dippit's been trying to provide medical care for the injured. Plus, I think it's about twenty minutes until the end of the world. Sorry, I only just got your messages." Stan tried to ease the tension with a very misguided jest. His lack of repetition was testament as to how stressed he was. Stan only managed to get

down to Hell through some tricky subterfuge. He had sneakily withheld Dippit's Guiness and herb infusion so that she would turn green and fall into a deep faint. He could then hide her away in a bombproof shelter. It was the only way he could guarantee a modicum of safety for his wife, child and wee-ish horse. A wife who had categorically refused to abandon the sick and was willing to risk everything to tend to another burn victim.

"We've no time for your stupid jokes. Look at the boards. Look at them! Use your lucky pen... or whatever it is you have. Solve this. Get him back. Now." Bub sarcastically told the traumatised man. Harry noticed a slight bump forming on Bub's forehead and his words were accompanied by a pronounced hissing sound. She feared that her Bub was on the brink of tipping into full demon too. This was bad. Really bad.

"I'm so, so sorry. My luck's all dried up. Gone. I've used it all helping others and leading searches through damaged buildings for survivors." Harry took the time to study Stan. He was clearly exhausted. And he was unable to do his usual, and repeat parts of his conversation. He was also covered in a range of bodily fluids and debris. He had obviously been going through hell on earth.

"Then what use are you?" Bub snarled again and turned away from the apologetic man.

"Stop, just stop. That's unfair and you know it. We can't turn on each other. Not now. Not when we're so close to being able to give Devil Keith and Nora justice. Justice that just might help Devil Keith recover. Stop with all the bitching and throwing stuff. I need everyone to read the boards and tell us what we've missed." Dr Riel forcefully stated. Harry tried to console Bub but he initially resisted her attention. He quietly whispered an apology in Harry's ear and shook Stan's shaky hand.

The Hell team, the Faeries, the ogres, the Oracles, HR Sarah, Jonathan and the Atlantean's all lined up. One by one they checked the contents of the crowded boards. Vinnie stopped, tilted his head and looked puzzled. He whipped his head around and looked over at John O with a questioning frown. *"That's not right. That's not what happ..."*

The lights went off and there was the unmistakable sound of a Drill moving against a wall. A dazzling light appeared and a powerful torch was directed at the sound...

"You. I knew it was you. I hoped it wasn't. I really and truly hoped I was wrong. I couldn't believe it when I realised it was you." Harry shrieked. There was an almighty roar and an Angel darted across the darkened room and into the bright light. The startled killer screamed as they were ruthlessly rugby tackled to the ground. There were feathers, wings, boots, hair and fists rolling around the messy floor. Blood and bits of broken teeth splattered against the furniture, the walls and the terrified onlookers. Bone's crunched and a jaw dislocated to the back of a skull.

"Give me a knife, now. I want a knife or an axe. So help me. I'm having this bastard's head, so help me god." Nora screamed and shook. She held the killer up by the throat. Their booted feet dangling off the floor and their clothing hanging in shreds.

"Yes, dearie how can I help? Oh dear me. What are you doing to poor Willing? And why is she turning blue? Where did that Angel come from? This is all very irregular." a bedraggled God popped into the middle of the chaos and dropped onto a tilting, three-legged office chair.

CHAPTER SEVENTY-THREE

Willing was chained to the sturdiest chair in the room...

"Willing, why did you do it? Why did you kill our Nora?" Karen had taken over the questioning from Bub, as all he wanted to do was release Nora and let her rip Willing apart.

"How did you know it was me? I got such a shock when the torch picked me out." Willing belligerently asked and tugged at her restraints.

"Turns out Stan still had a tiny bit of luck left. Or, maybe it was just part of his safety gear that switched on by accident. Either way we were going to get you.

We didn't want to believe it at first, but the look Vinnie gave John O confined our worst fears. We suspected that he wasn't your alibi for that night. He was barely speaking then, so he couldn't have held a long conversation with you. We concluded that rather than talking to the curtains John O was, in fact, talking with a partially hidden Vinnie. Vinnie was John O's alibi instead. Clever of you to offer to check off the alibis for us. So why? Why did you do it?" Harry clarified. She was so hurt that her sister had not only destroyed Nora and Devil Keith, but Willing was also happy to demolish Fachance's opportunity for happiness too.

"I take it that the backpack you're always carrying held the missing Drill and it has the murder weapon in it too." Karen

added, and carefully searched through the bag.

"Yes, it was my escape plan if everything went pear-shaped." Willing angrily confirmed and rattled around in her chair.

"Where is my Gab? What did you do to him? How could you do this to me? I thought you loved me. We're sisters." Fachance tearfully whispered and refused the offer of a biscuit.

"No idea where he is. I just made a hole and shoved him through it. Afterall, I couldn't have him using the truth telling soap powder and discovering it was me. It was survival of the fittest and I was willing to do anything to succeed. Anything. It is my name, afterall.

By the way. I don't understand why you're still calling me a killer and causing such a fuss. Nora's very much alive and she looks better than ever. She's even lost that annoying squint and I think she's dropped a few necessary pounds. Haven't you chubby? I gave her wings, a waist and shiny hair. She should be kissing my boot-clad feet." Willing had the audacity to smile and awkwardly pat her own shoulder. Nora growled and tried to bite through Willing's restraints. That Horsewoman was dead-meat.

"That still doesn't explain why. Please, this is your only chance to try to salvage some kind of a relationship with us. Tell us why." Harry pleaded and gently moved Nora away from the chair.

The reason Willing murdered our Nora....

"I suppose I can, but only for Fachance's sake. She's annoying but I do love her...in my own way. So... us Horsewomen of the Apocalypse, were all raised in turbulent times, but at least ***you*** *all saw some honour and progress as a result of all the fighting. It had a purpose. A meaning.*

One of my first memories, when I was a little girl, was when I saw the remnants of the soldiers returning from World War One. They were mentally and physically broken. Used up. They were honoured with a ticker-tape parade, chants and cheers. Promises were made, then they were given nothing. No respect, no jobs and no dignity. They saw Wall Street crash and their lives crumbled further. Their children were dying in the streets from hunger and disease. But the rich got richer. The poor man in the street...their lives collapsed and they were forced to swallow their dignity and queue for scraps of food and miserly hand-outs.

My first real taste of violence was when I was a teenager. I witnessed the street fighting of the bootlegging gangsters of the nineteen-twenties and thirties. They scrabbled around for money and loose women to tend to their sordid needs, but they had no honour. No discipline. They scrambled in the mud and pulled everyone down with them.

We were promised no more wars. But they all lied. Then came World War Two, where a fanatic murdered and experimented on millions of people because he couldn't get a job as an artist, so he went in the huff. I know people give other, more complex, reasons for that war but that's how I saw it. It wasn't war...it was murder. Plain and simple. Haunted men returned from that war with limbs missing and their sight stolen. I would hear the ex-soldier in the apartment next to me scream out during the night and his children would cower away from him in fear. His wife left one day for work and just never came back.

Those wars and conflicts targeted the vulnerable: the weak, the very young and the elderly. Money and resources were wasted or hoarded. Religion was used to justify horrendous acts of torture and genocide.

The Cold War went on for years with costly spies and with, ultimately, no winners. Paranoia kept that war going and people starved whilst others were bloated due to their ill-gotten wealth.

So, I withdrew into books where myths, legends and goddesses ruled. Where promises were kept and war was a last resort. And war had strict rules where only soldiers fought and children were treasured. I read about the courageous Goddess Athena. She was one of the twelve chief Olympian deities. She was worshipped due to her wisdom and warfare skills. Her brother Ares displayed rage, violence and impulsiveness but he still had boundaries. Limits and rules that he followed.

In ancient times war also happened due to true love. Helen of Troy was the wife of Menelaus, King of Spartan. She was abducted by the Trojan Prince Paris. That sparked off the Trojan war and the magnificently brave Spartan's won. I used to dream about being loved like that. Inspiring that sacrifice and devotion in a partner.

When I landed here, and I was told I was the Horsewoman of War I was overjoyed. Finally I could make and enforce the rules. Really change things for the better. Punish the wrongdoers and make sure that the right people were victorious. That just hasn't happened. No matter what I do, I can't shape the outcomes of conflicts and save the people.

Even here, in Hell number one I'm disregarded. I'm only invited after all the action and the stories have been written. I'm marginalised and left alone to keep Fachance from descending into total cannibalism. You all laugh at my trusty mallet, but it's helped stop you lot from waking up to find Fachance chewing through your duvets and nibbling your giblets. But I'm unwanted and ridiculed… 'good old Willing she won't mind not getting invited to a wedding' or 'good old Willing she doesn't need affection'. Well I was sick of it.

Devil Keith was the only hero I've ever found here. He saved me from King Adrian and made sure I was bandaged and cared for. Then that no-good temptress, Nora, comes and steals him from me. A mere human burrows her way into his affections and takes him. ***From me!*** " Willing screamed and tried to kick out at Nora.

"My Nora, didn't…"

"From me!" Willing exploded from her chair and charged at Nora. Willing dropped to the floor and held her throat. She was choking and sputtering.

"That's me just paying my debt to Devil Keith for the shuttlecock entrapment incident. Although, to be fair to Willing here, he is a bit of a hero and a bit lush." Faery Lynn dusted off her hands and karate chopped her way out of the room. Her magnificent throat punch instantly becoming a thing of legends.

CHAPTER SEVENTY-FOUR

Karen's office and things are looking better...

It was a poorly Devil Keith who tried to tell Willing that Nora didn't steal him from her. Unfortunately, he was interrupted before he could make his big speech about loving his Nora, and only her. The eighty-six page speech can be broken down into this...Devil Keith loves his Nora, and he's not keen on anyone else, plus he'll beat the living shit outta anyone who says otherwise. If you want the full transcript of the speech please contact the authors, and they'll risk another dose of carpal tunnel syndrome typing it up for you.

Bub, Devil Keith, Nora, Karen, Dr Riel and frankly everyone else affected by Nora's death and the Apocalypse wanted Willing dead. That's well over nine billion individuals baying for blood, viscera and fresh entrails. Quite a crowd. God agreed with their sentiment, but firmly stated that they couldn't do that. The reason: although Willing felt she didn't positively impact on the outcome of conflicts she did, in fact, help. She also prevented a great number of Fachance induced famines. God concluded that Willing helped a great deal more than she could ever imagine and it was tragic that she just couldn't see her worth. So, God agreed to take Willing into her care and give her some time to heal, and to get over her bizarre infatuation with Devil Keith. The Hell team sorta understood and they very, very, very, very reluctantly agreed with the plan. Although they demanded daily progress reports and a celestial restraining order issued against Willing. A celestial restraining order makes the sound of a barking fox every time it's broken, so it's not really all that effective, especially when you're out rambling in the countryside.

God didn't seem at all surprised when she noticed that it was Nora that was now an Angel. She thought that Nora's selfless acts had given her a lovely pair of wings and a black belt in Mixed Martial Arts. She offered to enrol our Nora in the esteemed, "*Angel School of Flying and Carrot Cake Baking*". A true honour as most goody-two-shoes had to pass a difficult entrance exam in order to get a place. However, Devil Keith wasn't quite ready to let his beautiful wife out of his sight. Nora vigorously agreed with her rapidly healing man and snatched up a couple of giant Toblerones, then headed off to bed. To finish reading her naughty book to the even naughtier Devil Keith.

Unfortunately Gab was still missing but Harry and Bub are on the case. Now that they have their Interdimensional Drill back, they think that finding him should be easy-peasy. Good luck with that, the authors sarcastically laugh and open another packet of Tunnock's caramel wafers to have with their morning cuppa.

Fachance continues to be deeply upset by Willing's deceit. She can't believe that Willing did all of that on an empty stomach. She is also distressed by Gab's absence but she was comforted when God assured her that Gab was definitely alive and probably well. Fachance decided that she'd only do good deeds from now on in as it might increase their chances of finding her Gab. Plus, she has discovered a new love of all things plastic so she is currently working her way through the oceans cleaning up plastic bottles and general junk. So, be very wary if you see a beautiful, flaxen haired woman doing the backstroke towards you; she may just eat through your boat or yacht or cruise ship. Her appetite is back and raring to go.

Karen, Dr Riel, Vinnie and John O are planning a long trip. They're taking the Oracles to apologise to every Atlantean descendant. Seemingly, if you have varicose veins then you may receive a knock at your door and have a fun sized Milky Way chocolate shoved through your letter box. If you are an Atlantean descent then you have the author's permission to slap the Oracles around the head with a can of baked beans. Should you so wish. Even if you're not a descent just give them a whack.

After they locate Gab, Harry and Bub are planning on returning to Venice to do some repairs and apologise to some innocent olive growers. However, only if HR Sarah authorises their holiday request and releases their passports.

The Apocalypse update...

Justice being served and Wiling having a mighty impressive black eye and a sore throat, did indeed help with Devil Keith's recovery. That and the application of many, many boxes of Power Puff Girl plasters. Oh yes, and Nora kissing Devil Keith's boo-boos all better. Although the nightmares still persist and will do for quite some time.

C.C. helped the world by turning back time thirty-five minutes at a time, but even he had his limits. The world is still at peril but the rabbits have stopped shouting at their young, the lava rivers have receded and the swans are no longer dodging about Falkirk High Street. Everyone, not in the room when C.C. did his thing, has no memory of the Apocalypse. However C.C. does have rules to follow so everyone is now very aware of the impact of Global Warming.

Stan and Dippit are awaiting the birth of their superstar. That's another story...

CHAPTER SEVENTY-FIVE

The entrance to Hell number one…

"Father, what are you doing here?"

◆ ◆ ◆

CHAPTER SEVENTY-SIX

The other entrance to Hell number one…

"Hi, is there anyone here? Roger sent me. I'm the Horsewoman of Woke. Cooey!"

Good old Roger…. the authors have just frisbeed their laptop out of their upstairs window.

◆ ◆ ◆

BOOKS IN THIS SERIES

The Devil's a ...

The Devil's A Courting

The Devil's A Fighting

The Devil's A Hunting

The Devil's A Learning

Printed in Great Britain
by Amazon